SWEET TORMENT

"Amanda Jo, I can't believe you're such an innocent." In fact, the more Ryder thought about it, the more he knew she couldn't be as naive as she sounded, not living with such a family of cutthroats. His fingers dug into her shoulders as he lifted her up to look into her forest-green eyes. His voice grated on his own ears as he asked, "Just how many men have fallen for your pure and innocent act? How many men have you lured into your traps?"

When he saw the unfeigned hurt and disbelief in her eyes, he swore at himself for being twice a fool and captured her lips with his before she could utter a word in self-defense.

After the frenzied kiss eased into a relaxed reconnaissance of her flushed and heated cheeks, Mandy raised her head and gazed dreamily into the blackest, shiniest eyes she'd ever seen. They softened as she watched, and she sighed in bewilderment. This man could change moods in less than a heartbeat. And here she was, lying in his arms when he probably had every intention of using her to destroy her family.

For a moment, when he'd spoken so harshly, she'd been afraid. Now, looking into his smiling, handsome face, all she felt was a languorous warmth seeping through her veins. She wanted to bask in his arms and never move, never think, never worry about anything but loving him for the rest of her days. . . .

Lawman's Loving

Judith Steel

ZEBRA BOOKS

KENSINGTON PUBLISHING CORP.

ZEBRA BOOKS

are published by

Kensington Publishing Corp.
475 Park Avenue South
New York, NY 10016

First printing: August, 1988

Printed in the United States of America

To Grandpa, with love and many thanks.

Chapter One

Tears of happiness rolled freely down Amanda Jo Coulter's flushed cheeks as six men lowered the wooden coffin into the extra-deep grave. Lord, this was the best funeral she had ever attended.

The nondescript coverall-clad figure sitting next to her on the splintery buckboard seat moved gingerly to place a consoling arm around her shoulders.

"Amanda Jo, honey, if you don't quit grinnin' and cover those pearly whites, folks are goin' to get suspicious about just how grieved you are over the loss of our dearly beloved." The voice was low and whispered, as if the person was afraid of drawing attention to himself during the quiet ceremony.

Realizing how dangerous her lack of attention could have been for more than a few bereaved mourners, Mandy hung her head in heartfelt shame. She'd known better, yet had sat right there in plain sight of all the newspaper reporters, detectives and lawmen, and had almost made a spectacle of herself that could have been fatal to the dearest person in her limited world.

The horror written across her stricken features at

that particular moment would have been enough to convince any skeptic of her deep distress.

"That's good, hon. I'm gettin' a little choked up myself," her companion mumbled out of the side of his mouth.

The silence that had settled over the subdued group of people standing around the ugly pit was almost eerie. The April wind whipped dust from the mounded dirt into scores of eyes, but still they stood, awed and stunned, as the preacher intoned, "Ashes to ashes, dust to dust . . ."

For the two people on the buckboard, it felt as if the sun were trying to roast them alive between chilly gusts of wind. The heat and nervous tension were becoming so intense that sweat rolled from every pore enshrouded by the loose coveralls and flannel shirts. They weren't even aware of the goose bumps dotting their skin as the breeze dried the perspiration.

Mandy's second-hand hat had been through so many storms that the crown caved in, and the brim drooped so that she had to tilt her head to see out. Bless that hat! It may have saved the day from disaster. She would have to be much more careful in the future and watch her impetuous nature if they were going to pull off this escapade.

Drops of sweat continued to trickle between her breasts and down the back of her neck as she reached up to shift the heavy mass of hair beneath the floppy felt hat. All of a sudden her hand stopped in midair, and her skin began to crawl with a second layer of bumps that had nothing to do with the bite in the air. Mandy curbed the impulse to frantically swivel her head. She knew without a doubt that someone was watching her.

She nonchalantly continued the movement of her hand to rub the moisture from her neck, then shifted

8

her tender bottom and slowly scanned the fidgety crowd. Hrumph! They had pleaded that the burial be private, for family members only. Just look at all the inconsiderate thrill-seekers standing on tiptoe to get a better look at the coffin, she thought. It made her sick to her stomach.

Then a jolt rocked through her system when her gaze locked with that of a tall, intense-looking stranger standing just beyond the shade of the huge coffee bean tree, beneath which the seven-foot grave had been dug. Somebody was watching her all right, and the impact of the startling black eyes sent shivers down her spine as surprise gave way to a very real sensation of fear. Why was he looking at their wagon—at her—and not at the casket like everyone else?

Her eyes widened, and she inhaled deeply as she took in the trail-worn leather shirt and breeches, stained with sweat and grime as if the man had been traveling hard for a long period of time. His features were dark and brooding, and the fathomless eyes bored into her as if they intended to discover every deceitful thought and hidden secret.

Mandy stiffened her spine and gathered every ounce of courage to remain calm and unruffled under the severity of that calculating stare. She looked away first and swept her gaze onward as if making a casual surveillance of the people thronging the small yard before staring once more at the hands folded quietly in her lap.

Without moving her lips more than absolutely necessary, she whispered to her partner, "Don't turn around. Just act natural. We're being watched. He's the tall, Indian-looking fellow standing behind the tree." Again Mandy blessed her old hat, which she had been threatening to throw away, for hiding the

9

greater part of her face.

When she next ventured to peer from beneath the sagging brim, it appeared the man was making a move to walk in their direction. She was concentrating on the stranger so completely that she almost jumped off the seat of the wagon when a loud commotion erupted from the graveside.

A distraught, bitterly weeping, gray-haired woman began to shout as the casket was lowered into the earth. "Dear Lord, I beg of you, don't let the murder of my son go unavenged. I pray for justice against the traitors who brought about this cowardly deed." Shaking her fists to the sky, the woman then collapsed in a fit of tears.

All eyes had been riveted on the old woman, and people began to shuffle their feet and look aside nervously as if waiting for a bolt of lightning or clap of thunder from the heavens to acknowledge the vehement plea.

When the still figure sitting next to her on the buckboard trembled violently, Mandy slipped her hand into his and squeezed his fingers reassuringly. His pale blue eyes blinked rapidly as they lifted to meet her sympathetic gaze, and all of the love and devotion she had ever felt for this man came pouring forth as she clasped him in a comforting embrace.

It was hard for her to understand why God would heap so many catastrophies upon one family, and especially upon one man. She had only been two years old when the Union Army harassed his family the first time. They had strung up his stepfather and left him for dead beneath that same coffee bean tree, and then had beaten the man beside her up and down the freshly furrowed rows of his fields with horse whips. And he was only a boy of sixteen at the time.

Of course, no family had escaped unscathed along

10

the Missouri border during those years. Perhaps in no other area were families, friends and neighbors torn apart by their beliefs and convictions worse than in Missouri before and even after the Civil War. And in no other state did the hatred and persecutions continue with such long-lasting repercussions.

The weeping of the old woman grew louder, bringing Mandy's thoughts back to the present. Her eyes automatically sought the buckskin-clad figure who had caused her blood to slink so cowardly through her veins. He was gone! Now her head did swivel back and forth, searching, almost slinging her hat from her head. Surely she hadn't just imagined him. She still felt the icy blast from those dark, accusing eyes.

"Okay, hon. It's over. Let's get the hell out of here." Her cousin's voice was harsh and raspy, and her heart constricted with love and compassion.

Forgetting the stranger momentarily, she tried to put her companion at ease. "It'll be all right. Everything's going to work out just as we planned. Wait and see."

The exuberant young voice, filled with confidence and innocence, brought a sad smile to the man's face. "Even if it kills us trying. Right?"

Mandy's grin deepened, and her eyes flashed conspiratorially as she rebounded, "Right!"

Mandy's bottom was already sore, so the long jolting ride back to the homestead over the ruts and lumps of bunchgrass in the road did nothing to improve her flagging spirits.

The cheerful chirps and soaring antics of the mockingbirds and bright-colored meadowlarks, the fresh scent of the newly blossomed wild flowers, or

11

the unfurling of new green leaves on the blackjack and walnut trees, nothing detracted her thoughts from the scary uncertainty of the days to come.

Would she be able to carry out her role if someone were to ask questions? But why ask for trouble? Everything had gone smoothly. No one seemed suspicious. So why did those unrelenting black eyes keep haunting her so? What was it about the stranger that was so compelling and yet, at the same time, so alarming?

When they passed through the densest area of the lane winding to her home, the silent figure reclining beside her roused and pulled back on her hand which controlled the reins to the two thin, lop-eared mules leading the wagon.

"Okay, hon, this is where I get off. Now remember, I've got everything I need for now. Stay close to home and meet me at the cave in three days. Take your time and be sure you're not followed." He looked into her wide, too-bright green eyes and held her shoulder for support as he clambered to the wheel of the buckboard. "You're not scared, are you?"

Mandy swallowed a lump in her sandpapery throat as she nodded. "I've had a terrible feeling"— she thumped her chest—"right here, ever since I saw that man at the funreal. There's something about him . . . I can't explain why, but I know he's going to be trouble."

"Aw, Amanda, don't go gettin' melodramatic on me. He's just some drifter who wanted to be a part of the sideshow." A bitter note crept into his voice. "It was a damned carnival, wasn't it? Never knew I was so popular."

When he saw the real fear and concern etched on his favorite cousin's face, he smiled and blew her a kiss as he jumped from the wagon and faded into the undergrowth. She could barely hear his words as they trailed from the bushes. "Don't worry, hon. Hey, see if you can sneak a bottle of your pa's shine when you come."

Alone, Mandy presented a forlorn picture as she slumped on the seat of the ancient wagon and looked into the faded-blue sky. "Lord? Please watch after the fool. I don't know what I'd do without him."

She clucked to the weary team, and they bumped on down the lane to enter a small clearing at the base of a brush-covered hill. It was a lonely, isolated spot, but it was home. The house sat back in the trees, and she could just make out the sagging eaves of the porch. The mules walked on through the clearing, past the hen house and pig pen, to the dilapidated old barn. As the team passed through the open door and into the shade of the low-ceilinged building, she had to duck her head to avoid cracking it against the overhead beam. The soothing odors of old leather and freshly cut hay helped to settle her jumpy nerves.

"Whoa, Jen. Whoa, Zeke." She wondered why she even bothered to give the command since the mules had already come to a standstill. Maybe she needed to pretend that she had control over *something* in her life, whether she actually did or not.

The cracked leather on the aged harness snagged Mandy's hands when she hung it on a wooden peg. It needed to be greased again, along with numerous other chores, soon. As she forked a flake of hay into the nearest manger, Zeke's long ears flicked toward the door. Immediately alert, Mandy stepped back to the wagon and grabbed the old Sharps rifle that was her constant companion lately.

A horse's soft snort carried on the breeze through the open doorway before a deep voice called, "Howdy! Anybody home?"

13

The tiny hairs on the back of Mandy's neck prickled and stood on end. The same feeling of dread and apprehension that she'd experienced at the funeral now shivered its way down every individual vertebra of her spine.

With a deep breath, she cocked the hammer on her rifle and stepped from the shadows of the barn just as a tall, dark man in buckskins started to dismount from a long-legged, rangy mustang.

"Hold it right there, mister. Don't bother getting off that pony. You won't be staying that long." Wasn't fate something? She'd known who it was before ever stepping out of the barn.

The stranger settled back in the saddle and eyed the little kid with the big rifle warily. His jet-black eyes narrowed as he recognized the flop hat and soiled, baggy overalls. It was the same scrawny figure he'd noticed at the funeral. When his gaze locked with the bright emerald green ones of the youngster, an unsettling stir wormed through his belly.

Mandy's mind was going through recriminations of its own as she took in the features of the man she'd spotted under the shadowy limbs of the coffee bean tree. The only impression she'd received then was of glittering black eyes. Now she was close enough to see just how perfectly those eyes fit the rest of his lean, weather-worn face. Sure enough, he did resemble an Indian with his deeply tanned skin, high chiseled cheekbones, long aquiline nose and thin shapely lips.

Oh yes, shapely. He had the most beautiful lips Mandy had ever seen on a man—wide and narrow with a full lower lip that beckoned to her with sensual entreaty. Mandy shook her head in disgust when she felt her tongue moisten her dry mouth as she wondered what it would feel like to touch those lips with her own. Fool! How could she stand there with a rifle pointed at a man's mid-section and at the same time wonder what it would be like to kiss his lips?

Silence settled ominously over the clearing as the two eyed each other warily. With every shift in the saddle by the stranger, Mandy raised the gun a little higher. And having noticed that the hammer was already cocked on the rifle, the man was beginning to fidget under the continued glaring of the nervous kid.

"Is your father or mother around, sonny?"

Sonny? Sonny! Nineteen-year-old Amanda Jo Coulter straightened to her full five feet four inches and thrust out her indignant, full-bosomed chest. Then a thought struck her. If the stranger wasn't aware that she was a woman, couldn't she use that to her advantage until she found out just what he was doing snooping around her place?

Mandy slumped her shoulders and lowered her voice to aid and abet the misconception as she told him, "I'm the only one in charge here. Now, who are you? And what do you want?"

The stranger tilted his gorgeous lips in what some might call a grin. "You don't believe in polite conversation or wasting any time, do you? Right to the point. Well, I can't blame you, I guess." Again he shifted and lifted his weight in the stirrups as he gazed around the grounds of the run-down buildings. Someone was sure letting what used to be a nice farm go to ruin. It was a damned shame, too. More than half of the places he'd passed on his way out there were in the same shape.

Mandy's anger began to build as she saw what looked like contempt on the hawklike features of the stranger while he surveyed her home. It wasn't much now; but it was all she had, and she worked hard to keep what there was left in operating condition. How dare he turn up his nose at her only worldly possession.

"Mister, you don't have any business here, so get off my property."

The coal-black eyes came back to regard the kid thoughtfully. He still couldn't figure out what it was that caused his guts to churn at the sight of the ragamuffin, and it was setting his nerves on edge. "I was told that this farm belonged to a George Coulter. Do I dare to presume that's you?"

Mandy eyed him coldly, her arm tiring from holding the heavy Sharps for so long. "That's my pa. But I'm in charge when he's not around. And—" the rifle swung in a half arc and back again—"he's not around."

The man's eyes were not amused as he continued to stare a hole through Mandy's chest and the fullness of her shirt. She slouched a little lower.

"All right, you're the boss. I reckon I'll deal with you."

He started to swing his leg over the saddle to stand and state his business when the kid growled, "I told you once to stay mounted, mister, and I won't repeat it." The rifle pointed a trifle lower than his mid-section, and his belly quivered instinctively.

If he had any sense at all he'd turn around and leave before he was tempted any further to haul the brat over his knee. "Have it your way, then." He settled back on the horse and touched the brim of his hat. "The name's Ryder Manning. I've been on the road for quite a spell and would be willing to work for a while for room and board." Looking around the clearing, he applauded himself for thinking of such a good cover. If ever a place needed a hand, this was it.

The kid never flicked an eyelash. "Sorry, mister. It don't cut. You don't look like any drifter I've ever seen, and I don't need help." Mandy mentally apologized for the lie, and her face fell a little as she also surveyed her surroundings.

When the stranger snorted in derision and eyed the sagging barn, Mandy's finger tightened on the trigger. Why not? There was no one around for miles to hear the shot, and there were any number of caves in the area where she could hide the body.

Ry saw the icy glint in the hard green eyes, saw the finger jerk, and knew he'd made a terrible tactical error. As Ryder's hand tightened on the reins, the horse backed away a step or two and rolled its eyes balefully, lowering its neck to relieve the pressure on the bit.

Ry forced himself to relax and shrugged his shoulders. "Sorry, it's just that it looked like you could use some help fixin' up the place. You being a kid and here all alone." Maybe he could get to the inconsiderate brat another way. Use a little honey.

Mandy would've laughed out loud if she wasn't so angry. Who did he think he was dealing with? Some stupid, hick child? Then it dawned on her. That was exactly who he thought he was conning. In fact, if it wasn't so dangerous, she'd almost consider his proposition just to keep an eye on him.

"Look, I told you I don't need any help, and I'm getting bored with all the chatter. Now for the last time, turn that cayuse and get on down the road." She pointed to the weed-congested lane with the muzzle of her rifle. The best thing she could do was to get rid of the obnoxious, good-looking man and as soon as possible. No doubt about it!

Ryder's hand lifted to tilt his hat. The little monster. He hadn't seen the last of Ryder Manning.

17

Not by a long shot. "Well, no harm in asking, is there?" Not expecting an answer, he turned the long-legged grulla and was starting toward the lane when he pulled back on the reins and turned in the saddle. "I don't suppose you'd spare a hungry traveler a decent meal?"

Without a word, Mandy put the rifle stock to her shoulder and sighted down the barrel.

"No, I didn't think so. Thanks for the hospitality, sonny."

As she watched the broad-shouldered back diminishing through the sight of the Sharps, Mandy felt a curious stirring in her chest. Ryder Manning. What a beautiful, masculine name for a handsome, virile man. When he'd called her "sonny," it had taken every bit of her self-control not to whip off her clothes and prove to him that she was a woman, a full-grown, ready-to-be-kissed woman. Under all the shapeless mounds of cloth, she possessed a great variety of generous curves in all of the appropriate places.

Sonny, indeed. She'd show him. A feeling of desolation settled over her thin back as she hunched her shoulders and trudged back into the barn to finish her chores. More than likely, she'd never see the blasted man again, anyway. And, much more than likely, it would be for the best. The man had a dangerous quality about him that was definitely disturbing. He wasn't a common drifter by any means.

In two days time she would see her cousin. He'd know what to do about the stranger.

As the man called Ryder Manning loped down the barely discernable road, he couldn't dispel the niggling suspicion that things were not as they seemed, and at the root of his uncertainty was that gangly, wet-behind-the-ears lad with the oversized weapon.

He chuckled to himself as he recalled the angry tilt to those incredibly green eyes and the way the boy's finger twitched on the rifle's trigger. Ry had no doubts but what the little spitfire would've blown a hole right through his middle with further provocation. It was wondering what he'd said to rile the kid so that was bothering Ry. All he'd done was offer to work for room and board, like every other drifter. The damn scraggly place sure as hell needed all the work it could get. It didn't look like there'd been a man around to do repairs for years.

Suddenly Ryder remembered the moist sheen to the sea-green eyes when he'd inferred that the place was run-down. Had he inadvertently hurt the brat's feelings? Poor kid. He was probably the only one at home to do the work, and the job was just more than he could handle.

Ry cursed at the memory of those slanted eyes and the perfect cream-colored complexion. The kid was too pretty for his own good and would sure have to watch out for himself with all of the desperate characters still roaming these backwoods. Most of the riffraff and cutthroats were cut off from bodily pleasures by wanted posters or other such social deterrents. A scrawny boy could be just as appealing to some men as a voluptuous woman.

The mustang jumped when his rider threw back his head and roared with laughter. Ry pitied the desperado who dared go up against the half-pint and his Sharps. Ry would put his money on the brat any day.

* * *

19

Mandy was halfway through a breakfast of freshly baked sourdough biscuits and fried bacon when she first heard whistling and then footsteps coming down the path behind the kitchen.

When a young voice broke into a jaunty rendition of a local barroom ditty, her face flamed crimson even as her taut nerves relaxed. She'd been as jumpy as a long-tailed cat in a room full of rocking chairs ever since her encounter with the man named Ryder Manning yesterday afternoon. And now, on top of everything else, her younger brother decided to honor her with his presence after a long, unannounced absence.

The kitchen door swung open with a bang as a tall, gangly youth followed his twitching nose to the pan of biscuits warming on the shelf in the antiquated stove.

"Mornin', sis. Them biscuits sure smell good. Got any gravy ta go on 'em?"

Mandy's eyes flashed a bright green as she eyed her brother's rumpled, dusty clothes and sleep tousled hair. Where in the world had he spent the night? The past few nights, come to think of it?

Before she could issue a civil "good morning" she asked, "Is that all you've got to say? Mornin', sis? And all you've got to worry about—whether there's gravy for the biscuits? You . . . you . . ." She began to sputter and stammer, wrestling with a fit of angry words, but not knowing exactly how to reprimand the young scoundrel.

Her brother flopped into a rickety chair and raised a pair of sheepish green eyes to plead ruefully with the spitting fury in the eyes equalled in brilliance only by his own.

As always, Mandy's anger abated as she gazed lovingly at her sibling. The color of their eyes was the only outward link of resemblance, but there was a closeness of spirit that few mothers and sons were privileged enough to share. For ten years she'd been mother, sister, friend, confidante and provider for the younger Jeremy Coulter, and she could almost read what was going through his mind right now. Suffering from growing pains, he was rebelling against her overprotective nature.

Instead of hanging his head, Jeremy jutted out his chin in youthful defiance. "I'm not a kid anymore, Amanda Jo. I can come and go as I please."

Her jaws worked convulsively, but it was several seconds before Mandy had her temper in control enough to speak calmly to the young boy yearning too hard to become a man. "Jeremy, you're only sixteen . . . already a man in many respects . . . still a boy in others. And you'll always be my baby brother."

As Jeremy's chest swelled and his face turned red, she hurried on to explain, "Don't you think I worry when you take off for three days and don't even see fit to tell me where you're going? You didn't even go to the funeral!"

Jeremy's eyes took on an excited glow. "We were busy. I . . . uh . . . couldn't get away."

"And you couldn't take the time to tell me you were leaving either, I suppose." The hurt in her voice caused a guilty flush to stain the boy's face a dark shade of motley pink, but his newfound independence made him lift his chin even higher as he puffed his thin chest out proudly.

"You make me sound like I'm still a baby, and I'm not! I don't have to report my whereabouts like a damn—darned prisoner."

The tears he saw rolling down his sister's face before she turned her back stopped him cold. He

21

hadn't seen her cry for almost ten years, not since he, Reno, Amanda and their father had returned from Liberty one afternoon to find their mother had run off—taking the three smaller children with her. But after the initial burst of tears at finding themselves deserted, Amanda Jo had straightened her back, rolled up her sleeves and dug in to take responsibility for the family. She had replaced her mother in the eyes of her two brothers and her father in a way only a ten-year-old could.

As Jeremy looked around the old, dilapidated house, he marveled that there wasn't a speck of dust or grease; not even a picture frame dared to slant askew. Mandy had done the best she could with what she had to work with, and she didn't deserve his harsh words. However, it did harden his resolve to continue working with Reno whenever possible.

"I didn't mean it, sis. Nothing in this world would make me hurt you. It's just that Reno and me and some of the guys had some . . . uh . . . business . . . to tend to. . . ."

Mandy's heart sank. So, he'd been with Reno. She should've known. Who could blame a sixteen-year-old boy for admiring a handsome, dashing, devil-may-care older brother? But she was afraid that older brother was traveling a trail to destruction, and she didn't want to see Jeremy follow blindly behind. She had to salvage something from this wretched life, and she was determined that Jeremy would grow up to make something of himself, even if it was too late for the rest of them.

Rather than getting Jeremy's back up by denouncing his association with Reno, Mandy walked calmly over to the skillet she'd used to fry the bacon and placed it over the flames to heat the grease. It took her only a minute to round up the ingredients

22

for the gravy.

Casually she asked, "What kind of business would keep you from your cousin's funeral?"

Again an excited glow set off Jeremy's eyes. "Oh, uh, nothing important, really. We just found some stray horses and took them to Liberty to the sale." A hand slid down from his belt to pat his bulging pocket, but he wasn't about to reveal the amount of money he carried. He didn't want to lie to Amanda Jo any more than was absolutely necessary. She had an uncanny knack for ferreting out the truth when she suspected him of lying to her.

Mandy snorted through her nose but didn't say anything about her brother's hemming and hawing. She knew the foolhardy Reno better than that. He'd grown-up with a lot of frustration and anger, and if he wasn't careful, that anger would drive him to his grave.

Reno, older than Mandy by two years, had been even more aware than she of the persecution by the Yankee carpetbaggers who literally took over after the fall of the South. They controlled the lawmen, the banks and the railroads. Her father had watched as his neighbors had lost their land after the war because of excessive taxes, or just because they'd worn the Gray uniform. By the skin of his teeth, George Coulter had saved their farm, but the taxes kept them penniless.

Looking longingly out the window, she pictured in her mind's eye the grand farm she'd known as a child. Poor Reno had watched, too, as everything important to a young child-adult went awry. He cried when he saw his mother aging before her time as she brought yet another baby into a life of poverty, and he hardened his heart as he stood by helplessly and watched his father drink his life and farm away.

She couldn't blame Reno for harboring so much hatred and aggression. He'd grown up with it as a way of life. Mandy hated the ruthless tactics of the Yankee controlled government too, but she didn't let her hate control her every waking thought.

"Aw, Amanda Jo. The gravy's burnin'." Jeremy had already cut three biscuits in half and spread them with cool butter. He watched in dismay as the thick bubbling liquid in the pan began to smoke and turn a brackish brown color.

Chapter Two

After finally managing to make a perfect pan of cream gravy for her brother's biscuits and tidying the kitchen, Mandy began the long trek up the worn path to her father's still. She dreaded having to see him. He was always drunk, unkempt and terribly foul-mouthed, even to his own daughter, but this mission was important enough to make the effort if there was the slightest chance that he could help her with Jeremy. Maybe he could sober up long enough to talk some sense to his son.

Pausing outside a thick growth of blackjack trees, Mandy took a deep breath, leaned down and pushed through the sharp, scratchy limbs. Even over the loud snapping of twigs she could hear the nasal buzz of a man snoring and knew the trip had probably been wasted.

Amanda broke through the clinging brush to enter a small littered clearing. Shards of broken crocks lay scattered about, along with pieces of burlap sacking. George Coulter lay sprawled against an upright barrel connected to the cooling still. A half-empty bottle of his freshest batch of corn whiskey was tilted in his lap, dribbling away drop by drop.

As Mandy reached down to set the bottle straight, George's hand shot out and grabbed her arm. Mandy, caught by surprise, yelled out in fear and pain.

"Ah, daughter, that's what ya git fer sneakin' up on an old man that way. Don't ya have no respect?"

"Sneak?" she cried. "Pa, how can anyone sneak through all that dry, crackly brush?"

"Now ya see how smart yore ole man is, huh? It'd take a powerful crafty fella to find this still."

The snorty, gurgling laugh that foamed through George's mouth turned Mandy's stomach. If only he were the same man he used to be: proud, hard working . . . clean. Now she could hardly bear to be near the unwashed, odorous body of the lazy, good-for-nothing man she was ashamed to call her parent.

Enough years had passed since her mother had left and the carpetbaggers had taken over that he could have put the past behind him and gone on with his life like the majority of their neighbors had done. But no, George continued to wallow in self-pity and exaggerated grief until no one came by to visit or even check on the welfare of his children anymore. Of course, the *children* were almost grown now, and Mandy had taken care of the boys and her pa the best she could. She hadn't needed or wanted any help, but still, it was a lonely life.

"Where's yore head, gal? Ain't ya listenin' ta me? I said, what'd ya come up here for? Don'tcha need ta be home puttin' in that garden and gettin' them fields cleared and ready for the hay crop?"

That did it! Mandy put her hands on her hips and threw the long tresses of her wavy chestnut hair over her shoulder where they were left to coil in thick strands down her straight, proud back.

26

"Oh yes, there're lots of things I could be doin' right now, but I mistakenly climbed all the way up here to ask my pa for a little help. But don't worry, I know better now. Just sit up here on your fat behind and drink your life away. I don't care anymore. And when Jeremy is brought home in a casket for buryin', I won't ask for your help diggin' the grave."

Mandy covered her mouth with her hand. She'd never spoken to her father that way before. Tears burned behind her eyelids, but she'd be darned if she was going to break down and cry. She'd been the backbone of the family for almost ten years, and she wouldn't be weak and weepy now. She had Jeremy to think about.

George Coulter scratched under his arm, snorted and fussed before grumbling, "You kids is most growed now. Nothin' I kin do ta make a difference. Go on an' git! You've got enough ta do ta keep ya out'n my hair."

Mandy's heart pounded painfully within her breast at her father's callous words. But what more had she expected? Remembering her cousin's request, she walked over to the pile of jugs and picked up a full one.

"Just put this on my bill," she said over her shoulder as she disappeared into the trees.

George ran a shaking hand over his eyes and squeezed the bridge of his nose between a thumb and forefinger. He remembered something he would like to have said to his daughter just before he fell back into an exhausted, drink-laden slumber. Soft snores again permeated the air as the sweet trills of nesting birds filled the now peaceful clearing.

*   *   *

The early afternoon sun had warmed the air enough to start a trickle of perspiration running in a tiny rivulet between Mandy's rounded breasts. The long walk back down the mountain had cooled her temper, and the burning anger directed at her father had lessened. She wished with all her heart that their confrontations didn't always end in a battle of wits and words. She really did love the man.

As she wiped the dampness from around her neck, she felt a film of dust and grime. Jeremy had taken off to heaven only knew where, and her pa was never home anymore; so what was to stop her from taking an hour off from chores and soaking in a nice relaxing tub bath? She usually just sponged off at the creek until it got warm enough to dunk herself in the water, and a real bath would be quite a treat.

Her pixie face lit up with a flashing smile as the thought dug in and took root. She'd have to work a little later tonight to make up the time, but a bath would definitely be worth it. Mandy spun in a circle and flung her head back to look up into the cloud-flecked sky. The breeze was just enough to whisk a few stray tendrils of her chestnut hair across her flushed cheeks. The sun's rays shone directly on her head, causing red highlights to glisten in the shimmering strands. What a glorious day to be alive.

Mandy finished dragging the large wooden tub from the shed beside the house and went into the kitchen to put a kettle of water on the stove to heat. As she reached for a towel to dry her hands, a flicker of movement outside the window caught her eye. A covey of quail flew from the bushes at the top of the hill just to the right of the house. Then she noticed a rabbit sprinting away from the same area, zigzagging from bush to bush.

Her eyes widened and her breath caught in her

28

throat, but Amanda Jo Coulter quickly swallowed her fear. This was her home. There was no one else around to defend it, so it was up to her to handle the situation. Her father and brothers had always accused her of being too independent for a woman, but to her way of thinking it was a good thing. Where were they now when she needed them? Where were they *anytime* she needed them?

Quickly Mandy ran into the living room and grabbed the flop hat. She took the few extra seconds to tuck her hair up under the headband, then took the Sharps from above the mantle. She checked to make sure it was loaded, then left the house by the front door in case there was someone watching the back where she had first detected movement.

She crept through the short brush as quietly as possible with her eyes searching ahead for twigs and dried leaves. She didn't want to announce her presence by sounding like an elephant tiptoeing through the forest. The faded shirt and pants she had saved as castoffs from her brothers blended in with the background—at least she hoped that they did.

Mandy was within about a hundred yards of where the quail had flown when she stopped to listen for any sound or movement. The birds could've flown for any number of reasons, but she wasn't going to take any chances, especially not now. She had to meet her cousin tomorrow and couldn't afford to have any nosey busybodies sneaking around to follow her.

Ry hunkered down between a couple of budding oak trees and scooted back into a clump of sumac. Damn! He thought he knew this country better than he evidently did. He'd intended to come out on the other side of this little ridge.

29

When his shoulder accidently brushed a bush concealing a covey of quail, he'd dropped to the ground and used his elbows and knees to crawl to a different position. Any good woodsman in the area could've spotted the way those birds were startled from their roost.

All he could do right now was stay quiet and keep his fingers crossed that no one was around the Coulter cabin. It was the old man's still he was trying to locate, not an angry Coulter pup.

As he settled into a more comfortable position, a grudging smile curved the corners of his lips. He still pictured the grubby kid with the big Sharps running him out of the yard. Under different circumstances, he would've shown the brat the hard end of his belt, but right now he figured it was easier to catch flies with honey than with vinegar. He couldn't afford to get the Coulters suspicious of him this early in the game.

Mandy held her position for several minutes and was about to move on when she heard the rustling of leaves. Her eyes scanned the trees but couldn't detect any trace of the breeze that had been blowing earlier. Her quarry, whatever or whomever it was, had to be close.

She crept forward, taking pains not to disturb the dry brush. Her brothers had taken a lot of time and effort teaching her how to hunt and stalk prey. Now was as good a time as any to put those skills to use. But what if it was a human animal? Would she be able to pull the trigger?

Mandy's eyes hardened and her pointed chin jutted firmly. Damn right she could, if he was a threat to her family. And at this moment, the life of a prized member was in dire jeopardy.

At the same time, every instinct at Ry's command was tuned to his surroundings. There was someone, or something, close by. He could *feel* it. He reached to the scabbard on his belt and pulled his knife, testing the blade down the back of his hand for sharpness. When a length of black, curly hair floated to the ground, his mouth curved in satisfaction.

Mandy was crouched as low to the ground as her body could get without crawling. Just a few more feet and she would make it to a niche between the trees. Once behind that tall sumac, she could straighten her position and take a better look around. She hadn't heard a thing except the rapid pounding of her own heart for several minutes. Just another foot or so . . .

Now was the time for Ry to make his move if he was ever going to do so. He almost groaned as his muscles protested the quick rise from the ground.

"Oooff!" was the simultaneous explosion of breath as two bodies collided with a solid "thunk."

Green eyes widened with horror as they caught the glint of sunlight off a deadly bowie knife. In a lightning-quick reflex action, Mandy launched herself at the buckskin-clad arm holding the weapon.

Ryder was so taken by surprise at the unexpected impact that he was momentarily stunned. How could something like this have happened? In all of his twenty-five years he'd never relaxed his guard enough to allow anyone to slip up on him. He'd never be able to face his grandfather again.

The shock of the moment began to wear off as he became aware of his hand being twisted by a surprisingly hard grip from such a small attacker. When a solid knee in the belly pushed the air from his lungs, he realized that he had better concentrate on defending, rather than castigating himself.

31

Ry's left arm wrapped around the aggressive body's neck and jerked the head back against his own shoulder, pinning the squirming form to his chest. His right arm, longer and stronger than the person's gripping it, jerked swiftly and came away with only a long furrow or two of skin left underneath the fingernails of the persistant boy. He had finally recognized the clothing of the Coulter kid and was trying to get off his back into a sitting position to subdue the brat when the kid's now free arms went back over his head and started pulling hair and trying to get his fingers in Ry's eyes. Ryder's right arm instinctively drew forward to close around the boy's body.

Mandy was fighting every way she knew how: scratching, gouging, kicking. If she could only turn to face her opponent, she could inflict a lot more damage. She had thrown her arms over the back of her head to get a grip on the intruder when she again saw the glint of sun on metal as the stranger moved to protect himself.

Immediately, her hands released the thick, curly hair to attach themselves around the wrist holding the long, lethal blade. Her heels began to beat and pound at the assailant's legs in an effort to take his attention away from the knife.

With the insistent pain in his shin, Ryder had had enough! "Ouch! You damn brat! Quick kicking me. I'm not trying to hurt you." Not yet anyway, he thought as he promised himself the privilege at the next opportunity.

Mandy didn't quit fighting, but her strength was diminishing. She felt the muscles beneath her back flex and tighten as the man pushed himself off the ground high enough to make a twisting turn.

Suddenly she found herself pinned to the earth and looking directly into angry, obsidian eyes.

Neither spoke for several moments as they both fought for breath after the quick but vicious struggle.

During the brief respite, Mandy was in a quandry. Here she was, lying under a terribly frightening, extremely handsome man. What would any red-blooded . . . boy do in such a situation? She had to think fast or succumb to a typically female reaction.

When Ry let out an unconscious moan from the pain suffusing his shins, she reacted out of pure self-preservation. "Pardon me all to hell, mister, if I'm a hurtin' ya, but git yore damned elbow out of my chest." She kept her voice pitched low, imitating her father's abuse of the English language.

Ryder had been about to do just that until he felt a familiar softness under the baggy flannel shirt. Was it possible? Naw! No way could this ragged urchin be a girl . . . woman? He moved the exploring elbow in a semi-circle and smothered a lecherous grin. No, by damn! No child, this—but a woman full blown. His mind began to race. Now that he had made the startling discovery, just what did he intend to do about it?

Mandy's anger gave her a strength she never dreamed of possessing as she put her hands on the stranger's chest and shoved violently. Her heart gave a sudden lurch as he moved just enough to allow her to scramble backward, out from under his disturbingly masculine body, but he still trapped her legs with his chest. Suddenly she became aware of a tingling pain in her right hand.

When she'd pushed against the solid mass of his chest, something hard and metallic had pierced the

33

heel of her palm through the material of his shirt pocket. The object was kind of round . . . with sharp points. As dawning apprehension changed her angry features to a look of confusion, she was almost certain that what she'd felt had been a badge . . . almost positive. Or was it just over-zealous suspicion?

As the boy's—woman's—struggles came to an abrupt halt, Ry wrapped his left arm around her ankles to keep her in his grasp while he slid the knife back in its sheath with his right hand. There wouldn't be any need for it now, he hoped. Surely he was man enough to keep the little spitfire under control now that he knew her gender. After all, she was a small woman but very voluptuous. Now, why did he have to think of that?

The image of the adept way she'd handled that Sharps came unbidden to his mind, and he realized the possibility of his underestimating her abilities. In one fluid motion he pushed off the ground and grabbed the back of her jacket, holding her at arm's length by the fold of her collar just like he'd hold an angry kitten by the scruff of its neck.

Mandy felt like a rag doll dangling from the strong grip of the stranger's fingers. She'd known all along he was a big man, but he towered over her petite frame by at least a foot. He might have intimidated her at any other time, but at the moment she was too mad to think clearly.

"Put me down, you stupid . . . I mean. . . . Damn it! Take yore paws off'n me, ya big bully."

It had taken a lot of time and patience on her cousin's part to teach Mandy to speak and act like a lady, but now definitely was not the time to show off her accomplishments. The longer she could fool this oaf into thinking she was a boy, the better off she'd be—especially until she could find out what he was up to.

Ry couldn't help the grin that twitched at one corner of his mouth. He remembered every word the little wildcat had spoken yesterday, and she had used perfect grammar, for a while. Why was she going along with this idiotic charade?

"All right, I'll let you up. But will you promise not to shoot or knife me in the back?" he jokingly teased.

"What? Why, only a low-down, yella-bellied, chicken-livered Yankee'd do somethin' as cowardly as that. Besides, yore the hooligan that's sneakin' 'round whar ya ain't welcome." Mandy was so indignant that she was almost sputtering. To think that he'd accuse her of being a back stabber.

Ry's hand loosened its grip on Mandy's collar, and she plunked ungracefully to her feet. "I told you yesterday that I was looking for George Coulter, and I intend to find him—one way or another."

"An' I tole you yesterday that he ain't here. Now git off this property fore I fix it so's yore stay is permanent." Mandy's eyes searched the ground around her feet as she sought her Sharps.

The movement of Ry's hand was as swift as a rattlesnake's as he grabbed her collar once again and jerked her to her toes. "Oh, no you don't . . . sonny. We'll just leave that gun where it's at and go down to the house and wait. I'm sure old George will turn up sooner or later."

Mandy began to panic when she remembered all of the feminine paraphernalia she'd laid out in preparation for her bath. She couldn't let him go to the house under any circumstances. That meant she was going to have to tell him where to find George, her father. Besides, from the shape he was in when she left him, he wouldn't be of any use to this man.

She quit wriggling and trying to kick herself free of the unbreakable grip and favored the poor fool with an ingratiating smile. "If ya put me down, I'll tell ya where to find George. Deal?"

Her eyes roamed over the stranger's face while he was still looking off toward the house. He was undeniably the most handsome man she'd seen around these parts. Even his hair was beautiful now that his hat was lying on the ground after the scuffle. The ebony tendrils had natural curls and waves that put her own straight tresses to shame, but at least her long locks were easily tied back and quickly stuffed under a hat if need be.

Ry brought his gaze from the house back to Mandy, wondering why she didn't want him in her home. Reluctantly he released her from his grasp and set her down more gently this time. At least she was willing to tell him where to find George Coulter.

"Deal."

It was much later that evening, after Mandy had successfully taken her bath and was preparing for another lonely meal, when she heard the loud rap on the front door. Her head tilted warily. She hadn't heard anyone approach the house, and she prided herself on her ability to detect any strange noises that didn't belong in the peaceful clearing surrounding most of the house.

Since the knife she'd used to slice a loaf of freshly baked bread was lying close by, she picked it up and held it hidden behind her leg. Thank heavens she'd once again donned her brother's castoffs. With that stranger lurking about, she couldn't be too careful.

As Mandy passed the broken mirror hanging in the hallway leading to the front of the house, she happened to notice the long, clean strands of chestnut hair hanging down her back. She'd just made it to the chair by the door where she had dropped her coat and hat earlier when another loud knock rattled the door.

She laid the knife down and with one or two quick twists had her hair hidden beneath the dented crown of her hat. Remembering the knife at the last minute, she held it behind her back as she opened the door just enough to see through the small crack. When the door was suddenly pushed from the outside, she barely moved her head in time to avoid a black eye.

Ryder Manning had been waiting on the sagging porch, hat in hand, much longer than he ever waited on anything. And after spending the entire afternoon with his friend George and a couple of jugs of George's home brew, he was anxious to get on with his business. He knew the brat was home; he'd seen her silhouette in the kitchen window when he'd ridden up. Of course, he hadn't ridden right to the porch, as he'd wanted to take a look around the place first. So far, he hadn't found what he was looking for.

When the door creaked open inch by inch, Ry's impatience finally got the better of him. He slapped it open with the palm of his hand and bulled his way into the living room. The girl was standing silently behind the door, staring, while his head spun and he staggered to keep his feet. Damn, that homemade liquor was hard on a man's equilibrium.

One quick glance around the room encompassed all there was to see as far as furnishings. A rocking chair with hand-sewn cushions sat in front of a limestone and granite fireplace. The girl's Sharps hung above the oak mantle. The rest of the furnishings consisted of a couple of hardback chairs and a table placed in front of the only window. The table had a delicate lace doily centered beneath a cracked vase containing dried cattails. There were no wall hangings except for several winter coats, and the curtains were old and tattered; but the room shone with cleanliness. Even the worn-out boards on the floor fairly sparkled.

Ryder's flesh quivered with surprise when he felt the tip of a sharp blade poke through his leather shirt. The cold sensation ran all the way to his toes. Hell and damnation! This was the second time in one day the little minx had gotten the best of him.

It hadn't taken tremendous intelligence to figure out that the stranger was drunk on his feet, but what Mandy didn't know was why he would come to the house after she'd warned him off—twice.

Her voice was low and throaty as she pressed the knife a little harder and said, "Mister, you'd better have a powerful good reason for bustin' in here like some wild bull. Start talkin' or I'm liable ta shove this knife right between them ticklish ribs of yorn."

Standing so close to the big man's body, she couldn't help but admit what a shame it would be to puncture such a superb specimen of male strength and virility. Not only were his lips and hair beautiful, but he even smelled good. Kind of horsey and leathery and . . . outdoorsy, like the freshness of a spring breeze.

Ry teetered back and forth from his toes to his heels, his voice slurring when he said, "Ryder Manning, sonny, reporting for duty. Where shall I start first?"

Mandy's eyes bugged out, and her jaw drooped. "What? What're ya babblin' 'bout now?"

The grin Ry plastered across his lips was somewhat lopsided as he tipped his hat and almost lost his balance. "I'm your new hired hand, ma'-sonny. Hic!

And if youse don't believe me, jhust ashk your pa."

There was no way Mandy could manhandle the man back out the door as he was wobbling farther and farther into the room. And she could take no satisfaction in killing a man who wouldn't even feel the pain, so she let the knife drop to her side. He'd probably forgotten she had it, anyway.

"Somethin' shure shmells good in there." Ry was making his way toward the kitchen with the brat trailing behind. Damned woman was going to kill him on an empty stomach. She had no heart; she didn't.

Exasperated beyond belief, Mandy finally gave in. "Oh, all right, some on. There's enough for one more. Besides, I can't talk to you very well in the condition you're in now." Too late she realized she'd dropped her backwoods drawl, but she hoped he was inebriated enough not to notice. The way her day had gone so far, it was almost more than she could expect.

Mandy sat in awed silence while she watched Ryder Manning—if she remembered the name correctly—sop up the remaining gravy with the last piece of warm-from-the-oven bread. He had eaten more rabbit stew than Reno and Jeremy put together and was looking around the table as if still ravenous. There was half of a dried apple pie left from yesterday, but she'd planned to save it until Jeremy was home. Of course, with her wayward brother pulling his disappearing act yet again this afternoon, why should she bother? It was fun watching a hungry man, a non-related hungry man, enjoy her cooking for a change.

Mandy's thoughts took a startled turn when the man asked, "What's your name, sonny? Or should I just call you boss?" She watched studiously as Ry licked a small drop of gravy from his index finger, and her eyes followed the movement of his hand as he reached for the napkin in his lap to wipe his oh-so-perfectly-shaped lips.

Her own mouth felt dry, and she licked her lips before carefully answering his abrupt question. "Ah, just call me . . . A.J. Yes, that's what folks around here c-call me."

Ry leaned back in his chair, rocking on the two back legs as he patted his lean belly. "Okay, A.J. it is. That was a mighty fine spread, son. It's not often I find a busy youngster like yourself with such culinary skills. Surely you didn't learn how to cook all by yourself?"

Mandy Jo could've kicked herself. She hadn't even thought about that. Maybe she should keep the pie hidden after all. It sure wouldn't be too much of a chore to finish it off all by herself. Unconsciously she licked her lips again, drawing Ryder's attention to the moist, pink tip of her tongue as it glided sensuously over the full bottom layer of flesh.

He watched as A.J.'s face contorted into a worried frown and wondered again how he could have so mistakenly thought of her as a boy. His stomach knotted in frustration. It was going to take a super-human effort on his part to maintain discipline and self-control through the continuation of this game they were both enacting.

The girl's eyes were turned to a window, giving Ry time to study the near-perfect features. Her eyes were the most arresting he had ever seen—a luminous green—brilliant and sparkling like precious stones. The piquant nose was short and thin, turned up slightly at the tip, lending her an elfish quality that was most endearing. And that mouth—the fullness of her lips—invited him to taste and touch. . . . Ry shook his head to clear his muddled brain and, instead of waiting any longer for her to answer his question, scolded, "Do you always wear your hat at the table? Hasn't anyone taken the time to teach you any manners?"

Mandy puffed up with indignation. She had forgotten more manners than that insufferable bore could ever hope to learn. But he was right! Everyone knew better than to wear a hat at the table. Even her incorrigible brothers. Somehow she had to change the subject without making him suspicious.

"Would ya eat a slab of apple pie?" She plopped her elbows on the table and rested her chin on top of her hands as she stared at her "guest" to see if he was still inebriated enough to be so easily misled.

Sure enough, Ry almost salivated at the thought of apple pie. God, it'd been months since he'd eaten homemade pie. But he had to get in one more dig and repeated his earlier questions, curious as to how she would answer. "Sure I'd like a piece of pie. But when did a young scalawag like yourself ever learn to bake a pie? I assume you did the baking?"

Mandy was almost to the point of not caring whether or not he learned she was a woman. "Listen, mister, cut out the wisecracks 'bout ma cookin'. I may be a . . . boy, but when I had ta learn ta cook or starve, I decided I might's well learn ta do it right. If'n ya stay 'round here, ya'll find that I don't do anything halfway. Now, if'n ya want pie, fine. Just shut yore yap and I'll get it." As she turned, she missed Ry's slight nod as he silently saluted her spirit.

While she walked to the cupboard and pulled out the pie tin, she couldn't help but think that having the stranger around where she could keep an eye on him might be for the best. Knowing his whereabouts at all times would surely relieve some of her tension and worrying.

Mandy placed a good-sized portion of the pie on two plates, literally threw Ry's plate in front of him, then sat down and began to eat with obvious relish. It was a curse from Mother Nature that she was born with so many sweet teeth.

When the girl had shoved the pie in front of him, the back of her fingers had brushed lightly across the bare skin of Ry's wrist. He was flabbergasted at the jolt of electricity that still tingled where she had unknowingly touched his flesh. Was there no end to the torment he was to experience at the hands of this . . . this . . . innocent child—wanton courtesan? No completely apt description of the luscious scamp came to mind at present.

After cleaning her plate of every last flake of crust, Mandy stared unseeing out of the kitchen window, her mind working furiously as she tried to figure out how to get to her cousin tomorrow unobserved, not only by the stranger, but by any number of enemies that might be watching her movements. So far it had been quiet and peaceful, no one even coming by to offer condolences. But if this man was suspicious and snooping around, others could be doing the same thing.

She had been staring so intently at nothing that her eyes hurt when she blinked, and her hand trembled slightly as she reached up to rub the tension from her forehead. It was scary to think of herself as being all alone with the fate of her dearest friend resting in her own slim hands. What if she couldn't handle it? What if she made a mistake? What if—

At a moment that couldn't have been more opportune, Ryder Manning interrupted Mandy's rapid descent into panic. He had once again pushed back his chair to rock on the back legs as he stretched his arms over his head and yawned. The good food and black coffee had cleared the fog from his brain, but he suspected he'd still suffer from the afternoon's indulgence in the morning.

"That was a good supper, A.J.. If you do everything else the way you cook . . ." Ry left the rest of his sentence unfinished as he ogled curves even the baggy clothes were unable to hide. In one swift, only slightly wobbly movement, he stood up and began to gather his dishes. "Let's get these washed, and then you can show me where to bed down."

For one daring moment, Mandy glimpsed the image of the long, muscular frame stretched across her feather quilt. The most disconcerting part of the image though, was that she was lying full length next to him. With a suppressed groan, she placed her palms on the table and pushed herself erect. She had enough problems without her nighttime fantasy creeping into daylight hours. "N-No, never mind. It's no trouble, and I can do them faster by myself."

Mandy almost dropped her plate as Ry's elbow grazed hers when they both turned toward the sink at the same time. A porcelain basin was already filled with warm water and soap, and they placed the dishes into the suds.

Ry's voice was deep and soft as he rubbed filmy bubbles between his fingers. "It's been so long since I washed a plate with anything but sand that I'd consider it a treat if I could do the honors."

Mandy couldn't catch the giggle that erupted from her throat in time, and then melted at the flash of white teeth as Ry reciprocated. "Well, if ya think doin' dishes is a treat, I'd hate ta have ta do yore

43

chores." Worry over whether or not she was consistently keeping up with her hillbilly accent faded in her awe of this unpredictable man. In all of her nineteen years, never had Mandy seen one of her brothers, or her father, willingly offer to dunk a calloused hand in dishwater. This was an evening she would have to store away in her memories for future reference.

Ry rubbed the back of his neck, feeling the tiredness from the past few days of hard traveling begin to settle in his mucles and joints. "Well, after tonight, I'll be doing *your* chores. Speaking of which, where shall I start first in the morning?" In his mind's eye he saw himself carrying a tray into the girl's room at dawn and pictured the lithe grace of her slender form as she stretched and smiled at him. The sheet slipped low on her naked body as he sat down on the edge of the bed and reached out to—

"Watch out! We don't have very many good plates left."

The startled cry brought Ry back to reality as he watched the alert reflexes that enabled her to catch the plate that had slipped through his fingers while daydreaming. "Uh oh, I'm sure sorry ma'-A.J. Don't know what came over me. Must be more tired than I thought." He then turned away, flicking soap from his long fingers, so she couldn't see the state of his arousal from the so-called daydream.

Mandy took his place before the dishpan and told Ry to go on to the barn and go to bed; she'd finish in the kitchen. Her eyes rounded, and she gritted her teeth with frustration when she heard the next words.

"Oh, but your pa said I was to have your brother's room. Said he'd been gone for some time now and that I'd surely be done before he'd have need of it again."

44

Mandy duly noted the sly grin spreading over the stranger's face. "But you can't . . . I mean, it wouldn't . . . it's not . . ." How could she explain? Why couldn't he stay under the same roof, and why wouldn't it be proper or decent for a man to live in the same house with a *boy?* Oh, what had she gotten herself into now?

Chapter Three

Distant thunks of sound intruded Mandy's dreams as she slowly awakened, one eye at a time, to find that she'd overslept by at least two hours, probably because she'd tossed and turned all night thinking about the intriguing stranger now occupying the room across the hall. Stretching her arms over her head, she felt the sheet slip down to expose vast amounts of sleep-warmed flesh to the chill morning air. How tempting it was to take a day off and just lie in bed for a change.

But it was impossible to relax again. It bothered her to still feel the intensity of Ryder Manning's eagle eyes as they bored into her across the grave the morning of the funeral. Her skin rose in goosebumps as once again a sick feeling of dread invaded the beautiful spring morning.

It had nothing to do with her knowledge of the suspected badge. There was something . . . threatening . . . about the man. It was as if he could see through her and knew what she was thinking, hiding.

Gratefully, upon hearing the kitchen door slam, Mandy put aside her dark musings and languidly rolled to the edge of the bed, ready to don her cherished shirt and overalls. As she twitched her nose in delicate fashion, she decided it was about time to wash the well-worn articles before she started smelling like the ragamuffin she appeared to be. If only her disguise would fool him a little while longer.

"Mandy! Amanda Jo Coulter, where in the devil are you? Man—"

"Shush up right now, Jeremy, before I plant my knuckles between your teeth." Mandy spoke in husky gasps, out of breath from running to the kitchen in hopes of silencing her brother before the stranger heard the loud raving. "What's gotten into you, Jeremy? Didn't you see that stranger? Keep your voice down, for heaven's sake."

Jeremy's face was beet red, and he was also breathing heavily. Angry, he continued to shout. "That stranger is exactly why I'm a yellin', Mandy Jo. What the heck's he doin' here? And he said somethin' 'bout sleepin' here in the house last night . . . with you? It's not true, is it, Mandy?"

The youngster's voice sounded so childish as it cracked, and so wistful at the same time, that Mandy had to stifle a giggle. Poor Jeremy had been trying to talk himself into being the man of the house for two years now, especially since he'd grown and filled out so in the last year. It must've been quite a shock to find his sister and a perfect stranger sleeping in the same house, unchaperoned, the minute his back was turned.

As he paced back and forth across the bare floor with his fingers laced behind his back, Jeremy's thoughts weren't trained so much on his sister's misdeeds as on his own stupidity in leaving a poor defenseless girl alone so often. But if Reno and he were ever going to get ahead and carry out their plan . . . well, he just wouldn't always be around.

As he looked up and opened his mouth to ask Mandy about the stranger, he noticed her attire for the first time. Instead of his beautiful sister, Amanda Jo, he was gawking at a sloppily dressed, bedraggled urchin with its finger pressed to its lips asking for silence. Bewildered, Jeremy nodded his head to show he understood—whether he actually did or not.

He let Mandy draw him into his bedroom and waited while she closed the door. He even listened attentively as she whispered, "Jeremy, I'm so glad you're here. And just hold on a minute; he doesn't know I'm not a boy. These old clothes have fooled him from the very start."

Jeremy's mouth twitched as his eyes followed the curves protruding at various strategic locations in his old coveralls and figured the stranger was either blind or stupid, or maybe both. At least that assumption eased his peace of mind. More softly he conceded, "Well, if you say so. But what's he doin' here?" Jeremy's brows narrowed as he frowned at his sister. "And what do you mean by 'from the start'? It sounds like you've seen a lot of him." Surely Mandy couldn't be interested. . . . Naw!

"It's a long-story, brother dear, and I promise to fill you in later. Right now I need to get breakfast started." As the two walked toward the kitchen, Mandy tried to explain about their father supposedly hiring the stranger to help out around the farm.

Jeremy guiltily darted his gaze out of the side window, then with real enhtusiasm told Mandy, "Gee, that's great, sis. The place could sure use some sprucin' up."

"But we wouldn't need him if you'd—" Mandy clamped her jaw shut. They'd been through this

48

before, and she hadn't been able to keep him close to home; so why should now be any different? There was something he *could* do, though. "Jeremy, please stay around here today. I've got something very important to do. Will you keep an eye on him? Please?"

Mandy dipped the dishes out of the rinse water and placed them on a clean, cup towel to drain. As hard as she tried, she couldn't keep her eyes from straying to Ryder Manning and her brother as they repaired the fence around the chicken coop.

Jeremy, in his mid-teens, had the thin, lanky, angular frame of a growing boy. Ryder, on the other hand, though still a young man, had filled out and fleshed over all of the jutting bones and sinewy muscles. Both men had removed their shirts as the sun warmed their bodies, and their skin glistened with perspiration.

The sun seemed to reflect from the whiteness of Jeremy's skin, while soaking familiarly into the smooth, rich-brown tones of Ryder's lustrous flesh. The muscles across Ry's upper back and shoulders bunched and flexed as he lifted a board to hold it in place while Jeremy hammered the nails.

The back of Mandy's neck was wet, and her shirt clung to the surface of her chest and breasts as she became warm just watching the graceful movements of her stranger. It took the pain from the steaming water burning her submerged hand to bring her back to her senses. If she didn't get a move on, she'd never make it to the cave before midday.

Mandy quickly gathered flour, salt and pepper from her cupboards, then lit a candle to find bacon and half a smoked ham in the cellar. She then added

49

the biscuits she'd hidden from breakfast. Her cousin always loved her flaky baking powder biscuits, bless him.

She placed all of the items into a large gunnysack and was on her way out the door before she remembered the important jug of corn liquor. He'd probably make her come all the way back if she forgot it. To play it safe, she made a mental list to be sure she had everything else before edging her way to the door and looking carefully around. It wasn't that she couldn't depend on Jeremy, she just didn't know how the stranger would react if he caught her sneaking off.

She made a dash across the open space between the house and the barn, then crept into the safety of the tall bushes at the base of the hill. When the birds began to chirp overhead and all was calm again, she moved as quietly as any woodland creature through the undergrowth until reaching the path that led to a dry creek bed. She followed the shallow gulch until it dipped down and broke from the woods into a small clearing.

At the far edge of the clearing was a shed and corral containing, in Mandy's opinion, the most beautiful sorrel thoroughbred in the county. He'd heard her approach, and with all four legs planted in picturesque form, head held high, ears pricked forward alertly, he greeted her with a loud, guttural nicker.

"Good morning, Red Fox. Have you missed me, boy?" Mandy ran her palm over the horse's forehead and murmured sweet nothings in his ear while brushing the sleek, red coat. "We haven't gone for a ride for two whole days, have we fella? Well, today we're going to get a lot of exercise." She finished cinching the saddle in place and then slipped the bit between the horse's teeth, all the while talking in her

50

sweet, sing-song monologue. She knew by watching the flick of Red Fox's ears and the movements of his head that he understood every word.

"We're going to see your old master today, fella. Hope he's doing okay all alone in that ole cave." There was a muted shuffle as Mandy mounted and Red Fox's unshod feet clipped the dusty ground. The horse's head bobbed up and down as Mandy peered between his ears and watched for the turnoff to the cave.

Finally, she spotted the barely perceptible game trail that angled off and disappeared behind two large boulders. She'd never have known where to look for the trail if her cousin hadn't pointed out the odd markings on the trees behind the rocks. Dismounting, she wrapped and tied burlap around her horse's feet to mute any sign of her passing. Then she stepped into the saddle again and worked her way across an old rock slide before merging into the trees and winding up the steep slope of the hill.

Mandy rode slowly and carefully over the faint path that sifted through the Missouri countryside. Her mind was so distant that she missed the spectacular beauty of the green, tree-studded swells rising to either side as her horse plodded methodically along.

As Red Fox snorted and shook his head, Mandy reached down to pat his strong, muscled neck. Her cousin had presented her with Red Fox when he'd moved back from Tennessee, and she'd never been more pleased with a gift. Red Fox was such a proud animal and could outrun any horse within a thirty mile radius. Always appreciative of good horseflesh, the image of the stranger's compact, sturdy little mustang flashed into her mind. Now there was another fine specimen. Mandy couldn't help but feel a thrill as she wondered who would win if they ever matched a race.

It took almost two hours of strenuous riding before Mandy and Red Fox reached the cave. The trail they followed had disappeared half an hour earlier because the same route to the cave was never used more than once, therefore leaving no distinct trail into the area.

Mandy dismounted and walked to within ten feet of a thick growth of weeds and bushes. She whistled a fair imitation of the call of the bobwhite, with one planned variation, several times before the wall of brush rustled and began to shift. Red Fox, who had been trained to ground-tie, snorted, then stood patiently and watched as his rider gripped one of the protruding branches and helped to move the hand-crafted barrier.

Mandy and her cousin had worked for hours on the clever device, using limbs for the outside frame and crisscrossing the interior space with rope. They then wove weeds and branches throughout to create a natural look that blended with the rest of the scenery. It was easy to remove the brush after it wilted and then replace it with fresh. No one would guess what was hidden behind the dense barricade without having previous knowledge of the cave's existence.

Mandy gasped and giggled with pleasure when her cousin appeared and swung her off her feet to twirl around and around until she was giddy with dizziness. "My goodness, Jesse, I hope you don't greet all of your visitors this enthusiastically. It'd scare them off faster than that old buffalo gun you used to carry."

Jesse laughed and stated, "I haven't had to worry much about visitors, but you can rest assured that the only ones I'd hug and kiss would be those of the female persuasion." He stopped spinning and held Mandy in place until she regained her equilibrium. "But I must admit, it sure is good to see a familiar face. Even old man Crittenden would look good right now."

At the mention of Governor Crittenden, Mandy's face sobered instantly, and Jesse wondered at the worried expression that quickly gained control. "What is it, Amanda Jo? What's causing that beautiful face to look so sad?"

Jesse had always been family oriented and was extremely loyal and protective of all its membeers. But there was something special about Amanda Jo, and she was his favorite. Maybe it was because her mother had deserted her at such a young age, and in reality her father, too; while Jesse had always had such strong support from his own.

At first, he'd just felt sorry for her and brought presents of hair brushes and new dresses to help ease her loss. But it was Mandy's adoration and free gift of unqualified love that made all of his offerings pale in comparison. And now in return for that love and trust, he was placing her future in jeopardy.

"Speaking of our illustrious governor reminded me all too soon of something we really need to talk about." Mandy looked over her shoulder and tried to see through the encompassing woods. "Let's go inside first. You need to stay out of sight as much as possible."

Jesse had taken hold of Red Fox's reins and accepted the big horse's affectionate nuzzling as they walked through the narrow entrance of the cave. Then he and Mandy carefully replaced the concealing frame in front of the opening. The cave was long and ran down a slope where candles were spaced intermittently to allow enough light to alleviate most of the danger from the descent.

The slope leveled off as they entered a large cavern illuminated by a flickering fire. Supplies were stacked neatly on shelves built against the rock surface of the right wall. There were canned goods of all kinds and various pots and pans. A large skillet rested on a flat rock next to the flames. Beyond the fire and straight ahead, a large pallet was neatly made up with blankets folded and stacked at the foot.

Jesse walked Red Fox around the left side of the cave and through an entrance that led to another smaller cavern than the one used for living. Hay was stacked high against one wall, and ropes had been strung against the other to partition off several stalls for horses. Toward the back of the room was a small indention to the floor filled with water from some sort of hidden spring. There was another covered opening that Mandy knew led out onto a narrow ledge from which there was almost a thirty-foot drop to the gulch below. Her cousin had chipped away rock and dirt from the face of the cliff, making enough room for a horse and rider to leave the cave in case of emergency. It was dangerous, but it could be done.

Mandy forked hay into one of the stalls while Jesse unsaddled and brushed Red Fox. "You know how lonely I've been? I haven't even had a horse to talk to. So, I looked out the back door over there and chatted with a mother hawk until I scared her off. I wonder if that says anything about my gift for gab? Oh well, I've never been accused of being a brilliant conversationalist."

Taking a deep breath, Jesse seemed to realize that he was rambling and finished currying the horse in silence since Mandy seemed too preoccupied to notice one way or the other.

In the living quarters of the cave, several large stones had been rolled beside the fire to use as seats. Taking one, Mandy held her palms out to the flames to ward off the perpetual chill of the damp interior of the cave.

Jesse sat on another of the rocks as amusement twinkled in his pale blue eyes. Evidently his cousin agreed with his statement about being a poor conversationalist. But as her silence continued and she stared into the flames, he began to absorb some of her worry.

"Okay, Amanda Jo, what's bothering you? I don't like to see you so upset. Does it have anything to do with what you wanted to talk to me about?"

Mandy leaned forward, placing her elbows on her knees as she turned her head toward her cousin. "You remember the stranger I pointed out to you at the funeral, right before your mother started crying?"

His mind had been so preoccupied that day that it was hard for Jesse to recall much about that particular incident. "Just barely, hon. I'd just begun to look in that direction when all of the commotion started. I never really saw him."

"Well, he's at the house now."

The information was as subtly dropped as a thunderbolt. "What? Why? When?" Jesse stopped, unable to put his thoughts into more articulate sentences. But he was relieved to see Mandy's eyes light up and the corners of her mouth lift in even a semblance of a grin.

"Let's see . . . *what* he's doing there is working. He hunted George up and swears Dad gave him a job. *Why* he's there is anybody's guess. . . . *He* says he was broke and hungry. *When* he first came by was the afternoon of the funeral, and then again yesterday."

Jesse pulled at his ear thoughtfully. "So, he was at

the funeral, then just accidently showed up at your place looking for a job. That's not really so—"

"But that's not all. We got in sort of a scuffle yesterday and . . . well, I'm almost positive I felt a badge hidden in his, ah, shirt pocket." Mandy tried to hide her blush by covering her burning cheeks with her palms. It was almost a relief when Jesse reprimanded her.

"Amanda Jo Coulter! What were your hands doing on a strange man's chest in the first place?" As concerned as Jesse was about the news of the stranger, he couldn't help the slight quirk of his lips at his cousin's obvious embarrassment and absolute naiveté.

Mandy felt a lot better when she realized Jesse was teasing her and reached over to slap at his knee. "Quit that! This is serious. What are we going to do about him?"

Jesse shook his head. "I don't know, Amanda Jo. Do you know his name?"

"Yes, it's . . . Ryder Manning." She'd thought of him as "the stranger" for so long that she'd almost forgotten he had a name.

Jesse stood up and began to pace back and forth in front of the flickering flames, causing shadows to dance along the walls of the cave. "That name's familiar, but I don't know from where. I'll have to think on it for a while." He grinned and held his hands in the air, looking around the small interior of his enforced dwelling. "And I don't seem to have anything better to do right now."

Mandy watched her cousin pace the dirt floor with a nervous energy that'd been his mainspring for as long as she could remember. He even reminded her of a taut, coiled spring, ready to unwind with only the slightest pressure.

With her palms braced on her knees, Mandy rose and went to her cousin to give him a reassuring hug. "I'm sorry, Jesse. Just have patience. It won't be much longer until you can start over again; no fears, no worries."

There was a bleak look of desperate hope in Jesse's eyes as he blinked uncontrollably. "Do you think so, Amanda? Will it really happen?"

Despite her own doubts and gloomy forebodings, Mandy smiled brightly and nodded. "Yes, Jesse. Everything'll be fine. You just wait and see." She was getting in such a rut repeating those words of encouragement. If only she could believe them. . . .

As Mandy rode leisurely away from the cave and its solitary inhabitant, her spirits lightened while she grinned and blushed again at her cousin's parting words. He'd told her, "Now, Amanda Jo, keep your hands to yourself from now on and leave that poor cowboy be. I don't want to be hearing any rumors about my favorite girl goin' 'round and friskin' strange men. Folks could get the wrong impression, you know?"

How funny that he'd exaggerated his drawl to make his point. And how humiliating! She hadn't manhandled the man on purpose. After all, she'd found out about the badge, or what she imagined was a badge, hadn't she? The very thought of the feel of the hard muscles beneath the rough exterior of Ryder Manning's shirt, and the weight of his large body crushing hers to the ground, and the clean, manly scent of his—my God, even now her flesh tingled in anticipation of his touching her again. Surely he *would* touch her— *Stop it, Mandy!* That kind of thinking would only lead to trouble.

The pink flush on Mandy's freckled cheeks and the flashing sparkle in her evergreen eyes presented a fetching sight to the man hidden in the forest. His beady brown eyes glinted with malice as he blessed his good fortune to finally find the woman alone. Usually she was surrounded by her brothers or that overprotective cousin. Of course, Bob had eliminated that source of annoyance. And Reno was long gone chasing some trumped up dream. That left only Jeremy, and no snot-nosed kid was going to stand in his way. Not now. He'd waited too long for this moment. With a savage kick of his heels, Hank Ford sent his scrawny horse careening into the path of Amanda and Red Fox.

Mandy cursed her stupidity for daydreaming and not paying attention to her surroundings. If she hadn't been thinking lascivious thoughts about that stranger, she might've been able to prevent this unwelcome confrontation with her enemy. She'd thought he was out of her life for good after the thrashing he'd taken from Jesse and Reno, but evidently it hadn't been warning enough. She mentally took tally of the dagger hidden inside the top of her boot and the derringer riding easily in her overall pocket. Just let the snake try something.

"Howdy, Amanda. Nice day fer a ride. Were ya headin' anywhere's special, or was ya jest out lookin' fer me?" The crooked grin exposed several brown teeth with spaces in between, testimony to a hard life frequented often with drunken brawling.

As he rode even closer, placing his horse's head even with Red Fox's tail, Mandy could smell the foul odor ensuing from his breath and unwashed body as he leaned into her face. "I've been lookin' fer ya fer quite a spell now. I owe ya one, gal, 'member?"

For the first time since laying eyes on Hank,

Mandy felt a jolt of fear. Even with her weapons, it would take some doing to get away from the brute if he really intended to do her harm. And she suddenly realized that he did.

Hank Ford was a bear of a man. He wasn't really tall, but he was solid and thick muscled, a man used to having to fight for what he wanted out of life. And he had always wanted Mandy. The fact that Mandy loathed and despised Hank was of little consequence to his way of thinking.

Although never classically handsome, some would have thought Hank an attractive man before time and hard living had ravaged his face into cruel, sadistic features. Saliva frothed from the sides of his mouth as he contemplated the ways he was going to make Amanda Coulter pay for years of snubbing and spurning his company. If she put up even half the fight of his last woman . . .

When Hank's eyes glazed and he licked his lips, Mandy knew that it was time to make her move. Luckily, she was left-handed and Hank had drawn alongside her right. As her left arm moved slightly to allow room for her hand reach into the pocket concealing her gun, Hank reached suddenly to grab her right hand and the reins controlling Red Fox.

Mandy was trying to get her hand out of the overall pocket and keep control of her horse while at the same time fighting down her panic. She knew that to best a man of three times her strength she'd need a cool head. She actually thought escape was near when Hank's hand let loose of the reins, so she gave her horse a swift kick in the ribs, knowing his speed was far superior to the nag Hank was riding.

What she hadn't counted on was that in releasing her horse's reins, Hank had instead gone for her person. As Red Fox lunged forward, Hank's arm

59

wrapped around Mandy's waist, pulling her from the saddle. What Hank hadn't counted on was the bundle of flailing arms and legs that battered him from every direction once he had her within his grasp. They both rolled from the top of Hank's horse to land with a hard thud with Hank directly on top of Mandy. Her finger instinctively triggered the derringer before it jarred loose from her hand to land somewhere in a pile of brush.

Her last conscious observation was the flapping stirrups of her saddle as Red Fox thundered through the trees, narrowly escaping the wild bullet that struck the tree to the left of his rump.

Ry and Jeremy only stopped working once, for about half an hour during lunch, and even then Jeremy had a heck of a time trying to cover for Mandy's absence while they relaxed in the relative coolness of the kitchen.

It had been a definite relief when the older man had pushed back his chair, stating that it was time to dig more post holes. If the truth were told, it was probably the first time Jeremy had ever been *eager* to work.

By the middle of the afternoon, Jeremy was sweating as much from the contemplative glances cast in his direction by Ryder as from the heat and humidity. He didn't know if his chest was caving under the pressure from the lack of air or from the weight of the black, brooding eyes. The stranger was definitely wearing on his nerves.

Ry had just dug the tip of his shovel into the earth and rested his hands on the rounded end of the handle when he felt the vibrations of rapidly pounding hooves. His keen eyes searched every direction before catching a glint of red flashing through the trees on the north side of the house. He also saw that Jeremy had seen the horse and noted the boy's pale features as the youngster dropped the post he was carrying to run in the same direction as the riderless horse. Ry's shovel was embedded so deeply into the soil that it didn't even topple as he abandoned it to follow Jeremy.

His stride lengthened to catch up with the boy when he feared losing him in the brush or up the sides of the twisting ravine they followed. Ry's breath came in huge gasps, and his feet smarted from running in boots meant for riding when he broke into the clearing containing the small barn and corral. He couldn't believe it. He'd scoured the surrounding area thoroughly and had never come close to this beautiful spot. It was a perfect place to conceal a mount—or several mounts—if the need arose.

Ry's eyes narrowed, and he frowned at Jeremy's behavior. The boy was running his hands over the sweating horse, feeling carefully. Then he checked the saddle . . . searching. For what? And why was he looking in the direction from which the horse had come with such concern?

Then it hit him with the fierceness of a kick in the gut: the small saddle, the shortness of the stirrups. A.J.'s absence from the farm.

With a nonchalance he was far from feeling, Ry sauntered up to the fence. "That's a fine looking animal. Whose is he?"

Jeremy visibly jumped, apparently unaware that the stranger had followed his mad dash after Red Fox. "Uh . . . I . . . that is . . . he belongs to . . ."

The boy looked straight into Ry's fathomless, knowing eyes and suddenly knew that the big man was much smarter than either he or Mandy had given him credit for. What should he do? Should he lie and then search for his sister alone? Or should he tell the truth, partial truth, and enlist this man's help? Amanda could be in terrible trouble. She was too good a rider for Red Fox to just turn up like this, and the horse's eyes were still rolling and wide as if he'd had a bad scare.

Ry had been watching the conflicting emotions running over the lad's face and decided to take the initiative. "You don't need to think up a story, boy. I think I can put two and two together and come up with A.J. Now, do you want to tell me what's going on, or shall we play more games?"

Jeremy's Adam's apple bounced up and down in his throat. A.J.? A.J.! Ah, Amanda Jo. She'd said the stranger thought she was a boy, so she must've given her initials as a name. That was good thinking—real good. Well, the man looked so fierce and formidable that he'd sure rather have him on their side.

"Y-yes, this is Am-A.J.'s horse." Then the fear he felt for his sister's safety began to creep into his voice. "And I can't . . . I mean . . . oh, damn! Something must've happened. This horse wouldn't have run off and left he—iim unless it was really spooked."

Ry was beginning to feel some of Jeremy's concern. Over the last few days he'd come to admire the little brat for her determination and courage. And he didn't want anything to happen to her before he had a chance to know her better . . . all of her. There was something about the girl that tugged at his insides the way no other woman ever had.

Too, there was something strange going on

around here. If his instincts were true and he wasn't playing a false hunch, he'd find what he was looking for in this area. And he had a gut feeling that A.J. Coulter was his key to the puzzle.

"Jeremy, why don't you go on back to the house and wait, just in case A.J. comes in after a while." At the stubborn expression closing the boy's face, Ry hurried on. "If he's close, and hurt, it would be best if you were the one at home. I'll take this horse and backtrack and try to find out what's happened on the other end."

Ry softened the commanding tone of his voice when Jeremy's face began to crumple. "The horse probably just pulled loose while A.J. was getting a drink or something and decided to come on home for some oats. I'll fetch h-him back, one way or the other." Hell, that sure ought to reassure the boy.

Jeremy knew that the stranger didn't believe those words any more than he did, but the boy appreciated the effort. The older man had a hard-bitten way about him that didn't allow much room for soft feelings. He only hoped the man wouldn't take his anger out on Mandy when he found out how he'd been duped by a nineteen-year-old girl.

"Okay, I guess. If you think it's best. But . . . ah, A.J.'s still a little wet behind the ears, if ya know what I mean . . . and I'd appreciate it if . . . ah, just handle him—"

"Don't worry, son. I'll use kid gloves." Ry smiled in such an assured manner that the boy's fears were somewhat put to rest. The more he was around the younger Coulters, the more he envied their fierce protectiveness of family. He hadn't known much family himself, and being a half-breed had alienated him from both Indian and white alike. Damn, he hated to even think about it. He could get maudlin real easy.

"C'mon horse, let's get crackin'. We don't want to waste time. . . ." He let the rest of the sentence trail off. No need to worry, yet. Ry was one of the best trackers in the Cherokee Nation, and it didn't take him long to find the crushed grass and broken twigs indicating the path the horse had taken through the hills. *Hang on, A.J. Coulter, Ryder Manning is on his way.*

Chapter Four

When Mandy regained consciousness, she was lying on her side on a dilapidated cot, trussed up like a Christmas goose and feeling just as helpless. A handkerchief wadded in her mouth stifled the moan that arose in her throat when she tried to shift position and move her aching body. Her head throbbed abominably as the fuzziness dimmed from her eyes and she took in her barren prison. Besides the cot, there was one chair and a peeling washstand. Boards covered the only window, so she assumed it was still daylight for there to be any visibility at all.

As she tried to flex her hands and move her fingers, she picked up the sound of voices filtering beneath the crack of the closed door. She recognized Hank Ford's gravelly voice at once, and goosebumps shivered their way over her cold flesh. She'd made a grave mistake in underestimating the madman's threats before this. No matter how brave and independent she professed to be, she hadn't been man enough to handle this situation.

As she moved her wrists and ankles, she felt the leather of her boots and the bulge along her shin. At least they hadn't taken her boots and must've failed to search her carefully, for the knife was still hidden in the scabbard.

Cool air drifted across her chest as she once again attempted to move. Her shirt gaped open, and one bare breast peeked out of the flannel material. Now she knew why her boots and knife had been left alone. Slowly and surely anger bgan to replace her fear and confusion. Damn the mangy beast! No one touched Amanda Jo Coulter's body without her permission. She wouldn't stand for it! At least not without putting up a good fight.

Footsteps sounded just outside the door. It was pushed open, quietly, one inch at a time. Mandy closed her eyes and willed her breath to come slowly and evenly, as if still unconscious.

When fingers brushed the bare skin of her exposed breast, it took every ounce of willpower she possessed to keep from flinching and lashing out in any way she could. She stifled a groan and never blinked an eyelash when the tender flesh was cruelly pinched.

"Damn, woman! You've got ta come around soon," Hank muttered maliciously. "I want ta look into yore eyes when I take ya, ya bitch." With one more vicious twist to Mandy's breast, he turned and left the room, letting the door slam behind him.

Tears of pain trickled from Mandy's green eyes as she breathed deeply and sighed with relief. She had to make her escape from this place, and fast. Men's voices from the other room rose in unison, clamoring for Hank to "share the little piece," conscious or no.

There was no doubt in her mind that Hank would do just that very soon. Rumors had circulated about Hank's sexual idiosyncrasies for years. Wriggling her fingers, trying to restore the circulation, she bent her knees and moved her legs upward toward her bound hands. She had to arch her back enough to

66

reach into her boot top.

Hours sped by in the space of a few minutes as Mandy struggled and contorted her body. Her fingers finally touched the top of her boot and inched slowly, painfully, toward the knife. When she touched the cold metal, she almost shouted out loud, but she still had to grasp it within her numbed fingers. The ache in her fingers as they closed around the hilt was almost more than she could bear, but close they did as she raised her hands and arms away from her legs. Now what? She had the knife in the clear, but how was she going to hold the blade steady enough to saw through the stiff cords around her wrists?

For another agonizing minute, Mandy lay still, taking deep breaths and trying to think calmly and rationally. Aha! Again bending her knees, she turned the knife in her fingers until the hilt was toward her feet. She placed it between her ankles and squeezed them tightly together. Then she began to move her wrists back and forth, sawing the cord against the blade.

Mandy bit her tongue to keep from cursing the wasted seconds when she realized she was trying to cut against the blunt edge and had to start all over.

However, once she started moving with the sharp side, it didn't take long to cut through the bindings. She lay still, panting softly, and sent a prayer of thanks heavenward, which probably saved her life as the door to her room was suddenly thrown open and a rough voice called back, "She's still out, boys. We'll fix us some vittles, then have us some fun."

The door was left partially open as the man turned, rubbing his crotch, to recount how he was going to take Mandy, and how many times, to his cohorts.

Mandy took a deep breath, slid her legs off the bed and waited a lifetime for the circulation to painfully resurge into her limbs. She was alone, with no one she could count on to help her out of a desperate situation. If she was going to escape with her life, she'd have to call on all of her resources. She wasn't afraid, much.

Ryder had tracked Red Fox's dash through the hills easily and now studied an area where it appeared a scuffle had taken place. There was also an extra set of hoofprints mingled with the dust and debris.

It was late afternoon, and he didn't have long to follow the extra tracks. He was turning his mount onto the trail when the sun reflected on a piece of shiny metal. If it hadn't been the right time of day, he never would've found the little derringer hidden halfway under the weeds and grass. It had been fired and looked suspiciously the right size for a small woman to carry. She'd probably had delusions that it could protect her, too.

Of course, he was only assuming that the gun belonged to A.J.; but it was here, and since he'd backtracked her horse to this location, it was a fairly sensible deduction. She'd evidently run into trouble . . . dangerous trouble.

As Ry followed the tracks of the unknown rider, he noticed they were deeper than they had been, as if carrying more weight, perhaps riding double. Again fear clutched at his insides. It didn't matter that the little minx had bested him on several occasions. He didn't care why she went along with his first assumption that she was a boy. So what if she was hiding something? He just wanted to find her alive and safe. They'd get down to the particulars later, after he'd proven that she was a woman. He even had visions of making her *his* woman, at least for as long as it took to finish his mission.

As darkness settled over the horse and rider, Ry fantasized about the taming of A.J. Coulter, even while concentrating on following the dim trail. Just as the tracks led around a low, mound-shaped hill, Ry pulled sharply on Red Fox's reins. Directly to his right was a log cabin and an open corral containing six or seven horses. A guard was posted on the end of the covered porch. Another foot farther and he would've been spotted.

A kerosene lantern burned invitingly through a drapeless window as the moon hid behind a thick layer of clouds. Ry hated the thought of working in the rain, but if a storm was brewing, it could be to his advantage, providing A.J. was indeed in the cabin. Finding her location was number one on his list of priorities.

Ry dismounted and led Red Fox back behind the cover of the hill and tethered him to a dead dogwood tree. Its shape would be easy to pick out later if he was in a hurry. He removed the saddle and blankets and, taking fistsfull of dry grass, began to rub the horse's back and sides. They'd stopped for water earlier, so that was no problem, but he did pull more grass for the horse to munch before resaddling and giving it a good pat. This was some fine animal and would probably have a long night ahead of it if things shaped up the way Ry was afraid they might.

As he moved away from the horse and worked his way slowly and carefully down the rocky slope, Ry cursed silently at not having the foresight to change into his moccasins before riding off so quickly that afternoon. Of course, he'd had no way of knowing that the woman would sneak away and get herself into such a dreadful mess. As he continued to worm

69

his way toward the cabin and to think about A.J., he realized that she was just enough of a spitfire that she wouldn't have to *look* for trouble; it would find her on its own. It clung to her aura like the static electricity crackling in the air around him at that very moment.

Approaching the corral, Ry tested the air and was disappointed to find there was barely even a breeze, although he could physically feel the turbulence in the low-hanging clouds. The atmosphere was so oppressive that he had a hard time breathing. The horses were already nervous and prancing along the fence, so he decided to take the risk of moving on.

He hadn't gone three feet when a light was held aloft on the end of the porch and he heard two voices. Noiselessly, he dropped to his stomach and slithered the rest of the way behind a large rock that partially concealed his body.

"What's got the horses so riled up, Harley? They were quiet till jest a while ago," whined a high, nasal voice.

It took several seconds for the second voice to answer, but Ry breathed a sigh of relief when he heard, "Jest feel the air, Simon. There's a storm comin', sure as shootin'. I s'pose the horses is nervous 'bout bein' out in the open. At least the fence is fixed an' should hold 'em if'n it gets bad. C'mon, relax. Hank'll be bringin' that gal in purty soon."

Ry gritted his teeth and clenched his fists to keep himself still when he heard the whiner say, "Oh, goody, Harley. Do ya think he'll let me have a turn, too? Do ya, huh?"

The voices were fading, but Ry still made out Harley's answer. "Sure ya can, Simon. We'll all get a chance to poke 'er, an' maybe more'n onct. I'm so hard now that I'm afeared I'll bust."

Ry's teeth glinted white in the dark night. He'd

send the sons of bitches to hell and gone before they'd ever get a chance to take A.J. Coulter. Besides, he'd reserved that pleasure all for himself. Quickly he climbed to his feet and darted between and behind every object of concealment he could find.

From a back room of the cabin, Mandy hobbled to the boarded window and ran her fingers around the edges. The wood was solidly nailed in place, and her hopes ebbed. What if she couldn't get away? What if they . . . ? No! She wouldn't allow herself to even *think* that way.

Squaring her shoulders, she put out her hands and began to examine every board and crack on the wall clear to the base. When the foray to the first corner turned up nothing encouraging, she started resolutely down the next wall.

Voices in the adjoining room were getting loud and boisterous, evidencing the anticipation building among the outlaws. Lewd comments concerning her body filtered alarmingly between and under chinks in the walls, inspiring Mandy to move more swiftly up and down and around each board, looking for a loose nail, a cracked board, anything she could use to her advantage.

Ryder reached the front corner of the cabin on a dead run. To his surprise and consternation it was surrounded by wild rose bushes. He stifled a groan as thorns tore through the material in his shirt and punctured his tender flesh. If only he had worn his buckskins and moccasins, he could move more stealthily and with better protection.

He slowly removed his hat to peer into the first

window on his left, away from the porch. A table in the center of the room was piled with dirty dishes and tin cups, and from the conversation between the four inhabitants, they were jovially debating whether to do the dishes, or the woman, first. At least he knew she was safe so far.

Picking each limb of the rose bush carefully away from his smarting flesh, he placed them to his right then moved slowly toward the next window. No light illuminated the interior of the room, but enough filtered through the crack under the door to allow Ryder's keen eyes to detect an empty cot and one chest of drawers. A pair of dirty denims and two shirts littered the bare floor. It didn't take but a few seconds to discern that the small area was vacant of human occupancy—for the time being.

When Ry reached the next corner of the building, there were no bushes or shrubs to use to conceal himself, so he straightened to his full six feet two inches and flattened his trim body against the peeling boards of the house. Still holding his hat in his right hand, he tilted his head away from the building and inched his forehead and right eye around the corner.

He couldn't believe his good luck. No guard was posted in back. Either the hoodlums were very confident or very stupid. Quite a few law enforcement officers had relaxed their vigils since the death of Jesse James, but Ryder and a lot of others knew it was too soon. There were still too many groups like this one in the cabin—hardcases that didn't fit in with the changing society. And besides that, Ry still wasn't convinced about Jesse. He'd ridden long and hard to get there in time to see the body, and—

A sudden cracking noise along the back wall splintered the quiet night. The rain was just a soft drizzle now, and the wind had died down considerably. He looked over his shoulder to make sure no one had come up on him from behind, then concentrated on piercing the darkness and searching for movement. He hadn't heard a sound since that one loud snap, and he wondered if maybe his nerves weren't playing tricks on him.

Mandy held her breath and dared not get overly excited when her fingers located a loose board. It was even a wide one, wide enough to squeeze her slender body through the opening if she could only— Before she even realized she'd done it, her fingers had inched under the dry wood and, in her excitement, had pulled.

Every nerve in her body jumped when the panel cracked and the bottom nail popped loose. A small cry of dismay escaped her trembling lips while she stood absolutely still and waited for the door to be thrown open. When only another burst of loud laughter greeted her straining ears, she collapsed in a heap to the floor.

Leaning her head against the wall, she inhaled deeply and wiped her sweaty palms on her jeans. That had been a close one. If those men weren't getting so drunk and telling those horrid stories, there was no telling what would be happening to her at this very moment.

Mandy rolled her head to the side and looked out the opening into the welcoming darkness. As soon as her legs quit shaking, she crawled on her hands and knees to the narrow slit and attempted to squeeze her upper body through the space. It was painfully small, but she didn't dare try to pull the board out any farther. No telling what kind of noises would penetrate the building, and she couldn't take the risk.

Turning on her side, she slid her head and one shoulder and arm up under the board. By wriggling and pushing with her heels, she was able to get enough of her upper body out sideways to free both shoulders and arms, but from her waist down she was still in a tight spot. If only she had her brother's narrow hips.

Ryder had eased his way around the corner and was inching along the back of the house. He had passed the only other window to the little bedroom and was continuing to feel his way. He kept hearing heavy breathing, but the night was so black and dense that he couldn't see a hand in front of his face. It might be the echo of his own breath sighing in his ears.

He froze in mid-step as a muffled grunt and low "Damn!" drifted into the black surroundings. He'd been thinking the same thing. Had he said it out loud? But then *he* hadn't had any cause to moan like that.

God, this was the blackest, eeriest night he'd ever had the misfortune to be out in. What would happen if he made a misstep? And what would become of the girl if he didn't get to her in time? Aw, damn! He knew the answer to that, but he didn't want to think about it. He shook his head to clear it of the image of one of those slobbering animals buried deep in her lovely, bloody body.

Mandy had twisted her shoulders through the opening enough that her hands were on the ground outside and helping to lever her weight out of the room. She had just about worked her hips through when the exposed nail caught in the backside of her overalls. There wasn't room to slip an arm back through to free herself, either. So, now what?

She laid her head on her arms and bit her lip to keep from shouting her frustration. There had to be a way to work herself free, so she kept her upper body flat on the ground and lifted her pelvis up, then down, in an effort to dislodge the errant nail from the loose material.

Meanwhile, Ryder made his way down the wall, stopping every so often to listen. He'd held his breath twice now and still heard the breathing, so he knew it wasn't his imagination. He wasn't alone.

He took one step with his left foot, then slid the right leg over, repeating this procedure until he was bored to tears. The pace was too slow; he was losing too much time. Whoever was out there was close. Did they know he was coming? Were they waiting?

He lifted his left foot, slid it over a few paces, then shifted his body weight to that side. When the foot landed on a soft, moving object, it startled him so badly that he couldn't hold his balance. In one swift movement, his body rolled over the lump, and he landed with a muffled thud against the back of the house and into another damn-it-to-hell rosebush.

Pain from the thorns was just surfacing in the nerve endings when he heard the now familiar "Damn!" and a loud ripping noise. With a move that left bits of shirt and flesh hanging on the prickly branches, Ry lunged from the bush and tackled the shadowy form crawling from the recesses of the wall. He didn't really *see* the body, he just sensed its presence and knew it was moving.

"Ooooff!" Ry's arms encircled a waist, and his weight drove the victim to the ground. All movement ceased, and he found his cheek pressed next to a smooth, satiny surface of skin. He moved one of his arms from under the body and felt his way over the still anatomy to discover that his face was resting on a partially exposed rump, a small, round, smooth derriere.

Ry levered himself to one knee and quickly turned the body. His hands grazed firm globes under the coverall top, and he breathed a long sigh of relief. His quarry had been found. A.J. was safe and—sound?

The buttons on the shirt front were gone, and his belly tightened at the temptation set so deliciously before him. But when his hand moved to the bare flesh and there was still no movement from the girl, he realized that she had either fainted from fright or collapsed from exhaustion. Or maybe *he* had hurt her when they fell.

Reluctantly he moved his hands away from the soft flesh of her breasts and ran his palms over her body, from her long, silky hair to her boot-clad feet. From the baggy clothes she wore, it had been impossible to detect the perfection of her luscious curves. He was very pleasantly surprised. Relieved to find no obvious injury, he decided it would be more prudent to move her to the waiting horse rather than have her come around there, where they risked eventual discovery.

With a tenderness he hadn't felt for a long time, Ry gathered the unconscious girl into his arms. As if carrying a load of breakable eggs, he moved carefully and stealthily across the open ground near the horse corral. His nerves strung as taut as a Cherokee bow, he stumbled and almost dropped his precious burden when the wind suddenly gusted and a loud clap of thunder spooked the horses. At least the lightning illuminated the rock behind which he'd hidden earlier. He was heading in the right direction.

Ry felt like the demons of hell were truly after his

hide when the heavens opened, cascading sheets of rain and hail upon the earth and his unprotected head. In the brief scuffle at the cabin, he'd lost his hat. Hell's bells! He'd paid twenty dollars for that hat.

When the next bolt of lightning lit the sky, he grinned in amazement. With everything that had happened to his little brat, she was still wearing that old piece of worn-out felt on her head. Well, it was certainly better than nothing.

As he hurried under the next large tree, he slid to a halt in the gooey mud and took his arm from under her knees. With his other arm still around her shoulders, he pressed her limp body against his firm length and jerked and pulled at the floppy brim of her hat until it popped off her head. No wonder it had survived the action. He then transferred it atop his own soaked head and smashed and tugged until it clung at a tilted angle over one ear. He'd probably have a headache by the time he got it off again, but better that than be knocked unconscious by the hail.

Before he scooped her into his arms again, he took a brief moment to enjoy the warm contact of her body next to his. The sensuous thrust of her mounded breasts against his chest—

A gunshot split the air not two seconds after the last streak of lightning, and Ry hid against the trunk of the tree, protecting A.J. with his body.

They couldn't have been seen from this location, but he knew that A.J.'s escape had now been discovered. So, if he could make it to the horse and get out of there without being detected, they'd think she just disappeared into thin air. What a good joke on a bunch of bumbling idiots.

Stepping away from the tree, Ry found that the hail had diminished, but the rain was still falling by bucketsful. He trod gingerly to keep his footing and was relieved to hit a rocky slope. Once they were away from the area, it wouldn't take long for the rain to wash away their tracks. His even white teeth flashed brightly in the night. It couldn't have worked out better if he'd planned it all himself.

There was only one problem that seemed to be of immediate import. It was too dark to see the damned tree where he'd left the horse, and the girl was beginning to stir and twist in his arms. A soft moan and muffled, "Oh, my head," brought a frown to Ry's face as he cocked his head to listen for pursuit. The frown changed swiftly to a grin when he heard the horse snuffle and paw at the ground hearing the sound of distress issuing from its mistress. Of course, the horse was a pet. She probably even took it carrots and sugar.

Walking in the direction of the snorting beast, Ry stubbed his toe under a dead branch. In trying to regain his balance, he managed to entangle both feet and fell to his knees, dumping his bundle in the mud and nearly under Red Fox's feet.

The next streak of lightning illuminated A.J., who was now fully conscious and ready to scream bloody murder. Ry quickly crawled the few feet separating them in time to grasp her by the waist and clamp a hand over her open mouth.

"Shut your damned mouth, A.J.. Do you want that bunch of roughnecks to find us? We're almost out of here. Don't spoil things now."

Once again Mandy found herself in the embarrassing position of lying on her backside under the stranger's long, lean, pleasurable body. Fear evaporated, leaving in its stead a prickly sensation that ran the length of her body. She was shivering from the cold rain and wind, yet her insides were mushy with molten warmth. It was a dreadful situation.

Even through the black of the night she could feel those fierce eyes penetrating and appraising her. He was waiting for her to speak, but her mouth was as dry as her mind was muddled.

"Uh-h, sorry 'bout tryin' ta yell like that. I-I didn't recognize ya. Those guys, they were—"

"Don't make up any lies, sonny." Ry sneered the last word, and Mandy began to fidget and move apprehensively beneath him. "Your buttons are scattered from here to who knows where, and unless my mammy told me wrong, there's no way in hell a boy could have a chest like that."

Warmth radiated throughout Mandy's body, and a hot poker branded her bosom. When she lifted a hand to investigate, she found a large, hairy hand ahead of her, its palm enclosing the full mound of her breast. She gasped and would've cried out except that Ry's head lowered and his mouth absorbed her breath.

Mandy had known all along that his lips would feel like that: warm, soft, demanding, moist, gentle and so persuasive. She lay under him and soaked up the pleasant sensations that vibrated through her very core. Suddenly she was very glad that he was aware of her femininity.

Then her eyes flew open, and she stiffened abruptly as she remembered who she was and what he was. My God, if he'd found out and was using his sexual expertise to purposely—

Loud voices on the other side of the low ridge penetrated their ringing ears, and they both lay still, aware of the close proximity of the other, aware of the danger of any further delay in their escape and aware of the temptation to stay right where they were, forever.

79

Water cascaded from the brim of her own hat directly into Mandy's nose and eyes, effectively dousing the passion that had burned so out of control only moments earlier. Thank heavens she'd come to her senses in time.

A shout from the direction of the corrals carried across the breeze, but Mandy and Ry remained still. Crunching footsteps were too close, and a lantern shone over the rough terrain to within a few feet of where they lay.

Several minutes passed before Ry rubbed his body sensuously against Mandy's pliant length then rolled reluctantly to his knees and helped her to her feet. He led her to the horse and chuckled knowingly as he watched her rub the horse's nose and whisper soothing nothings in its ear. A frown creased his features as he realized that he could actually *see* her movements.

One look at the sky and Ry knew they had to move quickly. The rain had all but stopped, and the clouds were skimming across the moon and stars like powder puffs blowing in the wind. He hated to admit it, but after saving the woman's life, he was now going to have to ask for her help.

"A.J.? You know this country better than I do. What's the best way to get out of here unseen?" Ry took off the battered hat and shook water off his head and shoulders like a drowned pup. "Better yet, is there a place we could hole up and dry off? I promised your brother I'd take you back safe and sound, not suffering from a case of a-a-aaachhooo-o . . . pneumonia."

Mandy's heart beat a rapid tatoo against her ribs. Naturally, the first place that came to mind was Jesse's cave, but that was out of the question. Then again, was her heart thrumming like a flamenco dancer because of her fear for Jesse or her fear of being alone with Ryder Manning? And why shouldn't she be afraid? He aroused her body and tender instincts like no man ever before. She couldn't allow herself to become involved with a man who might eventually cause her cousin's true demise.

Ry's impatient "C'mon, woman, where's your head?" hit her the wrong way, and she whispered as loud as she dared, "I'm thinking! I'm thinking! Damn it all, what do you expect from me? I've just been through a terrifying experience." From out of nowhere tears rolled down Mandy's cheeks, and her hands began to shake violently as the import of her situation sank in. She'd let him figure out to which experience she referred, though.

Ry couldn't distinguish the tears from the rain on her face, but he saw she was trembling and cursed his rough answer. She'd been through hell, and he didn't need to put her through more. Not trusting his reactions if he held her in his arms again, he stepped close and awkwardly patted her shoulder.

"I know, A.J., and I'm sorry. I'll tell you what; just pick a direction . . . lady's choice. And if Red Fox'll carry double, let's put some distance between us and your friends while you're thinking. Okay?"

Mandy snuffled and wiped her eyes. "Some friends! All right, Red Fox might carry double if I ask him to."

Ry snorted. "Be sure to ask real polite, please. It's a long walk home."

Without looking at the odious man, Mandy swung into the saddle without using the stirrups. She was sorely tempted to ride off and leave him stranded, but he'd gone to a lot of trouble to rescue her. Dadgum it, she'd rescued herself! It was *his* bumbling intrusion that'd caused all the mess. But she moved her left leg forward to give him access to the stirrup. He'd better count his lucky stars that she was in a benevolent mood just then.

Ry stepped into the stirrup and grabbed the saddle horn to pull himself up. Instead of swinging *behind* the saddle, he slid into the seat, pulling Mandy onto his lap, sort of, with his right arm. She had no opportunity to voice a protest before he kicked Red Fox into motion. Rather than objecting to the extra weight, the horse was eager to be away from the spot where he'd suffered through hail, thunder, lightning and drenching rain. A bucket of oats and a dry stall would be a welcome ending to a horrid night.

They rode in silence as Ry let Red Fox have his head. Occasionally he or A.J. slapped at a branch to keep from being scratched or knocked from the saddle.

His thoughts were troubled. He didn't like the possessive and tender feelings he was experiencing toward A.J. Coulter. She came from a vipers' den of outlaws and renegades. If the stories he'd heard were true, she was Jesse James's favorite relative. And look at her father: a drunken ne'er do well who couldn't even scratch out a living selling rotgut whiskey. He'd never met the older brother, but Ry had heard he was away from home conducting nefarious business of some sort. Then young Jeremy, such a nice seeming kid, had admitted outright that he worked with his older brother. Who knew whatever happened to the rest of the family.

So why, instead of despising A.J. for the whelp of the devil she was, did he want to take her in his arms and protect her from the wicked world? She had to have condoned what Jesse and Frank had done through the years. And what of the poor wretch buried in Jesse's grave? Of course, now he was going on pure speculation.

The crease between Ry's brows deepened as he became aware of A.J.'s squirming behind. As he drew his attention from his disturbed thoughts, he became even more distraught by the instinctive hardening of his groin. The bare half of the brat's bottom was rubbing suggestively against the front of his trousers. Apparently she was conscious of the solidifying lump, too, as she tried to draw away from the purely masculine reaction to her firm, round derriere.

With a decidedly roguish grin, Ry moved the hand that was still holding the horn and pulled her resisting body hard into his. "Hold still, damn it, or you're going to get something you hadn't bargained for." His fingers splayed across her belly with his thumb resting provocatively under the curve of a generous breast, which grazed the ridge of his knuckle with Red Fox's every step.

To get his mind off very unprotective desires, he decided to get some answers to a few questions. "Who were those men, A.J.? Do you have any idea why they were holding you?"

Mandy's skin felt pinpoints of electric current wherever the stranger's hand touched her. She knew that when he removed that hand she would be branded and left with the imprint of each and every finger, such was the heat generated from the contact. It was only with superhuman effort that she heard his words, much less concentrated on forming an answer.

"Ah-h, I only knew one of the men for sure, but I-I may have recognized another voice." Lord, what was he doing to her? His thumb was moving the flesh of her breast back and forth, and his breath teased the sensitive area on the side of her neck.

When Mandy's voice trailed off and he felt a shudder rack her body as his thumb grazed the tip of her nipple, Ry leaned forward and whispered in her ear, "And do these men have a name?"

Mandy's eyes were like saucers, and her mind drifted as she felt her body suffuse with some unknown emotion. Blood surged through her veins so fast that she felt dizzy and light-headed. Sweat beaded her forehead and upper lip, so she licked that lip to moisten her mouth in order to speak.

"Names? What men? Oh-h-h, oh yes. Ah-h, one of them is Hank Ford, and I think, uh, the other might've been a friend of his that's been hanging around lately; but I'm not really su-u-re."

Ry's tongue licked the outer curve of A.J.'s shell-shaped ear. God, but she tasted as good as she smelled, he thought, as he reached the sensitive skin under her ear and on her neck—a little salty, and rosey, and fresh as spring rain. His hand cupped her breast, and she leaned even more firmly into his chest as he gently kneaded the flannel-covered swell. Then that ever questing thumb moved under the button-less lapel of her shirt, rubbing, probing, seeking the other bare globe.

His lips blew softly into her ear as he nibbled and formed words at the same time. "So, who is this Hank Ford? Is he the one who took you?"

Mandy's back arched, and she reached desperately for the disturbing hand. "Stop that! I-I can't think. Hank's just a no-good who's been sniffing around the past couple of years. The last time, Reno and J-Jesse taught him a good lesson, I thought. But now, Reno's gone, and J-Jesse's d-dead, and—" A sob escaped her trembling lips, and she hoped the stranger mistook it for grief and not just the release of tension from the terrible scare Hank had given her. Just thinking about the maniacal look in Hank's eyes started an uncontrollable quaking in the pit of her stomach.

Chapter Five

Ry's dark brows shot up, and his arm tightened reflexively around A.J. when he realized what had just happened. She'd mentioned Jesse on her own accord, had said he was dead and sounded genuinely upset. Could he be wrong? Was he wasting his time following a misguided hunch? He shook his head. No! He'd seen the body. Then again, maybe the officer he'd talked to in St. Louis had been mistaken. Maybe the man had hit the other outlaw. Well, he had to find out, and whatever bag of bones was unlocked, the little brat in his arms held the key. He just knew it!

As he pulled Red Fox to a stop, he turned A.J. sideways in the saddle to enable him to wrap both strong arms around her body. She was so soft and so vulnerable. He *almost* felt like a heel for even thinking of using her to his own ends.

Mandy didn't resist as Ry helped her get a leg over the saddle horn so she could nestle in his welcoming arms. He was so warm, so gentle, and she'd been so frightened and alone for so long. She could almost pretend that he was someone who cared for her. So she wrapped her arms around his ribs and pressed her cheek against his shirt. Short, wiry curls tickled her nose from the open vee of his collar, and she inhaled the enticing aroma of spice and sweat and leather. He was solid, hard as a rock, someone to cling to when her emotions were set adrift. She knew better, of course, but a girl could always pretend.

Neither noticed the rocking motion of the horse as he turned off the faint trail and walked a few feet into the woods. But they did notice when he stopped and the wind no longer chilled their soaked clothing. Mandy lifted her head and looked around, then laughed with delight. "Oh, Red Fox, bless you! You're cold and tired, too, aren't you, boy?"

She slid down Ry's leg and wrapped her arms around the horse's neck while Ryder mused over how long it would take after the fire was built before she'd hug *his* neck that way.

A wry chuckle escaped his lips as Mandy darted a quick, embarrassed look in his direction. She was holding the front of her shirt in a manner that made him wonder if she'd read his thoughts that accurately. "I'll take care of your Red Fox if you'll rustle up some dry wood. Get a move on it, gal," he teased.

He was removing the saddle from the horse's back when he heard her foraging through some dry leaves to the left of the entrance. Taking the wet blanket in hand, he spread it over the saddle in hopes it would dry once the fire was started. There was no sense in injuring the horse's back with it tomorrow.

Meanwhile, Mandy was making good in her search. With the high spring winds, lots of dead leaves and twigs had blown into the mouth of the cave. It was just lucky that they—or Red Fox—had had the good fortune to find one of this size. Most of the caves in the area were so small that only rodents or snakes made use of them.

She carried a load of twigs and branches and had just discovered a larger chunk of wood when there was an ominous rustle not two feet from her outstretched hand. Something slithered toward her, then rattled. Mandy gulped and froze. A rattlesnake! Good Lord, she'd been raised in these hills and knew that this was just the sort of spot a snake would seek out. She deserved to be bitten for letting the stranger fluster her so. He had gotten to her so badly that she'd forgotten the rules of nature. She'd forgotten *all* the rules where he was concerned.

She must've unknowingly whimpered when swallowing, for Ry cocked his head and turned to see what was happening. His keen ears picked up the sound of the snake even before his eyes found Mandy. With a swift, fluid motion, born from years of practice, he drew his pistol and fired at the sound of the rattle.

Within seconds he was kneeling beside A.J.'s slumped body, making sure that his bullet hadn't strayed to the wrong target. Finding she was just shaken up and not injured, he picked up a stick and poked through the debris until he found the snake. He poked the limb under a long, narrow body and held it aloft before walking to the entrance of the cave to toss it in the brush.

"It wasn't a very clean hit, but the snake's dead, A.J. Stay put for a while and let me look around in case there's another one."

He needn't have bothered telling her to stay put. Mandy was too limp to move a muscle. But he didn't have to treat her like such a child. Didn't he think she had sense enough to know that snakes generally ran in pairs. If she wasn't so tired, she'd sure give him a piece of her mind. So intent was she on nursing her hurt feelings, that she jumped when a hand squeezed her shoulder.

"C'mon, A.J., let's get that fire started."

Ry helped Mandy to her feet and then rolled a large rock to the center of the cave. "Sit here while I gather that tender."

She sat for hours it seemed while she watched Ryder try to strike a spark into a small pile of dry leaves. Her mouth turned up, and she tried to grin as she thought how ill-prepared they were for an overnight campout. Instead of a grin, though, her blue lips began to tremble as her body convulsed in shudders. She wrapped her arms around her body to gather heat, but it wasn't nearly enough.

Ry's deep voice echoed throughout the cavern with a jubilant "Finally!" as the leaves smoldered, then flared into a bright, heartening flame. He rubbed his hands over the small points of heat and added small twigs to encourage the fire. "C'mon, baby, burn."

When Ry lifted his head in a triumphant gesture, his wide smile died quickly as he looked closely at Mandy. Her body was shaking, and her eyes were dull and vacant as they stared through the flames. He imitated a good duck walk in his hurry to reach her side before she fainted, or something.

He picked up her hand, feeling her cold and clammy skin. She was in a state of shock; probably caused by the scare from the snake compounded with the terror of her kidnapping, he thought. Anyway, he had to warm her body—fast.

"A.J.? A.J., sweetheart? Can you hear me? We've got to get you out of those wet clothes. Would you like that? To get all warm and snuggly?" Ry had already undone the straps to her overalls and was working on what was left of the buttons on her shirt. The wet material resisted slipping over the buttons, and in his haste Ry managed to rip off several more. All the while he kept up a continual soothing chatter as if he were gentling a recalcitrant filly.

"Here we go, sweetheart. Let me have your arm. That's the way; only one more sleeve to go. My God!" Ry swallowed hard and kept his hands busy removing the soaked shirt, but his eyes were glued to A.J.'s firm, ripe breasts. The skin was as smooth as whipped cream and delicate as ivory. Her pert little nipples, hard and puckered from the chill, stood erect and beckoning.

"Damn, A.J., what am I going to do with you?" Or rather, How am I going to keep *from* doing you? he thought. And then he saw the bruises on that sweet flesh and realized why the buttons were missing from the shirt. The slime had touched her, hurt her.

"I make you one promise, sweetheart. No one's going to hurt you like this again as long as I'm around." Ry inhaled, blew out a deep breath and drew back the trembling hand that was reaching to caress and soothe the purple flesh. "Ah-h, okay now, you're going to have to stand up for a minute and help me get these overalls off. Think you can do it? For me?"

In a half-conscious daze, Mandy watched Ry's efforts to unclothe her. It would've been funny if it wasn't so sad. She really wanted to help; she just couldn't make her body obey her commands. But she trusted him implicitly to see to her welfare. Wasn't that strange? Through the fog, she heard Ry's pleas for help, and her muscles twitched as if she was trying to make the effort; but her legs wouldn't support her weight.

So Ry stood up, moved in front of her, and put his hands under her arms and lifted. The heels of his palms settled against the sides of her breasts, and he choked over the next gulp of air. Then he pressed her chest into his and wrapped one arm firmly around her back, holding her in position while his free hand drug the denim pants down her legs. He'd just *thought* he couldn't breathe when he held her like this under the tree; now he was literally suffocating.

At this point, Ry was stymied. He hadn't thought to remove her boots, and the overalls were hanging stubbornly around her ankles. "Well, hell, Ry, now what're you going to do?" Things were going great. He was even talking to himself like some dumb-struck teenager. Of course, with A.J.'s pebble-hard breasts grinding into his chest, it was sorta hard to keep his mind on his task. She felt so good in his arms, so soft and cuddly, so cold and icy! That fact sank in and brought him back to business in a hurry.

"A.J., I'm sorry, but we're in a bind here. We've got to lay you down and take off those boots. I know, let's move over to the saddle and get the blanket. Maybe the inside won't be too wet and we can put you down by the fire."

Ry felt like a marionette on a string as he took baby steps sideways toward the saddle, trying to keep his feet from tangling with A.J.'s. Lord, if they lived through this fiasco it would be a miracle. He was about as inept a hero as ever came out of a dime novel.

After finally stumbling across the cave, he was relieved to find that the inside of the blanket was a little damp but not as wet as the outside or the side next to the horse. It would just have to do. Still holding A.J. in one arm, he inched his way to the fire and spread the blanket with one flick of his wrist.

Reluctantly, he lifted A.J. away and then felt a

91

chill pass over the flesh where her body had seared into his. As he laid her down, he gasped when he realized she was naked as a newborn babe under her overalls. He quickly removed the boots and tugged the damp denim off her dainty ankles. Her toes were so cute, all curled up like that.

Once he had all of her clothes removed, Ry looked around the cave. Now what? The only blanket was the one she was lying on. He couldn't keep his eyes off the perfection of her lovely body. She was sleek, and firm, and oh-so-gently rounded. And she was shivering!

Ry didn't hesitate another minute as he began to shuck his own wet, cold clothes. He added more fuel to the fire until a cheery, warm blaze beat back the dark shadows. Then, as was his habit of late, he took another deep breath and sank down on the blanket beside A.J. on the side away from the fire. He turned toward her shaking limbs and cursed when he heard the sound of her chattering teeth. He immediately slid one arm under her shoulders and pulled her into a tight embrace with the other. He threw his leg over hers and hooked them with his heel until she was enfolded in a human cocoon.

Ry's voice barely quivered as he asked, "Now see, isn't this warmer?" At least her violent shaking had been reduced to only an occasional shudder, but Ry's own skin twitched reflexively when she curled into his warmth, melding her skin with his. "God, sweetheart, I'm about to burn up. I don't know if I can stand being this close to you all night."

He'd threatened all afternoon that he was going to be the one to take the little brat, but his conscience was about to get the better of him. Especially with her in this condition.

As he tucked her head under his chin and

smoothed his fingers through her silken locks, he thought of something that had been on his mind for some time. "Ah, while we're having this wonderful conversation, would you mind telling me what the A.J. stands for? Somehow, lying here together like this, it seems we ought to be on friendlier terms. Don't you agree? Are you awake?"

Placing his finger under A.J.'s chin, he tilted her face up so he could look into her glazed green eyes. As she focused on his mouth and the little grin that dimpled his cheek, her eyes cleared and she pursed her lips. Ry's eyes followed the pink tip of her tongue as it peeked out and ran over her lower lip, leaving it dewy and inviting with a faint trace of moisture.

His hand stroked up and down A.J.'s arm and then moved to her back where he smoothed his palm up and down her spine. He watched intently as her lips formed a word but wouldn't quite speak. "C'mon, sweetheart. Just tell me your name. You can do it."

Mandy stared helplessly into his obsidian eyes and saw the flickering flames reflecting back. Yes, there was heat everywhere—in his eyes, radiating from his hands to the pores of her skin, and flowing through her veins like molten lava. If she became any warmer, the moist area between her thighs might explode. Her lips still trembled, and she couldn't tell if it was from the cold or the intensity of her reaction to Ry's body pressed so intimately close. She licked her lips and tried to control their shape in an effort to form recognizable words. He did need to know her real name.

"A-Amanda . . . Amanda Jo."

The words were whispered, and Ry had to tuck his head to catch them. "Amanda Jo? Amanda Jo Coulter. Yes, it fits. A beautiful name for a luscious lady." Ry hugged her even closer, if that was possible, and kissed the top of her head. When he felt a tentative brush of fingers through the thick mat of hair on his chest, he shuddered. The fingers wound through the curls and grazed a flat, masculine nipple, causing him to suck in his belly and groan with pleasure.

"Oh! D-Did I hurt you?"

The innocence in Amanda's husky voice was almost his undoing, but Ry was in control enough to see the humor in the situation. He chuckled and said, "No, sweetheart, you didn't hurt me. But sometimes even the greatest pleasure is painful."

Mandy was silent for a long time. "C-Can a girl, I mean, a woman . . . I-I . . ." Her words trailed off as her face flushed with embarrassment.

Ry's hand moved from Mandy's back, and he ran a finger down her nose. "Yes, a woman can experience the pain of unfulfillment every bit as much as a man. Is that what you're feeling, Amanda?"

Mandy's brows drew together, and her nose wrinkled in a thoughtful frown. "I don't know. What do you mean?"

Ry shifted his body to where he lay on his back and pulled Amanda with him until she sprawled across his chest. Another groan escaped his gritted teeth when her thigh brushed his aching groin.

"Amanda Jo, I can't believe you're such an innocent." In fact, the more he thought about it, the more he knew she couldn't be as naive as she sounded, not living with such a family of cutthroats. His anger built and festered unjustly since he knew deep down that she was probably as innocent as she claimed, but he was mad at *himself* for having feelings for her that he didn't understand and couldn't control.

Ry's fingers dug cruelly into Mandy's shoulders as

he lifted her up to look into her forest-green eyes. The half-glazed expression of newly awakened passion just added fuel to the already smoldering heat of his desire. His voice grated on his own ears as he asked, "Just how many men have fallen for your pure and innocent act, Amanda? How many men have you lured into traps?"

When his eyes found the unfeigned hurt and disbelief in hers, he swore at himself for being twice a fool and pulled her down to capture her lips with his before she could utter a word in self-defense.

Mandy's eyes were as large and soulful as a wounded doe's when she heard what he had accused her of. Act? Traps? What in the world was he talking about? Did he think . . . ? But logical thought vanished when he yanked her back down onto his chest and ground his mouth against her teeth.

She balled her fists and tried to push her way off his hard, muscular body until the pressure on her lips eased and she felt Ry's tongue gliding over the bruised flesh. He pulled her lower lip into his mouth and sucked gently as his tongue moved over the ridges of her teeth. His hands were playing erotic games with her ribs and spine, and she opened her mouth in surprise when he grasped her buttocks and pulled the lower half of her body astraddle his. Before she could snap her teeth shut, he thrust his tongue swiftly through the barrier and plungered every nook and cranny until it finally wound around her own and coaxed it to join in a silent, sensuous, mutual exploration.

When the frenzied kiss wound down to a relaxed reconnaissance of eyes, cheeks and ears, Mandy raised her head and gazed dreamily into the shiniest, blackest eyes she'd ever seen. They softened and faded to velvet gloss right before her eyes, and she sighed in bewilderment. The man could change moods in less than a heartbeat. And here she was, lying alone and naked in a hidden cave, in the arms of a man who probably had every intention of using her to destroy her family.

For a minute, when he'd suddenly become so angry and had kissed her so brutally, she'd been afraid. Now, looking down into his smiling, handsome face, all she felt was a languorous warmth seeping through her veins and settling in her lower abdomen. She wanted to bask in his arms and never move, never think, never worry about Jesse or their tenuous future.

A soft tweak of a pink nipple brought her back to reality, and she again marveled at the wondrous features of the man beneath her. Laugh lines around his mouth and eyes deepened as he flashed his white teeth in a boyish smile. A dimple winked at her once, twice, then disappeared when he asked, "Where've you been, sweetheart? Don't you know it's damaging to my fragile male ego to be lying in all my naked splendor in a woman's arms and have her a million miles away?"

Mandy shrugged her shoulders, then quickly turned her head as her nose started twitching. "A-ah-ah-choo-o!"

Ry groaned and rolled her over on her back to place a wet kiss in the middle of her forehead, then rose to his knees. "Don't go away. I'll be right back."

After adding more wood to the fire, he walked to the cave entrance and scanned the surrounding area. He listened and waited but heard nothing other than the gentle dripping of water from the overhead leaves. A few scattered stars winked from a black sky where the clouds had broken.

When he turned back toward the little encampment in the cave, he stopped in mid-stride to stare at the lovely sight presented so delectably to his hungry eyes. Amanda had turned on her stomach, using her forearms as a pillow. Her eyes were closed and her body relaxed in peaceful slumber. From the red-gold strands of hair tumbled across her shoulders and back, to the twin mounds of her shapely buttocks, to the long slim legs, he devoured her.

It didn't matter who she was, or who her family was; right now he wanted her with a desperation he hadn't felt since he fled the reservation. If he believed in such nonsense, he'd almost think that fate had been leading him down a path to this one woman. It felt *that* right to be with her, to hold her, to make love to her.

He walked slowly to the blanket and stared down at the naked body like a panther stalking his prey. Ever so gently he laid down and pulled her into his arms as if sinking his claws into a delicate morsel. His lips moved over her flesh, lapping and savoring as if it were the first taste of blood. Then a deep growl erupted from his throat when the prey put a hand on his chest and stroked his curly pelt.

"Jeez, Amanda, I can hardly stand it, I want you so badly."

Mandy was still drowsy and curled into Ry's embrace like a foundling seeking a safe haven. It didn't matter anymore who or what Ryder Manning was; he had saved her life and was now offering warmth and, well, if not love, at least tenderness and compassion. To a woman starved for a gentle touch, a soft caress, he presented a temptation she couldn't, wouldn't, turn down.

Her lips followed the trail of her wandering fingers as they moved up the thick mat of hair on Ry's chest. She grinned mischievously at the low animal growl her touch evoked. The taut muscles on his belly and the cords standing out on his thighs were proof that she had as great an effect on him as he on her. And somehow that thought was very gratifying to a girl who'd never imagined herself as being attractive or pleasing to a man.

As her hand roved lower on his body and accidently brushed the satiny tip of his stiff manhood, she gasped with surprise when he grabbed her hand and almost crushed her fingers in his iron grip.

Ry was on fire with his need for Amanda, and when she touched him, he'd been afraid of exploding right then and there. Things were moving much too fast. Amanda was definitely inexperienced, and he wanted it to be good for her the first time.

However, his good intentions were put to the test when she caressed his chest and followed the trail of her fingers with tiny, moist kisses. She would be his tonight, and if in the future he could use his skill on her body to get some more answers to his questions, so much the better. He'd used a lot of women to his advantage and, in so doing, brought them a great deal of pleasure. He'd never felt any remorse before, so why was his conscience picking on him now?

Ry released the pressure on Mandy's hand when he heard her whimper. "Sorry, sweetheart, I didn't mean to hurt you. Let's just slow down a mite, okay? We've got a lot of time, and there's a lot I want—"

Mandy took the situation out of Ry's control when she leaned up and closed his mouth with her lips and tongue. She didn't understand what had come over her usually shy, reticent self; but he'd started something wonderful coursing through her body, and she was determined to reach the culmination of that exquisite pleasure. If she knew the correct words, she'd tell him what she wanted, if she knew what it *was* she wanted. So instead of words, her body arched and told him in the most explicit way possible.

Ry sighed with unsurpassed pleasure when Amanda's tongue explored the inside of his mouth with tentative probings. God, what a surprise and delight she was, his little adorable brat. Her touch was so innocent, yet so accomplished. In all of his experiences with the opposite sex, never had he felt so alive, with every nerve ending begging for the brush of her fingers, the caress of her soft lips. When had his body ever ached so with the need for tender fulfillment? It was almost more than he could stand, but he wanted to prolong every torturous moment.

He rested his weight on his elbows propped on either side of Amanda's chest. His fingers slipped easily through the silken tresses of her hair and massaged her scalp and neck as his mouth worked quickly over her eyes and cheeks, finally settling for a brief moment on the sensitive underside of her ear lobe. He smiled as he felt her body quiver with anticipation and reveled in the feel of her pebble-hard nipples pressed urgently into the thick fur of his chest.

Keeping his weight resting on just one arm, he moved the other hand slowly around her neck to smooth over the satin skin of her shoulder to the bony ridges of her ribs. He rubbed and kneaded until the heel of his hand raised the generous flesh of her breast, and he cupped the fullness in his palm. Ry's forefinger circled and teased until the burgeoning nipple stood erect and at attention.

He waited calmly, watching Amanda's eyes darken to a deep sea green, and noted the droopy, sensual relaxation of her lids. When her hands encircled his neck and pulled his head to her breast, he wet his lips and ran his tongue over the soft, nubby surface surrounding the nipple until it puckered and she offered more for his worshipful adoration.

Mandy wanted to lift her body until it blended and molded into one with Ryder Manning's. She'd never experienced such intense feelings and sensations before in her life. She didn't even understand the pleasure, the joy, the pain and the longing, but she knew it was wonderful and something she would treasure when replayed in her memory in the days, months and probably even years to come.

Ryder groaned and clasped Amanda's body to his in a hard embrace when she rubbed and undulated beneath him. He wanted to thrust himself inside her and plumb the silken depths until she cried out for more, but there was something he needed to do first. He didn't want there to be any tearful recriminations later, no shotgun wedding prodded by an angry father, or brothers.

With a gentle nudge of his knee, Ry moved Mandy's leg and slid his own legs between her warm, welcoming thighs. A surge of adrenaline shot through his body, giving him such a feeling of power, of masculine superiority, of gentle tenderness, that he could hardly control himself. This was the ultimate in sensation. He was home.

"Amanda Jo, sweetheart? Look at me, darlin'." He waited until her passion-glazed eyes were revealed by the slow, languorous opening of her lids.

"You're beautiful, you know. You're everything a man could want all rolled into one adorable package. And I want you. I want to be one with you, to feel you surrounding me with your softness." He rocked his hips back and forth until the tip of his engorged staff found the moist entrance to her pulsating sheath, all the while holding her eyes with his drugging stare.

He stopped moving but could feel her lower body

quiver and contract with rhythmic movements of its own design. "What do *you* want, Amanda? Do you want me to stop? Tell me, sweetheart. It's lady's choice." God, if she wanted him to quit now, he'd die a slow, agonizing death. Why did he have to go and give her a choice? It would almost be worth whatever would be forced on him later to keep her, to always have her near.

Then his eyes released their heated gaze and traveled down the sweat-dampened length of her body. He watched as her movements became more sensuous and teasing and waited until her hips rocked and enclosed him more fully with each undulation. Was he the first? Could an innocent maiden seduce a man so skillfully?

His irrational musings halted instantly when he heard the small, trembling voice say, "I-I want you to . . . to n-not stop. I like what you're doing. There's a pressure . . . like I might explode . . . like I'm on fire. Is that the w-way . . . ?"

As Ry'e eyes came back to Amanda's, the anxious pleading in their evergreen depths swept away any doubt. "Shh, sweetheart. Don't be afraid. Yes, that's the way you're supposed to feel." He kissed her eyelids shut, then sipped from her honeyed lips. "I feel the same way, you know? Like I'd die if something didn't happen soon. Come with me? Let me show you?"

Mandy kept her eyes tightly closed but nodded her head vigorously. Her insides were churning, and the flesh that touched the hot silkiness of his manhood burned with a need that she was past controlling. Her body had taken command of her mind at his first touch. Now all she could do was wait and see what was going to happen, what was to be the next step.

So she thought until Ry's lips trailed a fiery path

101

down her neck and chest and engulfed an engorged nipple into his mouth until his tongue laved the sensitive bud and a tingling sensation rippled all the way to her loins. Then her hips reacted by bucking upward until she impaled herself ever more deeply upon his hardness. The farther she enclosed him, the less she burned, but that horrid, thrilling ache was building and spreading until her whole body was taut and yearning for—for what?

Ry was almost buried in Amanda's heated softness. He'd tried to move slowly, to penetrate the barrier and cause as little pain as possible; but when she dug her nails into his shoulders and raked down the sides of his ribs to his buttocks, he lost it. With a swift plunge, he drove deeper with each thrust.

Mandy rocked with Ryder and moved instinctively, meeting him, backing away, then coming together until the pressure inside centered in one intense spiral, building and burning until every thought, every nerve ending, sought a common goal. Just when little electric shocks began to ripple, when flashes of light exploded behind her eyes and she opened her mouth to scream, Ry's lips smothered the sound and drained the fear that had so unwittingly claimed her.

He held her so tightly as her body jerked beneath his that she knew he'd never let anything harm her. And when her hands felt his rigid muscles and moved over the contracting planes of his lower back, she knew he was experiencing the same feelings. So she relaxed and let him lead her. It was right.

They lay together, spent and entangled, for long moments afterward. Neither dared to break the spell of contentment. Mandy was speechless, not knowing what to say or how to say it. Was it always like that?

Ry was breathless, luxuriating in the blissful

afterglow. It had never been like that before, and somehow he'd known it would be special even before they'd started. But as he held the soft, warm body and felt her chest heaving from the exertion, his brows narrowed into a thoughtful frown. She was an innocent. He knew it to be true with both his body and his heart, but there had been no proof. Had he been right about her in the first place? Had she fooled him with her maidenly act? Maybe she'd been the one to attack that cabin full of— No! He was letting his imagination get the best of him.

Ry shook his head. Who knew what was behind the woman's reactions? But there were questions he wanted the answers to. "Amanda Jo? Sweetheart, are you awake?"

Chapter Six

Ry's hands moved over Mandy's body in such a way that she didn't want to move, didn't want to rouse herself from the languorous state of satisfaction that now enveloped her. But she'd heard the underlying note of harshness in his voice and felt the change in the movement of his hands. What had she done?

"Amanda, I know you're awake. Answer me."

"Y-yes? What's wrong? Wasn't I . . . ?"

The fear in Amanda's voice and the hurt in her eyes when she looked up at him like a wounded kitten melted Ry's resolve. He bent his head and kissed her with the tenderest emotion he'd ever shown. He wouldn't hurt her for anything, but he had to know.

"Sweetheart, I don't quite know how to put this, but have you done this before? Made love?"

As Mandy gaped at Ry, all the wonderful feelings she'd been nurturing evaporated in one big burst of pain. How could he ask such a thing? Did he think she could be *that* kind of woman after what they'd just shared? How could she have been such a fool?

Before she even knew she was going to do it, Mandy swung back a fist and socked him on the jaw.

"Odious creature." She heard the click of his teeth and gloated over the pain she saw reflected in the obsidian eyes, but before she could move fast enough, he had her arms pinioned to her sides and had clamped her body between his rock-hard thighs.

"Amanda, I'm sorry . . . I think. I don't like to hurt you, but I want an honest answer."

His voice was soft, but Mandy could sense the iron firmness of his determination. What right did he have to ask such a question? It wasn't as if she meant anything to him. Not if he had to ask *that!*

"Damn you, Ryder Manning! I could kill you with my bare hands. If you don't know that you're the first man I've ever . . . that's ever . . ." Not only had the beast insulted her virtue, but he'd made her so mad that she couldn't even talk or think coherently. And to top it off, embarrassing tears began to stream down her flushed cheeks. "D-damn you!"

Mandy tried to twist out of Ry's arms, but he held her too tightly. Given no other choice, she buried her head on his chest and sobbed out her frustration. Never! would she ever! have anything to do with a man again. She couldn't stand the humiliation, the degradation. What had been a beautiful, memorable experience was now a wanton, shameful act. What had she been thinking of, anyway? Well, she hadn't been thinking at all. She should've known better than to melt into soft putty after he'd had the gall to hurt her only moments earlier.

Ry felt a remorse so deep that it was acutely painful. He could see by the look on Amanda's face that he'd made a damnably stupid mistake. He'd known in his own mind that she'd been a virgin, yet his superior male pride wanted confirmation, had to hear it from her own lips. And for what good reason? Now he'd bungled the chance of using her to help in

105

his investigation.

Well, maybe he could redeem himself by trying to explain. "Amanda, I know . . . what I'm trying to . . . oh, hell! I knew you hadn't. Really. It's just that . . ." How could he put this delicately? She was looking at him like some lost little waif with huge misty eyes and those luscious lips pulled into a cute little pout. God! "You don't have the slightest notion of what I'm trying to say, do you?"

Mandy stared into Ry's eyes, trying to ascertain his sincerity. Was there really a reason as to why he'd acted so, so assinine? She chuckled to herself, despite her anger, that Jeremy had taught her some of his vocabulary. But seriously, she couldn't help but wonder if she was flawed in some unspeakable way. She slowly shook her head from side to side and, unable to bear his condemnation, hid her face in the hollow of his neck.

Ryder wasn't going to let her get away with that. He wanted to look into her eyes and have her see his disgust and repulsion. So when his fingers urged her chin up, she drew in a deep breath and bravely met a look of sympathy and, yes, amusement. Double damn! What could he possibly find so funny about such a dreadful situation?

"Amanda, hasn't your mother ever explained the facts of life to you?"

Mandy sniffled and shook her head. In a little girl voice she said matter of factly, "M-my mother left us when I was just ten years old. W-why? What's she got to do with this?" She raised her hand palm up and indicated their state of undress and the situation as a whole.

"Oh, my God, woman. What am I going to do with you? Take you to raise?" Ry hugged her to him and squeezed until she grinned. She acted so innocent, so

106

virginal. No, it couldn't be an act, not this time. It was real.

Maybe she had been raped at some time. No, she wasn't afraid. Actually, she'd responded quite aggressively. It was something he hadn't expected. And he was still recovering from the experience. He could still feel those long, smooth inner muscles as they pulled at him, drained him, exhausted him. Ah, the recovery process was being made with rapid ease.

"I imagine a pretty young thing like you has lots of boyfriends. It's a wonder you're not married." Or was there a really good reason no one would have her? He was going to find out, right now.

Mandy raised her eyes suspiciously. What was he getting at? Was he insinuating that she was an old maid? She knew that already. "It's not necessary for you to rub it in. Jeremy makes fun of me every chance he gets. Says if I was married, there'd be another hand around the farm, and he could take off any time he wanted. I guess he means even more often than now."

"So? Why haven't you taken a man?" As he cuddled her head on his chest and felt the softness of her hair under his rough palm, he blessed his lucky star that she'd waited until he arrived. Even the thought of another man touching her caused his blood to boil. One day, Hank Ford would make a mistake, and he, Ryder Manning, would be around to make sure the outlaw never made another.

The hairs on Ryder's chest tickled Mandy's nose, and she snorted. "There's never been a man brave enough, or stupid enough, however you want to put it, to hang around."

Now that was unbelievable. "What are you talking about? Why, even under those damnable overalls and behind that big old Sharps, any man with eyes could see you're a pretty woman." To himself he added,

107

"Well, maybe not right off."

"Ha! That's funny. Use all the flattery you want, but there's no way I'm pretty." She felt the calluses on her hands, then rubbed a finger down her freckled nose.

He couldn't understand it. The brat really didn't know she was gorgeous. "You're serious, then. You've never had a man come courtin'."

Embarrassed, Mandy admitted, "Well, one or two have tried, but they didn't last long. Jesse never liked any of my callers." Uh-oh. She hadn't meant to use his name. Somehow, she had to stay calm and act natural, not get flustered and make him any more suspicious.

Ry almost jumped when she said the name. "Jesse?"

"Yes, my cousin." As innocently as possible she explained, "I guess in some ways he was more of a father, or maybe a big brother."

The inference of "was" caused Ry to scowl, but he did not breathe easier.

"He always came by when he was anywhere near and made sure we kids were all right. He'd have a chicken or two, and supplies, and sometimes he'd even bring me a new dress, or a pretty comb."

Ry's deep "Harrumph!" went unnoticed as Mandy became lost in thoughts of Jesse and all he'd done for her family. For a long time, her father had stayed in town, too drunk to come home, until every last cent of his money was gone. Then he'd come back and built his own still, forgetting his youngsters all over again. But they could always depend on Jesse to see about them.

She had no idea of the emotional ups and downs Ryder was going through. He knew the cousin was Jesse James, knew the clothes and food were probably stolen from some other poor souls. How could she actually *love* or even be accepting of such a man? But then, how could such a hardened criminal be so caring and compassionate about a couple of ragamuffin kids? It didn't fit with his notions of Jesse James—outlaw—murderer.

"I guess you think a lot of this Jesse. Wasn't that what you called him?"

Mandy gulped and drew in her breath. "Uh, yes, that's right. And yes, I loved him with all my heart. We-we buried him the other day. You must have known. You were at the funeral." She lay still as corpse, waiting for his reply.

"Oh, so that was your Jesse. I didn't know." And it didn't appear she was going to offer any helpful information.

Sure you didn't. She closed her eyes. Lord, if this went on much longer, she would turn into a babbling idiot from the strain. She wriggled and slid her body sensuously against Ryder and almost purred when he began to explore her supple, pliant flesh with expert deftness.

Mandy reveled in the feel of Ry's hands and the glory of his lips; but he had hurt her, and she was upset. "Why did you act the way you did and say such ugly things to me after . . . after we . . . ? Do you think so little of me?"

He'd been expecting it, but he stopped her from continuing the unpleasantness with a deep, penetrating kiss. She had answered some of his questions fairly satisfactorily. "I'm sorry I hurt you, Amanda. No excuses, I was a fool." Failing to see Mandy's quick smirk, he went on in his own defense. "I knew you were innocent and had never been with a man. But when I entered you, there was no resistance. It's not all that unusual, but I jumped to the wrong conclusion. Somehow you've broken the barrier that symbolized your virginity. For some men, that symbol is all-important when they take a woman to bed the first time. And . . ." He paused, a strange emotion choking him from being placed in this position.

"Was it that important to you, then?" Mandy queried. "We aren't married or anything." *Not even friends, really*. But she was beginning to understand a few things now. If only she could figure out why he'd turned on her so viciously and ruined that beautiful moment.

Ry blushed for probably the second time in his life. "No! I mean, not usually. Oh, hell and damnation! It's never been important to me, and I don't know what possessed me tonight. I'm sorry, sweetheart." Damn! How could he explain to Amanda what he didn't understand himself?

Mandy stared at Ry for several minutes, then laid her head back on his shoulder to cover her smile. The anger was gone now, and in its place resided a feeling of smug satisfaction. She might be inexperienced, might be naive about her body, but one thing she understood with perfect clarity. Mr. Ryder Manning *cared*, about *her*. Maybe just a little, but it was enough to cause him to throw a jealous fit. Now the question was, how could she use this tidbit of information to her advantage?

Meanwhile, Ryder was fighting his possessive feelings. As he held her in his arms and tasted her velvet softness with his lips, he knew he'd never be satisfied until he held her like this every morning for the rest of his life. Dear Lord, the little brat had snagged him easier than a bass to a worm. But he couldn't afford these feelings now. He had things to do yet that would more than likely leave her with nothing but bitterness and hatred toward him.

He'd never thought of himself as the settling down type, either. He could pick up a willing woman in any town he passed through, and the thought of little chestnut-haired, green-eyed brats running around was . . . intriguing, and about halfway appealing.

Well, hell, why fight it? She'd never have to know, and he'd get over it soon. He always had before. There wasn't a woman born who could hold Ryder Manning's fancy for long. And to prove that he could get her out of his system, he'd take her again and again and again until he'd had enough. Then he'd leave and get on with the rest of his life.

Mandy reacted with a feline purr from deep within her throat when Ry began to stroke the still smoldering passion of her newly awakened body. Instead of holding back and waiting like a shy, virtuous maiden, she turned into his embrace and rubbed her body along his length, insinunating her knee between his legs and pressing upward in a most unladylike, suggestive fashion. She ran a hand over his ribs and down his lean hip to caress the firm hardness of his buttocks. And when she moved to the front of his hip and forward to find the burgeoning evidence of his male hunger, she grinned and slithered down his body until she met the tip of his erect hardness with her own moist softness.

Ry gasped with surprise when she held him in her hand and lowered her body to engulf him in her warm flesh. From the very beginning of this planned seduction, Amanda had taken control, and he wasn't sure how to respond until his body reacted of its own volition. Now he was caught up in a whirlwind of desire and passion, his mind spinning at a dizzying rate of speed as his hips bucked and kept time with her rhythm.

111

Mandy moved faster and faster, the core of her being driving her harder and harder until she felt Ry's frantic thrusts and his violent release. She was almost blinded by the explosion of lights behind her eyes as she reveled in her own mind boggling experience.

Ry was overwhelmed by her youthful exuberance, the way she returned his kisses and caresses with equal enthusiasm. It was a new experience, and he was exhausted. Instead of being shy and reticent, expressing shame and laying on a guilt trip, she was just . . . Amanda. Maybe it had to do with her being brought up in a household of men with no woman to tutor her in the art of making sex something nasty or unnatural.

When Mandy finally raised her head and looked into his face, she was startled by the whiteness of his features and the glazed look of shock permeating his eyes. She reached out to touch him.

"Don't talk, Amanda Jo. Don't say a word."

A pink hue was dawning in the scattered remnants of clouds when Ry woke Amanda the next morning. He smiled and handed her the dry clothes, then considerately left the cave to give her some privacy. He'd evidently been up for some time since he was already dressed and had Red Fox saddled and grazing outside. The fire was stoked and warmed her chilled body as she scooted closer and began to dress. She met an obstacle when she started to button her shirt and found most of the buttons missing. She overlapped the material and hoped the overall bib would cover her during the ride home. Hopefully, they would make it home today. She didn't trust herself around the stranger anymore. He led her to do wild and crazy

112

things she normally wouldn't consider.

She ducked her head when Ry came back into the cave and hunkered down on his heels beside her. He put a finger under her chin and pulled her face up until she looked him in the eye. She was amazed at the look of wonder and awe that gazed back at her, and neither spoke as they stared at and marveled over the other.

Finally Ry chuckled and rubbed his hands over the dying flames. "Sorry about breakfast, sweetheart. I don't know about you, but I worked up a terrific appetite last night."

Mandy blushed, then grinned and reached over to run her finger across the dimple in his cheek. "I didn't just sit idly by and watch the action, you know. I'm so hungry I could eat a bear." As if to emphasize the seriousness of her statement, her stomach picked that exact moment to let out a lusty grumble. "See?"

Ry stood up and held out his hand to help Amanda stand. "Okay, Woman-Who-Grumbles, let's get outta here and see if it's safe to rustle up some grub."

Slipping her hand in his somewhat timidly, Mandy let him pull her to her feet before asking, "Woman-Who-Grumbles? What's that supposed to mean?"

"I've just given you a Cherokee name. Aren't you pleased?"

Mandy knew he was teasing by the grin curving his sensitive lips. All she had to do was look at their thin, yet very attractive shape, and she remembered the way they had explored her body during the long, lovely night. If it wasn't for the more pressing obligations in her life, she'd be content to stay in this cave forever.

When she felt the sensation of staring eyes, she looked up from the study of those wonderful lips to find Ry laughing at her.

"Where were you, sweetheart?" His fingers rubbed his bottom lip as if to ease the heat from her scorching gaze.

"Oh, I was just thinking. From the first time I saw you at the funeral, I figured you were at least part Indian." She ran an adoring survey over his handsome features. "It's your high cheekbones and the fierce glare in your eyes, I think."

Ry moved closer, as if to take her in his arms, and in self-defense Mandy stepped back. She couldn't think when he was that close. "And no, I'm not pleased," she added.

"No? Why not?" Ry had been pleased with himself, coming up with such an appropriate name.

Mandy took another step backward. She had to keep Ry at a distance or be forever lost. She liked the way he moved so gracefully, liked the way his eyes shone when he smiled, and loved the way he touched her. Yes, if she wasn't careful, she could find herself love—*liking* the man too much, and there was too much at stake to let that happen now.

"Uh, I just don't happen to think that's a very good name. Can't you think of something more flattering?" Like Woman-With-Lovely-Body, or Woman-Who-Kisses-Well? Anything besides Woman-Who-Grumbles, she mumbled to herself.

"I don't know. I thought I did rather well. But just for you, I'll study on it as we travel today." With that said, he picked Amanda up and tossed her into the saddle before mounting behind her. "Okay, Red Fox, let's go. We've got a hungry woman on board, and you wouldn't want her taste to change in favor of horsemeat, would you?"

Red Fox snorted, shook his head and set off at a lively clip. It was a glorious morning, cool and fresh

114

smelling after the rain. The sun was just coming over the eastern horizon, a few birds were flitting and chirping about and it felt like the beginning of something new and exciting for the two riders.

They rode in peaceful silence, each thinking disturbing thoughts of the other, until the sun was high in the now cloudless sky. At the first creek they encountered with fairly clear water, they quenched their thirst and helped ease the emptiness in their stomachs. But as the journey lengthened, Mandy bgan to eye the robins and red birds with something more than appreciation for their beauty.

When a covey of quail took flight from a nearby bush, Ry dismounted and walked on ahead in the same direction as the birds. Several minutes and a few gunshots later, he walked back to Mandy with a proud expression of triumph glowing on his face.

"Breakfast! Woman, if you'll climb down from that beast and forage some dry tender, I'll clean these—" When Ry remembered Amanda's close call with the snake in the cave, he had second thoughts about delegating that particular chore.

Reading the worried expression on Ry's face correctly, Mandy put his mind at ease. "Don't worry, I'm not dumb enough to pull the same stunt twice. I promise I'll be careful. Go on, start pluckin' those birds before I tear into 'em now, feathers and all."

Ry grinned and confessed, "I'm with you, sweetheart." Then he reached into his pocket with his free hand and pulled out a small object. "By the way, I believe this belongs to you. I forgot all about it last night for some reason."

Mandy arched her eyebrows at his wicked leer, then squealed with delight and ran over to hold out her hand. Only when Ry placed the derringer in her palm did she believe that she really had her gun back.

"Oh, Ryder, thank you. Where did you find it? How'd you know it was mine?"

"Easy, girl, hold up for a minute. It's actually very simple. When Red Fox showed up so sudden back at your farm, I backtracked his trail. When I found the place where it looked like there'd been a scuffle, I just happened to see the gun under a bunch of brush. Since no self-respecting hombre'd carry a sissy little thing like that—"

Ry stopped his teasing abruptly when Mandy socked him in the belly with a hard little fist. "Okay, okay! I have seen a few city dudes and gamblers . . . ouch! Cut that out! I still carry the scars from where you beat me last night." Tilting his head at a daring angle, Ry warily pointed to the tiny bruise on his chin.

"You poor thing. Come a little closer and Mandy'll make it all better." Mandy's mouth quirked in a sly grin while she crooked her finger at Ry. The soreness between her thighs was proof that she carried a few scars of her own, but the memory of the battle wasn't at all unpleasant, just unsettling.

"Oh, no! No, you don't." Ry backed away very ungracefully as he stumbled over a rock. "Go on and get that wood so we can eat. Maybe that'll slacken your appetite and improve that nasty disposition."

As Ry bent over his cach and Mandy meekly started gathering dry twigs, she was sure she heard him mumbling something about, ". . . damn woman . . . think Woman-Who-Grumbles is a hell of a good name. . . ."

It was the middle of the afternoon when they heard

the first indication of trouble. Gunshots sounded in the distance, at first concentrated and heavy, then sporadic. Ry wanted to leave Amanda and scout ahead to see what was happening. If it was part of the outlaw gang, he didn't want her anywhere near the area.

"No, I won't be left behind. Why would you think I'd be safe here, and all alone? Besides, if we stick together, we'll present a more united front."

Ry blinked and shook his head at her weird reasoning. Two people on one horse presenting a united front? Oh yeah, that'd really scare off that bunch of hardcases.

"Well, sweetheart, I sure can't argue with that, now can I?" The arm holding Red Fox's reins rested just beneath Mandy's breasts, and he gave her an extra hard squeeze. "At least I'll know where you're at and can keep an eye on you if there's trouble."

With the decision finally made, Ry turned Red Fox in the direction from which the shots had come and kicked him into an easy lope. There was no sense in rushing headlong into something that might be too tough to handle. They'd take it slow and easy, one step at a time.

The second indication of trouble occurred when they spotted the riderless horse standing at the edge of a thick grove of trees. The body lying in front of the animal was trouble with a capital T.

Ry was just starting to order Amanda to stay back out of the way with Red Fox while he scouted the area when she suddenly jumped from his arms and off the horse at a dead run. When she fell to her knees beside the still form, tears were running down her cheeks, and Ry could see her hand shake as she reached out to touch the body.

117

Deciding the time for caution had already passed, he urged Red Fox to follow his mistress. As Ry dismounted and knelt next to Amanda, he heard her muttering, "Reno? Reno, are you all right? Who did this to you?"

Between the two of them, they managed to turn the man onto his back. Mandy wiped the dirt from the injured man's face while Ry unbuttoned the blood-soaked shirt to check the wound. The fellow had lost a lot of blood, but luckily the bullet had passed through his shoulder without breaking any bones or hitting a vital artery.

A ripping noise drew Ry's attention from the wounded man long enough for him to gape at Amanda tearing the bottom of her shirt. He watched in fascination as her breasts were presented for his consideration when the buttonless top opened wider and wider with each movement. In his estimation, she was the most gorgeous creature on God's green earth, and he didn't even try to control the jealous rage that burned through his gut as she murmured loving endearments to the handsome fellow lying at Ry's feet.

Reno! Now where had he heard that name before? Was he one of the outlaws who rode with Jesse James? Was that where Amanda knew him from? And what was he to her? Maybe he should go ahead and put the bastard out of his misery.

Ry's hand was hovering over the butt of his gun when Mandy turned soulful green eyes on him. "Will he live, Ryder? Can you help him? Please?"

A muscle beneath Ry's left eye jerked as he gritted his teeth and flexed his jaw. Damn! What should he do? Confess that he wouldn't mind watching the man die just so she couldn't run her hands so lovingly over the shallowly moving chest?

Instead he reached for the cloth she'd torn off her

shirt and folded two thick pads which he placed on either side of the oozing wound. Now, if he just had something to bind them in place. "Amanda, come here and unbutton my shirt while I try to stop the bleeding."

Mandy seemed uncertain, but when she looked down at the chalky features of her brother, she knew she'd not hesitate to do anything that Ryder asked. She stepped over Reno and knelt beside Ry, then tried to figure out the easiest method of accomplishing the task without coming into contact with the stranger's disturbing form. When she saw there was no help for it, she plunged right in and twined her arms through his in an effort to reach the buttons.

She finally freed all of the buttons she could reach and gripped the shirt on each side of Ry's ribs to pull until the tail was tugged free of his jeans and belt. That still left one more button before she could remove the garment from his muscled, bronzed torso. By the time she reached back around him, her hands were shaking so badly that she couldn't free the button.

Ry flinched and sucked in his breath every time Amanda's fingers brushed his flesh. Every sensitized nerve in his body lay in wait, anticipating her next touch. The skin along his hips and sides actually ached when the tail of the shirt was yanked from his pants. But when her knuckles beat rapidly against his belly while she fought with the last button, he felt as if his trousers had shrunk at least two inches.

The growl that rumbled from deep in his chest startled Mandy's already edgy nerves so severely that she jumped and fell back on her bottom, barely catching herself with one hand. The other jerked on the shirt just enough to pull it free of the blasted buttonhole.

"Damn, woman, what's the hold up? Do you want

this poor bastard to bleed to death while you fumble around all day?"

Amanda's watery gaze was almost his undoing. He hadn't meant to yell, but now that he'd started this business, they might as well try to save the sucker. "Get back up here and hold the bottom pad as tight as you can against the wound while I get out of this shirt." Ry traded arms as he held the pad and shrugged off the sleeves of the shirt.

"Here, Amanda, tear a couple of long strips off the bottom to use for binding, then rip up the rest for clean pads." Ry looked up and turned around, studying the surroundings. "How far are we from your homestead? Yoo hoo! Amanda? Are you listening?"

Mandy was totally absorbed in watching the play of muscles as they danced across Ry's broad back. She was remembering how supple and flexible they had felt beneath her hands the night before. It was amazing how his breeches molded to his rear and thighs, too, like a second skin, leaving nothing to the imagination. As if she needed it.

Ry's amused chuckle finally penetrated her rapt concentration, and she blushed at his knowing grin, telling her in no uncertain terms that he'd seen where her eyes had strayed.

"Oh, were you speaking to me?' she asked innocently. Quickly she finished tearing the shirt and handed him one length of binding.

Ry fought to control his body's reaction to Amanda's heated stare, and he cleared his throat before answering. "Yes, I was wondering how far it was to your home. We need to get this man somewhere so these wounds can be cared for properly, and fast."

The flush drained from Mandy's cheeks as she

turned to Ry. "He's got to make it, Ryder. He's got to! I-It's about ten miles, more or less, if we cross those hills. Do you think it'll be too rough?"

After studying the countryside with a calculating gaze, Ry responded, "I just don't know, Amanda. Would the going be any easier if we took another route?"

Shaking her head sadly, Mandy also surveyed the rough terrain that she had always loved before. "No, I guess not."

"Okay then, let's get started. Grab that extra horse and I'll ride it with . . . Romo, wasn't it? You can ride Red Fox."

Ry was already picking the wounded man up off the ground when he was stopped short by Mandy's vehement reply. "It's Reno, and *I'll* take care of him. Just head due east and find the safest trail possible. We'll be right behind you."

Again Ry had the desperate urge to finish off the so-called Rivo. It tore at his guts to watch Amanda tend to the fellow so tenderly and lovingly. God, what was happening to him? He'd never been jealous of another man in his life. It wasn't that he had anything against women, they just weren't a necessary item in his life. So what was there about this little scrap of a girl?

Thinking the better part of valor was to back off when in doubt, he didn't argue with the brat. Besides, scouting ahead, he wouldn't be forced to watch the tantalizing jiggle of those tempting mounds of flesh so visible beneath the edges of the unfastenable shirt. Amanda had definitely come up with the best plan.

They had been riding for over two hours with Ry doing his best to pick out the easiest path through the rock and tree-dappled hills. For the last thirty minutes he'd been surreptitiously keeping an eye on the stubborn woman trailing behind. She'd been holding up the weight of the unconscious rider with her arms and guiding Red Fox with her knees.

The strain was beginning to show in the grim lines around her tightly clamped lips and the droop in the usually straight shoulders. Every now and then, when Red Fox dodged a large rock or low branch, Robby's limp body would slip to one side, and Amanda would pull and tug until she had him securely upright once again.

Ry wondered if she would continue to fight and struggle, or would she eventually ask for help? He'd give her another half hour, then he'd insist on taking over the wearying task. Besides, the compresses were so soaked with blood that it wouldn't hurt to stop and put on fresh ones.

Upon topping the next rise, Ry looked over his shoulder and shook his head in exasperation. Red Fox was slowly picking his way up the slope; but Amanda's eyes were closed, and her head was slumped forward against the back of the now semi-conscious man. At least Rocky's head was up, and he was licking dry lips with a probably drier tongue. Ry decided it was time to take a much needed break when he detected the sound of running water coming from a few feet below the ridge.

He was dismounted and waiting when Red Fox stopped by the creek. Mandy and her burden were slumped to the left side of the saddle, and Ry barely made it over to the pair before they came sliding into his hastily raised arms. Unable to hold the combined weight, they all fell to the ground with Ry sprawled on the bottom.

Coming to her senses, Mandy sputtered and

apologized while trying to get to her feet. A knee slid into Ry's groin, and his groan of pain mingled with that of Reno's incoherent moaning as Mandy became more flustered than ever. "I-I must've fallen asleep. I'm so sorry. Didn't mean to . . . ah, I . . ."

"It's all right, sweetheart. I'll get over it . . . eventually. Right now, just help me out from under this man so we can change the pads and see if he can drink some of this fresh water. He's got to be at least as thirsty as I am."

Ry couldn't take his eyes off Amanda's pink tongue as she licked her cracked lips. "Me, too. I'd give anything to dunk myself in that creek and wash off . . ."

The words faded as she stared longingly toward the clear, clean water and recalled the filthy hands that had groped at her body—was it just yesterday? She turned her back and tore one last strip of cloth from her shirt, then went to the creek and dampened the cloth before kneeling to wipe Reno's face and neck.

Ry had been about to make a suggestive remark about dunking together until he noticed her pinched, strained features. When she clutched the remnants of her skimpy shirt in a clenched fist, he decided to let well enough alone. She needed some time right now.

He knelt beside her and cut away the bandages from Rufus's wounds. The bleeding was minimal at the moment, but how much blood could a man lose before running out completely?

The pain from the removal of the compresses roused Reno, and his eyes flickered open. They were glazed with pain, but when he focused on Mandy's face, his lips curved into a brave smile. His voice was hoarse and raspy, but he managed to say, "Howdy, darlin'. I thought I was dreamin' when I felt your . . . arms holdin' . . . safe . . . ah-h-h . . ."

Mandy's hands wrapped around Ry's neck with ferocious strength as she cried out hysterically, "He's not dead, is he? Oh, please, don't let him die!"

Ry grabbed her hands before she choked off his air, then pulled her into his arms. "No, sweetheart, he's not dead, yet. He's just weak from the loss of blood. Shh now, calm down. At least when he's out like this, he can't feel the pain."

"Oh, thank God!"

When Amanda collapsed in his arms, Ry looked down at the unconscious man as if to gloat that *he* had the woman in *his* arms. But even that thought was not much consolation as he imagined the handsome young man taking Amanda into his arms and kissing and fondling her as Ry had done. Ry's body quivered with the intensity of his reaction to the abhorent thought.

There wasn't any use in being jealous though. What woman would settle for the life of rejection and ridicule of a halfbreed's when she could have a nice, quiet existence with a young, personable man like this Rollo appeared to be, outlaw or no? The fellow had gazed at Amanda out of love-filled eyes if Ry had ever seen any. And look at his brat, displaying her feelings for the man for all the world to see. Right now, that world just happened to be one Ryder Manning.

More gruffly than he'd intended, Ry ordered, "Pull yourself together, Amanda. We have work to do if you want your . . . friend . . . to live."

Mandy wiped her eyes with the back of her hand, then chewed thoughtfully on a fingernail. "It's another mile or two to the house. Should I go get the wagon, or do you think he can make it the rest of the way like this?" She absently indicated the drinking horses, never taking her eyes from Reno's white, still face.

Ry was on his knees, using Amanda's wet cloth to clean the surface of the wounds before replacing the compresses. "I don't think we have enough time to wait on a wagon. We need to get him to a doctor as quickly as possible." Ry looked at her with a grave expression on his face. "You've got to prepare yourself for the worst, sweetheart. I'm afraid it's going to be touch and go whether we get him back or not."

She perked up as the word "sweetheart" bolstered her spirits, even if he didn't really mean it literally. He probably used it to make *all* of his women feel good . . . cared for . . . loved? But Mandy wisely put aside that notion as ludicrous while she nodded her head in understanding and helped hold the pads of cloth as Ry bound them in place.

She looked directly into his eyes and never wavered when he demanded, "When I get Ralston in the saddle, help balance him until I can get behind him. No argument, understand?"

It was such a relief to Mandy's tired, aching muscles to be relieved of the duty that they actually shuddered with the release of tension. It never even occurred to her to protest Ry's domineering manner. If the truth were told, she was grateful or it, no matter *what* he called her brother.

As she followed Ry and Reno, her spirits lifted, and she forgot her exhaustion as her eyes greedily devoured the bare form displayed so appetizingly before her. Muscles bulged across Ry's back and shoulders as he supported her brother in front of him. It was hard to believe that only hours earlier she had run her hands over every inch of that sinewy expanse of flesh. Lord help her, how had she gotten

125

into such a wretched situation?

But she felt no remorse, no self-condemnation. Instead she was invigorated, happy that she had experienced something so wonderful and exciting at least once in her life.

Then looking at the burden Ryder carried, her joy faded as she worried about Reno's chances. She tilted her head and looked into the late afternoon sky, and begged for her brother's life.

Chapter Seven

The first tinges of a soft, reddish-orange sunset were streaking the western horizon when the tired trio reined up in front of Mandy's home. Even the shabby appearance of the structure couldn't dispell the flooding relief and warm sensation of finally being home.

As Jeremy ran from the barn toward them, Mandy stepped away from Red Fox and intercepted her younger brother. "Jeremy, it's Reno. We found him wounded back in the hills. H-he's . . . in a bad way."

With his green eyes flashing fear and surprise, Jeremy just stared at Mandy, speechless, before putting his arms around her and holding her close.

"I-I just wanted to tell you before you saw him looking . . . looking so—"

"Hey, you two, isn't somebody going to give me a hand here?" Ry's voice was loud; but the brother and sister could hear the concern he implied, and both jumped into action to help lower Reno from the horse. As soon as Ry dismounted and tied the reins to a porch pillar, they all carried the inert form into the house and to the room used by Ry only two nights earlier.

127

Ry immediately began to give instructions as he started removing the injured man's blood-stained clothing. "Amanda, we'll need hot water and clean bandages. Jeremy, I've done about all I know how. Is there a doctor around here that you could bring back?"

Jeremy and Mandy exchanged apprehensive looks; but Mandy finally nodded, and Jeremy answered, "Yeah, there's a doc pretty close. I'll take old Zeke since the horses are about done for."

The boy had just started for the door when Ry looked over his shoulder. "Take my horse. He's fresh and could use the exercise. And Jeremy? Hurry!"

Jeremy gulped, nodded and was gone in a flash. Minutes later, as she was setting a large kettle of water on the stove to heat, Mandy heard the pounding of hooves disappearing into the distance. She silently prayed that this would be one time that nothing would go wrong.

When she walked into Reno's room, she was shocked by how pale and lifeless her usually exuberant brother appeared. It was scary, and she sent about the twentieth prayer of the day heavenward on his behalf before helping Ry finish removing her brother's clothes. She smiled when Ry looked askance before sliding off the undershorts and almost giggled at the horrified expression on his face when she innocently informed him she'd seen Reno without his clothing many times before.

She wouldn't have thought it so humorous if she'd known the murderous speculations roiling through Ry's head after her ill-stated confession.

Ry kicked himself mentally, over and over for being such a damned fool. Harboring tender, protective feelings for a tramp was ordinarily out of character for him. The little minx had really pulled the wool over his eyes—leading him to believe that she was a virgin—and all the time she and this, this Reno had been, been . . . what? In his anger he jerked the man's legs, causing Reno to moan and try to sit up.

"Don't just stand there, damn it! Hold his shoulders down." Ry was shouting, and it did his heart good to see the surprise and hurt in Amanda's eyes as she stared fixedly at him after taking Reno's upper body onto her lap. He hated to admit it, but he wasn't even surprised by the tightening in his chest when he saw her push a stray lock of hair out of the injured man's eyes. But he wouldn't let it bother him long. At least now he knew what she was—a damned beautiful, desirable liar and whore.

Mandy sat in stunned silence, contemplating the change that had come over Ryder since finding Reno. She was glad that she was seeing this side of the man since it would make it that much easier to forget what had happened between them and the feelings that she'd unwantedly experienced ever since. She didn't realize she was chewing on the edge of her fingernail until she hit sensitive skin and winced. Oh yes, she'd get over the obnoxious lout—no problem.

Ry had finally calmed down, glad to be in control of his emotions and senses again. "Amanda, there're some herbs in my saddlebags over there against the wall. If you'll get them for me, I may be able to control the swelling and fever in the wound." See how cool he could be? She didn't bother him at all. Getting her out of his mind was going to be easy.

Without a word, Mandy laid Reno's head gently back on a pillow, then went to search through Ryder's bags. In the first compartment she found nothing resembling herbs, but her lips thinned into a grim line as she thoughtfully closed the flap.

129

In the second bag she found an oilcloth carefully folded over several varieties of dried herbs. This packet she gingerly handed to Ryder.

Mandy was wiping Reno's forehead with a damp cloth when she heard the clattering of buggy wheels coming up the lane. Gently she stroked her brother's cheek and whispered, "Hang on, brother dear, this has got to be Doc Reilly. You're going to be fine, just fine."

Ry had been slumped in the rocker, catnapping before the doctor's arrival. He rubbed his eyes with the backs of his hands and stood on shaky legs until his equilibrium resumed. The last twenty-four hours had been more exhausting than he realized. Opening the door, he stepped onto the porch and took the doctor's bag while the middle-aged man climbed from the buggy.

"How do, young man. I hear you've got an emergency here. Bullet wound, no doubt?" Before Ry could offer comment, Doc Reilly stepped past him, entered the house and started toward the rear of the house.

Ry was bemused by the man's brusk manner, and he followed him through the hall, not even wondering how the doctor knew the location of Rafe's bedroom. Before Ry reached the room himself, he could hear Amanda welcoming the doctor and the low mumble of whispered words. When he strode through the door and saw Amanda's stricken expression, he naturally assumed it had to do with Rob's condition.

The doctor bent over the patient and examined the path of the bullet, remarking on the excellent job done of cleansing the wound and lowering the incidence of infection. "Young man, would you kindly hand me a few items from my bag? I'll need your help for a little while, if you don't mind. Amanda Jo, would you make me some strong coffee, please? It looks like I'll be here a couple of hours, at least."

A knowing look passed between the doctor and Mandy as Ry bent over the doc's bag. She nodded, mouthed "Thank you" and quickly disappeared from the room.

Almost forty-five minutes later Ry collapsed into a chair he'd just brought from the living room. Doc Reilly was already using the only other one in the room.

The doctor had kept him so busy running errands and doing little nit-picking chores that he'd lost all track of time. Sitting and relaxing, he had time to think, and regrettably, thoughts of Amanda Jo Coulter stole into his mind. Damn the woman for messing up his heretofore orderly existence.

As he looked at the quietly sleeping man on the bed, Ry pictured vague images of Amanda around the eyes and lips. Was just thinking about the brat always going to bring her so vividly near? And he still burned when he remembered Amanda's loving hands smoothing the rumpled blond locks of hair.

Ry then glanced at the doctor's profile and noted the worried expression that had remained fixed even after he'd pronounced that the patient would live, barring complications from the fever. Why was the man still so tense and agitated? Doc jumped at every little noise and cocked his head as if listening for something or someone.

Then it dawned on Ry that he'd seen nothing of Amanda, or Jeremy either, since the doctor had asked

131

for coffee. Maybe that was what he was waiting for. "It sure does take a long time to make coffee around here, huh, Doc?"

Doc Reilly started and looked nervously toward Ry before shifting his eyes back to the patient. "What? Oh, oh yes, I suppose it does." He sat quietly with his hands on his knees, absently bobbing his head up and down.

Ry thought to help ease the man's nerves and offered, "Why don't I go and see what's taking so long? I'll bring us both a cup when I come back."

He started to stand up, then sat back down with a perplexed look on his face when Doc answered, "No! Ah, don't bother, young man. I'm sure I'll get some, ah, when it's ready."

Ry watched the doctor fidget in his chair and wondered why the man kept sneaking looks out of the window. Suddenly, Ryder had an edgy, suspicious feeling all his own. When he stood, the chair tilted backward and almost fell, he moved so quickly. "Doctor, I'm going to the kitchen. Don't get up. You need to stay with your patient. I'll be right back."

The silence in the house was almost eerie as Ry stumbled his way to the kitchen in the dark. Lord, it had been a long day. Embers still glowed in the stove, illuminating the emptiness of the room. The pungent aroma of fresh-brewed coffee hung in the air, but where was Amanda? Why hadn't she returned to the bedroom to check on her lover and bring Doc his coffee? And where was Jeremy? Come to think of it, Ry didn't recall seeing him with the doctor when the older man had arrived.

Ry rubbed his chin and thought about Doc's nervous behavior, remembering the whispered conversation that had taken place with Amanda just before Ry had entered the bedroom with Doc's bag.

There was something going on around here, and he was going to get to the bottom of it, now.

Doc Reilly's back was turned to the room as he stared out of the window. When Ry opened the door, the older man turned with a noticeable expression of defeat written across his features, but before Ry could question the doctor, a low moan from the bed drew both of their attentions.

"Ma-an-ndy? Ma-andy, w-where are you?"

Reno tried to sit up, his eyes wide, as he frantically searched the room, but Ry hurriedly stepped over to push his shoulders down before the wound could reopen. "Easy, fella. Calm down before you hurt yourself."

"M-Mandy? She was here, w-wasn't she?" Reno grabbed hold of Ry's shirt sleeve, and Ry was amazed at the strength still remaining in the man's grip. By all rights, Rod shouldn't even be able to lift his head.

"Okay, okay. Yeah, she was around earlier; but I've just checked, and she's not here anymore." Ry didn't mean to worry the injured man, but he was bound and determined to get some answers to some questions, one way or another.

The grip on Ry's shirt loosened as Reno's hand fell back to the bed. Then the man's head turned, and he saw Doc Reilly. "Oh, hi, Doc. Will *you* tell me about Mandy Jo?" Then he slowly moved his head back around to glare as menacingly as possible in his weakened condition at the infuriating stranger. "And who's he? What's he doing here?"

Doc Reilly jumped at the second and third questions, totally ignoring the first. "Ah, I don't really know, Reno. All I *do* know is that this young man is probably responsible for saving your worthless hide." Doc's chuckle and twinkling eyes took the

133

bite out of his words, and Reno managed a facsimile of a smile.

Ry had locked gazes with Reno, and neither man backed down until Reno's face twitched and his eyes blinked with the pain from his shoulder. When the spasm had passed, Reno asked, "And just how did you happen to find me? Or know where to take me?"

There were so many thoughts running rampant through Ry's mind that he didn't answer right away. Some thanks he was getting for his trouble from this irritable fella. What should he tell the young man? Then Ry shook his head and laughed to himself. He sounded just like Doc Reilly. And how would he explain Amanda's abduction and their subsequent spending of the night together without bringing up ideas of shotgun shells and jealous lovers? Damn, speaking of Amanda, just where the hell was she?

Both Reno and Doc piped up at the same time. "Well?" The two men were curious about the stranger and wondered where he fit into the picture.

Ry sat back in his chair and propped his boot heels on the edge of Ralph's bed. Linking his hands behind his head, he looked to the men and sighed with resignation. "All right, gentlemen, where shall I begin?"

Doc cleared his throat and said, "Why not start with your name, young man."

"And what you're doing here." Reno was trying to get his elbows underneath his body to lift himself up but just couldn't manage it. Doc finally took pity and propped another pillow under his head.

Ry crossed his arms over his chest, deliberating over what to say. He might just as well stick as close to the truth as possible, in case something he said came back to haunt him later. "My name is Ryder Manning. And I'm here because—I work here." He grinned at the disbelieving gape on Rick's face. "In fact," Ry said, slanting a stern look in Rich's direction, "you're using my bed."

Reno was so flabbergasted that he was on the verge of shouting, yet the words came out as little more than a whisper through his dry, parched throat. "Since when?"

"Let's see, it seems like it's been months, but I guess the night before last was the first time I slept here."

Reno sputtered, and the doctor leaned over to hold his upper body still. "No! No, I meant since when do you work here."

"Oh, well, why didn't you say so? I started working the day before yesterday, too. Or I was hired then."

Ry looked innocently at the back of one hand, then calmly scraped a line of dirt from under a fingernail. Reno sat, red-faced, with his mouth opening and closing but unable to force words through his constricted throat. Doc Reilly sighed with relief as his patient quit fighting the restricting pressure from the doctor's hands.

"Young man, ah, Mr. Manning, was it?"

"Just call me Ry."

"Uh, may I be so presumptuous as to ask *who* hired you? Amanda Jo would never—"

"It was George. George Coulter." When the men remained silent and wary, he added, "You know, the man who sired Amanda and Jeremy? The one with the still up the hill there?" He pointed out of the room's only window in the direction of the Coulter corn liquor factory.

The doctor finally nodded his head and broke the stunned silence. "We know who you're talking about, young man, it's just hard to believe that the Coulters would be paying an extra hand."

135

"Well, George and I spent a very . . . intoxicating . . . afternoon at the still, and if my memory is correct, he talked me into working for room and board. Quite a sharp dealer is George Coulter, yessir."

Reno was in control of his temper enough to mutter, "I guess there's no telling what George might do when he's drunk, but what I really want to know is what you and Amanda Jo were doing so far from home, and alone?"

There were those horrid visions of shotguns again, but Ry could see no help for it. He would stick to the truth, up to a point, and maybe one of the men would help shed some light on some questions of his own. So Ry spent the next half hour relating the story of Red Fox's sudden and unexpected arrival at the homestead and Ry's subsequent tracing of Amanda's trail.

Ron's face was even more pinched and white by the time Ry had finished the part about Hank Ford and his cronies and the plans he'd overheard them making for inviting Amanda to a party being held in her honor. He left out some of the more embarrassing parts of his daring rescue and completely overlooked explaining about the weather and describing his surefire method for creating substantial body heat. If the two men should assume that he and Amanda had spent the night trying to elude their enemies, then far be it from Ry to dissuade them otherwise.

After Ry brought the story to its conclusion, as far as bringing the wounded man to Amanda's home, silence permeated the room. All three men seemed to be caught up in thoughts of their own. Finally the intense quiet was broken when Reno blurted, "I'll get that Hank Ford if it's the last thing I ever do."

"You'll have to stand in line." Ry's voice was hard

136

as he remembered his own frustration at not being able to do anything about the ruthless outlaw while making good their escape.

Reno's head tossed back and forth on the pillow as he rubbed his injured shoulder. "Jesse and I should've finished them off when . . . we had . . . the chance . . ." He dozed off, but sweat beaded his forehead and upper lip as he fretted and twisted in the damp sheets.

Doc reached over to feel Reno's face and sighed. "The worst is yet to come, but if he survives this fever, he'll be in the clear."

Ry shook his head at Doc's choice of words. In his own opinion, Rollo had damned himself when he'd admitted to being with Jesse. Of course, Ry hadn't seen any posters on any . . . Rafe? Rob? Let's see, he could remember Amanda distinctly emphasizing the name . . . ah, Rip . . . Reno! That was it! As if he really cared. But just who was this Reno? He'd never found out the man's full name, or even if it was his *real* name, or much about him period.

There were more important things he needed to worry about first, then he'd get back to—Reno. "Doc, who's this Hank Ford? And what's he to the Coulters?" Ry had wanted to ask the questions of Reno after observing the man's reaction to the name, but he was too far out of it now. Since Doc Reilly seemed to be a close friend of the family, maybe he could help just as well.

The doctor's Adam's apple bounced up and down in his throat as he swallowed nervously. "Oh, Hank Ford is a trouble maker, a no-good who has pestered Amanda Jo once too often." Then gathering up his courage, Doc looked Ryder in the eye. "If you were here for the funeral, as you claim, then you should know the name Ford. It was Hank's cousin Bob who

137

assassinated Jesse."

Doc's voice broke, and Ry was taken aback by the bitterness he detected in the doctor's sentiments toward the Fords. "But Doc, surely you don't disapprove of the Fords? They rid the world of a common thief, a vicious murderer." Supposedly.

Doc Reilly rounded on Ry with menacing eyes and clenched fists. "I'm not going to waste time tonight arguing with you on Jesse's sterling character, young man; but how can you condemn Jesse James on one hand, and then praise a man like Bob Ford on the other? The bastard shot Jesse in the back of the head like a low-down, dirty coward because he didn't have the guts to face him man to man. Now, young man, was that a law-abiding act performed by a fine, up-standing citizen? Or was it pure and simple—murder?"

Ry rubbed his chin and stood up to pace the floor of the small bedroom. "Maybe you're right, Doc. Murder's murder, any way you look at it, I guess." For the first time since his arrival in Missouri, the foundation of Ry's convictions was being shaken. He had always believed that a person's actions were either right or wrong, no in-between. And for the last forty-eight hours he'd been re-evaluating his stand on several things.

The younger man stopped pacing, stood stiffly in front of the window, glanced meaningfully at Doc, then clasped his hands behind his back, thinking. "Who was the doctor who identified Jesse's body, Doc? You?"

Again Doc's Adam's apple bobbed frantically as he visibly straightened his shoulders. "Y-yes, I examined the body and identified him. Why?"

"And you're positive that it *was* Jesse James?"

The doctor glanced hopefully toward his patient

138

but found that Reno was resting quietly for the first time in the last hour. He sagged heavily into his chair and rubbed his palms up and down his thighs. "The James family have been patients of mine for a long time, of course I knew Jesse. I've been patching him up for years."

"Did you have to do a lot of patching? I bet an outlaw like Jesse was at your door every time you turned around."

"No, not really. At the end of the war he suffered a chest wound that nearly killed him, but actually he was pretty lucky through the years. I hardly saw him at all."

"So, if you weren't around him very much, how could you be so sure when you identified the body?" Ry turned and watched the Doc's face closely.

Doc Reilly squirmed a little uncomfortably in his chair, then took a deep breath to answer confidently, "Jesse's appearance never changed that much, for one thing, and I recognized my own stitching on most of the wounds, for another." Having answered truthfully, Doc stood and faced Ryder. "Just what are you trying to say, boy?"

Ry decided to back off before riling the doctor and making him even more curious about a stranger asking such leading questions. "Don't mind me, Doc. You know what happens when a man starts thinking too hard sometimes. He gets crazy ideas that don't mean anything, nothing at all." He had read the truth in the doctor's eyes. Now where did that leave his theory?

Doc squinted his eyes and silently released a long, slow breath of air. If the young man's question had been stated any differently, he might not've been able to pull that answer off. He didn't have a poker face by any means and counted his lucky stars that he'd never had to lie before this incident. From the arrogance and the barely contained belligerence of the fellow, it was easy to see that he was sharp—and dangerous. Ryder Manning reminded Doc Reilly of a bull terrier he'd once owned—hardheaded and determined enough to gnaw and worry a bone until he'd eaten clear through to the marrow.

Ry glanced at his watch. Only five minutes had passed since the last time he'd looked. Where was Amanda? The doctor had been here over two hours. What could she be doing that could take this long? He must've transmitted his thoughts to the man on the bed, for Reno suddenly reared forward and shouted, "Mandy! No!"

Reno's eyes were still closed; but they suddenly flared open, and there was no doubt as to the genuine fear and pain located within their hazel depths. His good arm moved, but slowly, as he reached for the edge of the sheet covering his hips and legs. He was mumbling to himself as he attempted to rise from the bed. "Got to save her . . . Jeremy . . . got to hurry . . ."

Doc Reilly tried to hold Reno in the bed; but his own face was white with apprehension, and his hands shook so badly that Ry quickly stepped over to give him a hand. Luckily, the wounded man passed out before he could do any real damage to himself.

Ry turned a questioning gaze on the doctor as he watched the older man pace the floor beside the bed. Doc's smooth, tapered fingers wound themselves together as he talked to himself, not even realizing he was speaking aloud. "Oh, dear. Oh, Lord, what have I done? If anything happens to those children. Oh, dear."

It didn't take a genius to figure out what Ry had been suspecting for the last hour. He stepped in front of the doctor and put his hands on the man's shoulders to stop the irritating pacing. "All right, Doc. What's going on around here? Where is Amanda? And what was that gibberish Reno was spouting?"

Doc sighed and sat down, glad that he could unburden himself from the nefarious promise he'd given. After all, it wasn't as if he'd *volunteered* the information, and the young man looked ready to *beat* it out of him. "Sit down, young man. You make me nervous breathing down my neck like that." Doc Reilly cleared his throat and waited until Ry lowered his taut frame into a seat, his legs straddling the chair and his arms crossed over the carved back.

"I'd better start by putting things in sequence. First of all, Reno. He possesses a sort of . . . sixth sense, has had it ever since he was a boy. He knows when someone he loves or cares about is in danger, or hurt, things like that. I can't even begin to explain it. And that's the only reason I'm telling you this, because Jeremy, and more than likely Amanda, must be in some kind of trouble. You see, when Jeremy came to get me, the sheriff stopped us on the way out of town and arrested him for riding a stolen horse. Naturally, I hurried on out here to let Amanda know. I-I had to tell her."

Doc had stopped long enough to take a sip of water, and Ry took that opportunity to interrupt. "What do you mean, the sheriff arrested the boy? I told him to ride my horse."

"Young . . . Ryder, you've got to understand the situation around here to make sense of *anything*. The Coulters are close relatives of the James's. The sheriff is an ex-Pinkerton man who lost his job because of Jesse and Frank and their ability to outwit the incompetent bastard. Are you beginning to see the

141

picture? If it wasn't the horse, it would've been something else."

Ry rubbed his chin and nodded. "Yeah, I believe I do. This so-called sheriff has a grudge against Jesse and thereby takes every opportunity to harass those victims less hazardous to his health than the James's."

"That's about it. So when Amanda Jo asked about Jeremy, I had to tell her where he was. Which I assumed was in jail."

"But why would she take off like that, all by herself, and so late at night? What would she expect to accomplish?"

Doc chuckled and looked on the younger man with something akin to pity. "Ah, my boy, you don't know our Amanda Jo very well if you think she won't be able to come up with a few ideas of her own to take care of that precious younger brother." He looked down at the unconscious older brother and wished she'd been able to do as much for him. Reno was a good boy, but he'd been running wild for too long. Doc only hoped that he hadn't gotten himself into any trouble that would cause the family more pain and suffering.

Ry sat very still and very tense for several minutes, but outward appearances masked the frantic whirling of his mind and the churning of his stomach. Even sitting beside Amanda's wounded lover and knowing her feelings for the man, Ry experienced the outrage and fear that one could only feel for someone very . . . cared for? . . . loved? . . . whatever. What if she did something stupid and got hurt? What if he never saw her again? Would he really care after only knowing her for a few short days? Yes! Damn right he would! So what if she loved another man? Ry was experienced with women; surely he could put

142

that expertise to use and woo— Hold up one minute! What was he thinking? He was almost on the verge of forgetting why he was there, and in order to follow that lead, he had to have Amanda. That was the *only* reason for his going after her. After finally making that decision, he began to feel much more confident and lighthearted.

Doc Reilly had been watching the play of emotions across the usually unreadable Indian features. All evening he'd looked into an impassive, undemonstrative countenance, but suddenly he was privy to the inner workings of the man's mind, and he almost laughed out loud. The doctor could almost feel sorry for the young man. This Coulter bunch would surely lead him a merry chase.

"Doc, are you going to be around here for a while yet?" At the doctor's affirmative nod and choked "I wouldn't leave here right now for a million dollars," Ry cocked his head questioningly but decided the old man must be getting tired. "Okay then, I'm going into town and see what's going on. Just keep that—" Ry nodded toward Reno's still form—"that . . . Amanda's friend . . . from doing anything foolish."

Ry spun on his heel and was out of the door before the doctor said, "Friend? Oh, young man, this is even better than I thought."

It was almost ten o'clock by the time Mandy reached the outskirts of town. Rather than ride down the main street and advertise her presence, she angled left and rode behind the Kovat's general store and Mr. Moreley's blacksmith shop until she was within sight of the jail.

She breathed a sigh of relief when there was no light in the front office. Evidently Sheriff Pomeroy had already called it a night. Not that she wouldn't have been glad to confront the despicable man, it was just, well, she knew that it wouldn't have done a bit of good. The man was hardheaded and unyielding and was literally out to get her family.

There was a grove of elm trees not too far from the jail, and Mandy stopped there to tether Red Fox and Jeremy's old gray gelding, Dusty. It wouldn't do for her brother to leave town on Mr. Ryder Manning's horse. Then there really would be charges for horse stealing.

Mandy looked around the room carefully, then studied the shadows of the buildings on either side of the jailhouse. As far as she could tell, there was no one about. Even the traffic on Main Street was negligible at this time of night, except for the lights and music coming from the Busted Keg Saloon. It was just about time for business there to hit its peak, so maybe no one would be wandering in the jail's vicinity.

Fleet of foot, Mandy swiftly ran across the open space between the grove of trees and the back of the jail. Once in the shadows, she made a fast reconnissance around the building. Satisfied that she was alone, Mandy stepped onto the wooden planks that served as a porch for the jailhouse. Looking to the left and to the right, she moved with her back against the building until she reached the door. Slowly she reached out and tried the knob of the thick oak door and let out her breath when it turned easily under the pressure.

Quickly she slipped through the opening and closed the door behind her, almost sagging to the floor with the vibration from her trembling knees. So far, so good. But what if her brother wasn't there? What if Sheriff Pomeroy had already . . . ?

Chapter Eight

Ryder conserved his tired horse's energy on the ride to town, ignoring the urge to spur the beast into a hard gallop. There was no way to know for sure what the outcome of the night would be, but he hadn't lived twenty-five years on the edge of danger by careless thinking. He tried to plan ahead, to think rationally, and thereby survive any consequences.

Entering the town at a walk, the horse plodding stiffly, Ry's hooded eyes raked every nook and cranny of the buildings lining the street. As the bat-wing doors of the saloon on his right swung out and caught his attention, the form of a medium-height, stockily built man was silhouetted. Ry couldn't see the figure's features, but when the man turned to reenter the establishment, light reflected off shiny metal on the man's vest.

Indecision hung heavy in Ry's mind. Should he begin tearing through every building and alleyway in a mad rush to locate Amanda? Or should he slowly and methodically follow every lead? In the end, he took the middle road and hurried into the saloon after the man he had heard so much about from Doc Reilly.

He paused just inside the door, moved so his back was against the wall and waited for his eyes to adjust to the light. The saloon was smaller than he'd thought from the outside, but then the bar took up one entire wall and probably one-third of the space.

It was an ornate structure with carved mahogany panels inset into the front. The back bar was made of matching wood with round totemlike posts at either end, setting off the largest, cleanest mirror he'd ever seen. A brass foot and handrail ran the length of the front bar on bottom and top, embellishing the entire area with an air of lavishness. Quite a feat for such a small, backwater village.

The rest of the room was filled with round tables covered with red and white checked cloths, and a Steinway piano filled one corner. Yes, someone had put a lot of imagination and *money* into the joint. There were even padded seats on the chairs.

Several cowpunchers sat at one table, while another boasted nattily dressed townsmen. The illustrious sheriff sat alone, and at that very moment noticed Ry's presence inside the doors.

With a nonchalance he didn't really feel, Ry sauntered over to the bar and rested his left side against the brass rails. Out of the corner of his right eye he could watch every member of the clientele without actually appearing to do so. He wondered how long it would take for the ex-Pinkerton man to make his move.

When the barkeep asked his pleasure, Ry ordered a shot of the best bourbon the house offered and smiled when it went down smooth. The place had class all right. Leastwise, until a harsh voice rasped from directly behind, "You're a stranger to these parts." It was an accusation, not a question.

Ryder had seen the sheriff's approach reflected in

the monster mirror, and he turned slowly to rest both elbows on the railing while he studied the burly man standing in front of him.

Sheriff Pomeroy was of medium height, but the hard muscles on his stocky body lent him the appearance of a much larger man. His face was pitted, and his close-set eyes and long, sharp nose reminded Ry of the rat he'd killed in his last hotel room.

"You could say that."

"You just passin' through?" The harsh eastern accent didn't fit with the soft Missouri hill dialect one heard most often, but it suited the speaker perfectly.

"Maybe, maybe not."

The sheriff was becoming impatient and snapped, "You got business around here?"

"Guess you could say that."

Now the sheriff's face reddened, and his right hand twitched closer to the butt of his gun. "In case you haven't noticed, partner, I'm the sheriff of this here town, and I'm paid to ask questions. And when I ask those questions, I expect a clear answer. You understand me?"

Ry pushed away from the bar, placing himself within inches of the shorter man. He swallowed the last of his bourbon and placed the glass back on the counter before deigning to answer the surly sheriff. "Oh, I understand you all right, partner"—placing a certain emphasis on the word "partner"—"but I can't rightly give you a clear answer. I haven't made up my mind as to just what I'm going to do yet. Is there any law against my lookin' around for a spell?"

Ryder had leaned forward just enough to cause the sheriff to have to tilt his head back to look up at him and had moved his hands to his hips as his body tensed.

The threatening gesture was enough to make the sheriff retreat a step or two, then bluster, "Well, no, I can't think of any offhand. Just bein' neighborly, is all."

"That's real kind of you, Sheriff. Now, let me buy you a drink. I surely do admire a man willing to take on such a dangerous job during today's day and time. With all the outlaws and hardcases on the loose, it takes a mighty brave man to keep the peace, I imagine."

Ry almost laughed outloud as his conciliatory words of praise caused the man's chest to expand like a pompous toad in heat. What a conceited bastard he was. He was probably the type who got his thrills from kicking dogs and taking candy from babies.

"You got that right, ah, mister. This area's been a hideout for thieves and murderers for years, but I've been cleanin' up lately. Why, just a couple days ago we got the *famous* Jesse James right where he belonged—six feet under. That was a glorious day, mister . . . ?"

"Manning, Ryder Manning. Yeah, I heard all about it." Ry clapped the sheriff on the shoulders. "Guess you had a lot to do with that, huh, Sheriff?"

Sheriff Pomeroy winced from the blow to his back and looked nervously over his shoulder to see if any of the bar's patrons were paying any attention to their conversation. Seeing that the rest of the men were lost in their own thoughts or involved with decks of cards, he nevertheless lowered his voice.

"Naturally, I played a big part in bringing about the downfall of the little pip-squeak. He and his brother weren't so tough. If it hadn't been for all their family and friends, hiding and protecting them . . ."

The sheriff's words were choked and trailed off,

148

and Ry was taken aback by the hatred blazing from the man's eyes and the contorted features of his face. Even if he hadn't already been warned, now, more than ever, he feared for Amanda's and Jeremy's safety.

Ry cleared his throat. "So, you sound like all your troubles aren't over yet. Maybe you should call in some help from the government."

The sheriff's eyes darted warily toward Ry and, for the first time, really appraised the lean, young fellow. He noticed the calm self-assuredness, the wiry toughness of his body, and most disconcerting of all, the keen awareness of Ryder Manning's clear, dark eyes. A shudder worked its way unbidden down the sheriff's spine as those black orbs never wavered from his own shifty, muddy-brown ones.

"Nope, don't need no help from outsiders. I got things under control. Won't be long 'til these bloody nesters learn a few manners from Sheriff J.D. Pomeroy. Ain't nobody outsmarts . . . fools around with me and gets away with it. You'll see."

Ry could tell that the man had had too much to drink and wasn't talking to anybody but himself. It was hard to imagine what could go on in a person's mind to cause him to harbor such hate and vengeance.

"Well, Sheriff, it's been real . . . enlightening. I'll be seeing you around."

"Huh? Oh, yeah, I s'pose so. Take care, Mr. Manning." The sheriff's hands were both wrapped around his glass as he held it to his lips. He then wiped his mouth on his shirt sleeve and staggered back to his table to stare into the remaining amber liquid.

As Ry pushed out the swinging doors, he hoped the sheriff would remain occupied for at least a while

149

longer and smiled to himself when he saw a gaudily dressed woman seat herself in the man's lap. Ah yes, that should take care of him nicely.

Mandy moved to the only windows in the main room and closed the shutters. Then she felt around the massive oak desk until she found a tin containing matches. Her hands were shaking so badly that it took three tries before she could hold her hand steady enough to light the wick.

She moved almost reluctantly toward the door leading to the cells, as if afraid of what she might find. As the door creaked open, she looked nervously about, worried that Sheriff Pomeroy might somehow materialize out of the flickering shadows.

"Amanda Jo? My God, sis, I can't believe it's you! What're you doing here? Trying to get yourself killed?"

"You're welcome, Jeremy," Amanda said sweetly. "Shush up, will you? You want to wake the whole town?" She hated to sound so harsh, but she had to stop his tirade before it turned into hysteria. She knew how badly nerves could affect a person; she was bordering on a breakdown herself.

When she reached Jeremy's cell, he reached through the bars and gripped her free hand. "Put that lamp down, sis, and let me give you a hug, such as it is."

Jeremy's arms wrapped around Mandy's shoulders, pressing her chest into the cold steel. "I'm sorry to rant at you like that, Amanda, but you shouldn't have come. Pomeroy's hoping that the rest of the family will come in after me so's he can trap the bunch of us. Course, he doesn't know about Reno bein' back, an' hurt an' all." He finally stopped long enough to gulp in some air. He was so excited to have company and so afraid because Amanda Jo was there that he hardly knew how to react. "God, it's good to see someone, sis. I've been scared to death in here."

Mandy blinked back tears at her brother's admission. He was trying so hard to grow up so fast, but deep down he was still just a child. "I can't blame you. I'm more than a little frightened myself." She took Jeremy's hands in hers and squeezed. "But since I'm here, let's see what we can do about getting you out of there."

"That's what I've been prayin' for, but the last time I saw the keys, they were hangin' from Pomeroy's belt. Do you reckon he left 'em or took 'em with him?"

Mandy bent down to pick up the lamp. "Only one way to find out." With a parting grin, she quipped, "You wait here; I'll be right back."

"Oh, jeez sis, that's cute, really cute."

Back in the front office, Mandy looked carefully around the room. Along the right wall was a rumped cot and a chair with dirty clothes draped over the back. A pair of boots, bent and worn at the ankles, stuck out from beneath the bed. On the wall above the cot, suspended on nails, were a sheepskin jacket, a battered hat and a coiled rope.

To the left of the room was the big oak desk and chair, a gun case and a potbellied stove with a fairly new coffee pot sitting on the lid.

Naturally, the logical place for a set of keys would be the nail protruding from the gun case, but since the nail was empty, Mandy gave herself credit for having the intelligence to check out the desk. The top right drawer contained a stack of wanted posters similar to those she'd found earlier. The bottom drawer held the sheriff's life sustaining bottle of

151

Scotch and two glasses. She was tempted to take a swig to settle her nerves, but there was too much involved tonight to risk losing her head, like her pa.

The top drawer on the other side was locked, and the bottom contained an empty gunbelt. So, that left the locked drawer as the last hope. She sat in the chair and thought for several minutes, then lifted her pant leg and pulled out the long-bladed knife. Sticking the sharp tip into the groove of the lock, she jimmied and pried until the drawer began to rock and finally pulled free.

Her heart sank when she ran her hands through several pocket watches, a few rings and a bow tie. Bow tie? But no keys. The sheriff must've taken the keys with him after all.

Dejectedly, Mandy scuffed the soles of her boots along the plank flooring as she took the disappointing news back to her brother. "I'm afraid the keys aren't in the office. What're we going to do now?" She leaned back against the wall across from Jeremy's cell and slid down to a sitting position.

Jeremy had been pacing the interior of the small cell but stopped now to grasp the bars in his hands and lean his forehead against the cool pipe. In an effort to make Amanda feel better and to keep himself from breaking down and crying, he joked, "You don't have any dynamite on you, do ya, sis?"

Mandy raised her eyes and smiled crookedly. "Lucky for you, I'm fresh out tonight. I'd probably blow us both clear to St. Louis."

"Well, we'd be out of *here*, anyway."

The brother and sister stared into each other's eyes for long minutes, smiling, sharing their closeness. Finally, Mandy sighed and leaned her head back against the wall. She pictured the office in her mind in an effort to think if she might've missed something, someplace, where the sheriff could have hidden the keys.

It was like watching a fire fanned to life as Jeremy saw his sister's head come upright and watched the dullness in her eyes turn gradually to a brilliant flame. "What is it, Amanda Jo? You've got an idea, don't you? C'mon, c'mon, let me in on it." He was almost bouncing off the floor from the excitement in his body and the strength in the grip of his hands on the bars.

But she wasn't even looking at him. Her eyes were focused unwaveringly on the window in the back of his cell. He looked from Amanda to the window, then back to Amanda. "What? What's on your mind, sis? If it's the window you're thinking about, forget it! I've already tried that."

Mandy shook her head and also gripped the bars, her knuckles turning white with the pressure. "Jeremy," she whispered, "just how secure are those bars? Are any of them loose? Even one?"

Jeremy immediately ran to check, as he hadn't thought about that when he'd been gauging the distance between them earlier. He pushed and pulled on each bar and found some give in two of them. "These two are a little loose. Why?"

Excitement was building in Mandy's voice as she answered, "Remember when Jesse and Frank broke cousin Ezra out of jail up in Liberty? They wrapped a rope around the window bars and hooked it to their saddle horns and pulled the bars out. It could work, Jeremy. We could do it!"

"Aw, sis, that was fifteen years ago. They've reinforced jails since then."

"Not this one. Not yet. People've had enough trouble getting by around here since the war, let alone paying for county improvements. It's been a while,

153

but the last time Jesse came to the house for supper we spent a lot of time talking about how run-down the town was becoming. Remember? Let's try it, Jeremy!"

Jeremy rubbed his chin and let some of her enthusiasm sink in. "Okay, what've we got to lose? Yeah, it might just work. But how're we going to pull it off? And when?"

"Right now! There's a rope hanging in the office, and Red Fox and Dusty are tied in the trees behind the jail. Don't go away! I'll be right back."

"Don't joke, Amanda Jo. I'm too keyed up to appreciate it. Just hurry up, will you?"

But she was already gone, hurrying into the office for the rope before blowing out the lantern and opening the shutters on the windows. She looked out each window, watching the shadows and checking the activity on the street, then very carefully opened the door and tiptoed to the end of the porch. Her heart began to beat again the minute she was surrounded by the black shadow of the building.

When she reached the horses, she looped one end of the rope over her saddle horn and carried the rest still coiled in her left hand while she led the two horses behind the jail. She was as quick and careful as she could be, but if anyone had seen her crossing the open lot, there would've been nothing she could've done to prevent it. So far, luck was on her side.

"Jeremy? Which one are you in?" She whispered as loud as she could, then jumped in surprise when her brother stuck his arm out the window directly in front of her and touched the top of her head. "Eeegads! You just scared ten years off my life, you idiot!"

Mentally regaining her composure, she uncoiled the rest of the rope and handed the loose end to Jeremy to tie off on the bars. It was now or never.

154

"Okay Jer, stand back in case any bricks fall to the inside. It'd be a shame to go to all this trouble and have some stupid little thing like that do us in." She smiled and winked at her brother, then waited until he had moved to the other side of the cell before turning to mount Red Fox.

"Let's go, boy. Show 'em just what kind of heart belongs to Tennessee thoroughbreds."

The horse walked to the end of the rope, taking out all of the slack, and then took another step. The rope tautened, creaked from the additional stress, and held.

Ryder Manning had just pushed through the doors of the Busted Keg and stepped off the walk near the hitching rail when a loud grating noise exploded the stillness of the night. Several other passersby stopped to stare in the direction from which the noise had come, which also happened to be the direction of the jail according to the nearest spectator's excited ramblings.

Sudden comprehension blossomed in Ry's brain, and he made a flying leap into the saddle, simultaneously jerking loose the reins to his horse. He had ridden almost even with the jail before he heard one of the people in the street hollering into the saloon. It wouldn't take Sheriff Pomeroy long to pull out of his doldrums and make his way to the jail—especially after he realized he was losing his precious prisoner.

When the horse rounded the corner of the jail, it was just in time for Ry to see Amanda mounted on Red Fox holding the reins to a gray horse while Jeremy tried to swing up on the nervously prancing animal. He closed his eyes in hopes that he was dreaming the entire scene, but when he reopened them, sure enough, there were the same two lunatics, horses' tails turned and ready to charge into the blackness, or to their ends.

"Wait! Hold up a minute!"

Jeremy had just gathered Dusty's reins from Amanda and had turned to flee toward the nearest trees when he heard the shout. His and Amanda's eyes both rounded with the fear of being discovered and caught at a disadvantage until Jeremy finally located the source of the voice.

However, when Mandy noticed the rider, her fear only intensified. "Don't stop, Jer. You've got to get out of here. Now! I'll head him off and catch up with you at the river."

"But, sis, it's only Ryder. Maybe he'll help us."

"No, he won't. We don't have time to argue, just hurry. I'll explain everything to you later. Now go! You're the one they're after."

Jeremy pivoted his horse back and forth, undecided, until he heard the sound of footsteps running toward the jail. "All right, but I don't like this. Someone's coming, so you'd better make it quick."

Ry had pulled up to Amanda when the first voice shouted, "There he goes! It's the Coulter kid, and he's getting away."

Another voice chimed in, "Say, isn't that the boy's sister? Yeah, it's her, all right. I bet she's the one busted him out. Sheriff, over here."

Ry grabbed Amanda's reins, preventing her from riding after her brother. "Don't run, Amanda. It's too late, and you'll only make matters worse. Stay with me and I'll—"

He never got a chance to finish as a bullet whizzed between their bodies. Then he recognized the unmistakable voice of the sheriff shouting, "That's the way, partner. Grab her. I'm offering a hundred dollars to anyone who can bring her in. And that goes for the brother, too."

The rest of the rabble drew their guns and looked at each other incredulously. That was more money than most of them had heard of or seen in their entire lives, and they weren't about to let some stranger have it. Bullets soon filled the air with no care as to the target. After all, the sheriff hadn't said to bring her in *alive*.

Ry finally realized the hazard of posing as sitting ducks and yelled to Amanda, "It's no use; we've got to run. Follow me."

Mandy grinned, still feeling confident and exuberant over successfully pulling off her brother's escape. If the big, brave man wanted to play hero, it was fine with her. She'd follow him a ways, make sure he was out of danger, then break off and head for the river and Jeremy.

They had almost reached the trees when Mandy felt a stinging pain in the side of her back. In the excitement of the getaway, however, she just leaned lower in the saddle, grabbed hold of Red Fox's mane and ignored the discomfort as nothing more than a nuisance as she sped after Ryder Manning.

The wind was blowing, and the wee morning hours were cold. Mandy was still trailing after Ryder through the winding gullies and creek beds, even though sounds of pursuit had faded hours ago. At least it seemed like hours. She was riding in a rather numbed state, almost light-headed, which she attributed to exhaustion from the accumulated ride through the hills with Reno, then the trip to town to break Jeremy from jail and now this extra added trek to avoid a posse. Life hadn't been dull since meeting Ryder Manning.

Ry's thoughts were leaning in the same direction, but he was wondering how Amanda Jo Coulter had ever lived long enough to become such a beautiful, personable woman if she had gone through experiences like she had during the last forty-eight hours all her life. Damn! The woman definitely needed a keeper.

The most distressing thing on Ry's mind, however, was the fact that for the first time in his life he was running from the *law*. Here he'd been trying to talk Amanda into giving herself up, when the next thing he knew, people were trying to kill them. Yes, *them!* They didn't even know *him* or if he was friend or foe. Nor did they care; they had just started firing when the sheriff offered that one hundred dollar bounty.

Then something clicked in Ry's head. The sheriff had been standing there, looking directly at Amanda and himself, had seen that Ry had her stopped and under control, and had deliberately set the dogs on them. There had actually been no choice on his part. They'd either had to run or be killed.

For the first time, he wondered if any of the faces he carried in his saddlebags had wandered into the same kind of situation. Of course he'd never make excuses for anyone on the outlaw trail, but—

"Hey, Mr. Manning, do we have to ride all night? Can't we stop for a little while? My horse needs a breather." Mandy swayed in the saddle, then sat up straight and pretended that the rest would be for Red Fox more than for herself. If only the darn stinging in her side wasn't getting worse.

Ry grinned and turned in his saddle. "Sure, we can stop for the night, if you want. Guess I just didn't realize you'd be quite so anxious. I even had the foresight to bring a blanket." His voice was low and husky as he finished, and he raised one dark brow questioningly before he winked.

Mandy's face turned beet red. "Ooohh, you idiot. I only meant that we could take a break, not that we should, ah, sleep . . ."

"Why, Amanda Jo Coulter, where is your mind? Whatever did you think I was talking about? Surely you couldn't think that I'd use the blanket for any purpose other than stretching out and relaxing for a few minutes?"

"Oh, yes, I could. And you intended for me to, you no account—"

"Now, now, don't get testy. This is all an innocent misunderstanding, don't you think?"

"Well, I don't know about that." Mandy slid from the saddle and had to hold on to the horn while the pain in her side intensified, then lessened as she stood quietly. She thanked her lucky stars that Ryder had turned his back to see to Reno's horse, as she didn't think she was up to his irate questions at this time.

She'd seen the look on his face as he saw Jeremy and herself making their escape and had seen the terrible pain reflected in his eyes when he'd had to make the run out of town. Bounty hunter, lawman, whatever, he certainly couldn't be happy with the circumstances she'd more or less forced him into.

Mandy absently watched Ry as he searched his pockets for matches, and then straightened away from Red Fox with interest when he dropped a folded paper, apparently never noticing its presence. Slowly, she sauntered over to where he'd spread the blanket and just happened to reach down to fold a corner in the area of the dropped paper. She gasped in surprise when her brain informed her that a red-hot poker had been thrust into her side and almost

159

dropped the missive when Ry spun around at the sound and slammed into her chest just as she was rising.

Concentrating on nothing but the paper, she stuffed it into her back pocket as Ry's hands reached out to steady her. Another cry escaped her compressed lips as his hand grazed her ribcage, and she sagged into his sturdy frame, her knees suddenly buckling under her.

"Amanda? Hey, sweetheart, what's this?" Ry pulled one of his hands from her slim form when he encountered a wet, sticky substance. The moonlight was bright enough for him to make out a dark stain with a sickly sweet odor dripping from his fingers.

Blood! "Good God, you're bleeding like a stuck pig." Immediately he led her to the blanket and pushed her onto it, fumbling all the while at the buttons on her shirt.

Mandy closed her eyes and bit her lip to take her mind off the erotic sensations aroused in her body when his knuckles rubbed against the undersides of her breasts. Her voice was throaty and very seductive when she mumbled, "Go easy on the buttons, please, I don't have any extras on me."

"Ho, you don't, eh? Well, I'll have to see what I can do to spare these, then." His voice was teasing, not in the least betraying the fear that was clutching at his insides. Damn the brat! What did he ever do to deserve the troublesome woman?

"Okay, slip your arm out and let me look at your ribs." He watched her breasts rise and fall as Amanda bent her elbow and slipped her right arm free of the bloodstained shirt. A sigh of disappointment faded into the night as she shifted and brought the tail up around her chest, closing off the delectable view.

When he finally lowered his eyes to her ribs, he

sucked in his breath at the bloody scratch running across her ribs. He slowly let the air out of his lungs when he discovered the wound wasn't deep, just bloody as hell. "That's a bullet wound, Amanda. Why didn't you tell me before now that you'd been hit? Or had you decided that you'd rather *die* than have me touch you?"

Mandy couldn't figure out why Ryder was so upset. After all, it wasn't hurting *him*, and she hadn't complained or delayed their escape. So, a little angry herself, she responded, "I beg your pardon, your lordship, but your touch means nothing to me, one way or the other. And to tell you the truth, I didn't realize that I'd even been shot. I thought I had gotten a stitch in my side from riding bent over while they were shooting at us. There was never any pain, much, until I bent over to . . . straighten the blanket."

"Yeah, it looks like it scabbed over a little. You probably tore it open again when you stretched it." Ry's hands were probing the area around her ribs, feeling to see if any had been broken by the bullet, when he noticed how silky and smooth her flesh felt beneath his fingers. She was so trim and supple, her skin so vibrant and alive, quivering in response to his ticklish ministrations. So his touch didn't mean anything to her? Ha!

But she was injured, and they still had a ways to go before they could actually stop to rest. She needed his *help* more than anything else right now. So, to take his mind off the sensual urgings of his body, he lifted his head and looked toward the two horses. "Damn, but I did it again: came off on a heroic rescue mission about as prepared to face the world as a newborn babe."

He hadn't realized he'd spoken aloud until

161

Amanda's fingers on his arm regained his attention. She'd never appeared to openly want to touch him before, and he grinned when she sheepishly admitted, "Look in my saddlebags. I've got a few supplies that might come in handy."

He snorted and said, "Oh yeah, I forgot that you'd masterminded a daring jailbreak. You've probably got everything a worldly criminal would ever need." He stopped short and grimaced. He'd forgotten for a minute just who she was. More than likely she'd been trained by the best. And just look at the innocence shining from those enormous eyes. What a performance.

When he stood up, his knees hit Mandy's side, and she moaned with the added pain. But the pain ran even deeper when she heard Ry mumble, "Don't worry, sweetheart, it's a long way from your heart. I'm sure you'll live to pull off a few more escapades. Unless you're arrested and put behind bars where you belong."

She jerked her eyes from a penetrating surveilance of a broad expanse of shoulders that narrowed to lean hips, and buttocks that twitched ever so slightly when he walked. She'd never seen a man built so beautifully. But the words "arrested" and "behind bars" brought her reverie to a standstill as she remembered the wanted posters she'd seen in his saddlebags and the object that she was certain had been a badge.

Was he going to arrest her now? If so, what was his purpose in waiting so long? Maybe this was just a scheme of his to get her away from her family, to take her someplace where he wouldn't have to worry about anyone coming to *her* rescue.

Well, if that was his intention, he'd sadly underestimated Amanda Jo Coulter's ability to outsmart and outthink her enemies. In fact, she already had a plan.

They were back in the saddle again after Ryder had hastily cleaned Mandy's wound and bound it with strips from another shirt she had thoughtfully included for the speedily arranged excursion. Not a word had been spoken since his veiled threat, and personally, Mandy was relieved for the prolonged silence. She needed the time to plan her escape, and she was afraid he would hear the anger and resentment in her voice if she was forced to speak.

At the moment, her main problem was remaining upright in the saddle. She was so weak and dizzy, and her side was throbbing along with her head. But no way would she dare draw attention to herself. It was almost time.

Ry was lost in thought as he rode ahead. Every now and then the moon would beam down through a break in the trees and illuminate an easier path. He knew there should be a river coming up soon and wanted to be across it before daylight. He didn't underestimate Sheriff Pomeroy; the man had a definite mark of bulldog about him.

As Ryder topped the next rise, he looked back to see Amanda just starting the ascent. How he wished his gut didn't twist every time he looked at her. Even with her hair tangled and hanging in her face, and the deep hollows beneath her eyes, she was still a tantalizing sight.

Cresting the ridge, he continued down the other side, lost in thoughts of Amanda Jo. When the trail finally leveled out, he pulled his tired mount to a halt. It was past time to give the horses a much deserved break. Dismounting, he loosened the cinch and let the animal munch on nearby weeds while he waited for Amanda to join him. And waited . . . and waited.

Comprehension finally dawned in Ryder's exhausted state of mind that Amanda wasn't following him down the hill. As he tilted his head to listen, he was aware of none of the usual night sounds: no crickets chirping, no frogs croaking—it was too quiet. A chill ran down his spine while the hairs on the back of his neck stood on end. There was something ominous in the making, and he didn't like it.

He quickly pulled the horse to him and tightened the cinch before swinging into the saddle and reining about to retrace his trail. As often as he'd damned Amanda Jo Coulter during the past forty-eight hours, it was a wonder she didn't have pointed ears and carry a pitchfork. But by *damn*, he had to do it again. Maybe she'd even sprout a tail. . . . Ah, but what a tail she already had. Any addition would only be an embellishment to perfection.

On top of the ridge once again, he stopped the horse and listened to absolute stillness until he heard the shots!

Chapter Nine

Mandy continued to follow Ryder but trailed farther and farther behind until she found an opportunity to break off toward the river. Jeremy would be worried, might even circle back to try to find her and run into the posse. Of course, by now, most of the local barflies had probably gotten tired of the chase and returned home.

With that reassuring thought, she suddenly broke from the woods into bright moonlight and a clear expanse of undulating, grass-covered countryside. The going would be easier, but there was a greater risk of being observed when she topped the knolls and was silhouetted against the horizon. Why couldn't it have been cloudy and rainy tonight?

At least Red Fox had energy left and seemed eager to reach the hidden valley and the store of grain that awaited him there. She only hoped that what remaining strength she could muster would be enough to get *her* there, also. Right now she was holding the saddle horn with both hands and was still having trouble staying upright. If only she wasn't so sleepy.

As she rocked back and forth in the saddle, a feeling

of false security stole over her as she approached the nearest line of trees and safety. She hardly roused when a sudden rush of air and loud buzz whipped past her ear, but her attention was captured completely when, in the next instant, the report of a rifle echoed over the rolling landscape.

Ryder sat motionless upon the horse for a long moment—waiting—trying to pinpoint the direction from which he'd heard the gunfire. When the next volley erupted, he looked over a broad expanse of barren ground before noticing the dim, dark outline of a distant row of trees. It had to be the location of the river he'd heard Amanda mention earlier.

If he was to venture a guess, he'd wager that Amanda was on her way to her brother and had encountered the wandering posse. When he recalled her wound and the tiny pop-gun she carried, he dug his heels into his horse's ribs. Talk about a lamb to the slaughter.

When Mandy saw the line of horsemen riding toward her, she slid Red Fox to a stop, reined him back over his heels and took off at a dead run. If she hadn't been so tired, lulled into a sense of confidence by the easy motion of the long-legged thoroughbred, she'd have been paying closer attention to her surroundings and might've avoided the posse before so unwittingly blundering into them.

Now, as the round of shots whistled past her head, she had to find a way to cover without giving away her brother's protected location. With so many riders so close behind her, there was no way she could make contact with Jeremy tonight.

Mandy had almost reached the haven of the woods as she angled Red Fox over the empty plains, when a rider topped the knoll to her left. Was he a part of the posse? Had they set up outriders to try to trap her? But if so, why was he so far away from the river? He was going to catch up with her if she didn't do something—fast.

As she fumbled in her pocket for the little derringer, Mandy had a hard time making her tired, stiff muscles obey her commands. In fact, her actions were so sluggish that she barely reacted when a hand reached to grab her reins, but instead of pulling them to a stop, the rider kept the horses running for the line of trees now immediately to their right.

The posse was so close that they could be heard shouting words of encouragement to each other with Sheriff Pomeroy being the loudest of all.

As they ducked under branches while passing through the first group of trees, Mandy was startled into awareness by a now very familiar and, at this point, very welcome voice. "So we meet again. We started this thing together, sweetheart, and we might as well end it together. Just tell me where we are and how we can lose those bastards."

Ry couldn't believe she hadn't heard him and glanced back over his shoulder to see her give him a weak grin. "Hi. Let me have my reins, and maybe we'll get lucky." The shouting was sapping what was left of her strength, but she had to make herself be heard. "Ride close behind me. When I stop, be ready to get off and let your horse go. I'll explain why later, so please, just do it."

Ry started to argue about the folly of being stranded afoot at night but figured since she'd be stranded, too, maybe he should go along with her, for the time being. She at least had a plan, which was

167

more than he could say for himself.

He followed Amanda down the steep riverbank, the horses slipping and sliding in the loose dirt, until they reached the even softer surface of the riverbed. The water was high this time of year and there was little space between the bank and the water.

Amanda's shout caught him by surprise. "Okay, now!"

Ry saw Red Fox already racing ahead with the stirrups flapping against his sides and had just settled his feet on the ground when the report of a gun fired directly behind him took care of his having to scare his horse off with a slap from his hand. But it was too late to check his swing, and the force of the forward motion spun him around and into Amanda.

His arm knocked against her hand and discharged the second shot into the ground between his feet. "Damn, watch that little pepperbox, will you? There's enough bullets flying around here as it is."

Mandy didn't hear Ryder complain as she grabbed his hand and started running along the edge of the water, about ankle deep, to hide their trail. By now they could hear the posse members crashing through the brush close to where they'd left the horses.

"Those shots should slow down the brave mob behind us," Mandy whispered over her shoulder. "That'll give us a chance to duck out of sight, and the horses time to disappear."

Sure enough, just as they reached an overhang of dead branches and roots, Ry could hear the sheriff advising his followers to dismount and proceed with caution.

"Those shots were too close, men. Don't ride into a trap."

Then Mandy began tugging on his hand, motioning him to crawl under the jungle of roots. Of the two, it was Ryder who thought of the other inhabitants that might also be occupying the little den. He jerked her back against him and held her with one arm while he grabbed a loose branch and quickly poked it through the opening.

"Now let's see if we can squeeze ourselves in there." As he dubiously eyed the area, he winked and grinned. "I like your choice of cozy nests, sweetheart. This could be a mighty interestin' experience."

Mandy frowned, but the nearby sound of horseshoes clicking on gravel gave her the impetus to bend over and scoot through the narrow opening. She clinched her teeth from the pain tingling along the wound in her side every time she stretched her muscles but continued to squirm as far under the overhang as possible.

Ry waited until the scrape of cloth and leather grating against the dirt surface faded, then took his stick and traded it for a limb with dead leaves still attached. He went back to the spot where they had emerged from the water and began to obliterate their tracks. During daylight hours, his hasty scratching would more than likely be noticed, but since it was dark . . . they just might get away with it.

When he again reached the overhang, he laid on his back and imitated Amanda's scuffling motions. After finally pulling every limb connected to his large frame into the tiny area of concealment, he found there was no way to turn onto his side as his shoulders were broader than the space was high.

Mandy sucked in her stomach and tried to flatten herself farther into the hole, but Ry's shoulder and arm still dug into her chest and rubbed against the raw wound. As he continued to wriggle his upper body in an attempt to pull a few loose branches and leaves across their hiding place, she couldn't stop the pathetic groan that seeped between her gritted teeth.

Hearing Amanda moan, Ry twisted his shoulders in an effort to see what was wrong, unknowingly elbowing her ribs. A shriek would've erupted from her lips if he hadn't quickly slipped his right arm across his body to grab her shoulder and pull her upper body down onto his chest. His lips covered hers to absorb the hurtful cry at the same time footsteps fell on the top of their lair.

"I don't get it, Sheriff. They've got to be here somewhere."

"Yeah, unless those shots were just a ploy to slow us down. I'd lay odds that they just kept right on ridin'." Sheriff Pomeroy slapped the side of his leg with his hand, then kicked the mound of dead roots at his feet. "Go round up the others. We'll let the horses rest for a while. We can't very well track them in the dark, so we might as well take a break."

When Ry finally released her lips, Mandy let out the breath that had been constricted in her chest with a long, deep sigh. Unable to move from such intimate contact with the man since he had squished his way deeper into the hole, she had no choice but to rest her forehead against his collarbone and make the best of the situation.

Then to add to her consternation, her body began an ever more perceptible trembling and shaking. She was cold, tired, hurt and hungry, and if it wasn't for the presence of this strong, indomitable man, she'd probably break down and cry her heart out.

As if he were reading her mind, Ry reached up his right hand to gently smooth her hair. His breath, when he whispered in her ear, reverberated clear to her cramped, damp toes.

"Shh, it'll be all right. It sounds like we're going to

170

be stuck here for a while." He smiled to himself as he thought, in more ways than one. "As soon as they move on, we'll get you more comfortable."

Mandy sniffled and relaxed her upper body along the length of his chest. As the soft curves molded to his tough frame, Ry shifted his hips in an effort to relieve the growing tightness in his trousers. Inch by inch he wormed his left arm under her body until he could finally, and securely, hold her in place.

In her own mind, Mandy knew she shouldn't enjoy being held so tightly and so intimately by the stranger. She shouldn't, but she did. A feeling of euphoria prevailed, blocking the knowledge of who he was and what he was there for. She needed to be held, to be comforted, to feel that her life, and that of one she loved, was safe and that she didn't need to worry.

Ry could tell by the steady rise and fall of Amanda's chest and shoulders that she'd fallen asleep. What a blow to his male pride. He finally had the woman exactly where he wanted her, and she was oblivious to his growing need and obvious desire. What the hell, he'd just use the time to do what she probably wouldn't allow him to do if she were awake.

Slowly and surely his right hand massaged her tense muscles and worked methodically down each vertebra of her spine while his lips trailed feather-light kisses across her cheeks, eyes and nose before settling with sweet softness on her pliant lips. A feeling of intense tenderness and deep longing for something missing in his life swelled to such proportions that he wasn't even surprised at the moistness in his eyes.

If he'd been allowed to pick and choose a woman more perfectly suited to his way of life, he'd never

171

have found a better match than Amanda Jo Coulter. And, damn it, he was going to keep her, one way or another. All he had to do was get this stupid investigation out of the way.

Sheriff Pomeroy's loud voice interrupted Ryder's musings.

"Where in thunderation is the rest of the posse? They surely couldn't have gotten lost this close to the river!"

"Uh, sorry Sheriff, but it seems me an' Jack here are the only ones left. The rest of the, uh, boys went on back to town. Told Jack here that they was tired and that there wasn't no way, ah, to find no Coulters in the woods less'n they wanted to be found."

"Durn skunk-livered jackasses ran with their tails 'tween their legs when they figured the gal was goin' to fight back, Sheriff." Jack scratched his stomach and added, "Ya gotta have a healthy respect fer them Coulters. They's a mighty tricky lot, they are. Yep!"

"I don't have to be told that!" Sheriff Pomeroy turned away from the two men who had faithfully stayed by his side. All he needed was to turn the men away from him now. It was hard enough finding men who weren't relatives or close friends of the Coulter or James families and were willing to ride in a posse. He had to tread carefully.

"Ahem. Well, boys, since the last of the posse declared the girl free to go, I guess we might as well follow suit. There's nothing much we can do now, anyway."

"I wonder what happened to the fella that left town with the girl?" Jack scratched under his arm, and Sheriff Pomeroy moved away several steps.

The other man, Tom Jenkins, offered his explanation. "I saw a rider on a leggy bay, like the one the guy was riding, you know, back in town. Anyway, he

172

was comin' from over that first knoll. I figure they must've split up—"

The sheriff cut in on what could turn out to be a lengthy dissertation. "It's no matter. I saw him, too, but he's nothing to worry about. They're going to show up again, and when they do . . ." The voices trailed into the distance as the three men walked toward their tethered mounts.

Ry gritted his teeth and fumed, "Nothing to worry about, huh?" Well, he'd just have to see about that.

It was daybreak when Ry awakened and tried to move his aching body. He couldn't remember a time when his muscles had felt so cramped and sore. Then, when he felt the weight on his shoulder and smelled the sweet freshness of Amanda's hair, he remembered the disturbing events that had taken place during the night.

He turned his head to look out from between the loose covering of branches and started when he saw how closely the sheriff and his men had built their fire. If the wind had been blowing in the direction of their little den, they'd have been smoked out as sure as hell was hot.

Mandy had slept so deeply that she hadn't stirred once during the night. However, she came alertly awake when she felt the slight jerk of Ryder's body, and opened her eyes to find him staring at the ashes of the campfire.

"They were close, weren't they?"

When his head revolved in her direction, Mandy became mesmerized by the intensity in his eyes when their gazes locked. It was like looking into deep bottomless pools of oil, yet she could see a bright fire burning in their depths. How odd.

173

Later she could never quite remember who made the first move, but within seconds their lips were fused in a white-hot kiss. Their tongues twinned and separated, then met again in a duel as ageless as time itself. Her right arm was pinned beneath her body with no room to free it, but her left hand made up for the loss by caressing his neck and shoulders, then became entwined amid a forest of crisp curls as it slid into the open collar of his shirt.

Frustrated at not being able to turn, or hardly even move, Ry scooted to his right until he was free of the opening, yet still concealed by the branches and limbs he'd pulled over the top. Unhesitant, he turned on his side and crushed Amanda to him, eliciting a muffled moan from her pink-tinged lips.

Breathing heavily, Ry took a deep breath and panted, "Sorry, sweetheart, I didn't mean to hurt you."

"You didn't." She squirmed until she could touch her wounded side. "Darn it!" She had lain curled next to Ryder for as long as she could stand. The dressing on her ribs was itching. It felt like the cloth was stuck to the wound, and it was uncomfortable to move, especially when she breathed so hard during those passionate kisses.

Slyly she lifted her head and smiled at Ry. "Say, stranger, you wouldn't do a lady a favor, would you?"

Getting with the spirit of the situation, he replied, "Well, I don't know. Where's the lady and I'll see?"

Unable to free her right hand to do the deserved damage, she nuzzled her mouth into the soft fleshy spot where Ry's arm joined his shoulder and took a healthy nip.

"Yeowch!" Ry yelped, then turned his head toward the opening of the lair and looked hastily over the clearing. "Now why'd you do that? Can't you take a joke? You're going to get us in trouble if you're not careful." He reached down and soundly spanked one rounded globe of her delicately curved rear.

"Now, what's the favor, ma'am?" He smiled like a cat who'd outsmarted a wily mouse when he felt the tip of her tongue moistly lave the imprints of her teeth. "That's better. But don't ever do it again."

Mandy couldn't believe the playful banter taking place between them. In this tiny hideaway, away from all the problems facing them, they were just two people who would probably get along tremendously under different circumstances. It was a shame there was so much between them: an outlaw, a badge.

"No, sir. Never." But somehow she didn't sound too convincing. "If you don't mind, I'd like you to look at the bandage. My ribs feel stiff, and it hurts to move."

"Okay, give me a minute." Ry shifted until he could look outside. "Let me make sure there's no one around, then we'll move into the sunlight where I can see it better."

Mandy watched the rippling muscles on his chest and forearms as he maneuvered around in the small space. The lean length of his body rasped against hers, and tingling sensations shivered up and down her spine. She felt hot and flushed and desperately wanted to reach out and touch the black tendrils of hair that curled above his collar.

Embarrassed, she turned her head away and closed her eyes. Maybe if she couldn't see the temptation . . .

Ry turned back and realized his shirt had come unfastened during the night and had twisted around his body. He'd thought her teeth were sure sharp, and he hadn't even wondered why his body reacted so

175

acutely to the sensation of her tongue. Raising up on his elbows, he shrugged back into his shirt, then felt around Amanda's waist until he found the tie holding the cloth in place.

"We might as well go ahead and take the bandage off in here." Hoping to get his mind on something besides her soft, pliant lips, he pushed the top of her overalls down and hiked up her shirt until he could see what he was doing.

Feeling a tug on her ribs, Mandy turned her head down to see if she could see the wound. She'd never been shot before, had never really been seriously injured.

"Uh oh, no wonder it hurts. The binding is caked to the wound. The best thing to do is just . . . yank it off. It'll only hurt for a minute." While he was talking, and before Amanda had a chance to protest, he jerked the cloth free.

"Ouch! You did that on purpose to get even, didn't you?" Mandy's head was feeling strangely light. Blood oozed from where the scab had come away with the bandage, and a little trickle ran down her side, tickling her sensitive skin.

After all the times she had helped doctor the animals and Jesse and her brothers, for some reason the sight of her own blood worked crazy things with her equilibrium. Oh Lord, she felt like she might . . . faint.

Ry held the cloth to the wound, soaking up the small amount of blood. The seeping stopped immediately after he exerted only a small amount of pressure. He ran his hands up her back and hugged her. "Okay, I think it's safe to go out. I'll have you good as new in no time."

There was no response, no indignant huff of breath as he pulled her to him. Ry leaned over her

176

and touched his finger to her nose. "Hey, what's the matter, sweetheart? You're not going soft on—

"Damn! What have I done?" Mistaking the flushed state of Amanda's body for a sign of fever, he jumped up, sending an explosion of branches and leaves every which way. "Damn it to hell. Why didn't you tell me? You're not nearly as tough as you make out to be, are you?"

Lifting Amanda's slight body, he carried her out of the debris around the little den and laid her carefully on a carpet of grass near the river. His mind checked off a list of things he needed to do, the first of which was getting Amanda to her home before the doctor left. Then he remembered.

"The horses! Damn it all, the horses." His hands took hold of her shoulders and began to shake. "You never told me about the horses, Amanda." When he realized what he was doing, he abruptly stopped and lowered her back to the ground.

"All right, so we're stuck here. No big deal. We just have to get that fever down." He mumbled to himself and answered his own questions, all the while tenderly removing her grimy, sweat-streaked clothes.

As he pulled off her boots and slid the overalls from her dainty feet, his hands trembled. Glittering black eyes studiously traveled the length of her long curvaceous legs, to her rounded hips and over the flat plane of her belly. The heated gaze stopped briefly on the gentle rise and fall of her creamy rose-tipped breasts, before searching her delicate features for signs of consciousness. There were none. Afraid that she might be hurt worse than he originally thought, he moved quickly into action.

Using her shirt as a sponge cloth, Ry made trip after trip from the river to Amanda, wiping her forehead and entire body with the cooling liquid, but her body continued to feel hot and flushed.

During one of his sojourns to the river, Mandy came to. Drowsy and relaxed, she was just aware enough of her surroundings to recognize Ryder and to wonder at his strange behavior.

Funny, she didn't remember how beautiful his angular, hawkish features were or how deep and resonant his voice sounded as he mumbled to himself. Even though she couldn't bring herself to rouse, it was hard, oh so hard, to keep from quivering or trembling when he bent over her, telling her how sorry he was that she had been injured, berating himself for not taking better care of her.

As she let him continue to smooth the damp cloth over her heated flesh and luxuriated in the feel of his hands as they lifted each arm and leg or circled an aching breast, she knew it was cruel of her not to tell him she was perfectly all right.

But some perverse sense of punishment had taken hold in her mind. After all, if he hadn't been poking his nose in where it wasn't wanted, none of this would ever have happened. She deserved every bit of his guilty ministrations and was determined to thoroughly enjoy it.

Except she hadn't figured on the intense arousal, the deep longing his touch would elicit. If she had wanted him to kiss her, to caress her, to love her before, it was nothing compared to what she was experiencing now.

Ry trudged the last two steps to Amanda's side and collapsed on the grass next to her. Surely by now her fever should have lowered. Too exhausted to make

178

many more trips to the river, he squeezed the cloth, dribbling the excess moisture over Amanda's belly and thighs. At any other time, he would have followed the trail of sparkling drops with his mouth, lingering in the indention of her navel and twining in the curly thatch of hair at the juncture of her thighs.

He groaned and turned away, unable to endure the torture any longer. There was only one way he could think of to rapidly lower her temperature. He pulled off his boots, wriggling his toes with relief, and then unbuttoned his shirt. Standing, he pulled the long tail of his shirt from the waistband of his pants, then unhooked his buckle and began the process of removing the rest of his clothes.

Mandy missed Ry's presence by her side and opened her eyes to mere slits beneath the thick fringe of her lashes. Her heart thumped madly against her sore rib cage as she observed the tail end of Ry's disrobing. Her palms became sweaty, and a moist sheen covered her body, which, she discovered, was also nude. She closed her eyes and sighed, disgusted by her wanton thoughts.

Was this the real Amanda Jo Coulter emerging at last? It was a side of herself she'd never seen before. Few men had gotten beyond an ardent kiss or two before she primly turned them away. Now, in the space of a few short days, she'd let a man—no, encouraged a man to make love to her once and was yearning for him to do it again. Could there be something wrong with her? She hoped not, because she felt awfully good and very much a woman.

She was taken by surprise when two strong arms scooped her up and carried her toward the river. What was he up to? His skin was so supple, so warm next to hers. It was wonderful—

179

"Wait! No! Don't you dare drop me." Mandy shrieked and threw her arms around Ry's neck when she felt the pressure of his arms relax. He was standing waist deep in the river, and the water lapped and teased at her bare bottom.

Ry staggered and almost plunged them both into the gentle current. "Dear God, Amanda, you scared me. How long have you been conscious?"

When he noticed the shifty expression in her eyes and saw that they darted anywhere rather than to meet his own, a nasty suspicion began to dawn on him. "You did just now come to, didn't you? Didn't you?" He dipped her lower in the water until the cold waves licked at the tender flesh of her thighs and breasts.

Mandy held his neck tighter and slithered her body as high as she could along his tall length. "Well, I-I woke up a few minutes ago, that's all."

Ry's teeth flashed in a big grin. Now that he thought about it, there had been a change in her breathing. In fact, he remembered her breasts jiggling with the rapid intake of air. He'd been too worried to think she would be cagey enough to play tricks on him.

"You never had a fever at all. Why, I ought to . . ." He bent his knees to go down in the water, but Amanda twisted and squirmed until she faced him, climbing, trying to scramble from the water.

They would have been fine if she hadn't kicked her feet, hadn't tangled their legs, but as it turned out, there was no way Ry could prevent the dunking. Sputtering and splashing, they flailed in the water until Ryder finally found secure footing.

Mandy had a death grip around his neck, and he choked, "Ease up, sweetheart, I can't breathe."

"It's cold, darn it. Do something." Her legs gripped his hips and her heels dug into the backs of his thighs as he floundered awkwardly toward the bank.

"I'm trying, but you keep strangling me. Remember, we wouldn't be in this situation if you hadn't tricked me." Then he smiled. It was somewhat startling, yet tremendously exciting to find out she wasn't as immune to him as it often seemed. He raised his hands and slowly rubbed circles up her back.

Still clinging to Ryder, her arms and legs securely wrapped about his body, she leaned her head back to look into his smokey eyes. Shock waves shivered up her spine when his hands cupped her buttocks.

"It wasn't a trick, not really. I was just so tired, I couldn't move."

"And I suppose you couldn't gather the energy to let me know you were all right? You owe me for that, you know?"

Mandy blushed beguilingly, her cooled flesh warming quickly. The suddenly doused fire was fanned to life again as his smile reignited her desire. She let her body slide inch by slick, wet inch down his lean frame.

"Oh? And just how much do you think a little teasing is worth? I don't have a penny on me."

"That's not a problem. I have no use for money out here, especially when my hands are filled with something much more valuable." He smoothed his hands up and down her bare back, sending a spray of water droplets in their wake, the rough palms causing Amanda to arch against him until the tips of her breasts seared into his chest. He lowered his head when she tossed her wet hair behind her shoulders, and kissed her eyes and cheeks, than ran his tongue over the shell of her ear where his hot breath turned her spine to liquid fire.

She moaned, hugging him closer, and when he husked, "God, Amanda, I want you, now." She hesitated only a moment before nodding her head and clutching his shoulders as he sank to the grass.

Mandy stretched on top of Ry, her fingers sifting through his thick black hair, as he rediscovered her body with his mouth and hands. The once imagined fever was now raging full force between them, and Mandy groaned, protesting when Ryder suddenly stilled, placing his forefinger over his lips. "Shhh."

Ry took several calming breaths before turning his head so that his ear was next to the ground. Damn, but he'd been enjoying the taste of Amanda's succulent lips, the flavor of her shoulder and relishing the taste of her quivering breasts. Wait. There it was again. It was a sound that was out of place with the serene woodlands surrounding them.

Gathering his composure quickly, he lunged to his feet, pulling a recalcitrant woman up with him. He whispered over his shoulder as he started running toward a stand of sycamore, their broad trunks beckoning, offering sanctuary. "Don't argue, just come with me." He nodded approvingly, though, when she made a hasty grab for one of the sleeves of his shirt as she scurried after him.

Once behind a big tree, he helped her don the shirt and thought her exceptionally beautiful as the awkward garment hung to just above her knees. He placed her back against the concealing breadth of the tree and turned to look back toward the river. As he reached for the butt of his pistol, a bolt of panic raced through him. It was lying beside his pants on the bank of the river. Never once considering the consequences, he made the mad dash, swooped up his pants and gunbelt, and was beside Amanda again before she had a chance to utter a sound.

An unsettling stillness prevailed, in which there was no hint of the usually chattering squirrels, no barn swallows dipping and diving near the river. Ryder quietly cocked the hammer of his gun.

Chapter Ten

The sound of horses' hooves splashing through water invaded the eerie silence. Ry tensed and began to move away from the tree when Mandy placed an insistent hand on his arm, detaining him. "My derringer is down there in my overall pocket. I need it."

She leaned around him to look down on their forsaken lair. With the scattered clothes and all the fresh footprints, it was plain that someone had deserted the area in a hurry. They had been too careless.

Ryder reached out with his free hand to pull her back behind the sycamore. What a spitfire she was. Ready to fight at the drop of a hat. Then his face sobered. And why not? She'd been well trained by her outlaw relatives.

Before he could grab her, she squealed and darted around him to burst through the trees, running toward the overhang. Was the stupid fool that desperate for a gun? Couldn't she trust him to defend her? Taking a deep breath, he stepped from behind the tree and leveled his gun with both hands for better accuracy.

But instead of a posse with guns drawn and charging for Amanda, he found an excited brother and sister clinging to each other unashamedly, with three saddled horses standing calmly in the background. Sighing, Ry took the time to step into his pants and buckle the gunbelt around his narrow hips before joining the reunion.

"Jeez, Mandy Jo, when the horses showed up this morning without you, I almost went crazy. Especially when I found the dried blood on Red Fox's saddle. Are ya hurt, sis? Where? And what happened to Ryder? This is Reno's horse. Wasn't he riding Socks last night? What—"

Mandy couldn't stand it any longer. With a sudden lunge she threw herself into Jeremy's arms, wrapping one of her own arms around his neck for support while she placed the palm of her other hand across his mouth.

"For heaven's sake, Jer, slow down. I can't get a word in edgeways. Ouch!"

"See, sis, I knew you were hurt." Unknowingly he had given his sister a tender squeeze, pressuring her rib cage. His eyes traveled down her body and widened in horror at her scantily-clad form as he also took note of the approaching Ryder's nearly undressed state.

"Amanda Jo Coulter, I want an explanation of what's been going on here, and I mean now."

Still clinging to her brother, Mandy's body began an uncontrollable trembling, and she giggled, "You wouldn't believe in a million years what all's happened since we split up last night. I followed that . . . that man . . . all over creation, discovered I'd been shot in the getaway from town, broke off from him to come find you, met up with the posse and Ryder—" she stopped long enough to cast a suspicious glance toward Ryder—"at the same time, and then we . . . Ryder and I . . . hid in that deserted den all night. When we woke up this morning we . . . ah . . ."

Ry took hold of the arm Amanda had wrapped around her brother's neck and turned her around to feel her forehead and cheeks, effectively strangling any further explanation on her part.

"As you can see, Jeremy, your sister's in bad shape. She was running a terrific fever this morning, and I had to bathe her body to bring down the temperature." His look dared her to refute his words.

Jeremy looked from Mandy Jo's barely concealed thighs and long shapely calves to Ryder's bare chest. They were both still damp from head to toe, and he scowled threateningly. Meanwhile, Mandy slumped against Ry's chest as he supported her tenderly with his body.

Not enjoying having to explain the questionable situation to an angry brother, Ry snapped shortly, "Well, what would you have me do? If I'm not proper enough to suit you, I can't help it."

Ryder was being overly sarcastic, but Jeremy still ducked his head as he thoughtfully considered the appearance of things. "I didn't mean to sound so highfalutin. I'm just concerned about Mandy Jo. She's the only sister I know, and for a change, *I'd* like to see after her. She doesn't deserve to get hurt, you know what I mean?"

As he held the soft, curvaceous woman in his arms, Ry grinned at Jeremy. "Yeah, I know what you mean." Then, as he glanced at the suddenly restless horses, he told the boy, "We'd better get out of here. The posse could return any time."

Apprehension was palpable in the air, and Jeremy looked over his shoulder nervously as the horses stamped their feet impatiently. "Can Mandy Jo ride?" At Ry's shake of the head and his own observation of her rubbery form, he said, "No, I guess not." But he missed the warning squeeze Ry's arms gave his sister and her guilty grimace.

Before leaving, Ry gazed around their little hideaway rather wistfully until he noticed Amanda's overalls and boots. Bending to whisper in her ear, he suggested, "Just play the helpless female. I know it'll be hard, but we might get out of this yet." Then to Jeremy, he said, "Here, hold her until I get her things tied on the extra horse. Then you can boost her up to me after I get on Red Fox."

Jeremy frowned and looked warily at Ryder. "I don't know, it might be best if *I* took Mandy Jo."

"Don't be silly, son. You're going to have to lead us out of here and take the extra horse." He didn't understand why he suddenly felt so possessive over who was to carry the blasted brat, and he knew his excuse to hold her was flimsy; but he still breathed a sigh of relief when Jeremy capitulated and let him take her.

However, the younger brother was extremely adamant that they get Mandy Jo into her overalls before taking one step away.

Mandy awoke, snuggled firmly into the protective embrace of Ryder's arms, as they rode through country she recognized as being close to home. She closed her eyes, opened them again and lifted a hand from his chest to rub her nose. Lord, but she was tired. The last thing she remembered was Jeremy and Ryder helping her into her overalls, then being lifted

187

to ride in front of Ryder.

The overbearing oaf. Why hadn't he let her brother take her? He had to be sick of rescuing her and hers. The only reason he was hanging around was to find out for sure about Jesse. Of course, he'd never asked about Jesse, but since he was either a marshal or a bounty hunter, he was being sneaky and cautious in gathering news of her "late" cousin.

Mandy twitched her itchy nose and scratched it again. Having her around to fall all over him whenever she got a chance wasn't helping drive him away, either. She was behaving like such a fool. And she knew, deep in her logical woman's mind, that she should be grateful for Jer's timely interruption this morning, but instead, she was heartbroken. There was no other word to explain the pain that literally throbbed from her chest to her lower stomach. It was so intense that she actually felt sick. If only she could blame it on indigestion.

And what of Ryder? No matter *what,* if he didn't find clues regarding Jesse, he'd be gone in no time. And if he *did* somehow find out the truth, well, they'd have to get rid of him. Either way, he wasn't destined to be in her life long. How strange that the thought should leave her feeling so . . . weird.

As Ry looked questioningly down at her shaking body huddled so comfortably in his lap, Mandy started to hiccup between fits of giggles. If he only knew what she'd just been thinking, that she'd actually considered disposing of him with the same amount of concern she'd give to tossing the garbage.

How could she possibly harm the body that brought her so much pleasure and delight? Her hand raised to trace the edge of his jaw, then ran under his chin and around his collar to the first tuft of curly hair at the base of his throat. How she loved to feel the

188

warm vital texture of his skin beneath her fingers.

Ryder Manning was quite an enigma to a backwoods country girl. He was so strong and sure of himself most of the time, yet shy and almost vulnerable at others—so hard and tough, yet gentle and kind. She was becoming terribly fond of the man. Even though it worried her to death having him around, he'd been there when she really needed him.

Ry shivered as Amanda's finger trailed over his stubbly chin and neck, and his body tensed as the digit lowered to entwine several strands of hair to tease and tug playfully. Didn't the brat know what she was doing to him? If she wasn't careful, he'd lay her down right there in front of her brother, God and anyone else who happened along the trail.

But his passion cooled to waves of tenderness when he met her eyes and encountered only a dazed look of confusion. Poor darling, she was running a slight fever, and he hoped the doctor would still be with Reno. Reno! He hadn't given *that* man a thought since he'd walked out of the bedroom yesterday evening.

As if his thinking the name brought the man to life, Amanda suddenly lost her dazed expression to ask, "Ryder, I know it's a little late . . . please don't think me terrible . . . I feel so guilty, but there were so many other things—"

"What was it, sweetheart? What did you want to know?" Right now he was willing to share almost anything with this woman, and he could hardly recognize himself. Was this the *real* Ryder Manning?

"How was Reno when you left? Was he alive? Will he be all right?"

Of all the things he'd expected her to ask, that was the last. Damn! When would he ever learn? After all they'd been through together, how could she still think of Reno? His voice was cruel and harsh when he answered, "What's the matter, sweetheart? You mean you didn't even think of him once all the time you were making love to me? He's really important to you, huh?"

Mandy's eyes clouded, and tears coursed down her cheeks. He was being hateful and cruel, but he was right. She'd forgotten all about her brother lying at home on maybe his death bed. Even though she'd left for a good reason, there was no excuse for not asking about Reno sooner.

Ry failed to notice the agony in her face as he continued to snipe at her. "No thanks to you, he was doing as well as could be expected for a man with a bullet in his chest. The idiot even tried to get up to go after you, but the doc and I convinced him to stay in bed as soon as I offered to take his place." It wasn't completely the truth, but Ry couldn't care less. "The doc said if he made it through the fever he'd probably be all right. It'll really cheer Reno up to know how concerned his little Mandy's been over him."

She took a deep breath and released it slowly. Thank God, Reno had a chance. But even her guilt over not thinking about her brother didn't cut as deeply as the thought that Ryder had only come after her as a promise to Reno. Why should that surprise her? He didn't care anything for *her*, just what she could do for *him*. Well, Mr. Ryder Manning, it would be a cold day in hell before he learned anything from Amanda Jo Coulter.

Her voice was choked as she called to Jeremy. "Jer, Mr. Manning just told me that Reno was still alive when he left last night. Doc Reilly thought if he survived the fever he might make it."

Jeremy let out a whoop of joy. "That's good news! With everything else that's been going on, I'd completely forgotten about Reno's condition. Damn! I can hardly wait to see the old cuss!''

The rest of the ride to the Coulter cabin was made in silence, each person lost in his own churning thoughts and emotions. Mandy was suddenly uncomfortable in Ryder's stiff arms and was more than grateful when Jeremy lifted her to the ground in front of her porch.

Doc Reilly had been sitting outside soaking up the warm sunshine when he saw the group approaching. Being an intelligent person, he knew something was wrong when he saw the riderless horse and recognized the young Mr. Manning atop Red Fox. He was already there to solicitously take her elbow and offer his support the minute Amanda's feet hit the ground.

They were in terrible condition, haggard and dirty, on the verge of collapse. But tired though they were, Mandy and Jeremy were stunned when, of the three, the doctor chose Ryder to answer his questions.

"What's happening to this family, young man? First Reno is ambushed, and now you have to carry Amanda home. There are too many unusual occurrences to suit me.''

Ryder grinned sardonically and shrugged his shoulders. "I can't help you, Doc, but I'm relieved to hear that this family doesn't make it a common practice to cause this much mischief all the time.''

Mandy and Jeremy glared at Ryder before turning to Doc Reilly, with Jeremy being the first to speak. "Thanks for the votes of confidence, both of you, but while we're standin' here jawin', Mandy Jo's wound could be gettin' worse.''

Doc Reilly's mouth gaped. "Wound? Oh, my Lord! A gunshot wound, no doubt? Will it never end?''

As he led Mandy up the stairs, she placed her hand

191

on his arm, quietly gaining his attention. "How's Reno, Doc?"

Opening the door, he turned to speak to her and accidentally noted the nasty scowl that had appeared on Ryder's face at the mention of the name Reno. So, he still hadn't figured it out. Dare he interfere? Ah, but he was getting too old for these romantic games of intrigue. Besides, he wanted to be around to see what came of it.

Doc Reilly spoke more loudly than he needed when he told Amanda, "Good news, Amanda. Your brother is recovering quite nicely. Of course, he'll need to stay in bed . . . ahem. . . . Let's get you into your room and check that wound."

The doctor's eyes had been covertly watching the changing expressions on Ryder Manning's face, from the hateful scowl to disbelief, from questioning to anger again. It was time to remove the little lady from the line of fire until the young man had a chance to think over what he'd just learned. My, but it was invigorating playing cupid. Made him feel like a young man himself.

Ry was sitting alone in front of the fireplace, staring morosely into the cold ashes, thinking. So, Reno was her brother. And he'd played the fool. The more he thought of the things he'd said to Amanda, and how he'd mentally—thank the Lord for small favors—accused her of being calculating and a cheat, the worse he felt. Would she ever understand, much less forgive him?

Then Ry's natural instincts for survival started to take over. Hell, why should he care one way or the other? It had been a natural mistake. He'd just be damned glad to get his business done and leave this place in his dust.

When Jeremy sauntered into the room shaking droplets of water from his hair and buttoning a clean shirt, Ry looked at him closely. He and Amanda had exactly the same color of eyes and hair, but Reno and Amanda shared similar facial features. No wonder he'd conjured Amanda's image while studying Reno the other night. At least he wasn't completely crazy.

So intent was he on his scrutiny of the younger brother and his mental observations that he jumped when Jeremy spoke. His nerves were definitely shot, and that was dangerous for a man in his line of work.

"I wanted to thank you for taking care of my sister. She's not the easiest person to get along with, I know, and here you've risked your life for her, twice. We appreciate it more than we can say." Jeremy breathed a lot easier after finishing his little speech. It was something that had to be done, but he'd been uneasy about it. He liked Ryder Manning all right, but there was just something about the man he couldn't explain.

"You said 'we'?"

"Yeah, Reno and me." Then he snorted disgustedly. "And probably Dad, if he were sober enough to understand."

Ry had a lot of questions he wanted to ask about George Coulter, but right now he couldn't stand it; he had to hear it again. "Is Reno related to you and Amanda? I heard Doc mention something about it."

"Related? To Reno? Sure, man, he's our brother! You knew that, didn't you?" When Ry slowly uncrossed his legs and sat up straighter in the chair to give a dignified, if not threatening, shake of his head, Jeremy stammered, "Uh, sorry. I figured Mandy Jo'd surely told you when y'all first found him."

Ry stood up and rubbed the back of his neck. "No,

193

she didn't." Suddenly he felt hot, and particles of dirt were rubbing and irritating his skin. "I'm going to clean up. Catch you later."

"Yeah, sure." Jeremy stared after the stranger's retreating figure, wondering what had caused his hasty departure. Was it something he'd said?

"Ouch! Listen, Doc, you don't need . . . Ow! I'm fine, really. Quit that!"

"Oh, no you don't, young lady. I'm going to clean this nasty gash and make sure it doesn't get infected. You've seen firsthand what can happen with a fever. You don't want to go through that again, do you?"

Doc added the "do you?" with a sly gleam in his eye that Amanda didn't trust. "Of course not! Why would you ask a thing like that?" She wished she could explain about the fever.

"Oh, I don't know. That young Mr. Manning seems to be a nice, personable fellow. The Coulters have been lucky to have him around, don't you think?"

Mandy blushed a deep crimson. "Ah, sure, I guess so."

"And he's quite handsome, too, wouldn't you say?"

"For heaven's sake, Doc. You sound like you're in love with the man. For your information, he's a . . . he's . . ." No, now wasn't the time to burden Doctor Reilly with her suspicions.

"Yes? What *is* he, Amanda?"

"He's . . . all right, Doc. And yes, he's sure saved our bacon a couple of times this week."

The doctor was curious about what she had been going to say about Ryder, but started binding her side and let it drop. He'd already seen how flustered just

194

the mention of his name made her. Was there more going on here than he'd suspected? Yessir, he definitely have to make regular rounds to check up on the youngsters.

"Doc, I'd better warn you, the sheriff might be out sometime today . . ."

"Hush, my dear. Don't worry about him any more today. He's been and gone."

"What? He's been here? But what about Reno? He didn't—?"

"Oh, he tried. But I informed him that your brother had a bad case of pneumonia and might not live, and that even if he survived, he'd be bed ridden for a long while. That seemed to satisfy him, but I'm certain he'll be back. You watch out for that man, Amanda. There's something . . . unnatural . . . about this vendetta against the Coulters."

"I know. Believe me, I know. But it's Jesse that he hates . . . hated. Pomeroy just associates us with him."

"Well, that would explain it. Just be careful around him, that's all."

Mandy reached over and gave Doctor Reilly a hug. "I will. And Doc? Thanks."

"Ahem. Well, I, er, need to return to town now. My other patients will wonder what's happened to me and send out search parties. I'll give Jeremy and Mr. Manning instructions on taking care of my two invalids on the way out. Oh, no you don't. You lay right back down there. You're to stay in bed for at least two days."

"But, Doc."

"Oh, of course you can get up for *that*, but you know what I mean, young lady."

Mandy sighed and laid back against the pillow. It did feel good to relax. She was so tired and weak.

what you mean.'' And she was asleep.
...illy smiled. Given Amanda's young,
...dy, she'd be up and around, fit as a fiddle,
...e at all.

In open defiance of her doctor's orders to stay in bed, Mandy tiptoed to her brother's room. Visions of Reno's deathly pale and unconscious countenance had haunted her, and she was pleasantly surprised to find him propped up by several pillows with a grin denting each cheek.

She dropped all pretense of stealth and ran to him, enveloping him in a loving hug, but was careful not to hurt his wound. "Oh, Reno, I wasn't sure I'd ever see you alive again.''

Reno unwound his sister from his neck and, with both hands on her shoulders, held her at arm's length to study her hollow-eyed appearance. "My God, Mandy, you look worse than I feel.''

"Thanks a lot, brother dear, I needed that.'' Mandy's mouth rounded in a childish pout, but there was a new twinkle in her eye.

Then Reno's fingers squeezed her shoulders until she squirmed uncomfortably, and in a gruff voice he proclaimed, "I've missed you, Mandy.''

This serious side of Reno was unsettling, and Mandy gulped out, "I-I've missed you, too, Reno. You, and Jeremy, when he sneaks off to join you.'' Since he'd started this, she was going to add her sentiments. "And I worry about you. I'm afraid you and Jer will end up like Jesse. Please, promise me—''

"Now Mandy, don't. You know better than that.''

"No, Reno, I don't. You disappear for days, weeks, sometimes months at a time without telling me where you're going. Then suddenly Jeremy's gone, only to come back claiming to have been with you. What am I supposed to think?''

A rustle in the doorway drew their attentions to the tall, strikingly handsome man standing just inside the bedroom. The first thing Mandy noticed was the glistening lock of damp black hair that fell enticingly across his forehead. The sight naturally led her thoughts to the lustrous vitality of the thick strands as she ran her fingers through them. Was it only this morning?

A pink flush stained her cheeks and deepened to a brilliant shade of red when her eyes lowered to the mocking lips. He was laughing at her. He couldn't know what she was thinking, could he?

Reno released Mandy's shoulders when he felt them tense under his fingers. "How long have you been standing there, Manning?''

Ry sauntered casually into the room and leaned against the post at the foot of the bed. "I just got here, Coulter. What's the matter? Nervous?''

Red blotches appeared in Reno's cheeks, and anger blazed from his sky-blue eyes now turned navy. "We're having a private conversation here, and you—'' With a visible effort to regain control of his temper, Reno continued more calmly, "Look, I know we owe you for saving both of our lives, but I can't help but wonder how you've managed to so conveniently show up at just the right times. We've got a lot of friends, but even more enemies. I'd like to know just where you stand.''

It was a moment before Ry spoke, a moment during which he studied both Amanda and her brother. He found no guile in either pair of eyes and found himself suddenly drawn to the Coulter family's plight. He liked them. Even old George made no pretense of being other than he was. Again he doubted his mission. He could be completely mistaken, though his instinct had never failed him, yet.

"Believe it or not, I understand your predicament. And for what it's worth, you have my support for as long as I'm around, or as long as you need it." He walked to the side of the bed and extended his hand. He was standing so close to Amanda that his knee brushed her thigh. Her leg jerked at the contact, and he even felt the shock himself. Lord, help him!

Reno had taken his hand in a firm grip as they shook. "Thanks . . . Ryder."

"Call me Ry. I only came in here to take Amanda back to bed. Er, the doctor made it plain she was to get plenty of rest. I just meant, ah, you can have a few more minutes." He shook his finger under Amanda's nose. "Then I'll be back to escort you if you haven't already gone."

Mandy's eyes followed the graceful swing of his lithe body as he walked from the room. She could definitely see his Indian heritage by the easy, catlike strides and the silent, gliding motion of his big frame. He was beautiful, no way around it. Her heart did crazy things just to look at him.

"Mandy? What're you looking at? He's gone."

She slowly shook her head clear of thoughts of the inimitable stranger and turned back to her brother. "I know. I was just thinking."

"I've been thinking, too, Mandy, a lot. And I want you to think about something. Will you?"

His voice was unsteady and deep with some hidden emotion, and Mandy watched him carefully as she replied, "Sure I will, but you have to tell me what it is first."

Reno chuckled nervously. "Oh yeah, I guess that would be best. Well, here goes. Mandy, I've been

198

sittin' here in bed and studyin' that things just aren't good for us around here anymore. Jesse's gone. Most of our good friends have lost everything and moved away. We're barely livin' hand to mouth. And that damned Sheriff Pomeroy is breathing down our necks every time we spit wrong."

He took a deep breath and looked out of the window at the barn and the moldering appearance of the only home he'd ever known. "Let's get away from here, Mandy. Start a new life someplace where we're not recognized as being related to the James's, where it doesn't matter if we fought for the South or the North."

He grabbed Mandy's shoulders and stared her directly in the eye. Hazel and emerald green met and merged. "Let's do it, Mandy. Soon!"

She placed her hands atop his shoulders, squeezed and then stood up to pace back and forth in front of the window, seeing exactly what Reno had seen earlier, only in a different light: the patches on the roof that it'd taken her a week to fix; the corral where she'd held the head of her favorite milk cow in her lap until it died; three or four wild rose bushes and some yellow daisies which had managed to survive as long as she remembered to pull the weeds.

Leave? The farm? Missouri? How could she leave her home? She didn't *want* to leave, but she could understand why Reno and Jeremy would. When she turned to Reno again, tears streaked her face. "I don't know, Reno. I can't promise anything except that I'll think about it."

She ran from the room only to encounter Ryder Manning coming down the hall. In hopes of beating him to the door of her room, she continued running, but he was there ahead of her and stopped her escape easily.

"What is it, Amanda? Why, you're crying. Is it Reno? Is he worse?"

"N-no, no. Nothing like that. I . . . it's nothing. Just leave me alone. Please!" She jerked from his grasp and walked calmly into her room to quietly close him out.

He could hear sobs through the thin panel of wood, as if she were just on the other side, within his reach. But instead of crashing through the door, he went to Reno's room. The expression of anguish on the older brother's face was enough to stop him in his tracks.

"What's been going on in here? When I left five minutes ago everyone was happy; now I come back to find disaster's struck. Someone please tell me what's happening."

Reno couldn't hold Ry's gaze, so he scooted lower on the pillows and wiped a hand across his eyes. He trusted this Manning, in a way, but how much should he tell him?

Ryder was again sitting alone in the living room, his boot heels propped in front of the fireplace. He'd been considering the prospect of building a fire but so far had been unable to muster the energy to fetch the wood. The past two hours worth of thinking had momentarily drained his capacity for physical activity, and the conversation with Reno had been informative, but depressing.

It had never occurred to Ry that the Coulters might be persecuted for being related to Frank and Jesse James, especially here in their home stomping grounds, but then he'd never gotten very involved in the politics of an area before. Everyone knew that the states of Kansas and Missouri had declared war long before the actual confrontation. Even as a youngster back in the Territory, he'd heard about the bitter battles taking place over whether the states would enter the Union as free or slave states. It was a cryin' shame that repercussions from that terrible conflict were still influencing so many lives.

Ry himself, as a lawman, hadn't considered the fact that the James's would have as many enemies as friends in their home state, especially since they'd been so successful in avoiding arrest or capture due to help from numerous people in providing them with places to hide, fresh horses and false leads to pursuers. It had seemed like absolutely everybody was on their side. Two of the worst problems had been that people glorified in bragging that they'd been held up or robbed by the famous "James gang," and very few people, other than actual friends or neighbors, had ever gotten a very good look at the outlaws.

That was why Ry was here. He'd met a farmer in Tennessee several years ago who ran horses in county fairs. One horse in particular stood out in his mind as it had beaten his mustang every trip. At the time he hadn't known the farmer was Jesse James, but he'd have recognized Red Fox anywhere. A Pinkerton friend had given him the information on the identity of the farmer almost six months ago, and he'd been on Jesse's trail ever since.

Coming back to Amanda again, it seemed the woman was never very far from his thoughts lately, in one way or another. But right now he was concentrating on Reno and his reasons for wanting to leave Missouri, and why Amanda would probably be the cause for their staying. Maybe he could be of help in swaying her decision somehow.

The Coulter brothers were to be admired for

wanting to better themselves and provide a stable life for their family, but the thing that weighed on Ryder's mind was how they were getting the money to finance the move. He'd overheard most of Amanda's and Reno's conversation, accidental though it was, and he, like Amanda, hoped the young men weren't following the path of their cousins.

Damn, if he kept this up he'd take the whole damned family to raise, and he could ill afford that. With a determined sigh he pushed to his feet and walked to the corner where a small stack of wood was stored. A slight chill worked down his spine as he picked up a handful of kindling. Tomorrow morning he was going to make a trip up the hill and visit old George. He was definitely in need of a good stiff drink.

Chapter Eleven

Mandy and Reno recuperated quickly, though Mandy was naturally up and around much faster than her brother, which was a good thing as it took all three of them to keep Reno down when he started feeling better.

"Quit fussing over me and let me out of here." Reno pushed away the cloth Mandy was using to wipe the perspiration from his forehead. "I feel fine, Mandy, really. The only reason I'm sweatin' is because of these damned blankets you keep tucked under my chin."

He finally gave up trying to reason with his overly attentive nurse and bellowed, "Jeremy! Get in here and help me!"

Within seconds an anxious Jeremy crept into the room. "Whadaya want, Reno? Are ya hurtin' again?"

Reno looked at his brother with despair. "Quit cowerin', Jer. And talk right. Ain't I been tryin' ta git ya ta speak correct an' talk like ya was someone?"

Mandy and Jeremy looked at each other, then at Reno, and burst out laughing. Then Jeremy borrowed their hand's favorite phrase. "I guess you could say that. Aw, c'mon, big brother, lighten up. I do okay most of the time, don't I, sis?"

"Well, I hadn't thought about it, but it does seem like your grammar has improved lately." She looked at Reno and asked, "When did you guys start trying to improve your language? And why?"

Reno studied Mandy's face for a long minute while Jeremy backed against a wall and stuffed his hands in his pockets. Then Reno stated very seriously, "When we start our new life, in a new place, we don't want people pointin' their fingers and laughin', callin' us dumb hicks. We're goin' to make a good place for ourselves somewhere."

Mandy sucked in her breath, and her cheeks pinkened with her growing ire. "Are you saying you're ashamed of who you are, Reno? Does your family disgrace you? If that's the way you feel, you can darned well go . . . wherever . . . all by yourself." She glared at her brother in furious indignation, so mad she couldn't speak without sputtering, then turned on her heel to stalk from the room.

Reno shouted, "Don't you dare say things like that and turn your back on me, Mandy Coulter. Stop her, Jer. Don't let her leave this room."

Jeremy rolled his eyes to look at the ceiling, shrugged his shoulders and then obeyed his older brother's command by grabbing Mandy Jo's arm as she attemped to breeze by him. "He didn't mean it that way at all, sis. C'mon, let him finish."

Reno had thrown back the covers in an attempt to follow his sister, but when she was turned back toward the bed by Jeremy, she saw what he was trying to do and broke free to run to him. As she reached out to push him back, he swiftly captured her wrists and pulled her down to sit beside him on the bed.

"You know damned well I didn't mean anything against our family. You're just on a high horse 'cause

204

you don't want to leave this place, and you're getting back at me for suggesting it, aren't you?''

Mandy haughtily tilted her chin to stare into her brother's eyes. "All right, maybe I am. But I'm proud of my heritage, and proud to be a Coulter. I'll not run in shame.''

"Damn it, Mandy. I'm not goin' to change my name, just my way of life. You just don't *want* to understand.''

The validity of his words struck home, and Mandy's eyes lost their hard glare as she continued to gaze into Reno's anguished face. She *was* punishing him, and she knew it; but she couldn't seem to help herself. At this moment she almost hated her elder brother, yet she was also so proud of him that she could hardly stand it.

"You can let me go now. I won't run off." But as Reno released his fingers from around her wrists, she was sorely tempted to flee as fast as her feet could carry her, and as far, so she could bury herself in the woods and pretend none of this was happening.

As if they could read the fear in her eyes, nobody made an effort to speak until Reno again tried to remove himself from bed. Then Jeremy stalked forward to ask, "Just where do you think you're going, big brother?''

"I'm sorry, but we'll have to finish this conversation later. Everyone's too upset, and in case you've forgotten, it's about time for our illustrious sheriff to make a return visit. I want to move the extra horse from the barn and—''

"Then lay right back down. Old Jer has already seen to it. I moved all of the horses but yours and Ryder's to Mandy Jo's valley yesterday. And Mandy and I have taken precautions, ain't that a fine word?, to remove traces of our presence, just in case.''

Mandy couldn't suppress the grin that spread across her face as she listened to her younger brother. All the years that Jesse had spent helping her learn to read and write, and to speak with a semblance of intelligence, had seemed to wash off Jeremy like water off a duck. But now he had a purpose, a reason to want to learn and to improve his lot in life. Could she stand in his way? Hadn't she been determined to see to it herself not too long ago?

Reno looked at Jeremy with a puzzled frown on his face. "Why didn't you take Manning's horse, too?"

"He says he's going to hang around 'til Pomeroy shows. He wants to explain that he was just passin' by the jail when he heard a noise and went to inves-ti-gate."

"Does he think he'll be able to pull it off?"

"Seems to. And he says he wants to be free to move around town and keep an eye on things."

Mandy thought to herself, Yeah, and nose out all he can about Jesse. Whether he knew it or not, *she* was going to keep an eye on *him*.

It was hardly an hour later when Sheriff Pomeroy paid his respects at the Coulter farm. It was almost noon, a time when everyone should be at the table, even those who might not want to be found at home.

They pulled up where the lane entered the little clearing, and he sent two men in the barn, while two more went to the back of the house to watch the windows and the kitchen door. Then he and the rest of the posse members rode on to the hitching rail in front of the porch. So far, it had been almost too easy.

He knocked on the door and was reaching for the knob himself when it was suddenly jerked open. "Well, if it isn't Sheriff Pomeroy. What a surprise.

206

Come in, won't you?"

The sheriff looked Ryder up and down, noted the Smith & Wesson revolver holstered around his hips and turned to his men. "Tom, Jack, come with me. The rest of you take a look around. We want the kid brother *and* the girl."

When they entered the living room, the sheriff stopped Ryder and ordered, "And I'll take that gun. I'm placing you under arrest for aiding an unlawful—"

Ryder held up his hands in a placating manner and interrupted, "Now hold on a minute, Sheriff. I knew you were going to think I'd helped in pulling off that jailbreak, but just think for a minute. I'd been in the bar enjoying a drink with you while all that was taking place."

"Yeah, but you could've been sent in to keep me busy while the break was pulled off."

"*You* came to *me*, Sheriff, remember? I never tried to engage you in conversation, and I didn't stay longer than it took for that one drink. I would've bought a bottle and sat down with you if I'd been wanting to distract you. And I was on the walk in front of the saloon when I first heard something suspicious soundin' coming from the jail. There were other people around. They could tell you I was there."

"All I know is that you were with the Coulters when I got to the jail, and that's enough to arrest you on suspicion alone."

"Look, I admit I was there. I went to see what was goin' on like everyone else. But if you'd stopped to look first before pullin' your iron, you'd have seen that I had Amanda's reins. She was stopped. You tell me what *you* would've done in my position when the bullets started clippin' my ears. Would you have stayed around and tried to chew lead, or would you have done like I did, and run like hell?"

The sheriff lifted his hat and scratched his head, then smiled a little. "Guess I see your point, er, what was your name again?"

"Manning. Ryder Manning."

"Okay, Mr. Ryder Manning, you're off the hook this time, but just what are you doing here, on the Coulter's place?"

"I work here." At the skeptical look passing between the three men, he added, "No, I'm serious. George Coulter hired, well, offered me room and board for helping out around the place for a while. And since I've hit hard times lately, I gratefully accepted." Ry was getting so used to telling little white lies that they flowed from his mouth like sticky, sweet syrup.

"Well, that's a wonderful story, but you're going to have to let us search the house for the girl and the kid." Then before he left the room, the sheriff added, "Let me give you a little advice. This isn't the healthiest place to work. I'd head for greener pastures—soon—if I were you."

"Ah, I'll remember that. Guess there's nothing I can do to stop you from searchin', so go ahead." he couldn't help the show of nervous agitation. He'd been on his hands and knees looking through discarded leather articles in back of the kitchen when he'd first felt the vibrations of approaching horses. By the time he'd entered the house, he'd seen no sign of Amanda and Jeremy. Where could they have gotten to?

At least he was able to hide his surprise when the men came into the kitchen a few minutes later and the sheriff said, "Doesn't look like that older brother's going to make it. That'll make one less to

208

deal with."

One of the posse members approached the house from the barn. "There's no sign of anyone bein' in the barn, but there's two horses in the stalls."

"Thanks, Fred, that'd be right. Well, Mr. Manning, that's all for now, but I 'spect we'll be back. You remember what I said."

Ry started to ask the man if he was threatening him but decided to let well enough alone. He didn't want to start anything now, at least not yet.

"Good day to you, Mr. Manning."

"Ah, sure, Sheriff. Be seein' you around."

As the posse mounted their horses and started to ride toward the lane, their heads swiveled on their shoulders as they continued to look around. They'd been so sure.

Ry took a walk around the perimeter of the clearing, making certain that no one had been posted to stand guard, before he went back into the house and searched every nook and cranny on his way to Reno's room.

The injured man was lying still as a statue with only his deathly pale face showing above the covers. His breathing was shallow and hissed between his slightly parted lips. If Ry hadn't known better, he'd have thought he was looking at a man on his soon to be deathbed.

One of Reno's eyebrows slanted upward, and his lips curved in the barest hint of a smile. "Pretty good, huh?"

Ry laughed from deep in his chest. "Damned right. You almost had me convinced." As he watched the man's sudden transformation from invalid to animated human being, he had to ask, "Where's Amanda and Jeremy? How'd they get out of the house?"

Reno's face took on a guarded expression. "We have an escape route, ah, sorta built into the house."

Ry's interest was hardly feigned as he sat in the chair next to the bed. "No kidding? How'd you do that?"

After a short hesitation, Reno decided that since he'd trusted Ryder so far, he might as well continue. "We copied cousin Jesse, in a way, but not near as elaborate. We dug a tunnel under the house that ends in the gully just this side of the trees. Once you get in the woods, it's smooth goin'." He snapped his fingers in an expression of ease, but his listener was impressed.

"That's quite a scheme. But what do you mean, you copied your cousin Jesse? Did he use a similar plan?"

Reno's eyes lit up as he explained to Ryder, "Man, you wouldn't believe the setup he and Frank built at the farm in Clay County. They had a trap door in every room that led to one big tunnel under the house, and it was all shored up with rock. Then there was another rock tunnel covered over with sod that ran from the house to a deep canyon where they could work their way to the barn."

He stopped to catch his breath, then continued to describe the layout of Jesse's farm. "That barn was a masterpiece. You couldn't see it from the house, you know. The front was made of limestone, about two feet thick, and the top story was used for beds and all. They built square portholes starting from about six inches wide inside, flaring to about two feet wide on the outside. Their guns could cover the whole area in front of and to the sides of the barn."

Ry had constructed a good picture of the place in his mind. He was astounded at the work and imagination that must have gone into making the perfect outlaw lair.

"They kept the horses on the bottom floor, and if worse came to worse, they could ride right out from the barn and into that canyon. What a setup! They were geniuses."

Reno's face lost its animation as he sat in quiet contemplation. Then as his expression hardened to one of defiance, he made a fist and pounded the bed. "I don't care what anybody says, Jesse was a good man in a lot of ways. Damn, but I miss him." His head fell back against the pillows, and he drew in several deep breaths before looking once more at Ryder. "Bein' a stranger to these parts, I don't reckon you knew him."

Ryder had a hard time holding his eyes steady with Reno's. "Surprisingly enough, I did know him. We met back in Tennessee. But I didn't know at the time he was Jesse James."

Ry looked out the window as if suddenly noticing the time. "Say, I started the fire in the stove a while ago. What say I rustle us up something to eat?"

Reno gave Ryder a questioning look, but admitted, "Sounds good to me. I'm starved all of a sudden."

The next morning everyone sat around the breakfast table in no hurry to begin the long day ahead. They'd just finished a filling repast of fresh eggs, flaky biscuits and sausage gravy. This time the gravy was perfect, but then Ryder had made it.

Mandy was still in shock. She'd never had a man help her with the cooking before, at least not willingly. In fact, she'd never seen a man offer to do anything that was considered "woman's work." That didn't mean that she wasn't expected to muck

211

out the barn or repair broken boards or fix leaking roofs, of course. But Ryder, of all people. He was a man's man, every woman's dream, but didn't seem to think it a bit unmasculine that he should tie an apron around his waist and take spoon in hand to stir up a mean pan of delicious country gravy.

She watched as her two brothers and Ryder discussed the chores that needed to be done first. It felt good to enjoy such a friendly, enthusiastic atmosphere at her usually lonely table. Her brothers, especially Reno, were seldom ever home anymore, and she reveled in the thought that they'd be around for a few more days, if only because of Reno's injury.

Then her gaze settled on Ryder's strong profile. His full black hair fell over his forehead to just above his eyebrow and swept back to curl behind his ear. His nose was long and thin, and from the side his lips were narrow, with the bottom lip just a tad fuller than the top one. His mouth was curved upward in a rare smile at the moment that almost catapulted her heart into her stomach. The hard lines of his jaw set off a slightly square and quite stubborn chin. He was a wonderful addition to their family. So handsome and—

Mandy drew in her breath. What was she thinking? That she could become accustomed to his presence? That she'd like to have him around all the time? Phooey! He'd be gone and out of their lives in no time, and then where would that leave her?

She moved a hand to her stomach in an effort to still the butterflies fluttering there. Lonely again, that's where. And when Ryder Manning left, the loneliness would be more of an acute, empty feeling of loss, of something that could never be retrieved again. She knew deep in her heart that he would leave a void in her life that would never be refilled.

She shivered and straightened in her chair. She couldn't allow herself to dwell on such maudlin thoughts. She lifted her eyes from the scratch on the table that had been the center of her unseeing attention and started when her gaze locked with Ryder's. How long had he been staring at her like that? His lids were half-closed, but the heat from his gaze burned her skin as if she were sitting at the table completely nude. Didn't he realize her brothers were watching?

But they weren't. They were looking out the window at something. Embarrassed by Ry's blatant sensual stare, she mentally pulled herself together enough to turn in her chair to find out what had captured her family's earnest attention.

"Oh, my God, it's . . . Papa."

When George Coulter started down the path leading to the kitchen door of his home, his heart was filled with sadness. He'd been sober for almost two days now, and he welcomed the sickness of his body as one would welcome a friend. There was a jug hanging from his right hand, but he'd only picked it up out of habit.

As he reached out to open the door, he almost lost his courage, and he had actually taken the first step of the decision to turn back when the door was pulled open from the inside. Standing before him was a ghost, a nightmare come to haunt him for all of the mistakes he'd made in his life. He fell to his knees in the dirt trying desperately to lift the jug and uncork the stopper.

Reno, though still terribly stiff and sore from his wound, knelt down in front of his father and took the whiskey from his shaking hands. "Here Pa, let me do it."

But when George had the jug back in his hands and halfway to his lips, he stopped himself and put the spirits on the ground to instead reach out and touch his son.

"What's the matter, Pa? You're white as a sheet."

George touched Reno's shoulder, noticed his son's wince, then saw the white bandage under the shirt. So, they'd come close to killing him after all. It hadn't been a lie. "Th-they s-said you was dead, s-son. I-I grieved fer ya. F-fer two days, I sh-shorely did. B-but they was wrong. Yore a-alive."

Reno looked over his shoulder to where his brother and sister had come to stand behind him. "Must be drunk out of his mind. He's not making any sense."

Jeremy stepped around Reno and put his hand under his father's arm to help him to his feet. "Let's take him inside and see if we can get some solid food down him. Maybe it'll clear his head."

Once their father was seated at the table, Mandy fixed him a plate of biscuits and gravy. The food had been left on the stove and was still warm. She then poured a cup of coffee and set it by the plate. "Here you go, Papa. You must be hungry after the walk down the hill."

She knew she was prattling; it wasn't that far, but she was nervous and didn't know what to say to her father after their last dreadful encounter. And he hadn't been to the house for a long, long time.

George looked gratefully at his daughter. She'd turned into a beautiful young lady. Almost as beautiful as her . . . mother. The boys had grown into fine, handsome young men, too. How had they gotten involved with that scum, Hank Ford?

Then his eyes narrowed as he saw Ryder. "Who're

you? Are ya a friend of Reno's? He always was bringin' home strays, two-footed an' four." Just as quickly as he'd made the statement, George turned to his food, leaving Ry to face three pairs of warily watching eyes.

"Ahem, you know me, Mr. Coulter. I'm Ryder Manning. We met up at your still."

George forked another bite of biscuit into his mouth and chewed slowly while he carefully looked the young man over. There was something familiar about him, but his memory wasn't as good as it used to be. A lot of things could've happened while he was drunk and he wouldn't remember. . . . But wait!

"Shore, I'd forgotten about you. We'uns drank a whole jug, if'n I'm not mistaken."

Ry grinned at the relieved faces grouped around the table. "No sir, you're not. And I might add that you've got a good touch with that still. You cook a right powerful brew."

George frowned at the jug taking center position on the table. "Yeah, reckon I do. Jest takes practice, my boy, lots of practice."

Nobody spoke again until George had finished eating. Then Reno broke the silence by asking, "What's all this about hearing that I was dead? Who would've told you such a thing?"

By the way Jeremy and Reno looked at each other, George correctly guessed that they were questioning his good sense and were wondering if he hadn't imagined the whole thing. The problem was, he almost wished he had. Heaven only knew that he hadn't been much of a father to these kids, and now he was bringing more bad news. But they had to be warned.

"Had a visitor the other day. A friend of yourn, or used to be. Hank Ford."

Mandy's breath hissed through her teeth. Reno frowned and set his coffee down so hard that it sloshed all over the table. Ry's jaws clenched, and a muscle jerked under his eye. And Jeremy, oblivious to the reactions of the rest of the group, asked innocently, "Gosh, I haven't seen Hank for years. What's he up to these days?"

George wiped his dry mouth on the back of his sleeve. "He's up to no good, son, no good."

"The bastard shot me! And he stole my . . . our . . . ah, tradin' goods. Stole 'em right out from under me." Reno's voice was cold and hard, and no one at the table liked the terrible glint that was in his eyes. It boded trouble, for everyone.

"I'm afeered yore right. He out'n out told me he'd done ya in. But it's what he said later that skeerd me. Yep, it shorely did." George scooted his cup up close to the jug and pulled the cork. If he was goin' to tell this story right, he needed to wet his whistle.

Evidently the rest of the crew figured if they were going to have to listen to the story, they'd better join him. Everyone but Mandy pushed his cup forward to be filled. The three older men looked askance at Jeremy, but he steadfastly held his cup up until it, too, was full. Then Ry took the crock and splashed a drop or two into Mandy's, spilling some on her fingers as she tried to cover the top.

"Keep that; you might need it."

Finally, Jeremy took a swig from his cup, coughed and prodded his father to continue. "C'mon, Pa. What'd he say?"

George took a long, relaxing swallow of the whiskey, cleared his throat and then continued, "He come to me, tellin' me as how my boy, Reno, had got hisself killed. Said it was likely Jeremy'd meet the same fate anytime soon, and reckoned as how my

216

Amanda'd need a protector, a man to look after her once her family was gone."

Ry's eye twitched as he raised his cup, gulped the shine and then coughed. He started to say something after he'd finished choking, but George was speaking once again.

"I told Hank *I'd* look after my gal, that she warn't awful fond of him, but he allowed that I mightn't be long for this earth either. He figured as how he'd hitch up to Amanda, jest to keep 'er safe, ya know?"

Mandy had listened to enough. She sputtered and stammered but finally blurted out her feelings. "Why that low-down, mangy cur. That . . . that—"

Ry stood up and walked over to Amanda in an attempt to settle her down. She still looked a little peaked to him, and he was afraid of the anger he saw there. "Calm down, sweetheart. The man's just tryin' to do you a favor. He doesn't want you to grow up to be an old maid."

Mandy couldn't believe her ears. Was he mocking her? Trying to tell her that no respectable man would have her now? "Old maid! Old maid, huh? I'll have you know . . ." Before anyone realized her intention, she pulled back her fist and swung, clipping Ryder directly on the jaw. She was in the process of doing it again when she noted the dangerous glint in his eyes and thought better of it. "Damn you! Damn you to hell and gone."

She'd never really taken the time to think about what was going to happen to her now—now that she'd given herself to Ryder. And it was achingly apparent that *he'd* not thought about it, either. She'd known better. She'd just known she was going to let herself get too attached. Double damn him!

Ry finally managed to grab both of Amanda's wrists and pulled her up against him to twist her arms behind her back. Her breasts straining into his chest caused his heartbeat to race alarmingly. "Cut it out! I was only teasing." Then, in a voice so low that only she could hear, he said, "Settle down, wildcat. Your father and brothers are already wonderin' what's going on. You don't want to tell them about us right now, do you?"

Mandy lifted her chin and shook the hair out of her face. After piercing Ry with a look that would have joyfully killed, she lowered her lashes and gave a barely perceptible shake of her head.

"I thought not." He released her wrists and moved back a step or two, then turned to George and muttered, "No sense of humor. I don't think you have a thing to worry about, Mr. Coulter. Give him a week and Hank'll bring her back on bended knee, begging you to take her back."

Though everyone, with the lone exception of Mandy, laughed at his teasing, Ry still felt the chill that had run through his veins upon hearing George's words. Hank Ford was going to pay for threatening the Coulters, and especially for frightening Amanda. The man's time was running short.

George sighed and leaned back in his chair. "I didn't know what to say, so I jest pretended ta pass out, an' he finally left. But not 'til he robbed me blind. Took all the jugs he could carry, he did."

Jeremy looked at Reno, then at Ryder with young, frightened eyes. "What're we goin' to do? He'll wipe us out."

Reno's voice lashed out at his brother. "Shut up, Jer. He can try, but we damned sure aren't goin' to just roll over and let him have a free hand."

After watching Amanda reluctantly settle back into her chair, Ry joined the conversation. "You've already got the advantage. He doesn't know Reno is still alive and almost recovered, and he doesn't know I'm here. He thinks all he has to do is intimidate a young boy and an . . ."

George looked at them all defiantly. "Go on, say it. An old man, and a drunkard at that."

"I wasn't going to say that at all, George."

Reno saved the awkward situation. "No need for you to buy in on this madness, Manning. You've already done enough for the Coulter family. One of these days you won't be as lucky as you've been so far."

"Thanks for the concern, but as long as I'm workin' for the Coulters, I'm involved. Where I come from a man's loyal to his outfit, no matter what."

"Good. From the looks of things, we're goin' to need all the help we can get. Now, sit back down and let's work on a plan."

Chapter Twelve

It was late. Everyone had long since turned in for the night, but Mandy lay restless among the twisted sheets. All evening she'd felt helpless, trapped like a fly in a web of its own making, while listening to the men plan her safekeeping. Every chance they got, they paired her with Ryder—for her own protection.

How she wished she could stand up and shout out loud that it wouldn't protect her to throw her into constant contact with the man. The thought of losing her life wasn't nearly as scary as the reality of losing her heart and having it torn to shreds. And that's exactly what would happen, whether he found clues to lead him to Jesse, or if he just up and left. Either event would destroy her unless she could get a grip on her emotions and keep a safe distance between herself and Ryder.

Ryder. Even after making . . . love . . . with the man, she still knew nothing about him: his likes and dislikes, what made him happy or sad. It was best left that way, too.

Maybe she could work it out so that either Jeremy or Reno would be around to be her escort rather than Ryder. The theory of staying in pairs was quite acceptable, but why did she have to draw Ryder as her other half?

All she had to do was think of him, of his lean muscular body, the taut suppleness of his skin, and she broke out in a cold sweat. Even now her nightgown clung to her damp body and rubbed against her overly stimulated flesh until she couldn't stand it any longer.

Sitting up abruptly, she scooted to the edge of the bed and touched her bare feet to the cold floorboards. The moonlit porch beckoned until she silently glided down the hall and out the front door. A cool night breeze wafted across her heated skin as she leaned against the railing.

Without thinking, she unbuttoned the top two buttons of her gown and pulled the material from her chest to fan the perspiration causing her flesh to feel so hot and sticky. Then she gathered her hair from the back of her neck and raised her arms over her head as the air caressed the tender nape of her neck.

"You couldn't sleep either, huh?"

The rich timbred voice spoke from not more than two feet behind her, but when she turned her head to peer into the shadows, she couldn't even make out his outline. The red tip of a burning cheroot was the only indication of Ry's presence.

"Do you make it a habit to sneak up on unsuspecting females in the middle of the night?" she asked.

His chuckle rippled resonantly across the space separating them, and Mandy's skin broke out in goose bumps.

"It's easier that way. I don't give them a chance to run first."

Mandy thought to herself that no sane woman would even think about running from Ryder Manning. His sexual appeal would engender just the opposite effect. To take her mind off the sudden inclination to ravish the man, she said, "It's a beautiful night. I love springtime. Everything smells so fresh and new, especially at night, when there's a breeze."

Ry moved out of the shadows to lean next to her. He stubbed out the ashes of his cigar. "And the stars are so close you can reach out and touch them."

She looked at him in amazement, surprised he would notice such a thing, much less comment on it. She stood absolutely still, afraid to move or even breathe when she felt his fingers comb through her mussed and tangled hair.

"Your hair is beautiful. The moon reflects off the golden strands, and they shimmer like the stars. And the red gives the illusion of shadows, just like the heavens."

A shiver raced across her shoulders as she involuntarily swayed closer, as if to a magnetic force. Before she could realize what she'd done and recover, she found herself drawn into his arms and cuddled next to his chest. She couldn't deny the pleasure of the moment, even though a moment was all it would ever be.

Ryder was lost when she leaned toward him. He hadn't intended to touch her, had been doing his best to avoid her the past few days, but he couldn't help himself. It was the natural thing to do, to hold her close, to caress her hair and the bare skin of her arms, to feel the softness of her yielding body as it pressed against him. He could hold her like this forever.

He bent his head and captured her lips when she strained back enough to look into his eyes. Her mouth was parted as if she were preparing to speak, and Ry took advantage of the opportunity to explore the mysterious recess with his tongue. As he did so, he became aware of the heat between their bodies and the liquid sensation of the way they melted together.

Ry's hips thrust forward as his hands cupped Amanda's buttocks through the sheer material of her gown, and he was taken aback. For some reason he'd associated her with cotton and flannel, and the thin, gauzy material barely cloaking her heated flesh was somehow out of character.

When Mandy felt the hard evidence of Ryder's arousal against her abdomen, her blood boiled through her veins at a rate that left her clinging helplessly to his lean strength. Her limbs were like jelly and refused to support her. She'd never experienced the complete loss of self before. For the first time in years, she was dependent upon another person to take control, and she was willing to let herself be led.

Ry's breath was coming in short, ragged gasps as he raised his head and stared into Amanda's languorous, passion-filled face. The little smile on her lips reminded him of a cat that had gotten into the creamer. When she slowly licked her lips, he followed the path the pink tip of her tongue made as it slid over the sweet fullness of the flesh he'd just sampled.

"God, sweetheart, I want you."

Mandy buried her face on his chest, and her breath waved through the downy curls growing there as she whispered, "And I want you." Then, as if suddenly aware that his upper torso was bare, she reached around his waist to run her hands over the broad expanse of sinew and muscle cording his back.

Ry caught her arms and pushed her away, taking one of her hands in his as he started for the door. Remembering her brothers sleeping inside, he stopped and looked around the clearing. When his gaze settled on the barn, a wily grin curved the corners of his mouth.

"Follow me, sweetheart. Our palace awaits."

They ran across the space between the house and the barn like two kids out for a romp. The breeze fluffed the hair away from their faces, and Mandy's gown clung revealingly to her firm, young shape.

After opening the barn door, Ry led Mandy to the rear stall where he remembered dropping a sheaf of hay earlier in the day. Now he was glad he hadn't gotten around to cleaning it up. He untied the bedroll from the back of his saddle and spread it over the loose hay.

"What do you think, love? It'll be more comfortable than any place we've been so far."

Mandy was unaccountably shy as she backed against the stall partition. She ran nervous fingers through her hair before trying to nonchalantly cover her upper body with her arms. She wanted him, yes, but she was appalled by her brazen actions. This wasn't like her at all. What had happened to the cool, calm, indifferent Mandy Jo Coulter? Had she really changed so much in such a short time?

Ry stood with his hands on his buckle, hesitating as he watched the play of emotions cross Amanda's face. Where she'd been clinging and demanding earlier, she was now bashful and very reserved. She was like two different people confined to one body. And what a body.

He took the steps necessary to bring them together once more, and his hands smoothed down her neck to rub along the pulse that thrummed so rapidly at the base and over her trembling shoulders. "Don't be afraid, Amanda. I wouldn't hurt you for the world. You know that, don't you?"

224

FREE

BOOK CERTIFICATE

ZEBRA HOME SUBSCRIPTION SERVICE, INC.

YES! Please start my subscription to Zebra Historical Romances and send me my free Zebra Novel along with my first month's Romances. I understand that I may preview these four new Zebra Historical Romances Free for 10 days. If I'm not satisfied with them I may return the four books within 10 days and owe nothing. Otherwise I will pay just $3.50 each; a total of $14.00 (a $15.80 value—I save $1.80). Then each month I will receive the 4 newest titles as soon as they come off the press for the same 10 day Free preview and low price. I may return any shipment and I may cancel this arrangement at any time. There is no minimum number of books to buy and there are no shipping, handling or postage charges. Regardless of what I do, the **FREE** book is mine to keep.

Name _____

(Please Print)

Address _____ Apt. # _____

City _____ State _____ Zip _____

Telephone ( ) _____

Signature _____

(if under 18, parent or guardian must sign)

Terms and offer subject to change without notice.

MAIL IN THE COUPON BELOW TODAY

To get your Free ZEBRA HISTORICAL ROMANCE fill out the coupon below and send it in today. As soon as we receive the coupon, we'll send your first month's books to preview Free for 10 days along with your FREE NOVEL.

GET FREE GIFT

She nodded her head. Yes, she knew that. It wasn't him she was afraid of; it was herself. All of her recent actions, and reactions, were so alien to her nature, yet she felt good and enjoyed the new sense of freedom she was experiencing.

Ry bent his head, and his kiss was so tender and all-consuming that she knew whatever happened in the future would just have to happen. It was the present that was important, and whatever time she could spend with Ryder would be time remembered forever. It couldn't be wrong. She was doing it for love.

He put his hands on either side of Amanda's shoulders and braced his palms against the stall. He bent so that his eyes were level with hers. There were too many shadows dancing around them as the breeze ruffled wisps of hay and swung the rope hanging from the roof. He wanted to see the expression in her eyes as he asked, "Do you want to go back? If you're not comfortable, sweetheart, all you have to do is say so."

Mandy licked her lips with a tongue that was so dry it rasped over the sensitive flesh. Nothing she could say would make his opinion of her any better or worse after her previous behavior in his arms. So, why not be honest. "N-no." And when he stiffened and sighed in her ear as he started to rise, she placed her hands on his ribs and held him still. "No, I don't want to go back. It'd be a shame to let that soft pallet go to waste." Her hands moved up his back, and she pressed her body firmly to his warm, taut skin. She'd waited days for this moment.

"Ah, Amanda, sweetheart." Ry pushed the straps of Amanda's gown off her shoulders and watched as the garment slid sensuously over her curves to fall into a soft puddle at her feet. In seconds his jeans followed suit.

As he bent his knees and pulled them into the hay, he told her, "One of these days we're going to make love in a real bed, and we won't know how to act." They stretched out on the bedroll and lay face to face, their hands reaching and touching and exploring, finding the places that brought the most pleasure to the other.

Mandy's breasts swelled to aching as he gently cupped them in his palms and lifted first one and then the other to be nibbled and loved by his questing teeth and darting tongue. Her own hands were never idle as one glided over his hips and down the leg thrown across her lower body, and the other played with the curls between his flat, male nipples. Every once in a while she would tease and lightly pinch one of those nipples, and it would elicit a moan of near anguish from his heaving chest.

Her stomach muscles contracted as one of Ry's hands trailed down her front to allow his fingers to flutter over and encircle her navel. His other hand moved leisurely to the back of her head to burrow into her thick, shiny tresses, holding her head steady as his mouth assailed her lips. She quivered from head to toe and turned on her back as his body shifted to lay over her, most of his weight supported on the elbows on either side of her waist.

His legs rested between her thighs, and Mandy's skin was so sensitized that she could feel the slight tingle of the tiny hairs on his legs, up his groin and over his chest. They tickled and teased in turn until her flesh and bones mingled into a mass of jelly, responding and reaching for his every touch.

"I can't believe the way you make me feel. So alive and so . . . cherished." Mandy's face flamed when Ry chuckled and she realized she'd spoken her private

226

thoughts out loud. She was going to have to be more careful. No telling what she might blurt out when her mind was so fuzzy.

Ry wriggled his hips and teased with his throbbing organ at the apex of her thighs. "You do something special to me, too, sweetheart." As her hips lifted in anticipation of his entrance and her heels locked behind his legs, Ry confessed, "I need you, sweetheart. I love you."

But Amanda was beyond listening or understanding his words as he pushed inside her. If she whispered words of caring or loving herself, neither ever knew. Her body flamed and expanded to savor a depth of feeling and pleasure that she knew was impossible for any human to endure. But as she soared with the power of his nerve-shattering thrusts, she did indeed endure, and as they floated back through the heavens, clinging to and touching each other, as if wondering if the explosion were truly real, they cuddled and stroked and murmured incoherently. Their hair was damp and their bodies slick with perspiration as they recovered from the intensity of their joining.

"My God, Amanda, I've never . . ." Ry was at a loss for words. He didn't know how to describe the intensity of the emotions he had just undergone.

Mandy was shaking her head in wonder. "I've never hurt so badly or felt so excruciatingly happy all at the same time. For a minute, I thought I'd died."

As Ry ran his hands lingeringly over her silky skin, he said, "No, sweetheart, you didn't die. I can feel your heart beating everywhere we touch."

"I wish—" Mandy stopped herself. There was no use in spilling her dreams and desires now. There would be no future in it. Instead, she told a truth that was safely unrevealing. "I wish we could stay here all night.''

Ry hugged her to him and kissed her so lovingly that they both stared into each other's eyes as if they were the only two people left in the world. But there was reality to face and two brothers dangerously close. "No more than I, sweetheart, no more than I. But we don't have much choice in the matter."

As they walked toward the house hand in hand, there was a movement from the shadows on the porch. Jeremy stood at the top of the steps, his face suddenly illuminated as the moon came out from behind a long, wispy cloud. His eyes were round, and his mouth worked open and shut, as if he were choking on words that daren't come forth. Just as quickly, he turned and fled into the house.

Mandy stopped dead in her tracks, shamefully aware of the mussed and crumpled condition of the thin nightgown that left little enough to the imagination as it was. She raised a hand to her hair and pulled out a long piece of hay that was dangling behind her ear. She buried her face in her hands. "He knows! He can't help but know. Oh, God, what if he saw . . . ? What am I going to do?"

Ry put his arm around her shoulder and held her to him with a consoling embrace. "I wish I could give you some sage advice, Amanda, but I don't know any. I've never had to deal with anything like this before. Just leave him alone for now. We'll get a good night's sleep, or what's left of one, and talk to him in the morning when we're all feeling a little better. Okay?"

Unable to think of a better idea, she nodded her head as two big tears trailed down her cheeks. Ry captured them on the end of his finger and immediately licked the wet, salty digit. How he loved

228

the taste of her, the scent of her and the heart-stopping sight of her. He knew she was hurting, but was afraid of being rejected if he offered too much comfort. She was more than likely blaming him, and it made him uneasy.

"Go on in, sweetheart. I'm going back to the barn. See you in the morning."

Mandy stood silently, watching Ry's retreating back. What a time for something like this to happen. But instead of blaming Ryder, she was piling the guilt on her own shoulders until very soon she wouldn't be able to function under the heavy load.

Breakfast was a disaster. No one spoke, but the accusation and guilt being spread by cold, hard stares was unbearable, especially to Mandy, who'd been so happy to be surrounded by love and family only twenty-four hours earlier. What a difference a day could make to alter one's peaceful existence.

Over a bite of scrambled egg, Jeremy shot daggers at Ryder, while Mandy barely looked anywhere except at her plate. Ryder had eyes only for Amanda, while Reno looked back and forth between the three other people in utter astonishment.

"We've been sitting here for over half an hour and no one has spoken even one word. Who's going to fill me in? I've never seen my brother so hostile, and you two—" he gazed intently between Mandy's and Ryder's faces—"look like you've both been caught red-handed in the candy jar. Now, what's up?"

Jeremy pointed the end of his fork at Ryder, while he tried to hurry and gulp the mouthful of food he'd just begun chewing. Ryder, meanwhile, had captured the hand Amanda had been using to mutilate the napkin in her lap and held it under the table, giving her a reassuring squeeze.

Finally Jeremy lunged to his feet, throwing his napkin in his plate. With one final glare at Ryder and a denouncing glance directed at Mandy Jo, he shouted, "You'll have to ask them. As for me, I'm leavin'." The kitchen door slammed on his last words as he disappeared around the corner of the house.

Mandy would've jumped to her feet and followed him if Ryder hadn't maintained the pressure on her hand, forcing her to stay in her seat. Her eyes were a sad forest green, turned dark by her pain, when she entreated, "I've got to go after him. He needs me."

"No, sweetheart, let him cool off. He needs to be alone and have time to settle things in his own mind before you confuse him even more."

Reno sat in silent contemplation during the entire scene. By observing Mandy's behavior around Ryder Manning, and hearing him use the endearment, he could make a fair guess at what had Jeremy so upset. It made him damned angry, too, but Mandy was a grown woman, free to make her own choices. Still, it rankled that she'd chosen the stranger.

"Well, well. Evidently little brother must've caught you two sneakin' 'round. His angel's suddenly been toppled from the top of the tree. How's it feel to be human, Mandy?" He knew his tone was nasty, but it felt good to take his sister down a peg or two after all the sermons she'd given him during his life. It felt good, that is, until he saw her bury her face in her hands and begin to weep.

Reno looked at Ryder, and his temper rose. "Well, is it true?"

Ryder leaned back in his chair and crossed his fingers over his lean belly. He spoke very softly. "I guess you could say that."

Reno slapped his palm on the table and leaped to his feet. "Damn it! Either it is, or it isn't. You've either bedded my sister, or you haven't! I want to know, *now!*"

The noose was tightening around Ry's neck, and the dreaded vision of shotguns and weddings played over and over through his mind. Why hadn't he had the sense to control his lustful urges for once?

Both men's eyes turned to Mandy when they heard her meekly say, "It's true. We've made . . . been . . . together. And it's *my* fault, not his . . . Ryder's."

When he saw her standing in front of him, so regal and proud in her denim hand-me-downs, facing up to what, to her, had to be an embarrassing truth in front of her brother, Ryder knew he'd never had a chance. What man could resist such a woman? God, she was beautiful, independent, proud and such a brat.

"What do you mean, your fault? You think Reno's going to believe for one minute that his prim little darling threw the first available stranger down and seduced him? He's smarter than that."

Reno leaned over the table. "You're damned right I am. But that story sounds pretty believable the other way around. Is that the way you planned it, Manning? You found my sister alone and—"

"Stop it! Stop it, both of you. You make it sound so contrived, so . . . cheap. You can't plan something that—" Mandy clenched her fists, moving her tear-stained face back and forth between her brother and lover, trying to make them understand. But seeing the set, angry looks on their faces, she stomped her foot, let out a disgusted "Oooohh!" and fled the room with as much dignity as she could muster.

Her brother straightened his back and sighed as he sat back in his chair. All of the fight drained out of him as he said to Ryder, "I know I sound like the doting father, Manning, but I am the man in charge right now. And I love my sister. I don't want to see her hurt. It's a lousy situation, but I'd like to know what you plan to do about it."

Ry appreciated Reno's attempt to talk rationally, but he still had his hackles up. "Do? I don't plan on doing anything. You heard her. She admitted that nothing happened without her consent." He nervously ran his fingers through his hair before rising to pace the floor. This was going to be sticky, and he'd probably screwed up his investigation by letting his loins rule his head. Now he was getting pressured to "do the right thing." How he hated that old saying.

"Ah, since Mandy's shouldering the majority of the . . . consequences . . . you don't feel you have any duty toward her?"

"That's right, bucko. I'm not going to be trapped into anything."

Reno moved his hands slowly toward his hips, only to ball them into fists when he remembered his gun was hanging on the bedpost. He'd never been so angry with a human being in his entire life, but rather than turn into a raging demon, a deadly calm settled over him.

"Then I think you'd better get out while you're still able. Don't ever show your face around this farm again. Count your lucky stars that cousin Jesse's gone. You'd either be goin' to a weddin' or fertilizin' a plot of ground about now."

Mandy's brother turned on his heel and headed toward the living room, then stopped and looked over his shoulder. "You've got five minutes."

*　　　*　　　*

Ry's ride into town was made at a much slower pace than his last trip, and since he'd only seen parts of it at night, he wasn't too disappointed in daylight. It wasn't much of a town: a saloon, general store, blacksmith and stable, sheriff's office, and a church that set off the main street surrounded by a few rows of wood or stone houses. Some were a combination of both.

He reined to a stop in front of the general store and ran the fingers of one hand through his wind-tossed hair. He'd felt naked without his hat and was in dire need of a replacement. Then he'd find out where the nearest telegraph line was located. His superiors had to be worried.

As he stepped onto the boardwalk, he absently glanced in the front window. A pale green dress with a pink and blue flowered print caught his eye. The first thing he thought of was how pretty the dress would look on a certain auburn-haired brat. But chances were, she'd probably never wear anything that dainty.

Reno knocked on Mandy's door until he heard her stirring, then turned the knob and stepped into the room. His heart died a little when he saw her tear-streaked, unhappy face. Since she remained on the edge of the bed, he went over to sit beside her.

"Is there something, anything, I can do?"

Mandy sniffed, rubbed a finger under her nose and laid her head on her brother's shoulder. "You are helping, just by being here. And . . . and for not passing judgement on me."

"Ahem, ah, I'm not goin' to say that I *like* what you done, did. But I understand what it's been like for you, an attractive, inexperienced woman, living out

233

here in the backwoods, wantin' to find out what life's about. That Manning's good-looking, charming. Lots of women would've been attracted to him."

"Oh, Reno, if it were only that simple. You see, I-I liked him. He's—"

"Why, sure you did. What's not to like? I'm just glad I took care of him for you."

"Took care of him?" Mandy turned to face her brother and grabbed the front of his shirt with both hands. "What do you mean, 'took care of him'?"

"Mandy, quit tearin' my new shirt. I threw him out, is all. Right after you left the room. Don't worry, he left peaceable."

"But, he can't leave, Reno. He's got to stay here!" Her voice was rising to a pitch of near hysteria before she realized that Reno had no idea of the importance of keeping Mr. Ryder Manning under surveillance.

"Ain't no way that man is ever goin' to set foot in this house again, Mandy. No way."

What was she going to do now? How could she get Reno to bring Ryder back without telling him the whole story? It would have to be something really outlandish . . . devious, even.

"Reno, you know I don't want to go against you, but there's a good reason for keeping Mr. Manning around the place, at least for a while." She used her most placating and cajoling tone of voice.

"There ain't nothin' worth havin' that bum on this farm." He was dead set and earnest in his conviction to see the last of Ryder Manning.

"Wh-what if I . . . get pregnant? What if he leaves the country and never comes to see about m-me or the b-baby? You'd be stuck with having to see after us and wouldn't be able to leave." Hmm. The more she thought about it, the more she almost wished she would be carrying Ryder's baby. She might see the last of Ryder, but it would be one way to keep her family together—in Missouri.

Reno stood up and walked to the window. "Maybe you're right." But when he turned to face his sister, his eyes were hard. "But the minute you find out you're not, he's outta here. Is that clear?"

"Y-yes, I understand."

"And if you are . . . he's by damn goin' to marry you! Even if we have to tie him to the altar."

Mandy waited until Reno had been gone for some time before donning her boots and slipping the little derringer in her clean overalls. Now she was sitting in the rocker in the living room, holding the piece of paper she'd hidden from Ry. It had still been in the pocket of her old pants when she'd gone to find the gun. She didn't want to read it, but she had to.

So, she'd been right all along. He was a lawman—a deputy marshal out of St. Louis—and he was here looking for evidence to prove whether or not it was really Jesse James who was buried. Did they have some sort of proof that it wasn't? God help her, what a mess she'd gotten into.

She ran all the way to the valley where Red Fox was hidden. He greeted her with an enthusiastic whicker, and she gave him a hug around the neck in return.

"I've missed you, boy. Sometimes I think you're my only friend."

By the time she reached the area surrounding Jesse's cave, she'd gotten off Red Fox to lead him and study the ground. There were too many tracks crisscrossing the land to suit her. In the first place, no one had any business up here, and secondly, a lot of the tracks were made by unshod horses. There hadn't been any Indians in this part of the country for years, and the ground was much too rocky to ride a horse barefoot for any length of time. Something strange was going on here. She only hoped it didn't involve her cousin.

She remained in the trees outside the entrance to the cave for a long time as she scouted the area and made sure no one was near. Then after whistling several times, receiving no indication that she'd been heard, she decided to go on in, dreading what she might find.

Just as she was sliding the cover of branches and leaves to the side, it rustled and was pulled out of her hands. She was going for her gun when she recognized the familiar voice.

"Whoa, put that thing down. It's only me."

"Thank heavens, Jesse, I was worried about you."

"No need. I was in the back looking over the canyon when I caught the end of your signal. Have you been here long?"

They recovered the opening and walked side by side as they led Red Fox to the back room. "Not long actually, but I took a lot of time getting up here. I don't like the looks of things out there, Jesse."

"Yeah, I know what you mean. Come out back and I'll show you what I've been looking at for the last half hour."

As they stood on the trail leading out the back way from the cave, Jesse pointed out three riders, each leading two additional horses. "It's Hank Ford and a couple of his boys. They've made a trip through here almost every day, either leading or driving five to six head of horses. And they're darned good animals. Unbranded, well made. They're not Hank's usual brand of transportation. I'd give anything to know where he got them."

"And where they're taking them?"

"That, too. I'd wager they're going back in the hills to Hank's uncle's old place. Remember him? The old hermit? Never went to town. Raised or killed all his own food. That's the only place they *could* be headed for over in that country."

"You're talking about old Uncle Swiddell. But he's been dead for years."

"Yes, and he left his place to Hank. I was there when they found the old man's will. We couldn't believe the old fellow actually had one. It was worded like some educated, scholarly person wrote it. Never can tell about people, I guess."

As Hank and his cohorts faded to dots on the horizon, Mandy and Jesse turned back inside the cave. When they entered the main room and sat down on the large rocks, Jesse asked, "Speaking of people and strange behavior, what're you doing here so soon? I wasn't expecting you for another three or four days."

Mandy rubbed her hands up and down on the denim covering her thighs, then accepted the cup of coffee Jesse held out to her. "Thanks. I'm kind of cold all of a sudden." After several sips of the hot liquid, she sighed and scooted off the rock in order to sit on the ground and use it as a backrest as she stretched her feet to the fire.

She handed the piece of paper to Jesse. "I'm afraid we have trouble. I was right about Ryder Manning."

"Where'd you get this?"

"It fell out of his pocket one night. I, uh, kinda found it and kept it. But I didn't get a chance to read it until this morning."

Jesse read the missive, then silently studied the shadows on the back wall. The fire crackled, and sparks flew in all directions when a ball of sap exploded.

Mandy began to fidget. "What're we going to do?"

"Well, it's pretty safe to assume he's hanging around you to get any leads he can." When he turned to face Mandy, he couldn't get over how deathly pale she'd become. "Amanda, you're not sick, are you?"

"N-no, don't worry about me. Go on with what you were saying."

"Okay, but you tell me if you're not feeling well." Jesse's eyes blinked even more rapidly than usual as he rubbed his hand over them. "Has he been asking a lot of questions? Trying to find out anything in particular?"

"Not from me. And that's the strange part. He's never mentioned a thing about you unless I brought you up first."

"What about in town? Has anyone complained about his snooping around?"

"Well, no, but he hasn't had time to do much nosing about. He's, ah, been otherwise occupied."

Jesse leaned closer to Amanda in order to see her face. "Amanda, you're blushing. Just how 'occupied' has he been?"

Mandy took another swallow of coffee. "How much time do you have? It's rather a long story."

Jesse laughed and swung his arm in a half circle. "As you can see, my house is clean, the dishes are done and I'm at your disposal. Let's hear it."

Mandy filled him in on everything that had happened from the time she'd last seen him. Everything, that is, except the intimate details of her relationship with Ry. It would kill her if Jesse found out what she'd done. He'd be so disappointed in her. But as she'd feared, he wasn't going to let her off so easily.

"I'd say the Coulters have been a busy family lately. And I, for one, am grateful for the deputy's intervention. But tell me one thing. Why did Reno throw him out? I don't quite understand."

"Reno just thought it would be for the best. You know . . . he doesn't have any idea about why I was wanting to keep an eye on the man."

"I know that, hon. But something's not right. The man saved your life and Reno's, yet Reno turns around and kicks him out of the house. Reno wouldn't do something like that to a man he owed unless the man had committed some terrible—"

Jesse was still leaning toward Amanda and saw the flushed features and the moistness in her eyes. "Oh, my God." The tone of his voice was hushed and filled with comprehension.

Mandy scrubbed a tear off her cheek. "I-it's not what you think. Well, maybe it is. . . . Please, Jesse. Please don't hate me." She wrapped her hands around her arms and let her head drop to her raised knees as huge sobs began to rack her shoulders.

Jesse left his seat to kneel beside Amanda. He pulled her into his arms and held her as she let open the dam of tears and fears that had so frustrated her lately.

Later, after the tempest had ended, Jesse quipped, "I told you to keep a close watch over him, Amanda, but I didn't mean *that* close."

"I don't know what I'm going to do, Jesse. I-I think I love him."

Chapter Thirteen

Reno found Ry just after the deputy had wired his home office, informing them that progress was slower than he'd expected. At least now he'd checked in, and all he needed to do was wait for a reply to see if they wanted him to stay there or move on.

When Ry noticed Reno tying his horse to the hitching rail next to his own grulla, he tensed and watched the man warily. Had the older brother decided he needed to avenge his wronged sister? All Ry needed was for him to cause a scene. He'd been trying to keep a low profile and not cause any undue attention regarding his presence in town. The people around there were funny about strangers, and the better he blended in and made casual acquaintances, the better he'd get along.

Reno was also uneasy as he approached Ryder. He'd tried to think of any number of ways to logically request that he come back to the farm, but after what happened that morning, none of his ideas made any sense. And he'd promised Mandy that he wouldn't mention the *real* reason they wanted the man back, so he was stymied. Of course, he could always accidentally blurt it out and then swear the man to

240

secrecy. He should've just let his sister handle the whole mad scheme.

"Howdy, Manning. Wasn't sure if I'd find you here or not."

Ry looked at Reno with an almost comical expression on his face. He'd been expecting to have to defend himself from an irate Coulter, not this fairly civil greeting. "Afternoon, Coulter. Don't tell me you were looking for me?"

"Yeah, hard to believe, ain't it? Let's move over here out of everyone's way." And out of earshot of the local gossips, he thought. "Er, Mandy and I had a long talk after you left this mornin', and she convinced me that I'd, uh, overreacted. She wants you to come back to the farm. Says you need a place to stay."

Ry was flabbergasted. Reno had been defending his sister's honor, and now he was saying he'd overreacted? Something strange was going on here. "Well, that's real thoughtful of her, but there's a room over the saloon that I can use. She doesn't need to worry about me."

Ry had turned and started to walk toward the said establishment when Reno galvanized himself into action and blocked his way. "But what about the job? You told Pa you'd help out around the place. I won't be there much longer, and Mandy'll need help again."

Reno swung his injured arm around in a circle. "I'm almost as good as new, and I've got to be movin' on." He had to swallow the bile in his throat as he lied, "I'd feel a heap better knowin' there was someone there to kinda look after my sister."

Ry was smart enough to sense the duplicity of Reno's words, but he'd been worried about Amanda, too. He didn't like the threat of Hank Ford hanging over her head, and because of his own stupidity, her family was deserting her. But could he risk going back? Maybe there was still a slim chance. "What about Jeremy? Won't he be there?"

The shrug of Reno's shoulders gave Ry the answer he'd been afraid of. "Well, so much for family loyalty, all for one, and all that nonsense."

When Reno's already pale face blanched even whiter, Ry remembered his resolve to avoid a confrontation. He raised his arms and outstretched his hands, palms first. "Okay. Okay! Forget I said that. Your glib tongue has talked me into it. I'll be out to the farm later this evening."

"That's just, uh, great, Manning. See you later." Reno walked back to his horse, choking over the residue his words had left in his mouth. Damn Mandy for making him crawl to that bastard.

Mandy stood up and dusted the dirt off the bottom of her pants. It was getting late, and she needed to get back to the farm to find out if Reno had been successful in getting Ryder to return home. Home! For how much longer would she be able to call it that?

But first, there was something that had been nagging at the back of her mind. "Jesse, I know we covered our tracks well, and no more people know about this ruse than absolutely necessary, but is there something, anything, that could lead the deputy to suspect you're still alive?"

"I've been wondering that very thing, and there's nothing that I can think of. Since our man was at the funeral, I can only suppose he also viewed the body. But no one else seemed to notice anything unusual, and some of those people I've known for a very

242

long time.''

Mandy paced beside the fire, adding her shadow to those already hugging the wall of the cave. "Sheriff Pomeroy even footed half the bill just to make certain you were finally, and deeply, removed from his life.''

Jesse laughed. "Ah, how I'd love to haunt one of the great man's dreams some evening.''

"Don't you even think it! We've come too far and risked too much for you to pull a prank like that. Pomeroy's cagier than you've ever given him credit for.'' Mandy frowned and stomped over to stand in front of Jesse like a mother hen scolding a recalcitrant chick.

"I promise. Honest! Believe me, Amanda, I'm not going to do anything to screw up this chance. I know there'll never be another one. You know, I've been lucky. As many years as Frank and I have operated, and as many jobs as we've pulled, there're very few people who can actually say they know what Jesse James looks like.'' Jesse stood up and walked to a shelf to pick up some oil and a rag.

He looked at Amanda as he began to clean his Smith & Wesson Schofield .45. "That's the only hope I have that this deal's going to work.''

Mandy sat down next to her cousin and watched as he took the revolver apart. "Chuck looked enough like you to be your twin. I *know* it's going to work. Why, just think of all the years you took the blame for the jobs he pulled. I'm not saying I never liked the guy, but when he went to all the trouble of cutting off his finger to pretend he was you, I'd say that he was going a little too far.''

The outlaw shook his head in agreement. "Yeah, that was one of his crazier stunts. It was that chest wound he got a couple of years ago that finally did him in, you know.''

243

Mandy questioned the statement. "Why would you say that? He recovered, didn't he?"

"Sure, but he was never healthy again. He lost his desire for the chase, the thrill, the excitement. After that accident, all he wanted to do was sit at home and do the light chores, maybe read. And the scar matched mine."

Mandy heard the deep regret in her cousin's tone. He'd really liked Chuck Beggs. "How long had he been staying with you?"

Jesse thought for a minute as he ran the rag through the cylinder. "He'd been coming by the house to visit for years. Even stopped by when we were in Tennessee. But he'd only stayed over a time or two."

"Hmmm, I wonder why he was there when Bob—" Mandy couldn't finish. Just thinking about what a close call Jesse'd had caused her to choke up completely.

"I'd asked him to stay, Amanda. I'd needed to be in Texas for a few days, and I didn't want anyone to know I was gone."

"Oh." Mandy was tempted to ask him why he'd been gone but decided she really didn't want to know. Besides, there'd been no reports of any shootings or robberies during that time, so she knew he hadn't been up to his old mischief.

"Come on, Amanda, don't look at me like that. I feel guilty enough. I haven't committed any crimes against society for a long time. And there were times when you had Frank and I hidden in this very cave that we were accused of our worst sins."

"I know. It's just that every once in a while I think about Chuck, and what nearly happened to you, and . . . I just . . ."

Jesse refilled the cylinder with cartridges and

244

snapped it shut. "It was a fluke, that's all. God, I had no idea Bob and Charles would turn against me like that. And that damned coward, to shoot a man in the back. . . ."

Mandy put her hand on her cousin's shoulder. "He never knew what hit him. It was quick, and he didn't suffer."

"You think that makes me feel any better? Damn him for turning his back. I'd warned him not to trust anyone. And the fool even took off his gun. What could've gotten into him?"

"I guess we'll never know for sure. He probably thought Bob and Charles were part of the family, Jesse." She shivered and rubbed her hands up and down her arms. "Who knows, you might've done the same thing. You trusted them."

By now, Jesse's image was trying out the shadow routine. "You're right about one thing, hon. Who knows? But, God, I feel guilty as hell for letting something like that happen."

"Quit blaming yourself. *You* didn't *let* anything happen. It was fate, just one of those things, but it wasn't your fault."

Jesse didn't say anything. He just continued to pace back and forth, wearing a path in front of the fire.

She decided it might be best to partially change the subject. "Do you think Ryder Manning might be related to Chuck? Maybe that's why he's so interested in finding out about you?"

Finally he sat back down. "That's not likely. We had a lot of time to talk on several occasions, and Chuck never mentioned any lawmen or Indians in the family. I don't think he had a very big family, anyway."

Mandy had readily agreed to help Jesse in this wild

charade, but there were a lot of things she hadn't known, or had time to ask about. "What about the scars? Did he have *all* the same scars that you do?"

"Strangely enough, he did. All but this one on my arm." He rubbed his upper arm as if in remembrance of the painful wound.

"Is there any way that knowledge of that wound could hurt us?"

"I don't think so. Only myself, Jimmy Younger, the guy who shot me and Doc Reilly know anything about it." He had consciously stopped pacing only moments earlier, but nerves caused him to start again as he ran a hand over his eyes to try to control their rapidly blinking.

"Do you know who shot you?" Mandy was trying to sound casual while questioning her cousin, but deep down she had the feeling that this information was important to the probability of their getting away with the bizarre plan. And it seemed that Jesse thought so, too.

Jesse stretched his taut muscles and faced Amanda. "I don't really know for sure. James and I were mindin' our own business one day when this guy up and starts chasin' us. He fired; we fired back. Then he winged me, and the boy and I took to the hills to try and lose him. Shoot, he might not even know for sure whether or not he hit me. Anyway, we talked about it later and figured he had to be a Pinkerton or law of some sort to take out after us like he did."

"So, there was no proof you were hit, and . . . whoever . . . wouldn't have bragged about it?"

"That's what I'm hoping, hon. It was almost eight years ago. That's a long time."

Mandy had an uneasy feeling but thought that, in all likelihood, no one knew about or remembered that arm wound. "I hope so, too. Maybe if Reno has

246

been able to talk our Mr. Manning back to the farm, I'll have a chance to check his saddlebags again. There might be something besides wanted posters in them to give us a clue as to what he's looking for or why he's so intent on hanging around, especially since you're supposedly dead."

"You be careful around that man, Amanda. From all I've heard about him, he's a smart hombre. I don't want him doing anything to hurt you."

She gave Jesse a wan smile and went to get Red Fox. "Oh, he won't hurt me. But I'll be extra careful." If only she believed her own words. Wasn't she already hurting?

Ryder rested his hip and thigh on the porch railing, leaning his back against a post as he smoked a cheroot and watched the hill behind the house. Neither Amanda nor Reno were home, and from the looks of the kitchen stove, no one had been there for lunch. That meant Amanda had left early in the morning, probably shortly after he had gone to town.

Where did she go when she disappeared like that? He knew for a fact she hadn't been in town, and he hadn't met her on the road when he came back this afternoon. What could she find to do all day back in the hills? The smokehouse had venison and pork hanging in plentiful amounts, plus several rabbit carcasses, so she couldn't have gone hunting.

Ah ha. A faint movement caught his eye on the ridge directly over the valley where Amanda kept Red Fox. Another thing that had troubled him was why she kept the horse concealed. Of course, he was a valuable animal. Not a few men would certainly steal to get him.

The rider he'd seen had come from the east.

According to his map, there was nothing but wilderness in that direction. He'd have to bide his time and see what was so interesting in them there hills.

Mandy entered the Coulter living room only to halt her steps in an effort to lift her nose and inhale the enticing aroma drifting throughout the house. To the best of her knowledge, neither one of her brothers had ever learned to cook, and she distinctly remembered banking the fire in the stove.

Her nose led the way as she walked down the hall to the kitchen. She could hardly believe her eyes when she stepped through the door. None other than Ryder Manning—apron, spoon, and all—was standing over the stove supervising the ingredients of a bubbling kettle of the most delicious smelling stuff she'd ever had the pleasure of sniffing.

Mandy was nervous and excited over seeing Ryder again. She had no idea what Reno had said to get him to come back, but she only hoped her brother had stuck to their agreement.

"I see you decided to come back." What an inane thing to say. He'd think that it was no wonder she was such a pushover, she was stupid to boot. Then her breath caught in her throat and her heart began to thump madly against her chest when he turned around and smiled.

Ry gave the stew another stir before placing the lid over the pot. "Guess you could say that. I didn't really want to leave in the first place."

Mandy turned suddenly wary. She could believe that. "Well, I'm glad you're here again."

"Are you, really?" Ry's eyes narrowed, and he studied Amanda intently. His whole attitude had changed the minute she'd walked through the door. It felt so good to be around her. How long had he been gone today? Six hours, maybe? And he'd missed her like crazy. He'd never felt that way before, about anyone.

"Kinda. Ummm, what's that you're cooking? It smells scrumptious." Her lashes lowered to shyly hide her eyes from Ryder's scrutiny. If only her knees would quit shaking. Ry laughed and grinned a crooked grin that tore at her insides.

"Just like a woman. Always appreciative of any meal not of your own making. It's my special recipe of rabbit stew. Actually, it's my only recipe. If it wasn't for rabbits, I'd have starved to death long ago."

"You and my brothers. I'm still not sure how they manage to feed themselves when I'm not around to do the cooking."

"It looks like they've figured something out." Ry rubbed the back of his neck and darted his eyes around the room self-consciously. "It'll be a while before this is done, if you want to clean up, or something."

"Oh, sure, that'd be nice. I'm just . . . not used to this. I feel like I should be doing something."

"You can, later. You can set the table, make some biscuits, if you want. By the way, what happened to all the biscuits that were left over from this morning?"

Mandy put her hands in her pockets and scuffed her toe along a seam between the boards on the floor as she remembered the delight on Jesse's face when she handed him the biscuits this afternoon. Too quickly, she mumbled, "Oh, those. I threw them out for the birds. I do that, sometimes, when we have leftovers. You know . . ."

249

"Uh huh, I just wondered."

"Well, uh, I'll go . . . clean up."

"Good. I'll keep an eye on things in here."

As she backed through the kitchen door, Mandy let out a sigh of relief when the door swung closed, shutting her away from those insistent black eyes. They made her feel so itchy and squirmy, like they were penetrating to the dark depths of her soul. Just like the very first day she'd seen him.

Mandy entered her room, closed the door securely and climbed out of her overalls, tossing them haphazardly into a corner. Clean up. Put on a fresh pair of dungarees. She went to stand in front of her chest of drawers and picked up the brush lying on top of it. The cracked mirror hanging behind the chest gave a very distinct image of fly-away tresses as she ran the bristles vigorously through their length.

There was a smudge of dirt on her right cheek, so she licked her fingers and scrubbed it off. She'd put fresh water in the pitcher on her bedstand just that morning, but she'd save it to take a quick sponge bath before she dressed. Looking closer into the glass, she futilely rubbed the freckles on her nose. She'd hoped she would outgrow those annoying pests.

In the corner of the mirror, she noticed the reflection of something foreign sitting in the center of her bed. She turned to stare at an oblong package of some sort. Then tentatively, she took several steps toward the bed. When she reached the footboard, she stopped, afraid that the brown, paper-wrapped object would suddenly disappear before her eyes.

But it didn't, so she edged around the bed and gingerly sat on the side, holding her breath in case it might yet decide to jump and run. With a trembling hand, she reached out to gently run a finger over the top of the coarse paper, only to jerk it back when she felt something rough and lumpy.

Realizing that nothing was going to leap out at her, she let out a long breath of air and giggled like a little girl. A package! Was it for her? There was only one way to find out.

The same shaking hand reached forward, only this time her fingers took a firm grip on one corner and slowly pulled it to her. The rough object she'd encountered turned out to be another square of paper connected to the wrapping paper. And it had her name on it.

Mandy picked up the package and shook it before clutching it tenderly to her breast. This was an event to savor and treasure—unless someone was playing a trick on her. A practical joke? That would be too cruel. She couldn't stand the suspense a moment longer and slipped the string off the corners before furiously ripping open the paper.

Folds of material sifted onto her legs, and she audibly gasped. She dropped the paper to the floor, staring bemusedly at the beautiful green dress. It took several tries to stand, and she swayed as she held the dress in front of her, holding it securely against her waist with her arm. Again, she giggled, then spun in a circle as the material billowed around her.

A new dress. Tears of happiness rolled freely from her eyes as she sank down on the bed, taking the garment with her. How long had it been since she'd had a new dress? Or a dress of any kind? Jesse used to bring her presents, back in the good days—a dress, sometimes a brush, or pretty ribbons—but it had been several years since he'd been free to come and go as he pleased without worrying about leading the law or even bounty hunters to their door.

She'd outgrown the last dress a long time ago and hadn't felt the need for one since then. Overalls were much more practical for the work she'd been doing lately, and they were plenty good for her purposes.

Oh, God, a new dress. She sat on the bed, shoulders slumped, blurrily staring at the tiny pink flowers in the print. Who could have given her such a wonderful gift? Yes, who indeed.

As she entered the kitchen with catlike grace and little or no sound of movement, Ry was wondering if he'd done the right thing by purchasing the dress for Amanda. Would she take it as an insult, or maybe a peace offering? It was meant to be neither. He'd bought it because . . . because she'd look so pretty in it . . . because she deserved something frilly and feminine . . . because he wanted to do it . . . just because.

He stopped suddenly as if he'd run face first into a brick wall. Amanda was standing in the outside door to the kitchen. The setting sun was fading against the western horizon amidst a colorful display of pale pink and muted orange. Her figure was silhouetted, outlining a puffed sleeve, rounded bosom and full gathered skirt. On stealthy, moccasined feet he approached the lamp in the middle of the table and lit the wick. Light filtered quickly through the room, and when Amanda turned to face him, he felt as if he'd been dealt a severe blow to the gut.

She was even more beautiful than he'd ever imagined it possible for a mortal woman to be. Her cheeks were flushed a becoming shade of pink, almost matching the color of the sunset, and her eyes, if a bit red-rimmed, were mint green in their intensity. Her hair was brushed until it sparkled with ruby highlights and was tied back with the green velvet ribbon the store clerk had so generously included with the dress.

Then he grinned and smiled with a delight that also glittered from the depths of his dark eyes, for peeping beneath the hem of the gown were the worn, scuffed tips of Amanda's boots. With a hoot of laughter, he closed the space between them and lifted her in his arms to smother her in a gigantic bear hug.

"Sweetheart, you're somethin' else."

During the silence, and while suffering shyly through Ryder's obvious approval of her appearance, Mandy conducted a close perusal of her own. It was the first time she'd seen him so nattily attired. Was this some sort of special occasion? It wasn't her birthday. Maybe it was his?

Her thoughts and questions died a sudden death when he smiled. The brilliance of that look was enough to light the room. Lord, but he was beautiful. His jet-black hair was slicked back but fell naughtily to each side in a natural part on the left side of his head, causing a stray lock or two to dip across his forehead. The light-blue shirt he wore only heightened the blackness of his eyes and hair, and accented his deep, natural tan. A navy neckerchief added a jaunty air to his attire and matched new denim jeans that were rolled into a large cuff that rested atop the arch of his moccasined feet.

She stood stunned until he charged across the room and lifted her off her feet. Didn't the man realize she was heavy? He was going to hurt himself.

"Ryder, for heaven's sake, put me down this instant."

"I will." With one final spin, he let her slide down to touch her feet to the floor but still held her encircled within the confines of his arms. "Spoilsport. Can't a man have any fun?"

Mandy spouted as best she could while trying to catch her breath, "A man can enjoy all the fun he can stand, but hopefully, without risk of injury."

"Ha! A little mite like you? Hurt big ole me? It could never happen." But as he held her at arm's length, he remembered the spirit and determination camouflaged beneath the fragile beauty and charm, and he wasn't quite so sure of himself.

Mandy demurely lowered her lashes and clasped her hands together. Her voice was husky as she gathered the courage to ask, "Is the dress from you?"

Ry quickly walked over to the stove and lifted the lid off his stew. He sniffed, then stirred the brew, trying to nonchalanatly waste time. "I guess you could say that." He hadn't expected to be this embarrassed.

"Ooohh! If you say that one more time I'm going to personally wring your neck." She stomped around the table to stand beside the stove, but then she contritely added, "It was a dumb question. Of course the gown is from you. And I thank you for the kind thought. But . . ."

She ran a hand down a panel of the skirt and felt the material slide softly through her fingers. "But I can't accept it. I-I just couldn't help trying it on. I'm sorry."

Ry's hand jerked and accidentally flicked the spoon, scattering bits of stew in all directions. "What do you mean, you can't accept it? Of course you can. It's a perfect fit, and you look gorgeous. It was made for you."

Then he noticed Amanda frantically dipping a dish towel in cold water and wiping at the bodice of the dress. He sauntered over to get a closer view of her almost hysterical actions. "Aha! Now you *have* to take it. I'm afraid the store won't take a returned dress with rabbit gravy splattered on it."

He was doing his best to make light of the situation, even though he was hurt by her rejection of his gift. It was only a damned dress, after all. Wasn't as if he were trying to bargain for her soul. Then he saw the moisture staining her cheeks and felt it drip on his hand as he took the cloth from her shaking fingers. As he lifted her chin to look into her face, his heart skipped a beat, then took off like a runaway horse when he saw the forlorn expression she tried so hard to conceal.

He thought he would gladly lay down and stick a knife through his ribs when she spoke again. "It's ruined. The beautiful dress is ruined. I should never have put it on." His heart bled when she buried her face in her hands and her shoulders began to shake.

"Shush, now. It's not ruined. It was an accident. I'm the one who slung the stew. I didn't realize the spoon was full when I turned."

"I-I'm not used to such fancy clothes. I—"

"Fancy? That's not fancy. It's just a pretty, everyday kinda dress. Why, sweetheart, someday I'll show you fancy. I promise."

Ry pulled Amanda into his arms and hugged her until she relaxed and leaned against him. Then he took her hand and led her to the bucket. He still held the damp cloth, and he wet it one more time as he wiped at the final stain located on the material covering her right breast. Gently, he touched the cloth to the stain and dabbed with soft, circular motions.

He didn't realize what he was doing until he heard Amanda gasp and his eyes locked hungrily on the hard tip of her nipple pushing out the soft fabric. When he raised his eyes and met hers, they were round and luminous, filled with question.

This definitely was not the time for amorous seduction. "There you go; the stains are all gone. But I'm certain the storekeeper won't take it back now. Guess you're stuck with it." He chucked her under the chin and turned her toward the table. "Go on and set the table. The way the stew splattered all over everything, I'd say it was tender. I hereby proclaim the meal ready to be devoured."

All of a sudden, Ryder was inexplicably happy and content. Things hadn't exactly gone as planned; but he was certain now that she would keep the dress, and they had a nice, long evening ahead. Life was all right, sometimes.

"I don't know about you, woman, but I'm starved."

Mandy worked up a smile as she again fingered the material of her new dress. And it was her dress. She couldn't see anything *too* wrong in accepting it. She might as well give in and enjoy it. It might be the only thing she'd have to remember Ryder by.

"Then why don't *you* set the table while I stir up some biscuits. A growing boy like you needs to keep up his strength."

When Ryder laughed and winked at her, she realized what she'd just suggested and blushed from the tips of her toes clear to the roots of her hair.

"Well, get after it, sweetheart. I'm wastin' away."

Jeremy and Reno sat around a small campfire, watching as their beans heated over the flames. Jerky and cold biscuits comprised the rest of their meager fare.

"One of these days, one of us is goin' to have to learn how to cook." The younger brother reached

256

over to give the pan a shake, then swirled the contents.

"We're doin' okay. Hopefully we won't have to dine out much longer." Reno picked a rock from under his ground tarp and threw it into the underbrush. "What a time to get careless. Our last run, bringin' in the cream of the crop, and now it's all for nothin', thanks to our friend Hank Ford."

"At least we've got a lead on 'em. Pa said he saw Hank and his cousin Ed headin' this direction, leadin' a bunch of horses. Maybe we'll cut their trail tomorrow."

"God, I hope so. If they've done anything to hurt that black stallion, so help me, I'll make them wish they'd never laid eyes on that string of horses. I was countin' on that stud to be the foundation for our breedin' stock. Damn, Jer, how could I have been so stupid?"

Jeremy poked a long stick into the fire and stirred the embers. "It wasn't all your fault. If it hadn't been for Hank takin' off with Mandy Jo, I'd have been there to help you move the animals. There were too many for just one person to handle. Hey! Do ya think his grabbin' Mandy was a ruse to get our attention away from you and the string?"

Reno leaned back on his elbows and stretched his legs in front of him. "Don't kid yourself, little brother. The bastard wants Mandy. Wants her bad. But you've got a point. The two incidents couldn't have been coincidences. He had to have it all planned . . . with the exception of our man Manning."

Jeremy poked the end of his stick into the loose dirt and grumbled, "No matter what he's done, we were lucky he turned up when he did, weren't we?"

Reno gave a dubious snort but failed to respond

with anything to say in Ryder's favor.

The youngster cleared his throat, but his voice cracked anyway when he asked, "We aren't goin' ta be able ta make that last payment, are we?"

"Damn, Jer, quit askin' questions I don't have any answers for. We've still got seven days. If we can manage to get our horses back and trail them to the fort in a week's time, we might have a chance. If not . . ."

The brothers ate in silence, both lost in their own thoughts until Jeremy piped up. "We can do it, Reno. I know we can. We've gone through too much, come too far, ta let that scum ruin things now."

"I hope you're right. We've worked our tails off for a chance to make a new start, but it doesn't look like it'll make a bit of difference as far as Mandy's concerned. She won't go with us. You should've seen how upset she got when I mentioned leaving the farm. Some surprise, huh?"

"She'll come around. All she needs is a little time ta think about it. Remember? I felt the same way when you first came ta me with your ideas."

Reno chuckled. "Yeah, you said if a four-legged beast of burden didn't have long ears and a short back, you wouldn't know how to handle it. But I must admit, squirt, you've held up your end, and then some."

"Aw, shucks, t'weren't nothin'. You were the brains behind the deal. Contractin' with the Army to furnish all those remounts. But how was I to know you were goin' ta use wild horses?"

"But little brother, how else could poor folks like us come up with that many horses?"

"Okay. Okay. Ya did good."

Reno's face was sober and his voice hoarse when he told his brother, "So did you, Jer. Now, cut the jawin' and get some sleep. Mornin's goin' to come early."

The two turned in after Reno added more wood to the fire. The night was clear, and sounds seemed magnified as they heard the muffled munching of their hobbled mounts amid the chirruping of crickets and an occasional hoot from a nearby owl.

"Reno? You asleep?"

"Huh? Uh, not yet. What?"

"I was wonderin'. . . . You ever been west of the Territory?"

Reno yawned. "No, can't say that I have."

The young man's voice sounded almost childlike as he asked, "Are you afraid, Reno? I mean, we're just pickin' up and headin' out, to a place we've never even seen."

The woods came alive again during the long silence before Reno finally answered. "Yeah, squirt, I'm afraid. But I can hardly wait to get there."

Chapter Fourteen

Mandy yawned and stretched. What a beautiful morning. A smile creased her cheeks as she thought about the evening she and Ry had shared. After supper, he'd helped clean up the kitchen, almost as if he hadn't wanted to let her out of his sight. Then they'd gone into the living room, and he'd built a fire in the fireplace. They'd watched the flames for a while in easy, companionable silence before she answered some of his questions about her life on the farm.

Only now did it dawn on her that he'd never said a word about his own life. Of course, she'd been too nervous and cautious about what she'd been saying, that she'd never thought to ask him. She wouldn't overlook it next time.

And then . . . Ryder had kissed her, walked her to her bedroom door, kissed her again . . . and left. She remembered standing in her door, gaping after him, wondering what she could've done to turn him away. But when he'd stopped at the end of the hall and turned to look back, he'd flashed that brilliant, disarming smile and touched his fingers to his forehead in a jaunty salute, while she literally melted inside.

As Mandy walked a little timidly toward the barn, she had an uneasy feeling in the pit of her stomach. Maybe he'd had second thoughts about giving her the dress. Or . . . oh, God . . . had he tired of her so soon? But, no, his eyes had told her different.

Ry forked hay from the loft into his horse's manger. He was stiff and sore this morning from a long night of tossing and turning. Leaving Amanda had been the hardest thing he'd ever done. When he kissed her for the last time, her eyes had been soft and inviting, tempting him beyond endurance.

As he climbed down the ladder, he wondered for the hundredth time that morning what had brought on his sudden and unexpected attack of conscience. His only explanation was the dress. It was a gift he'd given for the pure pleasure of seeing another person's joy—or so he'd hoped. And he hadn't been disappointed. That is, after her initial refusal.

His reason for leaving the house and not making love to Amanda was entirely unselfish. He didn't want her to love him out of gratitude, thinking she *had* to make love in payment for the present. Women were funny that way. And now, this morning, he was suffering the aches and pains of the damned. He was damned if he *did*, and damned if he didn't.

If he was entirely truthful of the situation, he'd also abstained in consideration of Amanda and her relationship with her brothers. He was putting an undue strain on her as it was, and wasn't about to get caught with his pants down, so to speak, again. If and when they came together again, it would be where there wouldn't be any fear of recrimination from family or friends.

Ry was so caught up in his thoughts and with cleaning the stall that he didn't hear Mandy enter the barn. She silently watched as he forked manure into a pile, and lustfully eyed the way his muscles bunched and strained against the tight seams of the clean white shirt he was wearing.

When he turned toward her, she saw that the shirt was unbuttoned. The black hairs on his chest actually sparkled when a beam of light played across the rounded contours of his torso. Almost unwillingly, she felt drawn, as if by a magnetic force. Her eyes raised slowly and were immediately locked into a heated exchange with his gleaming black ones.

Mandy blushed and lowered her lashes, unable to meet the probing gaze. How long had he been watching her? Had he noticed the greedy way she'd been perusing his golden body? How embarrassing.

"Good morning, sweetheart. Sleep well?"

At least he'd called her sweetheart. That was encouraging. "Morning. Oh yes, I slept like a baby. Why, I never knew when my head hit the pillow," she blatantly lied.

"Me, too. Must've been the big meal."

"It was good, wasn't it?" She watched the way his fingers split his hair into four furrows, missing the wayward strand that continued to tease his brow. How she longed to put the errant lock in its place. She wanted to touch his lips and run her hand over his broad chest and lean ribs. She wanted . . . to love him. But she was uncertain of his reaction, so calmly stood her ground.

Ry watched as Amanda nervously licked her lips and turned to look out the broken window. He'd made the right decision. She was uneasy with him, probably wondering when he was going to ask her to return the favor of the gift. And that was fine. He'd

262

just show her that he didn't want anything from her that she didn't want to give, and give freely.

He amazed himself. He wanted something from this girl-woman that he'd never looked for before. He was asking for her commitment, maybe even her love.

It didn't seem to matter anymore who she was, or who she was related to. He had been wrong to think she could be anything like her cousin, to think she might have been involved in any crimes. She might act on impulse to save a family member's life, but she could never participate in a premediated wrong doing. And thanks, or no thanks, to Amanda Jo Coulter, even the importance of his assignment seemed to be diminishing in terms of priority.

Except he was worried about Reno and Jeremy. Why did they disappear so often? Why had Reno been shot? And what was the real reason behind Jeremy's arrest? Even though he didn't much care for Sheriff Pomeroy, was the man acting solely for purposes of revenge, or was Jeremy actually up to no good?

If he was going to do any serious thinking about a continuing relationship with Amanda, he was going to have to find the answers to the questions that kept nagging at him. And whether he liked it or not, that included his suspicions about the validity of Jesse James's death and Amanda's possible involvement in it.

Ry leaned the pitchfork against the stall and started brushing his mustang. The horse turned his head and rolled his near eye as if to say "a little higher," then returned to munching his hay with a contented sigh.

The deputy never looked up from his chore as he asked her, "Where are your brothers? I expected them both home last night."

Mandy chewed on a fingernail. Was that why he hadn't stayed with her last night? Because of her brothers? No, Ryder wasn't the type to be afraid of an angry brother, even though *she* was. A little angrily, she replied, "I don't know where my brothers are. I *never* know where they are."

Ry looked up, surprised at her outburst.

She met his eyes defiantly and added, "They're big boys now. They don't have to answer to me or anyone else." Her shoulders suddenly sagged, and her eyes broke their contact with Ryder's to stare fixedly at a beetle stoically working its way up, down and through stray pieces of hay. "At least that's what they tell me."

"Maybe they've got girlfriends they stay with."

"Well, maybe. But they must live a long way off."

Ry leaned against one of the barn's support posts but literally jumped away when it groaned a protest. He hated to think it, but the boys' long absences were certainly suspicious. And another reason he was here was to investigate the rash of robberies in the Liberty and St. Joseph areas.

"They'll turn up." And when they did, they'd not get away from him so easily again. "I'm just surprised they both took off . . . after yesterday." Damn, why'd he have to bring that up?

Mandy ducked her head, then straightened her shoulders and looked him in the eye. No, she'd not be ashamed of herself or her brothers. They'd only been trying to protect her, yet she knew it would do no good. How could they protect her from herself?

She'd enjoyed every precious moment spent in Ryder's arms and wished to spend many more. She shook her head. From his actions last evening and his standoffish behavior this morning, she'd do better to

264

just treasure her memories, for they were likely all she'd ever have.

Reno and Jeremy followed a set of tracks on the ridge opposite Jesse's cave. In fact, if they'd but known, their cousin had been watching their movement, or lack of it, all morning. The boys were disgusted that they hadn't been able to make better progress because of the hard, almost solid rock terrain.

Reno, especially, prided himself on his ability to track anything or anyone, but today, he was beginning to have doubts. "At this rate, the horses'll be too old to handle by the time we catch up with them."

Jeremy untied the scarf from his neck and wiped the sweat from his face with the dry ends. "Ain't it the truth." He stood on a flat rock and looked slowly and carefully at the bits of forest, wide-mouthed gullies and deceptive ridges. "Let's not get in too big a hurry, big brother. I'd like to live long enough to see that new ranch. I've got a strange feeling, like we're being watched, or something."

Reno tied his horse in the shade of a nearby tree and took a long drink from his canteen. "I'm glad you feel it, too. For a minute there, I thought I might be going crazy from the heat."

In an effort to relieve the tension, Jeremy laughed and joked, "You're crazy, all right, but don't try to blame it on the weather."

Before Reno could make a comeback, Jeremy's horse raised its head and cocked its ears. The men immediately fell silent and listened . . . waiting. The sound of metal striking rock could be heard in the distance.

They were stopped just a few feet short of a sloping ravine, so they carefully led their mounts down to the bottom. They secured the animals and covered their nostrils with their kerchiefs so the horses couldn't nicker and announce their presence.

Then they crawled back up the slope and hid behind a stand of scrub oak. Reno took off his hat and raised his head when the approaching sounds came close to their position. He dropped back down and put a hand on Jeremy's shoulder to keep him low and out of sight.

He whispered, "It's Hank. Ed and another man I don't know are with him."

The boys remained hidden until they could no longer hear any sound of the three riders. "Well, we were sure on the right track." Jeremy looked to Reno. "What do we do now?"

"They've made our job a bit easier by leaving a fresh trail. We'll just backtrack them. I'm curious as to where they've been."

The new trail sped things considerably. A little less than two hours later they were looking into a small valley that boasted a well-constructed log cabin and a set of corrals. To the right of the corrals was a creek that had been damned to allow a good-sized pond to form.

As they moved in closer, they counted almost thirty head of horses in the pens. "There they are, Jer. There's our final payment standin' in those corrals."

Jeremy looked at the horses, then to his brother. "Yep, let's go get 'em." He was about to let out a loud whoop until Reno grabbed his arm and put his hand over the younger boy's mouth.

"Hold it. Not so fast. We're still missin' about twenty head."

Jeremy nodded and moved Reno's hand. "Sorry,

just got a little excited.'' As he gazed down into the corrals, he said, "Yeah, and the black stallion's not there. So, what's the plan?''

"Give me a minute, I'm thinkin'.''

After tying their horses out of sight, they picked a good location to watch over the valley. Reno chewed thoughtfully on a blade of grass, then rested his head against a tree trunk. "The way I see it, Hank's got the rest of the horses hidden out somewhere else, but he's gradually bringing them here. Shucks, if we hadn't lucked out, we might never have found this place, so let's do it the lazy way—wait 'em out. Let 'em bring the horses to us and then make our play.''

Jeremy leaned back in the grass, his head resting in the palms of his hands. "Sure beats traipsin' back and forth through the woods and missin' 'em altogether, which'd be just our luck.''

"Hey, give me a little credit, would you? I could find 'em if I had to.''

"Aw, c'mon, I was just kiddin'. But seriously, how're we goin' to pull this off? Hank had two men with him, and there's at least two down at that cabin.''

Sure enough, a man came out of the door and threw a pan of water to the side of the cabin. Another was on his way back to the cabin after making a turn around the corrals. A rifle was cradled in his arms.

Reno slowly shook his head. "And there's got to be more watching the rest of the horses, wherever they are.''

Each brother looked at his respective pistol and gunbelt, then at the small sack of supplies hanging on Jeremy's saddle horn. "It doesn't look good, huh, big brother?''

"We are definitely underprepared. But it'll take Hank at least a day and a half to get back. We can make a run for ammo and supplies and still make it back here before he does."

"You go, Reno. I'll stay here and keep an eye on things. There's plenty of food left for just one."

"I don't know, Jer."

"Well, I do. I'm not a baby anymore. You can trust me."

"Jer, I do trust *you*, you idiot. It's those guys I worry about." Reno pointed toward the cabin and the rifle-toting outlaw. "I don't like the idea of leaving you alone."

Jeremy sat up and looked his older brother straight in the eye. "I can handle it."

Even though he wanted to argue, Reno remembered Mandy talking about how Jeremy was trying so hard, almost too hard, to become an adult. How he wished his sister were here now.

"You're sure that's what you want to do?"

For the first time, Jeremy smiled. "I'm positive. I won't let you down, Reno."

Reno put his hand on Jeremy's shoulder and squeezed. "I know you won't, squirt. But don't take any chances. Just stay right here and watch the place. That's all, you hear?"

Jeremy stood up and gave his brother a hug. "I will. And you be careful, too. I got a real strange feeling a while ago." Then, as if embarrassed by his childish display of emotion, he stepped away from Reno and crammed his hands into his pockets. "Take care."

As Reno mounted his pony, he waved and called, "Who knows, maybe it was our guardian angel just checking in."

Mandy worried about her brothers all day. She

didn't like the idea of Ryder quizzing her about their whereabouts. Why was he checking up on them? Did he think they were somehow connected to Jesse, or his gang? One thing she knew for certain; if she didn't get her mind off these worries, she'd wind up in an early grave herself.

She hadn't seen Ryder since lunch. He'd said he needed to clean his saddle and gear, but she knew he was trying to avoid being close to her. Darn him. If he was testing her, to see if she would go chasing after him, he would find himself awfully lonely before she would lower herself to such degrading behavior. Yet!

When she looked out the window and saw him walking toward the house, butterflies started fluttering against the walls of her stomach.

"Hello. Want some lemonade?"

Ryder's mouth watered as he thought about the offer. He was trying his damndest to give Amanda some room, but every time he saw her, his hands twitched and automatically reached for her. Could he calmly sit next to her and resist the temptation to take her in his arms? Ah, he could do anything for a tall glass of homemade lemonade.

"Do you really have lemonade? You're not just teasin' a poor ole country boy?"

"One never knows, does one? But yes, I made fresh lemonade. I've had the lemons stored in the cellar. My, uh, cousin always used to bring them. I don't know where he got them all."

Ryder figured he stole them, more than likely. Then he remembered he'd promised himself that he wasn't going to do that anymore. But, he corrected himself, he had made the promise about Amanda, not her cousin.

Ryder took a long drink of the tangy sweet liquid. "God, that's good."

Mandy drank in the sight of her lawman—the way his hair attractively plastered to his head, the drops of perspiration that trickled in tiny rivulets down his sideburns—but when he looked at her, she shyly lowered her lashes and stared at her own glass. "Thank you. I used to watch my mother make it a long time ago. We'd have it as a treat for special occasions."

Ry grinned. "Is this a special occasion, then?"

She rubbed her hands together and then down the sides of her dress. She'd changed clothes again. "Well, let's just say I wanted to do something nice for you."

Uh oh. Ry quickly changed the subject. "Whatever happened to your mother?"

She swallowed and shifted her gaze out the window. "I don't know."

Ry was surprised. She'd said her mother had left, but he figured the woman would've stayed somewhere close. "Didn't anyone ever try to find her?"

"Oh, Jesse said he'd keep his eyes and ears open, but he never ran across her; and that's as far as it went. Pa, well, you've seen Pa. He always thought she'd come back, and he kept the place up pretty good for a while. Then he just sorta gave up. Reno guessed that it was his pride that kept him from going after her."

"What about you? Did you miss her?"

Mandy snorted. "What kind of question is that? Of course, I missed her." She rubbed her nose and sniffed. "But I guess I suffer from an overdose of pride, too, 'cause I'll never go looking for her."

Ry sensed the underlying pain and hurt she must have suffered as as young girl growing up, responsible for a father and two brothers. His respect and admiration for her swelled until he felt his chest would burst.

"That's a shame. Your mother's missed getting to know a mighty fine woman."

Mandy's face glowed from the sincerity she heard in his voice, but she was gratefully saved from having to make some embarrassing reply by the sound of an approaching rider. She went to the window and looked out just as Reno swung out of the saddle. "It's Reno."

She didn't say so out loud, but Mandy was worried when she saw the exhausted, lathered horse. And there was no sign of Jeremy. She left Ryder as he was finishing the last of his lemonade and went to her brother.

Wiping the frown from her face, she cheerily asked, "Want some lemonade? I just made a fresh pitcher."

Reno gave her a blank stare. "Hi, sis. Did you say something?"

"Yes, I asked if you wanted some lemonade. What's wrong, Reno? You look tired."

"I am, a little. What makes you think something's wrong? I just came by to pick up a few things."

Now Mandy was really worried. Reno wouldn't meet her eyes, and she'd never seen him ride his horse so hard. "Are you leaving then, so soon?"

Reno was busy unsaddling his heaving horse. "Yeah, but not 'til the morning. I've got to gather up some supplies and give old Feller here a chance to rest."

As he led the horse into the barn and began to rub the animal down with dry hay, he looked over his shoulder at Mandy. "Where's Manning? I thought he was going to come back to work."

"He did. He's in the kitchen drinking some of that lemonade I mentioned—twice."

Reno chuckled and gave his horse's rear a slap as

271

he urged Feller into a stall. "Sorry about that. Guess I've got too many things on my mind."

"Care to share them?"

He studied his sister for a long time before answering. "Not right now. But soon. Jer and I'll have a surprise for you."

"For me? What kind of surprise? Wait! Jeremy? You've seen Jeremy?"

"Yeah, just left him. That's why I need supplies. That gangling monster'll eat you out of a week's supply of food in no time."

She giggled. "Tell me about it. The other morning he ate a dozen biscuits, that I know of, plus eight eggs, and drowned the whole lot with a tub of gravy. Where is he, Reno? Why didn't he come back with you?" Was he still upset with her? Would he stay away as long as Ryder was around?

Reno put his arm around Mandy's shoulders and led her toward the house. Suddenly, he moved his hand up and down her arm. "Hey, what's this? Why, Mandy, what a pretty dress." His eyes ran over her figure as if he couldn't believe what he was seeing. "You're beautiful, sis."

She ducked her head and pulled away from his arm. "Cut it out, brother dear. You act like you've never seen me in a dress before."

"My God, Mandy, it's been years. Ouch!"

"Now go on, and tell me about Jeremy."

Reno rubbed his shin as he hopped along next to Mandy, and he continued to cast appreciative glances in her direction. "Jeremy's testing his wings. But don't worry about him. I'll keep an eye on him. Let's go get some of that lemonade you've been harpin' on."

Mandy went peaceable but cocked a wary eye toward her older brother. So, he would watch after

Jeremy. That's exactly what she'd been afraid of.

Ryder was still seated at the kitchen table. "I helped myself to another glass. Howdy, Reno."

Reno glanced back and forth between his sister and Ryder. He picked up on a connection between the new dress, Mandy's pink complexion and Ryder's proprietary air toward her. For now, it was good.

"Yeah, howdy. I see you came back."

With an accusatory glare at Reno, Ry said, "It's a good thing, too. Otherwise your sister would've been here all alone last night."

Anger flashed in Reno's eyes, but he controlled himself. "Well, that shouldn't have been too disappointing. I'm sure you found some way to keep her . . . entertained." He looked knowingly at the dress and raised his eyebrow.

Mandy's face flushed crimson. "Reno! How could you?" But she didn't know if she was more upset over her brother's words, or the fact that Ryder hadn't seemed the least bit interested in entertaining her last night.

"I'm sorry, Mandy. I didn't mean that. It was stupid of me not to think of the danger of leaving you here alone all night."

"I could've taken care of myself. In fact, I did. Here's your lemonade." She handed him a glass, and with a disdainful look at Ryder, poured more for herself.

Ryder had been upset that both Reno and Jeremy had deserted the farm with the threat of Hank Ford hanging over their sister's head. "What if I'd stayed in town last night and come out this morning? What if your Mr. Ford had decided to come courting?"

Reno didn't think before he jumped in to answer, "Don't worry about Hank. He's real busy right now."

"Oh? You've seen him, then? Is he around here?"

"Uh, well, I don't rightly know where he is." That was the truth. "I, er, just heard that he had his hands full with a herd of horses." And that was mostly true.

"That's interesting. I wonder how he got involved with horses? I thought he was just a two-bit thief."

Reno's eyes flashed. "He stole 'em, the bastard. He's nothin' but a low down dry—" He stopped and took a gulp of lemonade, wishing fervently that it was some of his pa's shine.

Ryder had been studying Reno intently. The man wasn't telling everything he knew. Evidently he wasn't worried about Hank Ford coming after Amanda anytime soon. Why? And what was Reno's connection with the stolen horses?

Reno stood up abruptly, causing his chair to scrape across the floor. "Excuse me. I'm going to go rest for a while. Wake me for supper, will ya, Mandy?"

Mandy had silently watched the exchange between Reno and Ryder. She didn't like the way Ryder looked at her brother. His eyes were hooded, and his mouth was drawn in a grim line. And then there was Reno, acting so mysteriously—what was he up to?

For her brother's and Jesse's sakes, she had to find out just what Ryder knew. She'd have to search his saddlebags, and soon. "I'll wake you. And I'll look at Feller for you pretty soon."

"Thanks." Reno stepped toward his sister and kissed her on the cheek.

Several minutes must've passed since Reno left the room, but still she sat at the table with her fingers touching her face. How long had it been since her brother had kissed her?

*　　　*　　　*

Ry rocked back and forth in the chair in the living room. Amanda had called to her brother, and now he could hear the man rummaging through his room. It sounded like an extra pair of boots had just hit the floor, and a dresser drawer slammed shut.

Curiosity was about to send Ryder down the hall when Reno's bedroom door opened and the man himself stepped out carrying a large bedroll and holding a lever-action Winchester .44-40 rifle.

"Looks like you're leaving us again."

Reno jumped. He hadn't seen Manning sitting in the corner. "Yeah, I'm goin' on a business trip. Won't be gone long."

"Must be a dangerous one." Ryder had just noticed the extra cartridge belt slung over the boy's shoulder and the knife scabbard tied to the roll. What else was hidden under the layers of bedding? A small arsenal?

"Just being careful, is all. Never know who you'll run into these days."

"Here, let me give you a hand." Ry stood up and moved toward Reno with his hand out.

Reno shied away. "Uh, no. Thanks anyway, but I can carry it all fine. If you unbalance me, I'll have to repack everything. Is supper about ready?"

"I imagine so. I got run out of the kitchen a few minutes ago."

"Well, let's find out. My belly thinks my throat's been cut."

"I'm right behind you." And that's exactly where Ry intended to be whenever Reno decided to cut and run.

It was well after midnight when Reno made his move. He'd managed to get Mandy alone earlier and had said his goodbyes, telling her he'd be on his way

275

before daylight. He'd convinced her, he hoped, that Jeremy was all right and that they really did have business to take care of. She hadn't been at all pleased by his secretiveness, but he finally appeased her by promising that they'd both be home within the week. And they might—give or take a few days.

He quickly saddled Feller, glad to see that the horse was rested and rarin' to go. At the last minute, he decided to take old Zeke. The mule might come in handy when, and if, they retrieved the horses.

A pair of dark eyes glittered from the shadows of the porch, and as Reno rode toward the hill behind the house, the red glow of an inhaled cheroot flipped in the air, arched and buried itself in the dust. Silent, moccasined feet padded across the clearing and faded to the far side of the barn where an already saddled mustang waited.

Chapter Fifteen

The old rooster had to be just outside Mandy's room when he let loose a little before dawn. She stretched and rolled over, wishing for a false alarm, but the old buzzard was too reliable to be mistaken. Besides, the silence of the place was deafening, and she tossed and turned until her nightgown was wound so uncomfortably around her body that she had to get up.

She threw a robe over her shoulders and hurried to the kitchen to start the stove. Unable to do anything more than pick at her food the evening before as she sat between the two silent, hostile men, she was ravenous this morning.

As she stoked the fire to life, she decided to go ahead and throw some grounds into water for coffee. The much needed eye-opener would be made by the time she was dressed.

Walking back down the hall, she stopped outside of Reno's room. The rumpled bed was the only evidence of her brother's occupancy. She only hoped that whatever he and Jeremy were up to, they'd be safe and stay out of trouble. Turning to go on to her own room, a dark object caught her attention on the floor by the window.

It couldn't be! She hesitantly entered the room and stood in the middle of the floor. But it was. Ryder's saddlebags were in the same place he'd left them last week. Mandy put a hand to her chest in an effort to contain the rapid flutering of her heart. She looked around the room, out the window and down the hall. Did she dare?

The moment of indecision passed quickly as she remembered the promise she'd made to Jesse. She didn't have any choice. It had to be done. With determined resolve she marched to the bags and lifted them onto Reno's bed.

The strings on one side were already loose, so she opened the flap. She looked over her shoulder at the door, then stuck her hand into the compartment. It held a few articles of clothing and small packs of herbs like the ones he'd used on Reno's wound. That was all. No, there was a box of ammunition and some beef jerky.

Her hands shook as she tried to loosen the strings on the last bag, but after a few fumbling attempts, the flap was undone. She took a deep breath and carefully reached inside. There was a stack of wanted posters, and right on top was one offering a reward of five thousand dollars each for Frank and Jesse James—dead or alive. The descriptions of the two men were so outlandish that Mandy had no choice but to collapse onto the bed in a fit of giggles.

She quickly sobered, though, when a telegram floated from between the flyers to land face up on her lap. It was to the U.S. Marshal's office from a police district in St. Louis. The message briefly directed that Jesse's body be examined for any scars not previously noted. One of the district's officers claimed to have allegedly wounded the outlaw in a running gun

278

battle during the month of September, 1874.

Mandy's already strained heart plummeted to her roiling stomach. This was precisely what Jesse had feared. She chewed on her fingernail as her foot tapped a staccato rhythm on the floorboards. This didn't prove a thing. Jesse had so many scars on his body that one more couldn't prove or disprove his identity. Besides, the body was buried now, and there had been no outcry of suspicion either before or after the funeral. So what was Ryder up to?

Did he seriously suspect a hoax? Or was he working on hunches? Was he even there for the purpose she suspected? Maybe he was after Reno, or even Jeremy.

Mandy jumped to her feet and stuffed the telegram and posters back into the bag, then replaced it where she'd found it under the window. She had to get to Jesse with this information—fast.

Traveling at night was always slow going, especially when you were trying to follow someone and still stay far enough behind to remain undetected. Ryder rubbed a hand over his eyes and slumped in the saddle. Damn, but he was exhausted, and his eyes burned from the strain of trying to see through the wall of darkness. Where was the moon when you needed it?

He dismounted and loosened the cinch on the saddle to give his mustang a breather. There was no sense in glossing over the details—he'd lost Reno. Somewhere along the last creek bed, or over that ridge, or through that stand of trees, he'd lost the trail. Now he'd have to wait until daylight and backtrack.

How he wished he'd brought his saddlebags, but

instead, he'd packed light and had just tied on a blanket, an extra revolver and a few supplies. In utter frustration, and with nothing better to do, he pulled out a piece of venison jerky and methodically worked the hard slab with his mouth until he was able to chew it. He'd never liked jerky much, but it was sustaining and better than nothing at all.

Ry hobbled his horse to allow him to graze on the meager clumps of grass, then spread the blanket. As he tossed rocks and small branches from under his protesting body, he was grateful that it wasn't long until morning.

Reno kept a steady pace all night. At one time, he'd thought he heard someone following him, but when he took a switchback up the hill a little later and stopped to listen, he never heard another sound other than the yowl of a bobcat or the skitterings of tiny night creatures.

He hadn't waited for long because he was in a hurry. He'd had a premonition that something was wrong. No telling what, exactly, or why, but he knew. And it had something to do with Jeremy.

Having this sixth sense bothered Reno. Too many times he'd seen into the future, and it was scary. If anything had happened to his little brother, it would be all his fault for leaving him alone. But short of beating Jer over the head and dragging him off, what could he have done differently? When he'd been that age, he'd had the same cocky stubbornness, and no one could've told him what to do, either.

Even the heavy rationalizing didn't help dispell Reno's sense of foreboding. He just pushed Feller and Zeke harder.

*　　　*　　　*

280

By mid-morning Mandy was over halfway to Jesse's cave. Red Fox had fairly flown through the sparse patches of open ground but was now picking his way slowly up a rocky incline. She had taken what she thought was a short cut, but in all actuality, she was approaching the hideout from the north instead of her usual western direction. The country was much less familiar, but she could still see the top of the escarpment that marked Jesse's whereabouts.

She no sooner topped the slope and pulled Red Fox up to allow the horse to catch his breath than she heard the squeaking of saddle leather and the clopping of horse's hooves directly below her location. A familiar voice spoke, and chills ran down her spine.

"We're almost there, boys. Only one more trip and we can sell the beasts to the nearest glue factory."

Hank's cousin Ed was curious. "What about that big black devil, Hank? Ya gonna sell him, are ya?"

Hank let out an evil sounding laugh. "No way. That monster is mine. I'm going to get a lot of pleasure out of breaking that animal."

Mandy finally got a clear view of Hank and noticed he was rubbing his left arm, which was bound in a make-shift sling.

One of the other riders said, "Yore gonna larn 'im a thang of two fer fightin' ya back, ain'tcha, Hank?"

"You got that right, Simon. I aim to teach him a lesson he'll never forget."

As the outlaws passed from view, Mandy put a hand on Red Fox's mane to calm his nervous prancing. A shudder racked her body as she commiserated the fate of the poor animal Hank and his boys were discussing, or cussing, however you wanted to look at it. From firsthand experience, she knew that Hank had a cruel streak in him that wouldn't quit.

The urgency of her quest shifted as she considered the options of either going to Jesse or following Hank. As she saw the riders top the next crest, she remembered Reno's story of Hank and his involvement with stolen horses. Each of the men was leading two to three horses, depending on the docility of the animals. Where had the horses come from? And more important, where were they taking them?

Hank's uncle's place! It was around here someplace. Even Jesse had figured that much out. Then she thought about how upset Reno had been when talking about the horses. Could the stolen herd have anything to do with her brother's business trip? Knowing Reno's penchant for horses, she wouldn't be a bit surprised.

Without even realizing her decision had been made, she and Red Fox wound down to the gully. She could easily read Hank's trail, so they hung back a little, not at all anxious to be discovered by the group of hardcases.

Jeremy was fit to be tied. At least he was angry enough to throw a fit. He was already tied, hand and foot. And gagged. Why hadn't he realized there might've been a third man posted as a lookout somewhere close to the cabin? Of course, any tenderfoot could've picked him out when he slipped on a loose rock and rolled down the slope away from the camp. Nothing was hurt, except his pride.

And they didn't know about Reno. His brother was due back sometime today. All Jeremy could hope for was that Reno made it back before Hank. No telling what Hank would do when he found out that a Coulter had been spying on them. No one would be safe. Especially Pa . . . and Mandy.

Jeremy fought the ropes around his wrists one

more time but only succeeded in cutting into his flesh even deeper than before. He felt like such a fool, bragging about how grown up he was and how he could handle the situation. He'd never be trusted again. What a doggone mess he'd made of everything.

Ryder couldn't believe it. He couldn't pick up Reno's trail. His grandfather would laugh him out of the Territory if he ever found out. And he would. Ry would tell him himself he next time he went home.

He lifted his hat, combed his fingers through his hair and wiped the sweat from his forehead. He didn't know if the extra heat was generated by the sun or from acute embarrassment. He'd been riding through these hills for what seemed like days now, when in truth it was barely mid-morning.

He dismounted and led his horse to the creek to drink while he splashed the cool, refreshing water on his face and neck. Home! He hadn't been back for years, but he'd sent almost every penny of any paycheck he'd ever earned back to his family.

The Southerners here in Missouri griped and complained about their trials and tribulations following the war, but no one realized that the Cherokee in Indian Territory had been persecuted just as badly. At least these people were free to move on; his people were confined to a reservation and left with little choice as to what to do with their lives.

Ry took his gun out of his holster and checked the loads. For precaution's sake, he filled the chamber usually left empty under the hammer in case of an unforeseen accident. He leaned his arm against the saddle as he remembered the day the Army threw his family off their land for owning slaves.

They'd lost everything. And the worst part was

that the old Negro who farmed with his grandfather was a free man, paid for his labor. But the officer in charge wouldn't take the time or the patience to listen. He'd used the age old excuse of following orders. Of course, there were Cherokees who openly sided with the South and who'd held slaves. No one tried to deny that. But to indiscriminately take back such a large portion of the Cherokee land. . . . No one said life was fair.

Ry had been lucky. Thanks to his white father's encouragement, he'd been able to get away from the reservation and had then helped his grandfather rebuild over the years. Now he was making a new life of his own, far from the hatred and prejudices still so tenderly cultivated and nurtured. Would people never learn?

Ry mentally shook himself. It was time to move on. He could stand here all day and dream about his land and ponder the stupidity of man, but he still needed to find Reno.

He rode out of the creek bed and up the nearest slope in order to look over the countryside. Reno couldn't just disappear. However, what he encountered was startling. Instead of one man leading a mule, he found several riders leading a string of horses. They were a tough-looking bunch, with hats pulled low over their faces, and most of them wore scraggly beards and long mustaches.

They appeared trail worn and half asleep as they rode single file through the gully, but Ryder didn't doubt for a minute that they were alert and ready for anything under the layers of dirt and grime. He backed his horse below the top of the ridge so he wouldn't be outlined when they rode in front of his position.

As they neared, he recognized two of the riders as the men who'd inspected the horses during the storm the night he rescued Amanda from Hank Ford's clutches. The biggest man, riding lead, fit Amanda's description of the desperado quite accurately.

When Ry recalled his and Reno's conversation concerning Hank and stolen horses, everything fell into place. Evidently, Reno had known where they were keeping the animals or he wouldn't have ridden in this direction. Either that, or he was out hunting the horses, too. But what reason would Reno have for trailing a herd of stolen horses?

It seemed the only logical thing to do was to follow Hank and find out if his assumptions were correct. He'd be willing to bet a twenty dollar gold piece that he'd find Reno at the end of Hank's trail.

Keeping to the high side of the ridge, he followed the group, far enough back to keep from being seen or heard. At one point, the riders stopped to water their horses and to relieve themselves. Ry used the time to scan the area for recognizable landmarks. To his right loomed a large, craggy bluff. It was the face of the largest hill in the area and a piece of nature's handiwork that would stand out in one's memory.

The riders remounted and started forward again. Just as Ry swung into the saddle, he thought he heard a noise behind and to the left of the gully. Then, sure enough, he heard it again. Someone was following Hank and his crew. Was it another outlaw? Someone posted to bring up the rear in case of trouble? No, it wasn't likely.

Ryder rode to the opposite side of the ridge and dismounted. Maybe it was Reno, hot on Hank's trail. If so, should he announce his presence and join the man, or just keep following and wait and see what happened?

Mandy rode some distance behind the Ford gang,

moving carefully, taking few chances. She'd been watching the ground, making sure all of the heavier tracks, indicating horses being ridden, stayed in front of her. It was quite by accident that she stopped Red Fox to adjust a twisted rein at the same time she heard movement on the ridge to her right side.

She quickly got off Red Fox and took care to lead the horse over ground as bare of rocks and gravel as possible. A small grove of trees had caught her attention as she'd ridden by and was only a few yards behind, so she hid her mount in their midst. With a pat on the neck for Red Fox, she felt in her pocket for the reassuring contact of cold metal, then stealthily climbed to the top of the ridge. Once she reached flat ground, she knelt behind a large boulder and peeked around it.

There was nothing moving and no sound. Maybe her nerves had made her too edgy and cautious. It could've been a wild animal, after all. No, she definitely heard something now. It was a muted sound, but someone or something had stepped on gravel.

Ahead of her, and to the right, was a large elm tree. If she could sneak that far, she could climb up to get a better view. Thank goodness the weather had been warm and the leaves were full enough to offer cover. So, carefully placing her feet on ground bare of rocks and twigs, she took cover behind any bush or rock available until she reached the tree.

Ry cursed under his breath. He'd been trying to be so careful but had lost his balance and stepped on a bunch of small rocks. He was also worried that he hadn't heard anything more from Reno, or whoever it was following Hank Ford. Had he made too much

286

noise as he concealed his grulla? He hadn't thought so.

But now he needed to find a good vantage point to overlook the creek bed. If he had been lucky enough to go undetected, the man ought to show up soon. It was a good thing there were a lot of brush and trees to use for cover. All he had to do was watch where he stepped, which he'd found out wasn't always easy.

A little to his left was a huge elm that would suit his purposes perfectly, so he moved in that direction. Funny, how still the forest became when a person was trying to be quiet. Every little sound was magnified to screaming proportions. Once he reached the shelter of the tree, though, he could somewhat relax.

Mandy would've sighed with relief after reaching the big tree, but she had a prickling sensation in the back of her neck. Even the air felt electric, as if charged for some catastrophic event.

Disappointment seeped through her when she found all the lower branches still too high for her to reach. She'd have to work her way around to the other side. She put her back to the bark and skillfully maneuvered soundlessly around the base of the elm.

Looking up, she found a branch that would work if she could jump just a few feet. She moved away from the tree slightly and turned with knees bent, ready to leap for the limb. When she made her move, her head rammed into a hard, yet giving object. Her neck felt like it was broken as she tumbled back to earth.

Ry's breath whooshed from his chest when he was hit solidly in the stomach. He doubled over and fell to his knees from the pain of the impact, and before he could recover his breath, he was attacked again. A surprisingly light-weight form attached itself to his back, knocking his hat off and pinning his upper body to the ground.

His arms had been protecting his mid-section but now swung forward to catch the legs that were kicking on either side of his head. With a desperate lunge, he brought his knees forward and stood, dumping his assailant over his back.

Mandy felt herself falling headfirst as she was thrown over the man's shoulders, but she ducked her head and hit the ground with a slightly cushioned impact. Before she could move, or even attempt to get up, she found herself spread-eagled beneath one of Hank's men. She closed her eyes, knowing her time was up. He was too strong for her to fight, and she wouldn't give him the pleasure of seeing her cry or beg for mercy. Whatever happened, she was ready to die like a Coulter.

Still unable to take a good breath, Ry had acted out of sheer willpower and instinctive self-preservation. He had his man immobile beneath him, and even though he was surprised that the fellow didn't make an attempt to free himself, he gratefully buried his face in the sweet-smelling valley between the man's breasts until his own chest quit heaving so uncontrollably.

Suddenly, Ry's head shot up, his mouth hanging open as he gulped in air. The flower-fresh scent, the soft, rounded body, the faded overalls, could only belong to one person. "Good God, Amanda, are you trying to get yourself killed?"

Mandy's eyes flew open. She'd steeled herself against the possibility of death, but at the sound of the familiar, dear voice, husky and breathy as it was, the blood once again surged through her veins until

288

she was certain it would boil out her ears, or through the throbbing in the back of her neck.

"R-Ryder? What're you doing here? I thought you were still asleep in the barn. I-I mean—"

"Yes, I think I know what you mean. I thought you were tucked safely away at home, too. Now, brat, just what're you up to, roaming the hills? Don't you know it's dangerous?"

Mandy thought to herself that, so far, *he* was the most dangerous thing she'd encountered. And she naturally couldn't tell him that she'd been on her way to Jesse to tell him what she'd discovered in Ry's saddlebags. So, what could she say that he'd believe? "Uh, I . . . we . . . I was just exercising Red Fox. After all the activity last week, he's just been standing in the corral the last few days. He was stiff and sore and needed a workout."

Ry was proud of her. With anyone else, that explanation might've worked. "Uh huh, and you just happened to be riding down this particular gully, accidently following Hank Ford?"

Actually, her discovery of Hank *had* been an accident. "Yes, that pretty well says it. But how did you know I was following Hank?"

Ry snorted and ran his hands on either side of her head, threading his fingers through the auburn mass of hair curling around her ears. His body wriggled slightly, and he smiled at the way she squirmed beneath him. One more minute like this and he wouldn't be able to remember his vow to let her make the first move.

"Right now, why I'm here isn't what's important. I'm no fool, sweetheart. You're following that man for a reason, and I want to know what it is."

Only one thing came to mind, the truth. That is, about why she was trailing Hank Ford. "Okay, I'll tell you. I did accidently run across Hank and his gang. When I saw them leading extra horses, I remembered Reno talking about how Hank was supposedly connected to a stolen herd. I wanted to see where he was taking them. That's all. And that's the truth.''

Since that was exactly what had happened to Ry himself, he believed her, kind of.

"What about you? What're you doing out here?" Something was pressing between Mandy's shoulder blades, and she tried to move; but Ryder was too heavy. She was afraid to scoot around too much, afraid that he might be able to tell how much her body longed for his touch, for his caress. Her breasts ached where they made contact with his chest.

Unable to bear the pressure building in his loins from the intimate contact with the irresistable woman, Ry clambered to his feet and pulled Amanda up after him. His eyes narrowed and he cursed when he saw the crumpled mound where she'd been lying.

"Damn, that was a brand-new hat." He punched out the crown and tried to reshape the brim, but after all of his labor, it didn't look much better than Mandy's, which, of course, had managed to remain on her head during the entire ordeal.

Mandy rubbed between her shoulders and then massaged the muscles in her neck. "Well, I didn't do it on purpose, you know. It's a wonder you didn't break my neck."

"Your fool neck, you mean."

"That's a matter of opinion, Mr. Manning." She put her hands on her hips, unconsciously thrusting her chest and hardened nipples at Ryder. "Now, I'm waiting. What's your excuse for wandering the hills so far from home?"

Ry's eyes widened at the tempting sight, and he

swallowed hard. "Uh, I couldn't sleep last night, so I decided to take an early morning ride." He couldn't very well tell her that he was following her brother, could he? "I came upon Hank about the same way you did, I guess. And I was curious about the horses. So, here we are."

As Mandy gazed raptly at Ryder's handsome features, listened attentively to his deep, melodious voice and inhaled the alluring male scent of leather and horse combined with a somewhat smokey aroma, probably his cheroots, she knew without a doubt that he was the only man she would ever love. She knew also that she'd be bucking against fate if anything were to ever come of that love.

If only he wasn't snooping around after Jesse, if only he wasn't suspicious of her brothers, if only he wasn't using her. . . . There were too darned many "if onlys" to suit her; but it still didn't change the way she felt, and it probably never would.

Meanwhile, Ry was making an eye-opening discovery of his own. How he loved the way her piquant features squinted at him when she was angry, how the thick mass of hair shrouded her shoulders as it fell strand by strand from beneath the antiquated hat, how she so defiantly stood her ground against odds too heavy for her to handle, as though she wasn't aware of them. God, he just loved her, period.

Mandy finally broke the spell by saying, "Well, if we're both following Hank, and for the same reason, what're we doing wasting time standing here staring at each other? He's getting away." If she didn't get away from the man soon, she was literally going to attack him. Her body did strange things of its own whenever he was this near.

Ry chuckled. "Okay, brat, go get your horse. I'll

291

meet you in the creek bed in five minutes." He had to have a few minutes alone in order to compose himself. Never had a woman affected him this way before. She almost unmanned him.

Reno had been looking down on the cabin for almost half an hour. When he'd first arrived, he'd tethered Feller next to Dusty and left Zeke's lead rope tied to Feller's saddle horn. He'd expected Jeremy to pounce on the supply bag immediately and was more than a little surprised that he'd seen no sign of his brother. Where could he be?

He unloaded Zeke's pack and walked to where he'd left Jeremy standing the day he'd left to go back to the farm. Apprehension was building as he called Jeremy's name. If the kid had disobeyed him and gone down to check out the cabin, he'd murder the squirt, brother or no.

Reno sat down under a tree, bracing his rifle across his knees. He'd need a plan. Even though he considered himself a good fighter, two against one could prove deadly.

The sound of horseshoes clicking over rocks drew his attention, and Reno gritted his teeth at the sight of Hank coming back earlier than he'd expected. How could he hope to go against these numbers? But the first order of business was to be absolutely certain Jeremy had been taken.

Mandy was glad Ryder led the way. It left her free to greedily eye his broad, muscular form. He rode so easily in the saddle, with a natural grace that enabled him to move as one with the horse.

So intent was she in daydreaming about him that

she lurched in the saddle when Red Fox suddenly stopped. Ryder called over his shoulder, "Some one angled off in this direction." He pointed to the left, and Mandy could also see the barely discernable imprint of two animals. Only, one set of tracks belonged to a mule. Whoever went up the hill hadn't been with Hank.

Ry was overjoyed. They'd found Reno. Now to find out what he was up to. To Amanda he said, "Let's go this way, want to?"

"But Hank's trail leads this way. Reno didn't have a mule with him."

Damn! The girl was good. "I know, but we need to know what and who we're up against. Just humor me on this, will you?"

Mandy shrugged. She trusted him enough to know that following the unknown rider must be important. "Lead on."

They wound around for a time before breaking out of the trees to find themselves on the edge of a bluff overlooking a beautiful valley. Smoke rose from the chimney of a cabin at the far end, and from the number of horses in the corrals, they knew it had to be Hank's hideout.

Mandy reached over to touch Ryder's arm. "That's Hank's place. I knew it was back here someplace but forgot just where." She licked a finger that still tingled from touching Ry. Would he always do this to her? Even after he was gone, would his memory cause her body to burn and ache in this way?

"It's a good place to hide a bunch of horses. Who'd guess this kind of place was here?" Ry looked at Amanda strangely and rubbed his arm.

A loud bray suddenly split the air. Red Fox turned his head and cocked his ears toward the sound as Ryder smiled and kneed his horse in that direction.

Mandy couldn't believe it when they found Dusty, Feller, and Zeke. "Reno and Jeremy must be here. You don't think . . ."

Ry saw her glance toward the cabin and heard the worried inflection in her voice. "No, they're not part of that bunch."

It made her feel better to think that Ryder didn't think that her brothers were part of Hank's gang. "Then what're they doing up here?" She shot an accusing glare in Ry's direction. "Do you know?"

"No, I don't. But it's going to be interesting finding out."

Her eyes were wide and anxious as she looked frantically around the make-shift campsite. "Where are they, Ryder? Why aren't they here?"

"I reckon we'll find that out sooner or later. Right now, get down, and let's see what we can scrounge up to eat. I haven't eaten anything since supper last night. What about you?"

Mandy just shook her head. She had more things to worry about than whether or not she'd eaten. Were her brothers involved in some way with those stolen horses?

Ryder handed Mandy some bread and cheese and fumbled around until he found some jerky. "This'll have to do for now. We don't want to start a fire and let our friends down there know they've got company. C'mon, eat up."

She didn't realize how hungry she was until she obediently took a bite of cheese. Then she gobbled every bite before fetching her canteen to wash it down. Her eyes slid to Ryder, and she looked on with interest as he checked the loads in his pistol and lifted the flap of his knife scabbard just to make sure everything was in order.

"Where are you going?"

He knelt and readjusted the ties on his moccasins. "I thought I'd take a walk."

"Oh, sure, just a jaunt to the general store for a new hat, I suppose?"

Ry chuckled as he stood and put the crown of his battered hat over the horn on his saddle. "Not exactly, but I am going down there to take a look around. When I get back, maybe we'll know more about your brothers and can plan our next move."

Mandy moved closer to Ryder. "I'm going to go with you."

"Oh, no, you aren't. Someone has to stay here in case Reno or Jeremy should show up. And that someone is going to be you. Please, promise me you'll stay here so I won't have to worry about running over you at the least opportune moment."

She giggled, then chewed what was left of a fingernail. "All right, I'll stay, but only because I agree, someone should stick close up here, just in case. . . ." If Ryder got the impression that she would be around to back him up in case of a screw up, that was exactly what she intended.

He understood the implication perfectly. "Ahem, well, I'm glad that's settled. You keep a close look out and be careful." His eyes widened in surprise when Mandy boldly walked to him and planted a lingering kiss on his lips. His hands raised to pull her even closer, but she stepped out of reach and left him standing with frustration written over his entire body.

"Don't be gone too long. I'll be waiting for you," she teasingly promised.

With a curse and a groan, Ryder turned and started working his way down the bluff. It was slow going, and by the time he reached the valley floor, it was dusk, which worked to his favor as he angled across the valley to come up on the cabin from between the pond and the corrals.

One of the members of Hank's gang was making a tour of the corrals, so Ryder settled into the tall grass to wait until full darkness. From his observation earlier in the day, it appeared that at least one man checked the horses about every half hour. He didn't know if they'd change the routine at night or not.

The guard lit a smoke, cupping his hands around the flame to protect if from the gusting breezes. Ry saw the man's face during the brief illumination, and he thought he recognized Hank's cousin Ed. The match flipped in the air to land at Ry's feet. He fought the natural instinct to immediately snuff it out by doing the next best thing—watching it unwaveringly until it finally sputtered out.

An itch began to irritate Ry's foot. He stretched his toes, arched his foot, did everything he could besides reaching down to scratch it. Beads of sweat broke out on his forehead, and his whole body ached with the need to dig his fingernails into his leather-covered flesh.

It was almost as if the man felt the daggers piercing his back, for he turned in Ry's direction. But all he did was throw the butt of his smoke into the pond before taking a final glance at the horses and moseying toward the cabin once again.

Ry waited until he heard the distant click of a door before moving. He bent low and kept to the cover of the corrals as he silently made his way to the house. A feeling of déjà vu overwhelmed him as he leaned against the log siding and slithered along the wall to the back corner. It was dark and quiet, just the right atmosphere for snooping.

When he heard the cabin door open again, he ducked quickly around the corner, only to run full force into a solid body with the same intention as his but moving in the opposite direction. Acting purely by impulse, he grabbed a shirtfront and directed a punch in the area where the man's head should be.

The scuffle had been fast and quiet, and Ry pulled the inert form into the darker shadows of the cabin as he heard boots crunch across the yard. The outlaw didn't remain outside long, and when he spoke to the rest of the gang as he entered the cabin, Ry turned once more to the body at his feet.

Before he knew what was happening, his feet were jerked from under him, and he was pressed to the ground with a knife at his throat. A voice whispered in his face, "Don't even think about movin', bucko, or you'll be smilin' from ear to ear."

Ryder groaned. "Damn it all. I can't turn around without running into a damned Coulter."

Chapter Sixteen

The knife in Reno's trembling hand scraped a tiny chunk of skin from Ryder's neck before the shaken man finally pulled it away. "Lord, Manning, I could've killed you."

Ryder's voice was cool and calm. "Then we would've both gone."

It was at that precise moment that Reno felt the cold muzzle of the pistol pressing into his ribs. He levered himself off of Ryder and wiped the blade of his knife on the grass before replacing it in its scabbard. "I'd say we're both pretty lucky, wouldn't you?"

Ry's teeth flashed through the darkness. "Either that, or we're both awfully clumsy."

"Maybe a little of both, huh?" Reno leaned his head back against the cabin. "How'd you find this place?"

Ryder figured he didn't have anything to hide from the man at the present time, so he told him that he'd seen him leave the farm and had been curious and followed him. Ry left out the part about getting lost but explained about running across Hank Ford and then the subsequent meeting with Amanda.

Anger at Ryder for having the gall to spy on him was far outweighed by Reno's concern for his sister. "Amanda's here? Why'd you bring her along? It's dangerous, man." Reno took care to whisper, but his voice was agitated, nonetheless.

"I didn't have much choice. She was already on Hank's trail when I met up with her. She kinda brought me."

Reno was puzzled. "But what was she doing that for? How'd she run across him in the first place?"

"That's something you're going to have to ask her. All I *do* know is that we both saw the horses he was leading and remembered what you'd said about Hank having something to do with stolen horses. Our running into each other was just an accident." In more ways than one, he thought.

"Oh. That girl scares me sometimes, Manning. She's been poking in these hills too much lately. One of these days she's going to get hurt."

"I couldn't agree with you more." Ryder reached for a cheroot but thought better of it. One of Hank's gang might see the glow from his ashes or smell the different aroma. He'd just have to wait.

Reno stepped over to the corner and peered around toward the front of the house. "It's about time for someone to make the rounds of the corrals. I guess we'll be stuck here for a while longer."

They did move away from the cabin, however, and concealed themselves behind a stand of oaks. Ryder sat cross-legged on the ground and queried Reno, "Where's Jeremy? Amanda said that was his gray horse up there."

Reno sat down, dumbfounded. "I can't believe it. You even found our camp." Then he added seriously, "Jeremy's inside. I haven't seen him or anything, but I heard the men in there talking. They took him sometime this morning. What I can't figure out is, how? His horse and camp things were still where he'd left them. If those guys surprised him, they'd have brought Dusty along, too. That horse would be worth a lot to them."

Ry nodded in agreement. No telling what had happened to the kid. "Any idea on how many men there are?"

"I could only see five through the window; but Hank had three with him, and there were two staying here. So, there's six for sure. And I heard them say more are on the way tomorrow with what's left of the herd."

No one spoke as both men thought about the danger of the situation. Finally, Ry had to know something. "What's your connection to these horses?"

Reno was shocked. How could anyone know? Only he, Jer and Lieutenant Crump, who was miles away, knew about the remounts. He sighed. What difference did it make now whether it was a secret or not? If they didn't get Jeremy out of this mess alive, none of it would mean anything anyway. And Manning seemed like a good man to have on their side.

"Those are our horses. Jer's and mine. We caught them, broke them, and trained them, and I was on my way to sell them for Army remounts when Hank Ford shot me and ran them off." He remained silent for a few minutes, then spoke with determination. "But I'll get them back . . . one way or the other."

Ryder took a deep breath and let it out slowly. He believed Reno. It was a relief to know that the two boys hadn't been up to their cousin's old tricks. For a while, he'd been awfully suspicious of the two young Coulters.

300

"Maybe I can be of some help. What's your plan?"

"Well, Jer and I were going to wait until all the horses were brought here, then we thought we'd surprise Hank and get them back somehow. We really hadn't made any master plan, but now that Hank has Jeremy, even though he doesn't know I'm anywhere around, our chances of surprise are pretty well shot."

"Any idea when the rest of the gang is expected?"

"From the way they talked, I'd guess sometime tomorrow afternoon."

"Uh huh. How many horses are they bringing?"

Reno picked up a stick and scratched in the dirt with it. "There should be eight or ten left, besides my stallion."

"Stallion? What'd you boys do, trap a whole herd?" Ry had been kidding Reno, but when he saw the man's nod, his admiration for the eldest Coulter brother increased tenfold. No wonder the brothers had disappeared for days on end. They'd undertaken quite a chore.

"Does your sister know about all this?"

Reno slumped and shook his head. "No. Not about the horses. I mentioned that Jer and I wanted to leave Missouri, but I didn't tell her how we were getting the money. We wanted to surprise her."

Ryder was amazed. There was a lot more to this family than he'd ever imagined. "What was her reaction? I bet she was surprised, all right."

"Oh yeah, I guess some would call it surprised. She was damned mad, that's what. She never came right out and said so, but she'll never leave that ramshackle farm." His voice was low and despondent, like he carried the weight of the world on his shoulders.

Ry reached over and slapped him on the back, then remembered the houseful of outlaws and lowered his own voice. "Don't worry about it now. I might be able to help you out there, too." The thought of Amanda's moving away was depressing. After all this was over, would he ever see her again? "Just where are you boys planning to go if you decide to leave Missouri?"

As dark as it was, Ry could hear the excitement in Reno's voice and could picture the smile on his face and in his eyes as he listened to the young man talk.

"We've already got a place. Almost three thousand acres, west of the Territory, near Santa Fe. We haven't seen it yet; but these horses are our last payment, and then it's all ours. They say our land is south of Santa Fe, at the base of a mountain range along the Rio Grande. Plenty of water, tall grass. God, I can hardly wait to get there."

Reno's head cocked to one side as he listened to the description and location of the land. His own ranch had to be located just a little south of the Coulter's place. His lips curved into a slow smile. What a coincidence. Then he looked up into the twinkling heavens and watched as clouds skittered over the face of the moon. Or was it?

Jeremy tried to flex his fingers, but they were too stiff. His hands were swollen from the tight bonds, and his wrists were bloody from continued efforts to free himself. He was on the floor in a corner bedroom, with no light, no windows and, worst of all, no hope.

Once, he'd heard a scraping sound on the outside wall, and excitement had momentarily flared as he imagined Reno coming to his rescue. Then he thought about his brother single-handedly taking on the seven cutthroats and hoped he never found him.

He wouldn't be able to stand it if he thought his stupidity would lead to his brother's death.

He moaned when he moved his legs and felt the tenderness in his ribs and stomach. Hank had seen to it that Jeremy had paid for not answering his questions about what he was doing snooping around the valley. Then Hank had laughed and hit him harder when he'd lied and said he'd gotten lost.

Gritting his teeth, he fought the bindings again. Evidently rope wasn't like leather, for it didn't stretch when his blood soaked it through.

Mandy paced back and forth atop the bluff, never taking her eyes from the valley. Every now and then she tripped over the ends of the blanket dragging the ground; but it was cold, and she'd thrown it over her shoulders in deference to building a fire that might be seen from below.

Why had she promised to remain in camp? She was going crazy not knowing where her brothers were, or what was happening to Ryder. It seemed so strange that a man she'd known for only a few weeks could be lumped right up there in order of importance with her beloved brothers. She'd never thought that love could happen so fast.

The more she thought about it, the more leery she became. Just look what had happened to her father when her mother had left. Would the same thing happen to her when Ryder left? How could an emotion so exciting and so pleasurable be so destructive? At least he didn't know how strongly she felt toward him, and therefore couldn't use those feelings to hurt her even worse.

A twig snapped behind her, and she twisted so quickly that her feet became entangled in the blanket. She stumbled and fell to her knees. As she floundered off balance, she would've rolled off the bluff if a pair of strong arms hadn't reached out and scooped her up, blanket and all.

A deep voice spoke so close to her ear that goosebumps raised on her skin when his breath stirred wisps of her hair. "Didn't mean to scare you, sweetheart. You should've seen how high you jumped."

He was laughing at her, and Mandy sputtered with embarrassed indignation. "Put me down, you big oaf. It's not funny. I could've rolled over the edge."

The arms holding her too tightly already, squeezed her even harder. "Yes, I know."

Reno emerged from the trees behind Ryder. "What's all the commotion? I thought we were tryin' to blend in up here. You know, to not be seen or heard, silly unimportant things like that."

Mandy still pushed at Ryder, trying to persuade him to put her down. "It's all his fault, scaring a person half out of her wits, sneaking up on her."

"I beg your pardon. I did not sneak up on you."

"I don't know what else you'd call it. It's not normal for a person not to make any noise at all walking through the woods."

"C'mon, you two, cut out the bickering. We've got some plans to make." Reno went over to his pack and pulled out a jug. He tossed it to Ryder. "Here, wet your whistle with this. We could both stand to warm our innards a little."

Mandy found a rock to sit on, then looked in the direction from which Reno had come. "Where's Jeremy? Isn't he with you?"

Reno and Ryder looked at each other almost guiltily, took a swig of the whiskey, then joined Mandy on the ground. Reno finally raised his eyes to meet those of his sister, which also reminded him of his brother's. "We think Jeremy's hidden in the cabin. They've got him, Mandy, somewhere."

In one bound, Mandy was on her feet. "Then, we've got to go get him."

Ryder also stood and placed a restraining hand on Amanda's arm. "We're going to get your brother. But not now. There are at least six men down there. If we make a move now, the odds are too high that one of them will shoot Jeremy before we even make it to the front door."

Reclining on his bedroll, using his saddle as a backrest, Reno added, "And there's more of Hank's gang coming with the rest of the horses. If we wait and collect all of our eggs in one basket, we can fry the whole lot."

A snort of derision escaped Mandy's nose as she stated, "Or we find ourselves scrambled and in the pan."

"Well, it's the best shot we've got." Reno sounded hurt by Mandy's lack of confidence.

"At least they won't be expecting anything with the whole bunch together." Ryder gave Amanda's arm a reassuring squeeze and slanted her a lopsided grin before leaving her to slide down and lean against a fairly smooth barked tree. "We'll have the element of surprise on our side."

Mandy sighed rather dejectedly. "I hope it'll be enough."

It was after noon before the remaining members of Hank's gang made their appearance. Reno watched their descent into the valley closely. A disgusted "Aw, hell" drew the others' attentions.

"What's wrong, Reno?"

"Hell's fire, they don't have my stallion. I figured he'd have to be with this bunch." He slammed his right fist into his left palm. "What could they have done with him?" As his eyes darted to the cabin, they narrowed dangerously. "If that mad man hurt him . . ."

Mandy hissed air through her teeth. "Your stallion? What do you mean?"

Her older brother calmed himself and sat down beside her. In as short a time as possible, he explained how he and Jeremy had been capturing wild horses and selling them to the Army, how they'd invested the money in a ranch and how this last herd was to be the last payment.

Mandy shook her head at the enormity of her brothers' endeavors. Then she asked, "What color is this stallion you're missing?" She knew the answer even before he said the word "black."

"I don't know where he is, but Hank's keeping the horse for himself." She considered telling Reno about Hank's threats toward the animal but decided against it. They'd just have to find the stallion before Hank had a chance to hurt him.

"How could you know about the stallion?" Reno's mouth hung open as he questioned his sister. All the trouble he'd gone to, to keep it all a secret, and here she was, telling him about his horse.

"They rode right by me yesterday. I heard them talking about a black devil and just assumed it had to be the same horse."

"It's got to be." Reno hugged his sister. "Man, that's a relief. Now, after we get Jeremy back, all we'll have to do is get Hank to tell us where Ebony is."

"Ebony?" Ryder thought it a pretty sophisticated title to lay on a wild mustang.

"Well, I heard someone use the word once. It does

mean black, doesn't it?"

"Sure does. This must be some horse you've got."

Reno shrugged his shoulders and laughed. "Oh, I could tell you about him, all right, but you won't believe a word of it until you see him for yourself."

As Ryder put his hands in his back pockets and watched the activity surrounding the corrals and cabin, he said, "I hope to get the chance . . . soon."

Mandy's stomach growled, and she quickly covered it with her hands in an attempt to hide it. Finally she sighed and admitted, "I'm hungry, guys. And not for jerky and cold biscuits. Couldn't we build a fire and eat some hot food?"

Ryder stared at her for a long moment, then began gathering old, dry twigs. "If we use a small fire," he said, as he led her beneath a stand of trees, "and let the leaves and branches overhead diffuse what smoke we make, we can manage a hot meal." He smiled and let his eyes travel lingeringly over Amanda's trim figure. He'd give anything to be able to take her in his arms and slide the overall straps off her shoulders. To . . . just be able to touch her.

Mandy blushed furiously. She felt as if his eyes were stripping her naked, and she reveled in the feeling, wishing desperately that it were true. But Reno's timely approach rapidly quelled the inner fire as he knelt to help Ryder build the other one.

It was dark. The fire had long since been dashed, and the brother, sister and lawman watched the light glowing from the cabin window.

"One of us has got to go down there and see what's going on. We need to find out where Jer is and when they plan to move the horses out."

Mandy started to say she'd be glad to go, but both

307

men looked at her and shook their heads at the same time. "Don't even think it, sweetheart."

"Why not? Jeremy's my brother. And I'm as good at eavesdropping as either one of you. Probably better. I'm smaller and don't take up as much space and can move a lot lighter."

"Hon, we know all that; but you're not going, and that's final. Ryder, can I speak to you privately for a minute?"

The men walked into the trees, leaving a fuming Mandy to stare daggers at their retreating backs. How dare they treat her like such a child. Everything she'd said had been the truth, and they knew it. So, why were they plotting against her?

The men were only gone a few minutes. When they returned, Reno put his hat down by his saddle and checked his revolver. He'd have preferred to leave it behind, but it was too dangerous to be caught without it.

Ryder sat down close to Amanda and watched Reno make his preparations to leave. "Wear my moccasins. They'll be a tad big, but it shouldn't make that much difference."

"Thanks, Manning. I appreciate it." And he really did. Mandy's fella wasn't too bad. He looked back and forth between the two people, feeling the tension in the air as they tried to avoid looking at or touching each other. Yessir, that Manning was just the kind of man Mandy needed. Someone to keep her from being so headstrong and foolish. A man to love her as she deserved to be loved.

"Well, I'm off. With any luck, I'll be back by midnight."

When a knife cut through the rope binding

Jeremy's wrists and his arms fell to his sides, the boy thought he'd scream with pain as his circulation started flowing through his numbed hands and fingers. His jaw was stiff and unmoving as the wad of cloth was removed from his mouth. Two men dragged him to his feet, and he swayed dizzily.

"Bring him in here, boys. Let's see if he isn't ready to talk." Hank Ford's voice was deep and mean, its raspy quality only adding to his overall devil demeanor. He laughed when the youngster squinted his eyes in the bright light.

"So, have you had time to reconsider, boy? I don't believe for a minute that a Coulter was lost in these woods. That still the best you can do . . . boy?"

The backhand caught Jeremy by surprise. He hadn't quite gotten his equilibrium back as it was, and he fell to the floor—hard. If he lived through this, he was going to kill Hank Ford with his bare hands. With that thought in mind, he staggered to a standing position once more.

"As soon as I get my hands on that she-bitch of a sister of yours, I'm gonna teach her a few manners, too. I hope she holds up as long as you have, boy, it'll be lots more fun."

Hank roared with laughter as the baited boy lunged at him, and he deliberately kicked Jeremy in the groin and then delivered a punishing blow to the back of his neck. When the boy hit the floor and didn't move, he disappointedly told the two men, "Take him back and tie him good. By the time we're through with the kid, we won't have to worry about any more Coulters being sired, ever again."

It was a cruel howl of laughter that greeted Reno's ears as he finally worked his way to one of the front windows. The front windows were the only windows, and the front door the only door. That made any attempt to rescue Jeremy all the more dangerous.

As he raised his head ever so slowly, he saw a pair of legs and booted feet being dragged through a doorway. He gritted his teeth and barely refrained from drawing his pistol as he knew in his gut that the body belonged to his brother. But he couldn't help him, not just one man against so many.

Hank Ford sat at a table, his body shaking as he alone laughed at some joke told prior to Reno's arrival. Six more men lounged around a bunk, watching as a thin, cadaverous-looking man dealt a deck of cards. With seven men inside, Reno knew that at least two more had to be outside, somewhere around the cabin. He pressed himself closer to the wall, trying to blend in with the shadows.

One of the card players looked toward Reno's window and levered himself off the bunk. When he started walking toward him, Reno gradually pulled his head away from the window, resisting the urge to jerk and cause a movement that might be noticeable. Then he carefully side-stepped to the corner of the cabin and slipped around the edge just as he heard the scrape of a window being lifted.

"There, that's better. I was about to burn up in here."

Another outlaw called, "Open the other one, Fred. It's so smokey, I can hardly see."

"I'm not your flunky, Tom." But the other window squeaked open, regardless.

Reno released the breath he'd been holding. That was close. But now he could wait there, around the corner, and still hear some of the conversation going on inside.

Hank looked at Fred as the man returned to the poker game. "Did you tie that Coulter kid again?"

"Sure I did, boss. You told me to, didn't you?" Fred's voice was high and on the whiny side.

"Yeah, but I never know if you numbskulls are gonna follow orders, or not."

Another man threw in his hand. "Give us a break, huh, Hank. We're tired. We've been workin' hard, handlin' all them horses. We gonna get to stay here a few days and rest up?"

Hank stood up and scratched under one arm, then smoothed his hand over his belly. "Naw, I don't think so. I wanna get these horses outta here and collect the money for them. *Then* we'll have a few days to spend in town and a few extra dollars to blow."

One of the gang screwed his face up and was ready to argue. "Use your head, Tonio. If that kid"—he jerked his thumb toward the closed bedroom door—"was snooping around, don't you think there might be others? Hell, there might be someone out there watchin' us right now."

Six sets of eyes looked suspiciously toward the door and the open windows. Fred picked up the winnings from the game and agreed with Hank. "I'm with you, boss. I'd rather have money in my pockets when I . . . rest . . . or whatever. But what're we gonna do with the kid?"

"I haven't decided yet. May take him with us for a ways in case there's anyone trailin' us." Hank walked to the window nearest Reno's corner and stuck his head out to look around. "Tom, go out and relieve Ed for a while. Tell him I need to jaw with him a spell."

When the door opened, light swung in a wide arc

through the yard, and Reno flattened against the wall. The man called Tom walked to within ten feet of him. Reno melted back into the deeper shadows toward the rear of the cabin. He'd wait until things were settled down again before he'd try to return to camp. At least he had the information he needed. Now they had to figure out what to do with it.

Mandy hunkered over the dead ashes of the fire, poking a stick in and out and drawing meaningless diagrams. Ry sat under a tree, disinterestedly watching the stars twinkle against their black backdrop. Neither had spoken since Reno had left, and that had been over an hour ago.

From the corner of his eye, Ry watched Mandy. He liked the way her hair shimmered in the moonlight, and he enjoyed the pleasurable sensation his body experienced when he looked at her rounded, yet lithe, young form. His fingers dug into the ground to keep his arms from reaching for her.

Ever since the night he'd given her the dress, she'd been avoiding him, doing her best to stay out of his way even when they were in close company. If she didn't show some sign of wanting him soon, he was going to disregard his vow to wait her out.

With an angry thrust, Mandy scattered ashes every which way. They'd been alone for a long time now, and all the man did was sit and stare at the sky. Was he thinking of another woman? Did he have someone waiting for him somewhere? Why didn't he just grab her and . . . ravish her like she'd dreamed last night? Why didn't he at least say something?

Finally, she couldn't stand it any longer. She walked to where he was sitting and knelt down beside him. "Do you think Reno'll have any trouble?"

Ryder had been so caught up in remembrances of the way Amanda's satin flesh quivered as his hands roved over her delectable hills and valleys that he jumped when she spoke. He was surprised to find her sitting so near, but he noted she was on her knees, ready to flee at a moment's notice.

"What's that? Who?"

Exasperated that his thoughts had been so far away from her, she snapped, "I asked about my brother. Do you think he's all right?"

"Oh. Things have been pretty quiet down there. I'm sure if there'd been any trouble, we would've known about it. Reno's smart. He'll make it okay."

Mandy put her hands, palms together, between her knees, and her voice quivered with the emotion she was experiencing from being so close to Ryder, yet unable to touch him. Her upper body started to tilt toward him, but she caught herself in time. "I hope so. Poor Jeremy, he must be frightened to death."

"You underestimate your brothers, Amanda. They're both capable and intelligent. Just look at what they've done with those horses."

That was something Mandy didn't want to think about. The horses in those corrals represented the end of the only life she knew. She was tempted to sneak down there and open all of the gates.

"Amanda, what're you afraid of?" Ry wanted to beg and plead, to convince her to go west. After all, it sounded like they'd be neighbors. But if he told her that, she'd probably plant her feet like a stubborn mule and refuse to leave Missouri—ever.

"Afraid? Me? What makes you think that?"

"Reno told me that he didn't think you'd leave with them. That you were set on keeping the farm."

"He told you that? He barely even knows you. Why, I didn't find out about their plans until this afternoon. Well, about *all* of their plans, that is."

Ryder took hold of one of Amanda's arms and pried a hand from between her tightly clenched knees. "That's only because he wanted to surprise you, sweetheart. He thought it would make you happy."

"Happy? To pack up and leave our home, the farm? To go where? To what?"

"Aha! You are afraid."

A tear fell on the back of his hand, and he reached the other up to wipe away a wet trail from her cheeks. His arm just naturally wrapped around her shoulders, and he tugged until she literally fell into his lap and arms.

Mandy struggled. How could she regain her pride and composure when she was snuggled so protectively within Ryder's embrace? It was where she'd dreamed of being, but not like this. Still, he wouldn't release her.

"You don't need to pretend in front of me, sweetheart. I know what it's like to leave a family home, to lose everything, to move on to an unfamiliar place. It's certainly no fun, but it can be the start of a brand-new life. Think of the excitement, the adventure. Doesn't it appeal to you at all, just a little?"

Mandy's finger traced the hard line of his jaw, then down the tense cord in his neck, to swirl at the vee of his shirt collar. Everything was appealing when he was near. But how was she going to enjoy life anywhere, once he was gone?

The muscles on Ryder's chest tautened, clear down to his belly. His hand grabbed hers and held it, afraid of what might happen if it were allowed to continue its devastating exploration.

"I hadn't thought about anything except having to leave the farm. It's all I have, Ryder. It's kept me going for the past several years. I've put my life, and my dreams, into the place."

He pushed her head down on his chest and rested his cheek on the top of her hair. "I hear you; but think of the fun you'll have putting that time and energy on something brand-new that you can shape and build to suit *you*. You won't be keeping up something that someone else has built. It'll be your very own."

She sighed, and the curly hairs peeping above Ry's shirt waved with the gust of soft air. "No, whatever is built on Reno and Jeremy's place will be theirs. One day they'll marry and have families, and I'll just be extra baggage, a built-in baby sitter."

Ry managed to refrain from laughing at the picture she painted of her dreary life. "What if . . . you met a fella, fell in love, and *he* had a patch of land all his own? What if he wanted a partner to share a home . . . and a family? Wouldn't you feel it was a new beginning, something worth putting your dreams into?"

Her eyes closed, and she imagined following Ryder Manning to the ends of the earth, living in a sod hut, raising a passel of kids. It would be heaven. "That will never happen to me."

Ryder blinked. How could she sound so cold and determined? "Why not? What's wrong with you?"

"There's nothing wrong with me. It's just . . ." How could she explain that she'd never love anyone else the way she loved him—Ryder Manning—deputy U.S. Marshal? "You're right. It is me. I'm too old, and by the time we move and get a place built, who'd be interested?''

Ry's chest heaved with Amanda's head as he guffawed with laughter. ''Yeah, I've noticed you're getting a little long in the tooth. There's certainly no one less appealing than an *old* old maid.'' God help him, if she really believed that nonsense, maybe there was hope that she'd still be free after this was all over.

Mandy lifted her head to peer into Ryder's eyes the best she could in the dark. He sounded so serious. How could he be so cruel? Then she felt guilt wash over her. She'd been hoping he'd deny her words, that he'd tell her she was young and beautiful, that any man would be lucky to have her—especially him. It was dirty pool to resort to cheap tricks to trap him into making some sort of commitment, wasn't it?

His eyes sparkled with an emotion she couldn't fathom as he stared down at her. She watched his lips curve into that wonderful mocking grin, and the next thing she knew, her hands were winding through his hair and to the back of his neck as her lips clung greedily to his. Her breasts pressed heartily into his chest as she squirmed to get ever closer to his hard body.

She thought she'd die from the pleasure his touch wrought after such a long, tormenting interval. Their heads bobbed and twisted as their lips met, parted and met once again. They sipped and drank from each other as if just recovering from a devastating drought. Their hands were everywhere as they discovered each other all over again.

Suddenly, Ryder tensed, and he twisted his body until he had Amanda pinned to the ground beneath him. She opened her mouth to protest such rough treatment after his earlier tender ministrations, but a large hand clamped over her lips before she could

316

utter a sound. Then the click of a hammer being cocked next to her left ear alerted her to the possible presence of danger.

"Hello, the camp. It's me, Reno. I'm coming in."

Mandy closed her eyes and silently cursed her beloved brothers. They both possessed an uncanny knack for perfect timing.

Chapter Seventeen

The hammer was slowly eased back into place as Ryder whispered in Amanda's ear. "It was thoughtful of him to give us a warning, eh, sweetheart?"

Despite the scare she'd received upon being thrown to the ground, Mandy giggled at the teasing note in Ry's words. She pushed several stray locks of hair out of her eyes before reaching up to trace his lips with her fingers. "Uh hmmm, very."

"Hey, where is everyone?" Reno stomped back and forth between the dead fire and his pack. By force of habit he put a hand over his eyes to look around the camp, then realized what he had done and grumbled to himself as he quickly lowered his arm.

When he saw Ryder and Mandy emerging from the line of trees, and noticed their slightly disheveled appearance, his eyes narrowed ominously. "It's about time. Guess I needn't ask where you two've been. Can't leave you alone for a minute." The last sentence was muttered mostly to himself, but his look was accusing as he glared at Ryder.

Mandy's face flushed as she reached up to straighten her collar and pull the straps on her overalls back in place.

Ryder wasn't a bit remorseful of his actions but felt sorry that Amanda had to face her brother's condemnation. So, he stepped up beside her and hooked his arm around her stiff shoulders, while at the same time locking gazes with Reno. "We've done nothing to be ashamed of. You have no right to talk to your sister that way."

Mandy's jaw opened as if she were going to interrupt, but then it snapped shut. Her heart had thumped in double time when Ryder stood up for her, then she held her breath as Reno said the words she'd been wanting to say.

"I have every right. Mandy is my sister and I love her, and I'll be the one to pick up the pieces when you ride out of here a free and happy man with no responsibilities. That is what you plan on doing, isn't it?"

Reno watched Ryder's face closely to judge his reaction. For Mandy's sake, he hoped the man would be honest about his intentions. Any fool could see that Manning loved his sister. Then Reno's mouth quirked in a half grin. Except, maybe, the man himself.

Ryder felt the strain as two sets of eyes bored into him. He didn't know what he would do yet. He knew what he would *like* to do, but everything hinged on his investigation.

"I can't say right now what I'm going to do. Sorry, that's just the way it is. Besides, your sister has a stake in this, too. She might not want me to hang around."

Mandy's face had slowly crumpled into a deep frown at Ryder's first words, but by the time he'd finished, she'd composed herself. She stood straight and proud as she answered defiantly, "It doesn't matter to me what either one of you do. I never have, and don't intend to depend on a man to take care of me. Do you understand? Both of you?''

Reno opened his mouth and got as far as "But, what if—" before Mandy put her fists on her hips and turned to stare him down. He'd seen his sister mad before but never like this. Rather than push her any further, he quietly nodded his head. He guessed he understood.

Meanwhile, Ryder was totally captivated. He'd never seen Amanda look so wild and beautiful. His body burned with the need to make her his. Now— forever. Just the thought of her belonging to someone other than himself was enough to turn his blood to ice water. Another man might try to break her volatile spirit, to control her fiery temperament, and would destroy the sparkle in those emerald eyes. She could be tamed but never broken. So, with a thoughtful gleam in his eye, he nodded. He understood.

"Good. Now that we have that straight, tell us what you learned, brother dear.''

The blood drained from Reno's face as he recalled the frustration of being unable to aid his younger brother. "They've got Jeremy, all right. I didn't actually see him, but I recognized his boots.'' Knowing how Mandy would react, he left out the details of what he'd seen. "I also overheard them say that they were pulling out tomorrow and probably taking Jer with them.''

Mandy paced beside the embers of the fire. "But why? Why would they drag along a boy like Jeremy?''

Reno found it easy to produce an evil leer. "Because, our man Hank seems to think there might be vicious demons lurking about who'd think twice about confronting him if he had a hostage.''

Ry twisted the end of an invisible mustache. "Do tell.'' Then he looked at the sky and got serious. "We don't have much time before dawn, and we've got a lot to do. Let's concentrate on getting your brother first, then the horses. Any ideas?"

Dawn found the trio on top of the bluff, red eyed and weary. None had gotten any sleep, and all were tense and irritable. The horses were saddled, the pack repositioned on Zeke and evidence of their occupany of the area wiped out.

Ryder and Mandy looked on questioningly as Reno paced along the face of the cliff, cursing and staring at the cabin.

Mandy walked over to her brother and stopped in front of him. "Why so impatient? Everything's going to work out. You said so yourself last night."

Reno grinned and pinched the bridge of his nose between a thumb and forefinger. "Yeah, I know. It's just that I want to get it over with, now—last night. If they don't hurry and make their move, it'll be too late."

"Too late? Too late for what?" She didn't know they were on a schedule.

"We've only got three more days to get the horses to the fort, or we lost the contract. Three days." He turned to face the valley and almost shouted before he caught himself and pleaded in a low, earnest voice, "C'mon, you guys. Get goin'. What's the hold up down there?"

Mandy's heart had done a little song and dance when she discovered her brothers might not be able to make that last payment on the ranch. But then she scolded herself for being so childish and selfish. She hated herself for feeling so obstinate about sharing their dream, yet she couldn't help it.

A collective sigh exhaled from three chests when

Ryder joined Mandy and Reno and pointed to the cabin. Sure enough, it looked like little ants scurrying around the house and corrals. It was finally time.

They figured the outlaws would leave the valley the same way they'd entered, heading north to the railroad, or to the stockyards in St. Joseph. Still, they bided their time, watching to make certain they were right. But no matter which direction Hank chose to go, herding the horses would take time, and would take little effort to keep up with.

Ryder couldn't help the big grin that dimpled his cheeks, much to Mandy's enjoyment, when his idea was proven correct. When the corrals were opened and the horses bunched together in the middle of the valley, the men and animals then headed toward the northern entrance. Reno shook Ry's hand, and Mandy sent him a shy smile as they each moved to mount their horses and made their way down the steep slope to the much traveled creek bed.

Due to the rough terrain, the outlaws moved the horses slowly. There was only room enough for the horses to travel two or three abreast in the gully, so the riders had no trouble keeping them in control. The last horses had barely passed the ridge where Ry, Mandy and Reno lay in wait, when Ed brought up the rear, leading a bound and gagged Jeremy. Behind that pair rode another man with a scattergun held across his lap.

The trio held its place until the dust had settled. Reno looked at Ryder and said, "You're right again. A narrow place like this would be too dangerous to make a play. They should hit flatter country by mid-afternoon." He rubbed his hands together. "Then watch out, boys, here we come."

Mandy, who'd been silent during the entire ride,

now interrupted. "Did you see Jeremy's face? It was so bruised and swollen I hardly recognized him. It's a good thing Ryder grabbed my hand, or I'd have gladly s-shot them all, then and there." Her voice cracked, and she couldn't look the two men in the eyes.

Reno looked away, too. "That's why I didn't mention anything about him last night. I was afraid you might do something crazy. We just want to be sure we get him back alive, that's all."

She gulped and blinked moisture from her eyes. "Yes, that's the most important thing. But Hank Ford has a lot to answer for."

Ryder had been thinking the same thoughts as he watched the pain in her liquid green eyes. Hank Ford was one man he was tempted to try some so-called Indian torture tactics on.

As he pulled on Zeke's lead rope and rode the rest of the way down the slope, Reno called over his shoulder, "Let's follow a ways, just to be sure. There's plenty of time to set our trap."

Discovering that Hank was, in fact, moving the herd due north, made it easier for the Coulters and Ryder to choose a site that offered them concealment yet gave them space to make their attack.

The plan was for Ryder to take out the rear guard, while Reno and Amanda came from either side of Ed and got the drop on him. Amanda and Jeremy would then return to their lookout location, pick up Zeke and Dusty, and head back to the farm. Reno and Ry would trail the horses, picking off the outlaws one by one if necessary, until they were able to steal the animals back. They all knew the plan was by no means foolproof, but it was the best they could come up with.

They chose a long narrow clearing as their target area because there was no way the outlaws could miss it if they continued in their northerly direction. Mandy took the left side, Reno the right, and Ryder waited where the open country first began to thin. The clearing was perfect in that it ran up and over a small rise, ensuring that the riders in front wouldn't be able to see what was going on to the rear.

Only a short time had elapsed since they'd taken their positions before the sounds of approaching horses could be heard. A lot of horses. Mandy didn't know if Ry and Reno were as nervous as she, but she couldn't get over the urge to keep wiping her palms on her thighs. Her shirt stuck to her damp skin, and matted hair clung to the back of her neck.

For the millionth time, doubts assailed her. What if they couldn't pull it off? What if Reno, or Jeremy, or Ryder was killed? And worst of all, what if she froze and wasn't able to handle her end?

When the first rider and the leaders of the herd began to drift past her hiding place, she put a hand on Red Fox's arched neck while pulling the reins taut to keep him from nickering or prancing into the open. She knew he felt her nervousness, so made a concentrated effort to keep calm.

The first wave of horses had disappeared over the rise, and the main part of the herd was in the clearing. To the rear, the scragglers were just beginning to trail in. It wouldn't be long now. She took several deep breaths to still the thundering in her ribs and wiped her hands on her overalls, again.

Finally, or regrettably, the last of the horses reached her. As she trained her eyes on the trail entering the clearing, she saw Ed and Jeremy riding out. She held her breath, waiting. They had almost

324

ridden even with her before the last guard came into view.

She gasped aloud when Ryder dropped out of a tree onto the unsuspecting man's shoulders. That was her cue. As much as she wanted to wait and see if he made it safely, she knew she should already be on the move.

She pulled the revolver Ryder had given her that afternoon, and clucking softly to Red Fox, she nudged his ribs sharply. She and Reno came from the woods at the same time, a little behind Ed and their brother. In two jumps they were on either side of the pair, holding a surprised Ed at gunpoint.

Reno reached over to remove Ed's gun from its holster. "Don't move, friend. I've got a very nervous trigger finger."

Jeremy's puffed, swollen eyes opened as wide as they possibly could when he first heard the commotion around him. His cracked lips split to start a new trickle of blood as he grinned at his siblings. "God, I'm glad to see y'all."

While Reno kept Ed covered, Mandy slid out her knife and cut Jeremy's bonds. "It's good to see you, too, little brother." Her heart lodged in her throat as she searched his battered face. "Are you all right, Jer?"

Still smiling, he assured her, "I am now, sis. I am now." When he noted the wavering revolver in her hand, he reached over and took it from her. "Here, better let me have that gun. I may need it before we're out of this."

As if to verify Jeremy's words, a shot rang out from where Mandy had last seen Ryder. And while they were distracted, Ed knocked Reno's gun hand to the side and spurred his horse forward. He had disappeared over the rise before Reno could recover and take aim.

However, they quickly dismissed Ed from their minds as they turned their horses and rode to check on Ryder. He was just pulling himself from under the guard's body and, much to Mandy's heartfelt relief, dusted himself off, unhurt. He pointed to the woods on his left. "Get my horse, will you, Jeremy?"

Reno looked back over his shoulder, then to Ryder. "Ed got away. I figure he'll be back any minute with reinforcements."

Ryder mounted his mustang as soon as Jeremy led the horse to him. "Okay, Jeremy you go with Amanda. She knows what to do. Reno and I are going to fade into the woods and keep after the horses." His gaze locked on Amanda's with an indefinable intensity, raking her body from head to toe before finally settling once more on her emerald-green orbs. "Be careful" was all he said. Then he and Reno rode into the trees.

Mandy watched them go until she lost sight of them among the dense layers of brush and leaf-covered branches. When she turned to Jeremy, she saw that he was observing her reaction to Ryder's heated gaze. She was aware of her flaming cheeks, and every nerve in her body felt exposed and on edge. Quickly, she reined Red Fox around, and snapped, "Follow me."

They hadn't made their exit a minute too soon, as Hank, Ed and two more riders appeared over the rise, riding hard. When they found their fallen comrade, Hank swore viciously, then directed the other two men to search the area on one side of the clearing while he and Ed took the other.

Mandy and Jeremy hadn't ridden far before Mandy

noticed her brother lagging behind. When she turned to look back, she was dismayed to find that he was swaying dizzily and barely able to keep a hold on the horn. Without his guidance, the horse had dropped his head to pull at the tall weeds and grass along the way.

"Jeremy! Hold on. I'm coming." She whirled Red Fox around and rode back to her brother before he fell. "Jer, it's not much farther. Do you think you can hold on 'til we get to Zeke and Dusty? I'll be able to patch you up some then. You can do it, Jer. I know you can."

Jeremy's head rolled back until he was able to see his sister's blurry outline. His face was chalk white, and the pain in his ribs was almost unbearable. But he was well aware of their danger. "Lead the way, Mandy Jo, I'm right behind you."

She noted the death grip he'd taken on the horn and reached out to take his reins. "Hang on, then. Like I said, it's not far."

A rifle blast shattered the stillness of the afternoon, and Mandy jumped. The combination of her jerking on Red Fox's bit, causing him to rear, and Jeremy's mount's balking as she pulled on the reins, all contributed to her falling from the saddle. She landed square on her back and for several seconds was unable to catch a breath.

A muffled groan gave her the impetus to gather her wits and roll over. She screamed when she saw Jeremy sprawled on the ground, his face covered with fresh blood. On her hands and knees, she crawled to his side, and her hand shook as she felt for a pulse.

During all the confusion and the shock of finding Jeremy down, Mandy had forgotten about the shot until she heard a crashing in the brush off to her left. Her reflexes were operating in slow motion, and she

327

was unable to move fast enough to get away when a giant of a man stepped from out of the woods to grab her roughly by the collar.

A red haze blinded her vision when she saw the rifle held loosely in his other hand. Fury overwhelmed her good sense as she lunged off the ground to ram her head full force into his large midsection. The force of her blow caused him to free his hold on her shirt, and she pulled back her arm to aim a fist at the man's whiskered jaw.

She yelped from the pain shooting up her arm after landing the blow and never heard the roar that erupted from the giant's throat or felt the backhand that knocked her unconscious.

It didn't take Ryder and Reno long to catch up to the herd. Only four men were left to guard the horses, which caused them some worry; but it was a break they hadn't expected, and they took full advantage of it.

The four riders were grouped close together, talking across the backs of several horses about what could have happened to draw Hank away so fast. They couldn't believe their eyes when two armed men rode from behind a line of trees and ordered them to raise their hands away from their guns.

Fred Goins, like most of the rest, was a man with nothing to lose. Horse stealing was the least of the charges that would be brought against him if he were taken, so in desperation, he reached for his gun.

By the time the firing had ended, Fred and another outlaw lay dead on the ground, while the other two, one of them badly wounded, put the spurs to their horses. The money they'd been promised from the sale of the horses was worth far less than their lives.

Hank Ford's braggadocio meant little to men whose loyalty was questionable, to say the least.

When the smoke and dust had cleared, Reno looked at Ryder, saw that they were both unharmed, then watched the cloud of dust in the distance. "Well, I'd say we spooked the horses all to hell."

Ryder, his eyes hooded as he looked over the dead bodies, recognized one as a face he carried in his saddlebags. Finally realizing that Reno had spoken to him, he said, "Hmmm? Oh, yeah, couldn't blame them. But my guess is they won't run far. Let's go round them up, then come back by here and pick up these guys."

"Good enough." Reno didn't try to engage his riding partner in conversation as they trailed the horses. Ryder's face was set in hard lines, and his body was as tense as a coiled spring. Reno wasn't in much better shape himself. With all the bullets flying, it was hard to tell who'd killed whom, but it never set good with a man, or most men, anyway, to know he'd taken another life. Reno was glad to know that Manning was that type of man, too.

Mandy gradually opened her eyes. The sunlight exploded in her head, and she moaned. The throbbing pressure increased to match pace with an endless rocking motion that made her feel nauseous. She tried to lick her thick, sandpapery lips, but that tiny motion brought on a bout of pain so intense that she swayed dizzily.

She was caught and set upright by a huge, rough hand clamped forcefully over a tender bare breast. Suddenly Mandy remembered. Jeremy shot. The giant. The horrendous blow. And now she was aware of being held in front of a large, flabby body, her back pressed against a gelatinous mound of soft belly, her buttocks folded into a generous lap, the backs of her thighs adhered to massive legs.

His hips rocked forward to suggestively press her bottom, and she knew immediately that he was going to try to rape her. Panic gripped her, but good sense kept her from making a sudden move and giving away the fact that she was now conscious. Maybe if he didn't know. . . . His calloused hand scraped the sensitive flesh of her belly as it dipped lower, and she came close to screaming with fury.

Mandy's entire body flushed with the heat of indignation. She couldn't, wouldn't, let any man take by force what she'd given to Ryder. She refused to suffer through a brutal desicration of something that had been wonderful, so loving. She'd kill herself first. Flexing her leg and ankle as subtly as possible, she felt the presence of her knife scabbard. But whether the knife was still inside was another matter.

Time seemed to descend into slow motion for Mandy. As if through a haze, a lean, sun-bronzed figure appeared before her, a smile dimpling his extraordinary features. Wasn't it strange that while undergoing such a terrifying, degrading experience, she should think about Ryder, about his tender ministrations?

Suddenly the hand that had been in front of her holding the reins lifted, and a ham-sized forearm wedged beneath her breasts to slightly lift her weight. Startled, Mandy arched and kicked out as the ogre groped about the tender flesh of her belly and blew his foul breath by her cheek.

"Aha! I knowed you was awake, little gal." He massaged her stomach and smacked wet kisses over her earlobe and down her neck. His arm rubbed the undersides of her breasts as he pulled her tightly to

330

him, drowning her in the overwhelming odor of stale sweat and filth that was soaked into his shirt. "You like that, don'tcha, gal?"

Mandy forgot her blow to the jaw, opened her mouth to protest his abuse, and the pain hit her so hard that her head weakly fell back against his massive shoulder. Immediately his mouth slobbered over her collarbone. Her efforts to struggle proved futile when she discovered that her wrists were bound to the saddle horn. She'd never felt so helpless and frustrated in her life. Finally, she quit fighting, her chest heaving and stomach churning, knowing that she needed to conserve as much of her waning strength as possible. There was no doubt that the assault would continue as soon as he had her off the horse, and she was determined that he'd know he had a fight on his hands.

As they rode on, she became less and less familiar with the countryside. A trickle of fear that had begun an hour ago, now poured through her with dread certainty. She was alone, with no hope other than her will to survive.

Her stomach lurched and hit bottom when she saw the small shack in the distance. The madman rode his horse into the lean-to built against one side of the weather-worn shack, then dropped the reins to roughly cup both of Mandy's breasts as he kneaded and squeezed the soft flesh. "Yer gonna like it, gal." Then one of his hands dropped a breast and slid down to her thighs. "I bet yer ready fer me now, ain'tcha?"

His lips moved like slime over her bare neck and shoulder before he dismounted and tied his horse to the manger. When he turned back to Mandy, her body stiffened, and she fought the ropes on her wrists. The lust and fierce desire that shone in his evil little eyes horrified her. As drool bubbled from the corners of his mouth, she was afraid she would be sick all over herself.

When his beefy hands fumbled with the rope, she had a fleeting hope that she might be able to escape; but before she even had time to finish the thought, he jerked on the rope, and she fell into his arms. He hugged her breasts to his chest and sloppily rained kisses over her face as she arched and kicked wildly at his shins. She aimed a knee at his groin, but he saw her intention and grunted as he twisted and caught the blow on his thigh.

He grinned at her efforts to fight him and fell to his knees in the musty straw littering the ground. One of her wrists was still bound by the rope, and as he pinned her body to the dirt, he pulled both of her arms over her head and quickly secured them to a nearby post.

She twisted her body and flailed her legs in desperation, but he only laughed and pulled the overalls down her hips and legs to cast them aside. Then he stood, ugly and forbidding, leering down at her long, shapely legs and slim, naked body as he opened the fly on his trousers.

When he bent to remove her boots, the last covering left on her body, she kicked deftly out of his reach. If he succeeded in taking her boots, her last hope would be gone. For some reason, just the thought of the knife still being on her person gave her that last ounce of determination.

In a surprise move, the huge man grabbed both of her feet, stretched her legs out on the ground, then threw his tremendous bulk diagonally across her bucking form. There was no possible way for her to move, except to lift her head. She considered sinking her teeth into the odorous shirt, but remembered the blow she had taken earlier. Dare she antagonize the brute to that extent when she found herself in such a helpless situation?

She had decided that she could dare anything when she felt ground vibrate beneath her back and shoulders and heard the sound of horses being ridden hard and fast. Excitement flared to life as an undeniable joy lit her entire being. Ryder! It had to be Ryder. He had been there before when she was in need.

A shot rent the air and disrupted the man's heavy breathing and groping hands. "Get off her, Tiny. I told you no harm was to come to the girl. Get away. Now!"

Tears rolled from Mandy's eyes, and she giggled hysterically. Tiny? No harm? Now why would Hank Ford want to save her? Talk about from the frying pan into the fire. It was priceless. And then her heart sank in despair. Of course it wasn't Ryder. He couldn't know yet that Jeremy was dead, or that she'd been abducted.

She watched the scene unfolding as if from another world. The giant raised his head, growled from deep in his throat and drew his gun. His hand barely touched the butt before his body jerked repeatedly from the impact of several well-placed bullets. Blood dripped on Mandy's stomach and ran down her ribs.

Her abductor was still on his knees between her legs, dead, unmoving, when Hank strode over and pulled him backward, dragging the big man out of the lean-to. She watched, dispassionately, as his boots left twin trails in the dirt. Then she saw Ed on his horse, gun in hand, staring open mouthed at her nakedness. Hank returned to kneel beside her, and she cringed as he ran his hands slowly, almost lovingly, along her overly abused flesh.

Her eyes widened in disbelief when he reached up to cut her arms loose. But then she remembered he was anything but her savior when he opened his mouth. "Looks like Tiny had the right idea. Too bad we don't have time to take advantage of it." He tossed her a rag he'd found under the straw. "Clean yourself, then get dressed. We've got to ride."

Mandy toweled off the blood, then pulled on her overalls in full sight of the grinning men. Normally, she would've been shy and protested, but she was too grateful for the opportunity to clothe herself to make any fuss. When Hank threw her one of the extra shirts from his saddlebags, she took it without a thought to his kindness. She knew Hank Ford too well. She'd pay for it later.

Ryder and Reno caught up with the tiring band of horses even sooner than they'd expected. The mare in the lead had operated on her own, without the usual direction from the black stallion, and had enough sense to slow the grueling pace. The horses were already exhausted from the forced day's march and so, by the time the two men circled them, were docile and easy to gather.

They started back the way they had come, moving at a slow walk. Two saddled horses were among the herd, so Ryder picked them up and led them behind him until they reached the bodies. The horses shied, afraid of the smell of blood and death, but Ryder was finally able to get them loaded and took a position at the rear of the herd.

The sun was low in the sky by the time they reached the clearing where it had all begun. Reno rode back to Ryder and suggested they let the animals rest overnight there.

"I was just getting ready to say the same thing." Ry looked over the weary band and saw that some of them were already bedded down, while the rest had their muzzles buried in the new green grass. "It doesn't look like they'll give us much trouble tonight."

A creek bordered the western edge of the clearing, so the two men decided to make their camp nearby. Ryder wondered what he should do about the dead men. They'd be getting rank soon, and he wasn't looking forward to herding a bunch of nervous horses.

"Why don't we just bury those two and get it over with? No one's goin' to miss 'em," Reno said.

"It's not that easy. I . . . hell, let's do it. We'll remember where they're at if anyone asks." Ryder almost let it slip that he'd have to report the two . . . three deaths to his superiors. But it was true, he wouldn't need the bodies as proof, for they'd learned over the years that if Ryder Manning reported a man as dead, then dead he was. That was another reason, among many, why he'd been sent to Clay County.

Reno helped him haul the dead men down the creek to where the bed had washed out. They caved the bank over the bodies, hesitated a minute, then walked on. At one time they might've deserved a prayer, but now they were God's problem.

Ryder unsaddled the two horses and turned them with the rest of the herd, then gathered wood for a small fire. A pot of black coffee would go down real good.

He and Reno had just leaned back to each sip at a cup of the steaming brew when a horse snorted close by. They turned around to see the heads of most of the horses, ears pricked forward, staring at the opposite

335

line of trees.

They continued watching, and minutes later a horse emerged, carrying a slumped rider in the saddle. When he saw the other horses, the animal stopped, sniffed the air, trumpeted a greeting and pulled at the reins until they slipped low enough to allow him to lower his head to nibble at the grass. The rider just sat there, unmoving, as if he weren't aware of his surroundings.

Ryder looked at Reno, nodded his head toward his rifle, then the two men stood up and walked to the edge of the clearing. They split up so that each man would approach the figure from a different direction—just in case. It was almost dark, and it was hard to see.

Ryder walked faster and reached the horse first, but it shied at his approach. When the man swayed and started to fall, Ryder stepped in to catch the body.

Reno was within a few feet now, still unable to see what was going on, but he froze in his tracks when he heard Ryder exclaim, "My God, it's Jeremy."

Chapter Eighteen

Mandy's chin bounced off her chest for the second time before her head jerked up, her eyes blinking against the brilliance of the setting sun. How she wished she could crawl in a hole and hide, could nurse her aches and pains, could sleep for a week. But as she chewed on her lower lip, she straightened her back and held her head high. She wouldn't give Hank and Ed the satisfaction of knowing she was wearing down.

Her nose itched. She wrinkled it and curled her upper lip, but her wrists were once again lashed to the saddle horn. Finally, she hunched her shoulder and twisted her head until she could scratch against the rough fabric of Hank's shirt. It solved the problem temporarily.

Hank slowed his horse to ride beside her. The look in his eyes reminded her so much of the late Tiny that her stomach convulsed. She stared straight ahead in hopes that he would leave her alone.

"Well, Miss High and Mighty, we've taken quite a tumble, eh?" When she wouldn't look at him, or even acknowledge that she'd heard, he reached over and took hold of her bruised jaw. He laughed when she winced, and at the pain that filled her eyes. "That's better. When I speak to you, you look at me, and you listen. Understand?"

He squeezed her chin until she couldn't stand it any longer and nodded. "That's good. Remember it. Now, where was I? Oh yeah. I was going to tell you how lucky you were that Ed and I got to you in time. You know, I wouldn't want to take a bride that was . . . how should I say it . . . broken in? Yes, my dear, you're a very lucky woman."

Mandy stared after Hank, shocked at the strange-sounding cackle that drifted back as he loped ahead. Had everyone in the world gone crazy? Or was she caught in the middle of some weird dream? Maybe she'd wake up soon, safe and sound in her own bed back home on the farm. No, the pain in her body was too real to be a figment of her imagination.

It was long after dark before they stopped for the night. Hank cut Mandy's wrists loose, but her body was so tired and weak that she collapsed in a heap not two steps from her horse. She was barely aware of the men taking care of the animals and fixing bacon and beans for supper. It was the smell of coffee held directly under her nose that alerted her senses.

She lay on a blanket close to the warm blaze of the fire. Ed held the cup toward her. "Hank says to drink this, then grab some grub. We'll be dousin' the fire directly."

It galled her to be held as a prisoner, to be subjected to such abominable circumstances, but she couldn't help being grateful for the warming liquid. "Th-thank you."

Ed stood up and glared down at her. "The food's by the fire. You kin git it yer own self."

Her eyes widened, and she arched a brow at the hostility she heard in his voice. She hadn't expected to be catered to, but if anyone should be angry over the situation, it was herself. What had she done?

Hank spoke from across the fire. "Don't mind Ed. He's just mad 'cause I won't let him have my bride-to-be. Thinks I'm selfish as hell for not sharin' with him."

She willed herself to hold her temper and managed to half drag and half crawl her way to the plate of food. As hungry as she was, the meager fare tasted like a feast. The coffee finally took effect as warmth and energy seeped back into her lethargic body. The liquid was bitter and gritty, but she helped herself to a second cup.

Hank and Ed both watched her every move until she began to feel like some sideshow display. Her nerves got the better of her, and she had to put the coffee down or risk sloshing the hot brew over her lap. A coyote howled, and she jumped so quickly that she knocked the cup over just as she set it on a rock.

She wrapped her hands around her arms and huddled in miserable silence. God, how she wished they'd quit staring at her and do whatever it was they were going to do to her and get it over with.

When Hank spoke, his voice was so loud and harsh that she jumped again. "Take your blanket under that tree and get some sleep. I've decided that as long as I'm goin' to marry you, I might as well do it right." Then he smiled a gap-toothed leer and winked. "But I'll find us a parson first thing tomorrow, Miss High and Mighty Coulter, and then . . ."

She didn't wait to hear the gory details, so she just grabbed her blanket and ran to the shelter of the tree. Curled into a tight ball, she prayed that Ryder would find her in time. There she went again! Believing that Ryder Manning was the White Knight with nothing better to do with his life than to watch over her. There was no sense in getting her hopes up, for who knew if he was even alive? Tears trickled slowly down her cheeks to dampen the auburn locks under her face. She listened for every movement from the two outlaws, and her eyes searched every shadow. Sleep would be such blessed oblivion.

Ry awoke with a start. The first traces of dawn were streaking the eastern horizon, and he rubbed his eyes wearily. He'd had the weirdest dream last night. As he lay in his bedroll, reluctant to move, vague images formed in his mind. He'd been inside a church, his hands tied behind his back, and . . . yes, a hangman's noose knotted over his neck.

A shiver ran the length of his spine, but still the forms marched on. Jeremy had been standing beside him holding a shotgun five times the normal size of a gun, and a smug smile curved the boy's lips. And . . . there was Reno . . . wearing a black robe and holding a bible, grinning like a lobo wolf.

That was all. He couldn't remember any more. He must have awakened right after Reno's appearance in the nightmare. He stretched his arms up and rested his head in the palms of his hands. The memory of, the meaning of the . . . dream was clearly significant, but instead of the usual frown darkening his features, Ry's lips formed a slow, sensuous smile. When he rose, he whistled as he prepared to break camp. What a glorious morning.

As he saddled his horse, the somberness of the situation struck him again. He had no idea where Amanda was, or who had taken her, or if she was still alive. A trail that he figured had to belong to Hank and his cousin had intersected the one that Ry had been following once, but later he'd lost sign of either trail. So, he was backtracking to where he'd first run across Hank and his group before he'd met Amanda that morning, hoping that Hank would return to his place via the same route. If not, if he took another trail, then Ry was up shit creek without the proverbial paddle.

He finished the pot of coffee made the previous evening, ate a piece of jerky, cleaned his utensils, then packed his bedroll and tied it behind the cantle. As he swung into the saddle, he wondered how Jeremy was getting along.

The boy hadn't been badly injured. A bullet had just creased the top of his scalp. His worst problems were exhaustion and starvation. Evidently Hank and his crew were accomplished in the art of torture. It was going to give Ryder a great deal of pleasure to arrest the whole lot, or what was left of them.

But first, he wanted to take one alive for questioning. If he was right, and Hank was behind the robberies, it would solve a lot of problems. Might even clear up the mystery investigation. Then he'd be free to declare himself to Amanda.

As Ry passed beneath the face of the bluff he'd chosen earlier as his landmark, his eyes scanned the rugged hillside. It was steep, with small, gnarled trees jutting from the cliffs. There was something eerie about the place, yet he felt akin to its untamed wildness.

A little later he found the creek bed he'd been searching for. There were no new tracks, so he decided to lay up for a while and wait, and hope.

He concealed his mustang, then settled under a tree with low-hanging branches to enjoy a long awaited cheroot. It was while he inhaled the last drag that he heard the riders approaching. The cigar was stubbed into the dirt, and Ryder flattened out on his belly.

When he spotted only three horsemen, he was afraid it was a false alarm. Then he saw her, and his whole body tensed and quivered from the intensity of his rage.

Even from that distance he could see the swollen disfiguration of her jaw and the horrible yellowish-purple bruise along the side of her sweet face. The urge to kill ran rampant through his mind, but he took a deep breath and scooted lower to the ground as they rode past his hiding place. He kept his eyes on Amanda, and he saw her head perk up as she looked around with ill-concealed interest. Surely she couldn't know. He crossed his fingers and hoped her escorts weren't paying her any attention.

There was something different about Amanda. He couldn't put his finger on it, but something wasn't quite right. Something important was missing from the picture.

After Amanda and the two outlaws were out of sight, Ry rested his head on his arms and exhaled the breath he'd taken at the sight of Amanda's face. It was at that same time that he felt the weight of the pistol in his right hand. Damn, he didn't remember drawing the thing.

He got to his feet, reholstered the revolver and went to get his horse. It was time to make a decision. Should he follow the riders and find out for sure where Hank and his gang holed up? Or would it be better to charge right in and take Amanda while there were only two men to oppose? Whichever course he chose had to offer the least risk to Amanda.

Mandy was sunk about as low in self-pity as a person could get. Her body was one big ache, her mind was too tired to function properly and her

342

spirit was at its lowest ebb. And who should she conjure up in her darkest hour? Ryder Manning. She couldn't get what was left of her mind off the man. Why now? Why, when she looked upon the end of her life, was her only regret that of not realizing she loved the man sooner? Totally, irrevocably, with all her heart. Who cared that they had major, insurmountable differences?

As she calmly thought over their biggest obstacle, she rationalized that Jesse would soon be moving on and that to all intents and purposes, if—no, when—Ryder asked about her cousin, she could honestly say that Jesse James, the outlaw, was dead and buried. Then there would be no problem. Well, less problem. But he might not even return her love. He'd never indicated in any way that he did.

Suddenly, Mandy's head jerked up. It was almost as if thinking of him had brought him to her. She could feel his presence in such a tangible, physical way. Could it be possible? Was he actually out there somewhere? Ah, it had to be her imagination. She just wanted him so badly that she had believed he was there.

Ry decided to tail Hank, staying close enough to be of help to Amanda in case she needed him. No one was going to hurt her again, not as long as he could help it.

As he rode, his mind strayed to her brothers. When he'd left the boys, they'd planned to stay at the clearing until Jeremy regained some strength, then were going to start their herd toward the fort. If they drove the horses at a slow but steady pace, they could still get in just under the deadline.

One of the reasons Ryder had decided to follow

343

Hank instead of jumping right in after Amanda was his promise to Reno to do everything he could to retrieve the black stallion. But no way would he jeoparidze Amanda for a horse, no way.

Ryder grinned as he realized it sounded like he was trying to convince himself. Yes, he couldn't deny that spark of interest, that bit of curiosity that made him want to see this black stud. Like any horse lover, he was always on the lookout for that special animal, that individual that was a notch ahead of all the rest. And from the way Reno talked, this horse was of that caliber. How could Ry help but try to save the horse from the likes of Hank Ford?

Riding around the next bend, he discovered that Hank and Ed had pulled up at the outskirts of a small community. The men appeared to be arguing. As he waited in the background, he saw Ed lead Amanda's horse into the shade while Hank rode toward the nearest, and largest, building.

Curiosity got the better of him, and he dismounted, leading his horse closer to Amanda while looking for a place where he could get near enough to hear. What was Hank up to now?

It didn't take him long to figure it all out when he saw Hank returning with a short, somberly dressed individual, carrying a book tucked carefully under his arm.

A commotion nearby drew his attention from the settlement to find Ed dragging Amanda forward to greet the other pair. She was attempting to resist, but the outlaw's grip was too strong.

Ryder shifted his eyes once again to find Hank gesturing toward Amanda and smiling as he cajoled the preacher. Ry knew that the time for waiting was over. The only man to stand up with Amanda before

344

a preacher would be him.

"No. Let me go. You can't make me do this."
Mandy was desperate. She hadn't believed Hank
would go through with this crazy notion to marry
her. What purpose would it serve? Other than to
place her completely under his control and domina-
tion, to make her his legally to do with as he deemed
fit. Lord, the reasons were too depressing to consider
at all, let alone count.

She jerked her arm, hoping Ed's grip on her wrist
might've relaxed when he saw Hank approaching,
but no such luck. She even dug her heels into the dirt,
but she was no match against his brute strength.

When the preacher hesitated upon seeing her
resistance, she thought there might be a way out of it
yet, but then Hank started making gestures as if
explaining that she was mentally ill, crazy. And well
she might be if she allowed this farce to continue.

Pretending to stumble, Mandy slid her free hand to
the top of her left boot. Her heart hammered a
constant tattoo against her ribs. What if the knife was
gone? When her fingers brushed the smooth bone
hilt, she thought she would faint. She'd been so
worried, but it was there. At least she had a chance, a
slim one, perhaps, but it was better than none at all.

She twisted her head to check how far she'd have to
run to get back to the horses. Hank had his horse with
him, so she would have to be quick. Surprise was the
only thing she had going for her, and she held her
arm behind her back, effectively concealing her
weapon to wait for just the right moment.

Her arm felt like it was being wrenched from its
socket when Ed jerked her upright. "Stand up, bitch.

Watch where yore goin'. Yore nuthin' but trouble. Hank's gotta be plum locoed."

"So, let me go. I don't want this any more than you do, you know?"

Ed gave her a stern once over, almost as if seeing her for the first time. "No, I reckon ya don't, but Hank's got his mind made up."

Mandy opened her mouth to argue the point, but only succeeded in swallowing a scream when a horse shot out of the trees and came bearing down upon them. The mounted rider fired a shot, and she saw the gun in Hank's hand spin to the ground.

She thought she recognized the man just as Ed grabbed her shoulders and pulled her in front of his body. Then she saw Ry's face through the dust and confusion, and her legs went weak with relief. What a glorious sight he was.

Ed almost choked the air from her chest with his arm, and she cringed when he shouted in her ear, "Hold it. Drop yer gun or the gal gits it. Now!"

Disappointment dragged Mandy's spirits to the ground. They had been so close. Another minute and Ryder would've saved her. As her eyes and brain numbly put together a picture of the scene, she saw the preacher running frantically toward the village. Hank stood speechless, staring at the mounted stranger, who in turn stared warily at the gun being pointed at Mandy's head.

Mandy seemed to be standing in a suspended state of shock until she noticed Hank sidestepping ever so slowly toward his pistol. Her mind suddenly kicked into gear, and she raised her arms to try to keep Ed's arm from strangling her so she could yell a warning to Ryder.

Life poured through her body in a tremendous surge of adrenaline and hope when she remembered the knife still held so tenaciously in her hand. She didn't take the time to berate herself, however; she just sliced the blade across Ed's fingers until he dropped the gun.

A shout of exaltation escaped her lips when Ed screamed and released her to grasp his bloody hand. She sprinted as fast as she could toward Ryder, but his horse was nervous and shied away from her threatening approach.

"Watch out, Ryder. Hank has a gun." She pointed in the outlaw's direction, then stood perfectly still as Ryder kicked his horse into motion and very nearly rode her down.

"Give me your hand, Amanda. Quick!" He lifted her in front of him so smoothly, and so effortlessly, that she hardly knew it had happened. Then he bent low over her, shielding her body as he spurred his horse into a dead run. Bullets were buzzing so closely that she flinched and ducked, and once, she thought she heard a "thwack" and a grunt from Ryder; but he never slowed their pace, and the horse never faltered, so she assumed it was only her imagination.

When Mandy finally dared to peek over Ry's shoulder, she laughed excitedly to see the other three horses, stirrups flapping, reins flying through the air, following madly in the mustang's wake.

"We've made it, Ry. We're in the clear." She wrapped her arms around his waist and laid her head against his chest as she gave him a squeeze. But the smile on her lips faded, and the happiness in her eyes deepened to that of concern as one of her hands encountered a warm, sticky substance on his back. She quickly raised her head and noticed the pallor of his usually dark skin.

His eyes were even blacker than normal as he glanced down at her and tried to smile. "Yeah, we did it, sweetheart. You were good, real good."

Worry and a trace of fear crept into her voice as she whispered, "You're hurt, Ryder. Why didn't you tell me you'd been shot?"

Again the gorgeous lips tilted in what could either be taken for a grimace or a grin. "It's nothin'. Besides, we need to put more distance between us and them."

He slumped forward slightly, and Mandy twisted in the saddle until she had her legs on either side of the horn. "All right, now give me the reins and rest against me. I'll find us some help . . . somehow."

When Ry handed her the reins, she also grabbed his hand, then reached behind her to take his other hand and pulled them both around her waist so that she could hold them in place. At least now he couldn't fall off without her knowing about it.

She liked having his arms around her once more, the feel of his hard length pressed against her back, and the warm satisfaction that seeped through her body at having him close. She moved her shoulders until she could nuzzle her head against his beard-stubbled cheek. He'd actually come for her, had risked his life for hers, again.

She had to get him to a doctor. No, they would never make it, not in the condition he was in already. The wound was bad, and he was bleeding heavily. Yet she knew that if they stopped now, the chances of her being able to get him on the horse again were nil. She had to take him someplace close and somewhere safe.

As Mandy surveyed the country, she realized that they were within a mile, or maybe less, of the cave. Fear and indecision gripped her insides. Dear Lord, what was she to do? If she took Ry to Jesse, she'd be risking Jesse's life and future. If she didn't, Ry would surely die.

Her blood turned to ice, and she shivered violently with the enormity of her decision. She'd had a feeling it would come to this, almost from the first time she'd ever laid eyes on Ryder Manning. She'd sensed even then the danger of becoming involved with the man.

Mandy felt the weight of her burden in more ways than one when Ryder's head lolled to the side of her shoulder and she felt the slackness in his arms as his body sagged against her back. Panic assailed her as she realized he'd passed out, either from pain, or loss of blood, or maybe both.

Well, the decision was out of her hands now. She had no choice. If Ryder was to have any chance at all, she had to get him to Jesse. With new light in her eyes, and a determined nudge to the horse's ribs, she headed toward the cave in the most direct route possible.

She was so absorbed in holding Ryder on the horse and in trying to see through the rapidly descending dusk, that the horse's sudden stop almost jolted her and Ryder both from the saddle.

Mandy was terrified. The horse's ears were pricked in the direction of the cave, and he snorted and whickered. Damn! Someone was coming. She could hear the clop of horses' hooves. And here she sat, with her hands full, trying to get Ryder's weight distributed evenly on the saddle again, and she couldn't even get to a gun. Double damn!

She held her breath as the approaching horse stopped just under the branches of a nearby tree. It was too dark to see either the horse or the rider, if there was one. Had Hank, or Ed, gotten ahead of her somehow? Finally she could stand the suspense no

349

longer. She had to know who it was—now.

"W-who is it? Are you lost, or . . . l-looking for someone?"

There was movement under the tree, and her horse moved forward. God, was she going to die now?

"Amanda? Is that you?"

Mandy's heart started beating again. She drew a deep breath and sighed. "Jesse! Oh, God, Jesse. Thank heaven."

She was still mumbling almost incoherently when he rode over to her. Then she stopped suddenly and stared as the horse he rode snuffled and took the loose leg of her overalls in his teeth to tug playfully. "Red Fox." Tears flowed from her eyes at the marvelous revelation. She'd thought the horse lost, or maybe even dead.

Jesse eyed Amanda and her limp baggage thoughtfully. "He wandered up to the cave not more than half an hour ago. He was a Godsend because I'd just started out on foot to look for you."

"You had? But why?" Before she could find out what had brought Jesse out of the cave, Ryder began to slip to the side, and she frantically tugged at the unconscious body. "Catch him, Jesse. Don't let him fall."

Jesse quickly grabbed Ryder's shoulder and helped to get him balanced against Amanda's back. "Who is this man, Amanda? I've watched him poking around here several times this past week."

Mandy heard the suspicion and distrust in her cousin's voice but couldn't really blame him. She had taken a chance by bringing Ryder here. Now she had to see if it had been for nothing.

"This is Ryder Manning. The man I've been telling you about. He's been shot in the back, Jesse. He was wounded while saving me from Hank Ford

350

and . . . and his cousin Ed."

There was complete silence for a moment, just long enough for Mandy to hear the plaintive wail of a mourning dove. Its soulful cry did little to improve her spirits. "I was bringing him to you for help. He's hurt rather badly. I'm afraid. Please help us, Jesse?"

Jesse heard the desperate plea in her voice and knew he could refuse her nothing, anyway. He also knew his lovely cousin well enough to guess that this hadn't been an easy decision for her to make. "You knew I'd help or you wouldn't have brought him here. Come on, let's get him to the cave."

Mandy emitted a sound that could've been a nervous giggle. "I'd hoped you'd feel that way, but . . . I knew what it would mean. . . ."

"It's all right, Amanda. We both knew I couldn't stay here forever. It's been long enough. I can move on safely now."

"But . . ." She knew it was true. All the hoopla and commotion surrounding the death of the famous outlaw had settled. Only *Ryder* stood in the way of Jesse's making a clean break and starting over again.

But how could she let her beloved cousin walk out of her life so easily? He'd been the one bright light in her dismal life for more years than she cared to count. No matter what other people thought of him, he'd given her sound advice and guidance during her formative years when she'd had no one else. She loved him. She didn't want to lose him.

Sensing Amanda's turmoil, Jesse reined Red Fox to ride by her side, and he reached over to fold one of her small, cold hands into his large, warm fingers. "I know, hon, I know." They rode like that, in silence, the rest of the way to the cave. When they stopped, he squeezed her hand and said, "I love you, too. Ahem, wait until I get the opening cleared, then ride on in.

I'll be right behind you. Okay?"

They smiled at each other, and Mandy nodded bravely. It would be all right. Ryder would live. Jesse would leave. She'd survive. Please, God, help her to make it through it all.

Mandy sat still in the saddle, savoring the feel of Ryder's arms around her while she could. She watched Jesse pull blankets close to the fire and set a large cauldron of water over the flames. When he stood beside her at last, his face was solemn and grim as he held his arms up. "Let him slide off toward me, Amanda. I'll catch him. Don't worry."

She wondered what he'd seen in her face to say such a thing. Had he noticed her love, her concern, or her fear? Would he laugh if he knew how she really felt?

Ryder groaned, and he mumbled as his feet hit solid ground; but he never fully regained consciousness, so Mandy and Jesse had to drag him to the blankets. They eased him facedown onto the pallet, and Mandy covered her mouth with both hands as her eyes rounded with horror at the sight of his blood-drenched clothing. How could he possibly survive?

Jesse put a gentle hand on her shoulder and shook her until she looked at him instead of at the wounded marshal. "Get a grip on yourself, hon. I'm going to need your help. Use your knife and cut that shirt off. I've got to get a few more things together. Can you do it?"

Her eyes were still round and huge, a little too bright, but she'd do anything to be of help. She nodded, and Jesse left her alone. The knife had been returned to her boot, so she bent to get it, giving her another close up view of the bloody material. She took a deep, calming breath, steadied her shaking hands, then knelt beside Ryder.

She pulled the shirttail out of his pants and started

352

cutting from the bottom up. The material was damp and matted, and it stuck to the skin around the edges of the wound, making it difficult for her, knowing that she was hurting him. She stopped several times to swallow and turn her head to gulp fresh air. When she cut through the collar, she averted her eyes from the ugly hole that marred the otherwise perfection of the broad, smooth back. She pulled each half of the shirt from his arms, then tugged the material from under his inert form. She held his head tenderly, then softly caressed the black waves of his hair before placing his cheek on the rough blanket.

He was so pale, so still. His deep chest barely moved, and his eyelashes formed pools of shadow on his gaunt cheeks. She ran a loving finger over the gentle curve of his lips, loving the feel of their soft, sensuous texture. His kisses were so firm, so warm, so gentle, so— Sitting abruptly back on her heels, she buried her eyes in the palms of her hands in a futile attempt to stem the flow of her tears.

There was a change in the air the minute Jesse knelt beside her. He exuded confidence and determination as he placed clean rags and a long, thin-bladed knife on the rocks by the fire.

Jesse had been watching Amanda for quite a while. He'd guessed before that she had deep feelings for the man called Ryder Manning; now he knew it for a fact. Earlier, he'd been skeptical about saving the deputy marshal's miserable hide, but now he'd move heaven, or even hell if need be, to give her this life and a chance at happiness.

When he leaned down beside her, he touched the horrible bruise on the side of her face. He didn't like the exhaustion and desperation he saw mirrored in her delicate features, the hollow-eyed stare, and the way her hands shook so uncontrollably.

He'd been at the other end of the cave, watching this Ryder Manning circle the bottom of the hill, when his attention had been diverted to the approach of three more riders: Hank, Ed and his Amanda. He'd used his spy glass and seen that her wrists were bound. Hank was up to no good, and Jesse had started out on foot to see if there wasn't something he could do. If only for the reason that he'd saved Amanda, Jesse would do his best for Ryder.

He hugged his cousin to him, patted her hair and used his most calm and reassuring tone of voice. "Hon, there's a lot I need to do here. I want to get him undressed, then clean the wound. Now, there's something that you can do for me. Are you listening?" He cupped her face in his hands and stared into her eyes until she blinked and nodded that she'd heard.

"Good. Go back outside and make sure our tracks coming up to the cave are wiped out. We didn't try to hide them very well when we rode up 'cause we were in a hurry. Remember? Now, this is important. If Hank knows that this man is wounded, he'll be scouring the countryside looking for the two of you. Be a good girl and use the tricks you've learned to cover our trail. Okay?"

He smiled as he watched her gulp and then take a deep breath before getting unsteadily to her feet. "That's my girl. You do a good job. I'll take care of your man." When she looked questioningly at Ryder's jean-clad lower body, he shook his head. "Naw, I won't need your help. Now, go on, get out of here."

As he watched her small form moving toward the cave entrance, he breathed a heavy sigh of relief. His cousin was a strong woman, but she was on the verge of collapse. He didn't want her to have to go through what it would take to remove the bullet and cauterize the gaping wound in the man's back. Ryder was going to need the help of a strong, steady hand, and Jesse couldn't operate and watch Amanda, too.

As he turned to his task, holding the wicked-looking blade over the fire, he only hoped that *he* was strong enough to handle it. It was going to be a long, hard night.

Chapter Nineteen

Mandy felt better as she stepped into the brisk night air. For a moment inside, she'd felt dizzy, almost faint, but now she was alert and fully understood the importance of the task she'd been asked to do. She'd been so concerned about taking Ryder to the cave that she'd forgotten about concealing their tracks.

Bending down, she chose a long limb with a lot of smaller branches lying next to the entrance and started swishing it across the imprints of the horses' hooves. As she moved away from the cave, the dust resettled, and the ground she'd brushed became consistent with the rest. Any broken twigs encountered were snapped off completely, and she scattered dead leaves over the freshly scraped earth.

After working quite a ways from the cave, she stopped to take a breather and became instantly aware of the fact that she wasn't alone. She got the distinct impression that she was being watched, followed. A sad smile creased her cheeks as she realized that this time she wouldn't be tackled or have the breath knocked out of her by a dive from Ryder.

Her hand went immediately to her pocket, but the

derringer was gone, probably shaken from the pocket during the fracas with the giant. And her knife was in the cave where she'd put it down to finish removing Ryder's shirt. This was great. What if it was Hank, or Ed, or any of the number of cutthroats that could be found roaming these hills?

At least she had the limb, and she moved on, pretending that nothing had changed, that she hadn't noticed an alien presence. She only hoped they hadn't seen where she'd come from.

There was that noise again. Whoever, or whatever it was, was moving toward her, not bothering to hide or move very quietly. The sounds were close now, so she stepped under the cover of a tree where she would be harder to see, to kill. She didn't have to make it easy.

A loud snort from directly behind her almost caused Mandy to impale herself on the end of the dead branch. Another snort and a soft whicker, and she turned to stare eye to eye with the horse she'd abandoned earlier in the day. She laughed and threw her arms around the soft, sleek neck.

"What's the matter, boy? Are you lonely?"

It was amazing that the horse had come this far on his own. One rein was missing, and the saddle had slipped to the side; but otherwise, the animal was in good shape. It wouldn't do to leave him loose in this area, so she'd just take it along for Jesse to use. Besides, he was a nice horse, she decided as she gently rubbed its velvety muzzle.

Here she'd gone to all that trouble, obliterating all those tracks, and now she was going to make another set going back. She stepped back, looked the animal over and came up with a brainstorm. Taking the remaining rein from the bridle, she very carefully tied the limb to its tail. The horse turned his head and rolled his big brown eyes as if she were crazy, but he didn't put up a fuss.

As they returned to the cave, Mandy wound around through the trees and brush, every once in a while going back to see if the idea was actually working. Luckily, it was. So, taking hold of the side of the bridle, she led the horse to the cave entrance.

The closer she came to the opening, the weaker her knees became. Her stomach felt like a mass of butterflies, and her heart became involved somehow with the vicious fluttering. Guilt was a definite deterrent to returning inside. She had let Jesse talk her into leaving with no trace of an argument. What if Ryder was dead? What if he'd called out for her? Would she be able to live with herself for being such a coward?

Ry drifted into consciousness through a wave of dizzying fog. He couldn't move for the intense pain, and it hurt to blink his eyelids. It felt like he was lying on the back of a buckin' bronco, and his stomach was taking the brunt of the abuse. Gradually, his world stopped spinning, and efforts to throw him into infinity ceased.

He lay unmoving, hardly daring to open his eyes. As his mind began to function, too many questions caused him to feel uneasy, and he fidgeted, twisting the muscles along his shoulders and back. His brain literally screamed out his agony. The throbbing started at the top of his skull and hammered its way along every nerve in his body, the most intense area being over his back. As the pain eased somewhat, he realized that if he remained motionless he only experienced a dull ache, not the excruciating misery.

His eyelids blinked, then slit open. Everything was

blurry, hazy, as if he were in a dream world. It was dark, the only light given off by a fire burning close to his left side. Where was he? Had he died and gone to hell? It was easy enough to get that impression from the orange glow and flickering shadows that met his hooded gaze. Even the muted light was too much for his aching eyes, so he closed them and blessed the relief.

Time was meaningless. When he next opened his eyes a fraction, he had no way of knowing whether it had been ten minutes or ten hours, if he had slept or passed out. Everything was still in a haze, and even his mind was fuzzy. He couldn't remember where he was, how he'd gotten there, or . . . anything.

Suddenly, one of the shadows flickered, wavered, then drifted closer. When the image bent down by the fire, Ry knew that it was a human figure, a man. Or, wait. In the back of his mind he tried to put together something about a pair of overalls, but all that came to him was that the person didn't necessarily have to be a man.

There was nothing familiar about the face that turned toward him then. And it was definitely a male, with sandy-colored hair, nervous blue eyes, upturned nose and thin mobile lips. A very innocent, unthreatening face, all in all.

Everything had an innocent air, except for the gleam reflecting off a long, silver blade being turned over and over in the flames. When the blade was finally removed from the fire, its tip glowed red hot. Ryder had taken a distracted view of the scene until the man turned and started toward him, knife first.

This had to be a joke of some kind. Groggily, Ry tried to focus on the swaying tip of the blade, but everything was drifting in and out of his vision. He thought he felt a warm hand touch the back of his shoulder, but he couldn't be sure as the lights were suddenly blown out.

Jesse's hand shook slightly as he removed the knife blade from the flames and turned it over to be sure it was evenly heated. It had been a long time since he'd done this. Several years ago it had been nothing unusual to remove a bullet from someone, but today, and on a marshal, Mandy's love . . . the pressure could get to a man if he let it.

When he turned toward the patient, Jesse was surprised to see the fellow's eyes open. Barely, but they *were* open. The marshal was made of stern stuff. Jesse hadn't expected him to come around for some time, at least not before he was ready to take the bullet out.

As he put his hand on Ryder's shoulder, he felt the muscles bunch, then go slack. So much the better for the young man—he'd passed out again. Jesse moved the kettle of hot water nearer Ryder and washed off the fresh blood that had pooled around the wound. He inserted the tip of the knife into the hole and probed as quickly and as gently as possible. Yes, it had been a long time. And if he never did this again it would be too soon.

It was darker inside the cave than usual. As Mandy led the horse into the large cavern, she stopped so suddenly that his hoof clipped the side of her foot. "Ouch!" Then the horse nuzzled his head into her back and pushed her forward. "Oh, all right, you're forgiven, this time."

But the horse's antics were soon forgotten when she saw the long figure stretched so quietly on the pallet. A blanket covered his body as far as the stark white bandage between his shoulder blades. She dropped the rein that she had reattached to the bridle and tiptoed over to the unnaturally still form. The bleeding fingernail she'd been chewing went unnoticed as she forced herself to bend over and feel for a pulse.

Her knees gave out, and she flopped down beside Ryder. At least he was alive. She ran a hand through his hair, moving a lock that had fallen into his eye. His skin was hot and dry, so she dipped a rag into the cooled water and wiped it over his exposed flesh.

By the time she was finished, he was breathing easier and felt cooler when she smoothed her palm over the corded muscles of his shoulder and upper arm. It was painful to see such a strong, powerful man so helpless and vulnerable. It reminded her of the time Jesse . . . Jesse? Where was he?

Since Ryder seemed to be resting peacefully, she got up to go in search of her cousin. The horse, standing where she'd left him, pawed the ground impatiently to get her attention. "Okay, just hold your horses. Oops! Sorry 'bout that."

She led the animal into the smaller cavern and tied him beside Ryder's grulla. After she removed the saddle and rubbed him down with the blanket, he braced all four feet and shook, rippling the sorrel hide from neck to rump. The horse had such a contented look on his face as he stole a nibble of hay from his neighbor that she smiled for the first time in hours.

Then she noticed Jesse lounging against the back opening, not too far from Red Fox. He looked haggard, and his shoulders were slumped forward, his hands jammed into his pockets. She thought he must not have seen her until he nodded his head and asked, "Where'd you get the horse?"

She walked over to Red Fox and patted the horse's sleek coat. "He followed us. I rode him after . . . Hank killed his owner. I guess he liked me."

Jesse was glad to see Mandy smiling again. He'd been worried about her. "Your man'll be fine. It's not as bad as it looked."

"My man? I wish. No, even wishing won't make it true."

Jesse thought about the times the marshal had called out for Amanda and shrugged his shoulders, effectively hiding a grin. "You never know. Do you love him, Amanda? Really love him?"

She thought for a minute, combing her fingers through Red Fox's matted mane. "I think I do. In fact, I know I do. Is it stupid to feel this way over a man that's virtually a stranger, Jesse?" She didn't give her cousin a chance to answer, just continued, "Yesterday, when I thought I might . . . die . . . I would've given anything to have the chance to see him again. It's hard to explain. . . ."

"I know. It's something special, something between two people. I'm happy for you, hon. I hope everything works out for you."

She looked at her cousin long and hard. "I know you are, Jesse. And I thank you for all you've done for us."

They both stood looking out into the fading darkness. It was hard to believe it was almost morning.

Mandy swallowed, sniffed and stepped closer to Jesse. "Where will you go? Have you made any plans?"

"Oh, I don't really know for sure. I think I'll just start riding and see where I end up."

"W-will I ever see you again?"

Jesse put an arm around Mandy's shoulder and hugged her to his side. "Maybe. Maybe not. I'll never come back to Clay County. It would be too dangerous for too many people. But it's a small world. Someday you might travel some yourself, and who knows?"

Mandy couldn't help but think about Reno's and Jeremy's plans to move west. Yes, who knew what fate had in store for any of them.

"Amanda? What do you know about a black stallion?"

"I know that Reno had one stolen from him by Hank Ford, and he was really anxious about it." She explained about what they had been doing for the past few days: how they had attempted to steal the horse herd back, and Jeremy's being shot, and about her subsequent capture. "I don't know if they got the horses back, and worst of all, I don't know if Jeremy's alive or dead."

Silence settled over the pair as a soft array of pink and orange suffused the eastern sky. Suddenly, Mandy asked, "Why? What did you want to know about the horse?"

"It's just something that the deputy kept mumbling about. I only caught a few words: Reno, black stallion, Santa Fe. He seemed to be real worried about the horse."

Mandy sighed and glanced out of the corner of her eye toward the larger cave. "I might as well tell you all of it. The horse herd was intended to be a final payment for a ranch somewhere close to Santa Fe. Reno and Jer have been breaking and training wild horses and selling them to the Army in order to buy the land. Reno wanted to keep a few good mares and that stallion as his foundation stock for the ranch."

Jesse listened to the dull monotone of Amanda's voice. "The boys have really grown up this past year.

I'm proud of them. But I take it you aren't excited about the move?''

Her head was shaking as she answered, ''Surely you, of all people, understand, Jesse. You're being forced to leave your home, your family. Missouri's my home. I love it here. The farm is all I know. And . . . I can't just up and leave Pa all alone.''

''Take him with you.''

''You know Pa. He'll stay right there on that farm, operating his still, believing that Ma will come back someday.''

Jesse was stone-cold serious when he stared deeply into his cousin's eyes. ''Be honest, Amanda. Isn't that the real reason you stay on the farm? Deep down, aren't you waiting to see your ma again?'' It was something Jesse had thought for a long time. He'd just never had the chance to bring it up before.

''I . . . no, I don't. . . . No! She deserted us. Why should I care if she ever came back? Why would I want to punish myself like that? I never want to see her again as long as I live.''

''Oh, really? Then why do you always sit in the living room, staring out the window toward town? Why do you keep the place spotless, even when nobody else is home, or within fifty miles of the farm?''

''I . . . well, you never know who might happen to drop by sometime.''

''Sure. I bet the deputy in there is the first person to step a foot into your house, or sit at your table, for years. There's no one left to just drop by nowadays. Right?''

''Jesse, quit it. I don't know. Maybe you're right. I just know that I don't want to leave right now.''

Jesse shook Amanda's shoulders as he looked at her, his eyes blinking rapidly, an affliction caused

from a childhood illness. "I think you sho~~
with Reno and Jeremy. If things work out that they
got the horses sold and made that last payment, I
want you to encourage them to leave, and you, too.
Things aren't good here anymore, Amanda, especially now. The James's, the Coulter's, the Younger's are all going to have a rough time of it. People are
changing; their ways are different. Promise me,
Amanda. Promise me that you'll leave Missouri."

She continued to look into her cousin's eyes,
refusing to back down. "I promise . . . that I'll think
about it. That's all I can do."

"Well, at least it's better than a straight no. All
right, it'll have to do. But, hon, the best advice I'll
ever give you is telling you to leave, now."

Mandy just nodded. He was probably right, but
she couldn't bring herself to make that decision, not
yet. "I'd better go in and check on Ryder. He was
awfully hot a while ago."

"Okay, that's a good idea. After my expert surgery,
we've got to take good care of the man. Oh, hon? Do
you mind if I borrow Red Fox?"

Mandy's eyes rounded with worry. "You're going
out, Jesse? Do you think it's safe?"

"Probably not, but there's something I've got to
do. I'll make you a promise, though. I'll be careful.
Okay?"

She laughed and gave her cousin a hug. "Okay."

As Mandy sat with Ry's head cradled in her lap, she
thought about what Jesse had said about the times
changing so. And he was right. The old ways, as he'd
known them, were gone, as were the sympathies
toward his outlaw life. The only problem was that he
thought people had begun to put aside their

365

prejudice and hatred, as he had. But Mandy knew better.

It would take a long, long time to wipe out the hurt and hatred that had built for years before the war and then had only intensified during the fighting. There would still be persecution and prejudice, especially in Missouri and states like it where the fighting and bickering had started long before the actual declaration of war.

Maybe it would be best to move on, to start a new life for herself and her family. After all, her brothers were prone to find trouble easily.

Ry's head moved to nestle against her stomach. She'd propped a blanket under his chest so his head and neck would be more comfortable since it was probably too soon to turn him on his back. His body was hot; but she'd sponged him down again, and his color was better.

Her heart swelled with love as she gazed down on his drawn but handsome features. She could be happy forever just having him within her reach like this—where she could feast her eyes on his long, trim body, feel the muscled firmness of his flesh beneath her wandering fingers, smell the masculine scent of horses and cigars, and hear the soft breath hissing between his parted lips.

A shiver traced down her spine. It was cold in the cave, despite her warming thoughts, and the fire had burned down during her rambling thoughts of Ryder Manning. She gently lifted his head, pulling the blanket from beneath his chest, and laid him flat on the pallet.

Their wood supply was running dangerously low after last night, so she thought it a good idea to bring in another load. She looked at Ryder again before she

left, noted the even rise and fall of his chest and
walked away.

Ry would've protested when his head was lifted
from its soft cushiony pillow and placed on a rough
blanket, but nothing seemed to work. His arms and
legs wouldn't move, his neck was stiff and his mouth
and jaws refused to budge. What a frustrating
situation.

It took forever for his eyelids to finally blink and
then barely open, but at least he had enough vision to
make out a dim, foggy room. It seemed vaguely
familiar. And there was a figure bending over the fire.
It was like watching a replay of something that had
happened before, or that he had dreamed.

When the figure turned back, it was a woman, a
very beautiful woman, wearing those dirty overalls.
But that didn't seem to fit with his earlier version of
the scene. It had been a man then, hadn't it?

Everything was so confused and jumbled in his
mind. He was groggy and weak, and so sleepy. At
least he didn't hurt like before. Of that much he was
certain. If only he could will some part of his body to
move. A frightening thought occurred to him—
maybe he was paralyzed—but then he felt the weight
and the scratchy texure of a blanket covering his legs
and buttocks. If he was paralyzed he wouldn't be able
to feel, would he?

Just before his eyes blinked and closed for the final
time, he saw the woman stop and look down at him.
Even in his dazed state, he recognized the love and
longing etched on her lovely features, and his own
heart thumped a bit irregularly for a time. An
unfamiliar state of contentment seeped through his

body, and he fell asleep a very happy man.

It was late afternoon, and Mandy had curled up on the blanket near Ryder, unable to keep her eyes open a second longer. She had spent the day straightening things in the cave and taking care of the horses, besides bathing and looking after her patient.

It had been fun, and an unbidden picture of herself as a wife, looking after a home and caring for a husband, had flitted in and out of her head all day. She'd never thought of herself as a wife before, had never even considered marriage when it came right down to it. It had always been too painful a subject. Now, suddenly, she found herself almost skipping through her chores.

Ry had been sleeping peacefully, other than every once in a while when his muscles would quiver and tremble as if he were dreaming. He'd mumbled a few unintelligible words, then had been still ever since. It was over thirty-six hours since she'd slept, and it was telling on her.

Since she was afraid to leave Ryder untended, fearful that he'd run a temperature, she decided to lie down next to him. That way she'd be the first to know if he became agitated or hot, a condition that was fast taking control of her own body as she imagined the naked form separated from her by only a thin blanket.

She didn't know how long she'd been asleep, but when she awoke, she was lying half underneath Ry's heavy body. His head was tucked under her chin, his cheek pressed against her breast. One arm was wrapped around her waist, and his right leg was thrown over both of hers, effectively pinioning her to the pallet.

If she moved, he held her tighter, as if afraid to let go. When she felt the tremors that shook his body, it scared her to death. Had he taken a fever? Or was he cold and just attracted by the heat from her body? It wasn't the most romantic thought, but she enjoyed holding him close, no matter the reason.

When she put her arm around his waist to try to shift his weight so she could move, she found that the blanket had slipped. No wonder he was shivering, and . . . every naked, masculine inch of the man was pressed next to her. She was very proud of herself for remembering that he was a recently injured man, and she promised not to take advantage of him.

With that reminder running over and over through her head, she kept her hands still but snuggled as close as she could get. Then she squirmed until she could reach an end of the blanket and pulled it over their entwined bodies. The fire would just have to wait until his body built some extra heat before she could get up.

Something wet and warm tickled the lobe of Mandy's ear, and an electric jolt traveled the length of her body when something warm and hard teased the taut tip of her nipple. Surprise prompted her to jerk upright, but she was still immobile.

A gust of breath blew into her sensitive inner ear, and she shivered as a deep chuckle warmed whatever areas his touch couldn't reach. "Wake up, sleepy-head. Did anyone ever tell you that you snore?"

Her hand flew from around his back to catch the hand playing with her breast. He must've been awake for some time as her overall bib was unfastened, along with all the buttons on Hank's shirt. If she didn't stop him now, she wouldn't be able to remember all the questions that had been haunting her for the past few days. And no telling how long he'd remain conscious.

Still, she gave a throaty laugh and quipped, "No, I can't say that anyone's ever accused me of making noises when I sleep. Why? Do I?"

"No, I just wanted to be sure that no one else had heard you, either."

"Evidently you're feeling better. The bullet must've missed your funny bone."

Ry laid his head back on Mandy's shoulder, nuzzling his nose into her neck. He was soo tired. "So that's what happened. I couldn't remember."

Mandy put her hand under his chin and scooted down until she could look into his alarmingly cloudy eyes. "You don't remember? Anything?"

He closed his eyes and sighed. "Well, I don't really know. I guess I haven't tried."

"Think, Ryder. Think real hard. Did you and Reno get the horses back? Did you by any chance run across Jeremy? Was he alive?"

Ry's head was so fuzzy that he had a hard time keeping up with Amanda. "Hold on, sweetheart. I just remembered a little while ago who *you* were. Give me some time, please."

Everything was so quiet that Mandy could hear her heart beat, or hammer, whichever you wanted to call it. Why didn't he hurry? She consoled herself by knowing that he would if he could.

"Wait a minute, I saw Jeremy. Yes, I'm sure of it. He was hurt, but not too bad. He and Reno are together now."

"Oh, thank God. I was so sure Jeremy was dead. There was so much blood."

"Shh." Ry patted her shoulder and held her close against his chest. "It was just a crease on his scalp. As soon as his hair grows longer, you'll never be able to see it."

"You said my brothers were together. Do you know where they are?"

Ry's knee slipped between Mandy's legs, and his palm rubbed up and down her waist and ribs. "The last I knew, they were resting up, getting ready to take the horses on to the fort."

"Oh. I see."

His lips traveled over her shoulder to settle on the erratic pulse at the base of her throat. "I've let them down, Amanda. I promised to get that black stallion."

"Yes, that's what . . . I heard." That was close. For a minute, she'd almost said that's what Jesse had told her. "But it's certainly not your fault. They won't think you let them down."

She was beginning to fidget and squirm beneath Ryder's seemingly absent-minded manipulations of her extremely sensitive body. The hand smoothing over her ribs had brushed the lower side of her breast, and she now anticipated the next upward sweep.

"Besides, you saved the life of their favorite sister. They'll think they owe y-you-oooh."

Ry's hand cupped her breast, and he tweaked the hardened bud between his thumb and forefinger. "I didn't do it for them, sweetheart. But to tell you the truth, I was looking forward to seeing that black stud. He must be something else, according to Reno, anyway."

His knee slid higher but encountered the resistance of her overalls, so his lips explored her jaw and cheek and nipped her ear before sucking the lobe into his mouth.

"Well, I'm grateful you came after me first. Or did you just accidently stumble across me on the way to the horse?"

The hand on her breast moved, tickling slowly

down her ribs and over her belly. Her muscles flinched, and the silky flesh rippled beneath his fingers. "Uhmmm, now what do you think?"

Mandy's body was so aroused that she couldn't remember what they'd been talking about. When she'd caught his hand earlier, she'd had a momentary vision of Tiny and of the pain he'd inflicted. But it was Ryder touching her now, caressing her so sweetly, gently urging her on.

She lifted her hands to either side of his head and held him still long enough to fasten her lips to his. She kissed him until his lips parted and she gained free access to investigate the hard ridges of his teeth and then the honeyed recess beyond. His tongue met hers and then proceeded to take command away from her.

The kiss was long and satisfying, and when they came up for air, Ry took a deep breath and rested his head on Mandy's chest. They were both breathing heavily as she ran her fingers through the hair above Ry's ear.

Mandy's body was so stimulated that every nerve ending begged to be touched, so she turned more fully into Ry. Her hand trailed down his neck and over his shoulder to fondle the smooth, supple skin of his back and buttocks. She smiled when he groaned and nestled his cheek on her breast, and her nipple contracted as his moist breath huffed over the tingling nubbin.

"Ryder, there's something . . . I think you should know. I mean—" her hand rubbed and massaged up his body, and her fingers buried themselves in the rich black waves of his hair—"I-I wanted to tell you. . . ." She couldn't do it. What if he laughed at her, called her a fool?

But if he would only encourage her, prod her a little to finish what she'd started to say, maybe she could just blurt it out. Silence. Maybe he wasn't interested in anything she had to say. Maybe he didn't give a damn about her at all. When she shifted to the side to look into his eyes and see the truth of what she suspected, she halted all movement as his head fell to the side and she had to support it with her arm.

His eyes were closed, and his breathing was even but shallow. The man had gone to sleep during her big confession scene. She couldn't help herself; she just had to laugh. Her upper arm braced his head as she gave in to the urge. What a blow to her pride, yet she'd been saved from a very embarrassing moment— for the time being.

Mandy finally dozed, and when she came fully awake, what she had feared the most had happened. Ry's body was warm with fever, and he tossed restlessly in a fitful sleep. The bandage on his back was spotted with red, the bleeding probably started by his jerky movements.

For the next hour or so, she changed the dressing and bandages on the wound and soaked Ry's body with cold water from the spring. And it helped. He was resting better. Thank heavens it hadn't been as bad as she had thought.

Moving quietly so as not to disturb the sleeping man, she went into the back cavern, checked on the horses and went to the entrance for some fresh air. Now she knew why Jesse spent so much time at that spot. The view was magnificent, and you could shake the claustrophobic feeling of being cooped up inside a cave for days on end.

She sat there for some time, smelling the fresh spring air, noticing the contrasting browns, greens and grays below the brilliant blue and white skyline. She watched a red-tailed hawk swoop low over a cluster of summac, but as far as she could see, it failed

373

to scare up any prey.

Deciding to clean the manure from the horses' stalls, she'd just gotten up and dusted off her bottom when she heard a man yell. My God, it had to be Ryder.

She'd barely entered the main cavern when he sat upright and shouted, "No! Don't shoot. You can't kill her. I love her."

His eyes remained closed, though his body shook violently. Mandy let him lie on his back so she could put a cold cloth on his forehead. Then taking another rag, she sponged his chest. When the corded muscles relaxed and he breathed more evenly and calmly, she leaned her back against a rock and hung her head dejectedly.

She was so grateful that he'd fallen asleep earlier before she'd had a chance to prove what an idiot she was. But, damn, she was jealous as hell and hated the woman in his dreams. Was she alive? Had he gone to that woman's rescue the way he had hers? And the biggest question of all, just how much did he love her?

Chapter Twenty

As Ry slept peacefully all night and next day through, she held him in her arms, talking quietly, telling him soothing stories that she'd mostly made up through the years spent wishing and dreaming.

He now knew of her secret yearnings to be a fine lady, to wear fancy dresses and own sparkling jewels, to drive a light-weight buggy pulled by a matching pair of high-stepping horses, instead of the splintery buckboard and her pair of over-worked mules. But of course, he hadn't heard or understood, that's why she had told him.

Really, when it came down to it, she didn't want all of those expensive things, or to live the highfalutin life. But it was fun to dream, to imagine herself a lady of quality living in a big city. When she thought of the farm, though, and the freedom she had to dress as she pleased, to roam the quiet woodlands, either afoot or on horseback, to spend hours doing nothing but what she wanted to do—now that was her idea of living.

She'd never been raised to a life of high society and probably wouldn't be comfortable among the people who were. A country girl, born and bred, was what she was, and for the first time, she realized how happy she really was with her lifestyle. Maybe her mother'd had dreams, too, dreams that she couldn't shake, that had led her to a life that would make her happier, more content. Mandy hoped so; she honestly did.

Quite a ruckus was going on in the cavern where the horses were tethered, had been for some time, only she'd been reluctant to leave her comfortable spot, or to release her hold on Ryder. But she was afraid something might be threatening the animals, and they couldn't afford to lose the horses, for any reason.

As she slipped from beneath Ryder's head, she replaced her lap with a blanket. The air in the cave cooled the warm area on her overalls where his head had been, and she felt as if a part of her faded with the warmth. It was a scary feeling to love someone as much as she loved her stranger.

Quickly, she shook her head and walked to the back of the cave. Ryder's horse and Red Fox—Red Fox?—were tied where they should be, but they were staring toward the dark shadows near where the hay was stacked, laying back their ears and snorting with distrust.

She'd recovered her knife earlier, so she now drew it and started to move stealthily toward the pile of hay. It was probably some animal that had wandered into the cave for protection, and it caused her a moment's worth of hesitation as she imagined a mountain lion, or even a bear. But step by slow step, she made forward progress until a shrill whinny split the air and she jumped back in fright.

She could hear the animal's frantic movements and finally saw the whites of its eyes as they rolled warily in her direction. Another step and she could see the outline of a large, nervous horse. In the same low, monotonous voice that she used to calm all of her animals, she steadily walked toward the horse's head.

He was tied, but it looked like the knot had slipped with all the jerking and pulling the horse had subjected it to. Holding out her hand so the animal could get her scent, she continued to move forward. She wasn't afraid; he was just a poor frightened beast that needed reassuring.

His nostrils flared, and his huge eyes riveted on her hand as if waiting for it to jump out and hit him. Still she talked, telling him what a big, pretty boy he was and that she wasn't going to harm him, until his feet gradually quit stomping the ground and he snorted at the hand now so close to his quivering muzzle.

When she touched the velvet skin, his head jerked, but then lowered again as if to see if her second touch would be as gentle as the first. It was, and this knowledge seemed to calm the animal considerably. Mandy ran her hand over the horse's sweat-dampened hide, knocking away some of the nervous lather that had accumulated on his neck and chest.

The muscles that she encountered were long and hard, and as her eyes became adjusted to the darkness of the area, she saw that he was a tall, heavily muscled, well-proportioned black stallion.

It didn't take long for the significance of Red Fox's return and the presence of the black horse to sink in. Jesse had stolen the stallion back for them. But why hadn't he come in and talked to her? Where was he now? Her hand shook, and the horse moved nervously. Had there been a run-in with Hank Ford?

Surely if something were wrong he would've told her about it, but she couldn't help worrying about him. What if he was seen? It was still too dangerous for him to be roaming the countryside right now.

377

The stallion snorted and stamped a hoof close to the toe of Mandy's boot. She gave the horse a final pat and threw him some hay. Before returning to Ryder, she carried water to all three horses and breathed a sigh of relief that the stallion seemed more settled. Maybe he wouldn't cause too much trouble. It still hadn't occurred to her that she would have to explain the horse's mysterious appearance to Ryder.

Reno and Jeremy had just finished stabling their mounts and the six mares they'd selected from the herd. Reno's face was wreathed in smiles as he shouldered his saddlebags and slapped Jeremy on the back.

"Well, little brother, we did it. We've got the deed to our ranch and some spendin' money to boot." He laughed and suddenly kicked up his heels, causing Jeremy to wonder about his brother's state of mental health.

"Can you believe it, Jer? We actually *did* it!" His boisterous ravings trailed off as they approached the porch of their house and saw a piece of paper nailed to a post. "Damn! Damn the dirty, cheatin' bastard to hell." He was so caught up in his dark thoughts that he'd forgotten Jeremy was right behind him.

"Can they do this, Reno? I thought the taxes were paid until this fall."

"They are. Ole Pomeroy's up to somethin', Jer. It's got to be a trap. He can't catch us on our home turf, so he's tryin' to get us into town. Well, it won't work. Not this time."

"What're we gonna do, then? That notice says the farm'll be sold in May. That only leaves us a week."

"I know. I know. And that also gives us a week to think of somethin'. Right now I'm so hungry that my belly's makin' friends with my backbone, and I can't think on an empty stomach."

The boys dumped their gear on the living room floor and trooped into the kitchen. Reno stopped, did a double take and cursed. "I'll be go to hell. What's going on around here, anyway? Someone's left another callin' card. S'pose our sheriff left us a personal invitation to our own hangin'?"

Jeremy picked up the paper that had been propped against the oil lantern. "It's to you, Reno. Says that Mandy Jo's in some cave over in the hills. It's not her hand writin'. Do you think it's another trick?"

He handed the paper to his brother, then sank into the nearest chair. The dizziness was getting worse all of a sudden.

Reno took the note, but before he read it, he looked closely at his kid brother. The last few days had been tough on the boy, who still hadn't recovered his strength from his serious injuries at Hank Ford's hands. His face was deathly pale, and lines were etched too deeply into his youthful features. Reno had taped Jer's ribs, but that had been three days ago. The boy needed rest, and lots of it.

After reading the note, Reno said, "I remember that cave. Frank and Hank used to hole up there a lot a long time ago. Nobody's been over there for years now."

"Do you think it's really Mandy? We don't know for sure what's happened to her. What if that Manning didn't find her? What if—" Jeremy choked and couldn't finish.

"Okay, I get your drift. But there's no need to think the worst, yet." Reno was apprehensive himself. Reno had been shot, his sister had disappeared and he'd let Manning talk him into going on with the horses instead of looking for her. He'd argued, but

Ryder had insisted that he could handle it. What if Jeremy was right? What if something had happened to both of them? He'd never be able to forgive himself if he'd put the importance of his dreams over that of his sister's life.

"Jer, I'm going to the cave. I'll scrounge us up a bite of supper first, though."

"Good, I'm starved. But I'm goin' with you. You might need help if it's a trap."

Reno looked again at his brother's pinched features. The boy was in pain, had been for several days, but he'd never complained, had insisted on making the trip to the fort, and then on returning straight home. "Yeah, we'll see. I want to rewrap those ribs and put something on those cuts before we leave."

He left Jeremy slicing a slab of bacon and went to rummage through his room. Sure enough, he found the bottle of laudanum Doc Reilly had left. No way was Jeremy going to leave this house.

After supper, Reno cleaned the table while Jeremy rinsed off the plates. While his brother's back was turned, he mixed the laudanum into a cup of their pa's shine. As bad as the liquor was, he'd never notice it.

"Jer, come over here and sit down. I'm going to take the bindings off your ribs and put on clean ones. Drink this cup of whiskey before I start."

Jeremy sniffed and then sat down as ordered. "I'm not a baby anymore, Reno. Go ahead and do what you need to, but I don't need any of that stuff to fortify myself. Besides, I need to be alert when we go after Mandy Jo."

"Now, Jer, I'm not goin' to argue with you. You drink that or I'll not lift a finger to help you." At the stubborn expression settling over his brother's face, he added, "I wouldn't think twice about taking a drink if it were me. Anything to help dull the pain's worth it."

"You wouldn't? It is? You always told me to be tough, to take things like a man."

"Ahem, er, yes. And you have, Jer. I've been real proud of you. But we're home now, and I know you've been hurtin'. Forget about bein' tough and just get well. Okay?"

There was such relief in Jeremy's eyes when he picked up the cup that Reno could've kicked himself for ever saying those stupid, boastful words. And the worst part was, they sounded just like something he'd probably said.

"Yuk! Pa sure cooked up a bad batch last time. That stuff's terrible."

"Drink it all, anyway. I don't want you to holler when I fix your ribs."

Jeremy took another swallow before casting Reno a reproachful glance. "I never yelled the first time, did I?"

"No, but you've had several days of hard riding to work up a good soreness. Drink it all. That's the way."

The boy leaned toward the table and propped his elbow on the edge while trying to catch the cup with his mouth. "Damned stuff won't hold still. Wonder what all Pa put in it this time?"

"Not much tellin'." Reno decided to go ahead and fix Jer's ribs as long as he was going to the trouble of putting the boy to sleep. So, he told his brother to hold his arms to his side while he unbuttoned the shirt and slipped it off.

By the time he was finished, Jeremy could hardly sit in the chair. He helped him to his feet and half dragged, half carried him to his room. "C'mon, Jer.

Let's get you to your room so you can rest a spell."

"Can't. Ah gotta go . . . get Mandy Jo."

"We'll get her. Right after you take a nap. Okay?"
He helped Jeremy into his bed, then pulled the boy's
boots off.

"Gotta get Mandy." Jeremy was asleep by the time
his head hit the pillow. Reno pulled a blanket over
his brother and tucked it around his feet.

"Sleep tight, Jer. I'll get Mandy for you."
He spent the next few minutes packing enough
gear to last several days. No telling how long he'd be
gone, because he wasn't coming home without his
sister, one way or the other. Throwing his bags across
his shoulder, he headed out the door and was halfway
to the barn before he noticed the off-key whistling
getting closer and closer.

"Pa. What're you doing here? I was just going to
look for you."

"Were you? I'm glad I come by, then. I've been, uh,
kinda keepin' an eye on the place since that poster
was nailed up. Have ya been havin' troubles keepin'
the place up?"

Reno opened his mouth to tell his father exactly
what they'd gone through the past nine years, but
upon taking a closer look at the old, thin, fading man
before him, he snapped his jaw shut. He'd been
looking forward to the day he could tell the man just
what he thought of him for deserting his family and
obligations, but now that the opportunity had
presented itself, he found it impossible to accomplish.

"Yeah, Pa. We've had some troubles, but not all of
them have to do with the farm. Don't worry. The
taxes have been paid."

"Oh, well, that's good. I'd hate ta see ya havin' ta
sell her ta some stranger. I . . . never mind. Tell me,

son, why were ya lookin' fer me?''

Reno looked back toward the house, then at his father. ''I need a favor, Pa. Somethin's come up, and I need to leave Jeremy here. He doesn't think much of the idea, and I'd like you to see to it that he stays, and preferably in bed.''

''In bed? Is he hurt? Just what in tarnation's goin' on here, boy?''

''I don't have time to explain it all right now. Mandy may be in trouble, and I don't want to have to worry about Jeremy, too. Will you help me, or not?''

George Coulter licked his lips and stuffed in his shirttail. ''Why, sure. Sure I will, son.'' Then, as Reno turned toward the barn, he put a hand on his oldest boy's arm, detaining him. ''Ah, I just wanted to tell you . . . I know I haven't done . . . right by you kids. . . .''

Embarrassed by his own flare of emotions for a man he'd tried to hate for so long, Reno stepped back away from his father and stammered, ''Don't . . . don't worry about us, Pa. I-I think I understand. . . . We'll talk later, okay? I've gotta go.'' He almost tripped over his own feet, he took off in such a hurry. Damn! Why now? When it was too late.

Ry opened his eyes and was surprised to be able to see things clearly, not in the blurry or hazy condition he was accustomed to lately. He could even turn and lift his head without that dizzy, nauseous feeling taking hold. It was a surprise to find that he was in a cave, the only light coming from a cheery fire burning only a short distance away. No wonder he'd thought himself surrounded by shadows and eerie specters. He was.

His eyes, and an arm, then encountered Amanda,

lying only inches from his side. Her face was so angelic and sweet as she slept, yet he could read the tiredness from the lines about her eyes and mouth. Then he remembered how she'd been by his side every time he'd come to, caring for him. Oh yes, she'd said he'd been shot.

He tried to turn on his side, but felt the constriction between his shoulders, and then a slight pain. Maybe he'd be better off to remain as he was, flat on his back. At least he could move his arm quite freely, so he wriggled his fingers, his hand, then his wrist, and finally his arm under the indentation of the woman's waist and moved her closer until she moaned and rolled to where her head rested on his shoulder, her leg thrown over his.

The round globes of her breasts pressed into his ribs, and her flat belly melded to his hip. She was so perfect and fit against him so . . . perfectly. He had to have her—for always. It didn't matter how, or why, just when. And the sooner the better. Just maybe he'd scare up that little preacher.

Ry turned his head until he could see into her face. His lips kissed her eyelids and the tip of her pert little nose while his hand rubbed up and down her back. He hadn't realized it, but she was sleeping in only a shirt and a pair of cotton pantalets. As if by magic, the shirt began to ball in his fingers, and in no time at all, his hand was smoothing down the bony ridges of her back.

A tiny flutter of movement across his chest caught his attention, and his muscles contracted involuntarily as her small hand pushed down the blanket covering his heated flesh. He didn't mind because he definitely didn't need it any longer.

Her voice was soft and husky, and her breath waved the hairs on his chest as she asked, "How are you feeling this morning?"

"Is it morning? How can you tell?" Ry moved his hand under the band of her pantalets and cupped one round mound of soft flesh. "It depends on which part of me you're asking about."

Mandy leaned up and propped herself with her left arm. "Suppose I'm asking about all of you."

"Well, let's see. My head throbs. My shoulders are stiff. The old stomach is starving. My . . . lower anatomy . . . aches."

She laughed and ran the tip of her finger down the center of his forehead, between his eyes, along the bridge of his nose, and circled the firm line of his lips. "I'd better see what I can do to ease some of your pain. Where shall I start first?"

When his arm dragged her over until she was lying flat on top of him, she gasped and tried to pull away, but his other arm was able to reach up and hold her still without placing undue strain on his wound.

"Don't, Ryder. I'll hurt you."

Both arms now wrapped about her, pressing her length over his, imprisoning the swelling proof of his desire for her between their bodies. "The only way you can hurt me now is if you leave me."

"But—" Her protest was smothered when his lips captured hers and his tongue plunged inside the open recess of her mouth to probe and inflame until she forgot why she was complaining in the first place.

Her hands framed the sides of his cheeks, and her fingers buried themselves into the thick hair curling above his temples. When his lips released her mouth and traveled over her face to her ear and then down the slender column of her neck, she used the opportunity to make one last plea. "Please, Ryder, what if your wound opens again? It's just now starting to heal."

"You worry too much, sweetheart. Besides, I'm not moving my back." His palms massaged around her ribs and lingered on her breasts momentarily until they met at the top button of her shirt. "Let's take off these clothes, Amanda. I want to feel you next to me. You're so soft and sweet."

She couldn't help the smile that lit her eyes and curved her lips. It was his decision. And oh, how she wanted him. In seconds her scant clothing was removed and the blanket thrown aside as she resumed her place atop his powerful body.

"I don't want to hear any complaints if you're laid up an extra week because of this. Hear?"

His hips raised so that his hardness teased the curly mound at the juncture of her thighs. "I don't care if I'm stuck here for a month, as long as you're around to cure my . . . aches and pains."

She laughed and teased, "What if I have better things to do than play doctor?"

His hands spread over her bottom and pressed her hard against him. "Do you?"

Her mouth nipped at the taut flesh across his collarbone, and between nibbles she answered, "No."

"Then what are we arguing about? Kiss me, woman."

Mandy tried to keep from putting too much of her weight on Ryder's chest so that they wouldn't hurt his wound. But eventually, both were so wrapped up in the exquisite torture of the sensuous lovemaking that Ry's back was the last part of his body that they cared about.

When at last he instructed her to straddle his waist and sit back, she almost screamed with the intensity of the sensation as he bucked his hips and thrust deep inside her. He filled her to overflowing, and the heat and pleasure radiated clear to her fingertips—even her toenails tingled.

For a moment all she could do was rock with him; then her senses returned, and she leaned forward, placing her hands on his shoulders as she met each thrust with a downward plunge of her own. His hands squeezed her dangling breasts, and he laved their sensitized tips with his tongue before suckling greedily.

She threw her head back and closed her eyes as a nerve-shattering explosion rocked through her core. Wave after wave shook her muscles and bones and then subsided. As the final spasm ran its course, she found herself held tightly against Ry's slippery, sweat-streaked body.

Their hearts beat in time as they each struggled for breath. "Oh, God, Amanda."

Mandy was up and dressed, sitting on a nearby rock, watching Ryder sleep. She'd been fearful that their exertions would hurt his wound, or cause a recurrence of the fever, but so far, he was resting peacefully. He was still weak and had dozed off soon after their lovemaking. She had sponged his heated skin with all the loving care she could muster. Which was considerable.

Then she'd cleaned her own body, replacing Hank's detested shirt with one of Jesse's clean ones. She'd even borrowed an old pair of jeans folded away on a shelf and had belted them on with a length of rope. She wasn't the most beautiful sight in the world, but at least she was clean.

It was while she was combing through the matted strands of her hair that she heard the noise coming from the direction of the cave entrance. The comb dropped from her fingers as she ran for the Colt revolver Ry had given her. It was tempting to awaken him and lean on his strength for support; but it would mean he'd try to get up, and she wasn't willing to risk that. Not yet.

Moving stealthily up the narrow tunnel, she kept close to the wall, in the shadows. It was hard for her to see, but she had the advantage over whoever was outside. They wouldn't be accustomed to the darkness and would have a harder time than she.

When she reached the moveable partition at the opening, she flattened herself against the cold stone and waited, listening for a repetition of the sound that had alerted her. The door rattled, then shook, and she froze as a voice whispered loudly, "Mandy? Damn it, Amanda, are you in there?"

Her heart dropped to her knees when she recognized Reno's voice, but still she took no chances. There was a small separation of the branches at eye level, so she peeked out, making certain that it *was* Reno and that he was alone. As far as she could tell, he was.

"Just a minute, Reno, and I'll let you in."

Reno stopped pacing and breathed a sigh of relief. "Thank God. Hurry up, Mandy, will you?"

It took several efforts, but she finally managed to dislodge the partition and slide it open. The next thing she knew, she was being smashed in a gigantic bear hug by her brother. She did get to hug him back before putting her hands on his shoulders and pushing.

"I may be tough, but I am breakable. Unhand me, beast."

Reno stood back abashed. "I'm sorry, sis. It's just that I . . . we . . . were afraid. . . ."

"Don't you dare be sorry. I kinda enjoy being mauled by my brother every once in a while. You just don't need to squeeze so hard, is all."

He laughed and put an arm around her shoulders as he playfully hit her on the arm. "Okay, the point is made. Now, are you really all right? Are you going to invite me in, or not?"

"Yes, I'm fine, and I suppose you can come in. Where's your horse?"

"He's back down the trail a ways. I didn't know what to expect up here, so I came on foot. He'll be all right, for a while."

"Well, in that case, come on inside and help me shut the door."

On the way to the interior of the cave, Mandy explained what had happened to her after Jeremy had been wounded, and how Ryder had rescued her from Hank Ford. "He was shot in the back as we got away. It's been a pretty rough few days, but I think he's much better." Her face reddened as she remembered what had taken place only an hour earlier. Yes, he was definitely better.

"I've been wondering about you and Jeremy. Did you make it to the fort with the horses in time?" She hoped her voice sounded suitably interested and then surprised herself by finding that she actually was.

"It was close, Mandy. Jeremy was hurting but insisted we move on. I tried to keep the pace slow, for his sake, and we got there just at dusk. Henry had almost given up on us."

Reno stopped just short of entering the cavern and stared at the living quarters in awe. The look of wonder changed to that of extreme pride as he turned to face his sister. "We did it, Mandy. The ranch is ours, signed, sealed and waiting until we can deliver ourselves to it. God, I never thought it would really happen."

He couldn't help himself; he had to give his sister another hug, but this time he was careful and took it easy on her. Mandy blinked back tears as she held her brother to her breast. He and Jeremy had come so far, and she was bursting with pride, if not happiness.

As much as she hated to see it come, her brothers were growing away from her, ready to face life and its challenges without her help and guidance. And they would manage well. She wouldn't have to worry about them, much.

A sob escaped her throat, but she stopped it before Reno could hear. What was she going to do with herself? Jesse would be leaving soon, if not already. Her brothers would move on to Santa Fe, wherever that was. And Ryder? He'd probably be off to solve his next case, glad to leave the troublesome Coulters in his wake. She'd be alone, except for her father, who she never saw, anyway.

"I'm so happy for you, Reno. And Jeremy. You two have done something very wonderful for yourselves."

"And for you, too, sis, if you'll just see it that way."

"Yes, well, come on in and sit down while I put some coffee on." Mandy led the way to the fire and busied herself making the coffee while Reno bent over Ryder and felt his forehead.

"He's cool. You say he came out of the fever just this morning? How long ago did you take out the bullet?"

Mandy put the pot on a red-hot rock next to the fire and wiped her hands down the legs of her jeans. "Uh, inside this place it's sort of hard to keep track of time, but, uh, I'd say about two days ago."

"You must've done a helluva job. Did you have to cauterize the wound?"

She walked over to a large boulder and plopped down. How was she going to get out of this? The wound had been bleeding steadily, so Jesse would've had to have stopped it somehow. "Uh, yes, it was deep and just kept bleeding."

Reno came to sit by his sister. "I had no idea that you could do all that, Mandy. I'm real proud of you. Manning owes you his life."

Red color suffused her neck and worked up to pinken her cheeks. "I don't look at it that way. After all he saved you, and then me. I'd say we still owe him."

"Yep, I guess you're right. Hey! What's that?"

Loud squeals and heavy stomping noises were coming from the smaller cavern. Mandy sucked in her breath and cursed quietly. What else could possibly go wrong? How was she going to explain the black stallion? Damn that Jesse for being such a good guy. He'd sure left her with a mess.

She followed Reno as he ran into the back cave. When he halted dead in his tracks and just stared at the nervous, prancing stallion, she waited impatiently for him to flood her with questions—questions she was afraid she'd have no answers for.

But they never came. Instead, Reno walked over to the big horse and gentled him by talking calmly and rubbing his hands over the black coat and down the trim legs.

Mandy would've felt a lot safer if she'd known what was going on in Reno's mind at that moment. He was mentally praising Ryder Manning for being quite the hero. Not only had he rescued his sister but had retrieved the stallion as well. That was quite a feat for one man, and Reno admired Manning for being able to pull it all off in such a short space of time. He tipped his hat to the man.

When he came back to Mandy, all he said was "Now everything is set. We've got the ranch, the start of our horse herd, and . . . it's almost too good to be true."

Mandy shook her head. She knew what he was talking about. A month ago she'd had everything she needed or ever wanted and hadn't appreciated it. It was too scary to even think about.

The coffee was ready, and after they'd taken their seats again, both people stared into the flickering flames, each seeing the images of their futures taking shape: one bright and exciting, one dismal and depressing.

Reno finally dragged his eyes from the fire and gazed around the cave. "This is some setup. Didn't Jesse and Frank use this place as a hideout?"

Mandy blew into her cup, then sipped the hot coffee. "I think so, a long time ago. I thought you'd probably been here before."

"No. Well, not inside, anyway. But I'd heard Jesse talk about it some."

Wrapping her fingers around the warm tin cup, Mandy turned and looked intently at her brother. "Reno, did you ever ride with Jesse? You know, when he . . . pulled a job?"

Reno took a deep breath and studied the fire again. "Yeah, a couple of times."

She scooted down to sit cross-legged on the floor next to the warming flames. "I was afraid of that. I used to worry about you so when you were gone for days at a time. Always wondering if you'd ever come back. . . . Why did you quit?"

He choked on his coffee and stood up to pace the same ground Jesse had covered so many times before. "I don't really know how to explain it. It was just so different than I'd expected. The men were mean, always grumbling at each other. And they were too greedy. They weren't the close-knit, loyal gang of guys like in the old days, like I always dreamed about. I guess I realized that Jesse was just a man, not the super hero I'd made him out to be, trying to bring back those times; like I was just a boy, trying to live my fantasies."

He stopped pacing and went to check on Ryder before he sat back down. "Anyway, I couldn't handle it, so I quit. Jesse was good enough to see I didn't have any trouble with the other men when I left."

Since Mandy remained silent, he looked around the cave again and added, "You know, there's a feeling about this place, almost like Jesse was still here, looking over us, or something."

Mandy blinked, leaned closer to the fire, and said, "I know what you mean."

Chapter Twenty-One

Mandy and Reno were on their second cup of coffee when Ryder awoke. He felt weak but was sure it was nothing a good meal or two wouldn't cure. When he saw Reno sitting with Amanda, another load was taken from his sorely tested shoulders. It was a relief to know the boy was safe.

He'd thought it was Reno's voice he'd heard earlier when he roused somewhat, but had been too sleepy to pay much attention. "Hey, you two, it isn't healthy to ignore an injured man. For the man, that is."

"Manning, it's about time you woke up. We were afraid you were going to sleep forever."

"How long have I been out?"

Mandy got up and added a few more sticks to the fire. "Oh, three or four hours, I imagine."

"Getting a bullet cut out can be pretty exhausting for a feller, huh?"

Ryder looked at Reno, then shifted his gaze to Amanda. "That, among other things."

When Mandy blushed and turned away, Reno wondered at the electricity he felt in the air. It'd been the same that morning in their kitchen. These two seemed to have a knack for lighting a spark under each other.

As Ryder propped himself on an elbow and started to throw back the blanket, he remembered his state of undress. He'd have liked nothing better than to stand up and walk stark naked to Amanda and take her in his arms, but he wouldn't do that to her, not in front of her brother, yet. So, he politely inquired, "Would one of you kindly throw me those pants?"

Mandy looked from the freshly laundered clothes back to her patient. "Oh no you don't. You're going to stay right there. Anything you need, I'll get for you."

"Uhmm, Amanda, you better toss me the pants. There are some things that even you can't handle."

Her brother laughed, and Mandy turned a becoming shade of purple. Then Reno gave Ryder his pants and held out his hand for support in levering the weakened man to his feet. "C'mon, Manning. I'll hold your hand so Mandy won't worry. We'll be back shortly, sis."

By the time the pair returned, Mandy had the cave filled with so many mouth-watering aromas that Ryder's belly growled with welcome relief. The bacon, beans and cornbread were better than any steak and eggs he'd ever eaten.

"That was mighty good, swee—Amanda. Could I have another piece of that cornbread? And some more coffee? Thanks."

"Just be careful and don't eat too much. Your stomach isn't used to it." Mandy was afraid that he'd make himself sick if he ate any more.

Surprisingly, Reno came to Ryder's defense. "Aw, Mandy. Let the man be. It's the first meal he's had in a while." Reno reached over and poured himself another cup of coffee as Ry cleaned the last crumb from his plate.

"How's Jeremy? You two make it with the horses okay?" Ry didn't mention the black stallion. He figured Reno must surely know that he hadn't been able to get to him.

Mandy listened again as Reno repeated the story of his and Jeremy's trip, then she asked the question that had been plaguing her for some time. "Reno, I was going to ask you earlier, then forgot, but just what brought you up to the cave? You said you hadn't been here for years."

Reno shrugged his shoulders and shook his head. "It's the strangest thing. Someone put a note on the kitchen table telling me to look for you here. Does anyone else know where you are?"

She could've literally shot herself. What a dolt she was for even bringing the subject up. Jesse must've gone to the farm after delivering the stallion. And if that was the case, if he'd led Reno to the cave, then he was never coming back. A deep ache started in her heart and threatened to close off her throat as she tried to think up a plausible answer for her brother.

"N-no, not that I know of. That is strange."

Ryder leaned back and rubbed his full belly. Bits and pieces of dreams kept filtering in and out of his mind, but he couldn't differentiate between what was real and what was just fantasy. So much had happened.

But that face was so real: the blue eyes, the thin nose, and that smile as he came at Ry with the knife. No! It was a dream. He was still alive, wasn't he?

"Jeremy was afraid it might've been written by someone like Hank, setting us up. But I didn't see any tracks as I rode up, and it just doesn't sound like something Hank would do. Heck, I bet he can't even write."

Mandy smiled and tried not to laugh, afraid she

396

might break into hysteria. God, her nerves were shot. As much as she hated to lie, it looked like it would take some good ones to get out of this with the believability of Jesse's death intact. And if she could pull it off successfully, it could mean the start of a new and better life for a lot of people . . . if not—

Luckily, Ryder broke into the conversation and inadvertently changed the subject. "Speaking of Jeremy, where is he? He wasn't hurt worse than I thought, was he?"

Reno sighed and stretched his legs out. "No, but he was in pain and exhausted. He wanted to come, but I tricked him by lacing his whiskey with laudanum. Then I asked Pa to watch over him and make sure he stayed put."

"Pa? You saw Pa again?" Mandy couldn't believe it. What was making their father leave his precious still so often all of a sudden?

"Yeah, he was comin' down just as I was leavin'. Uh, he was kinda keepin' an eye on the place." Reno swung his eyes to the fire, hoping for an end to the subject.

But Mandy saw his nervous reaction and pounced. "Why? What's happened to make Pa so interested in the farm?"

"Ah, hell, Mandy, I didn't want ta have ta tell ya. Now see? I can't even concentrate on my language."

"You're stalling, Reno. Whatever it is can't be that bad. Can it?"

Reno looked to Ryder and rolled his eyes as if wishing the other man could magically ease the situation. But Ryder was as confused as Amanda and only shrugged his shoulders helplessly, the muscle under his eye twitching at the uncomfortable jolt delivered from his wound at the action.

"Yeah, it can, damn it all. When Jer and I got

home, there was a notice tacked on the porch that the farm is to be sold for back taxes if they aren't paid by May first.''

"But, Reno, we paid the taxes. Everyone knows we did.''

"Well, somethin's up, and I'm bettin' Pomeroy is at the bottom of it.''

Reno smiled. "Ah yes, Sheriff Pomeroy. A fine upstanding citizen of the community.''

Mandy stuffed her hands in the back pockets of her jeans and began to pace. The only security she'd looked forward to in her bleak future was being threatened. But what could she do? Then she swung around to face Ryder. He was a lawman. Would he have jurisdiction over a sheriff?

Without preliminary warning, she faced him down. "Isn't there anything you can do?''

Ryder was taken aback, but no emotion showed on his stony features. It almost sounded like the woman knew he was a lawman. But no, how could she? "Me? What could I possibly do?'' His mind had been buzzing like crazy for the past several minutes as he'd asked himself the same question. Given time, he'd come up with something.

Hands on her hips, feet spread apart, she glared angrily at the stranger. How dare he continue with this farce when something so important was on the line.

"Come off it, Deputy Marshal Manning. Just how long did you think you could get away with the roving cowboy routine?''

Reno's head swiveled back and forth between his sister and the man he'd taken such a grudging liking to. "What'd you say? Manning a marshal? Are you sure?''

"Oh, I'm absolutely positive. And I'd like his

explanation as to why he was at Jesse's funeral, and then decided to pick our place as his . . . his . . . headquarters. Is that the correct word, Deputy Manning?"

Ryder crossed his arms over his chest, his eyes and face betraying nothing of what was churning through his mind. She knew. What good would it do now to lie? But how much should he reveal? Then again, why should he hide anything? As he looked into the furious green eyes, he sensed that if there was ever going to be a tomorrow involving this beautiful woman, he'd better lay his cards on the table, face up.

"Well, Manning, or whoever you are. What do you have to say?" Reno was disappointed. He'd liked Manning, had even grown to trust him. But now?

"All right. Yes, I'm a deputy marshal, out of St. Louis. But I'm undercover, so don't spread the information around." He looked directly into glittering emerald eyes. "How'd you find out?"

Mandy's lips quirked in a smile that could also be taken as a sneer. "Since our first collision above the house. You don't take many pains to hide your badge for a man who's trying to hide his identity."

"Just what're you doin' in our part of the country? I can't see much reason for you to be hangin' around this long after Jesse's funeral." Actually, Reno was more concerned over when the marshal was leaving. From the look on his sister's face, she was really hurting.

"Well, I was sent here for several reasons. One had to do specifically with that burial. Rumors had it that maybe someone else had been substituted for the real Jesse James." Beneath thick black lashes he watched both Coulter faces intently. Both stared back at him, both with incredulous expressions, showing him nothing.

When no one else volunteered to speak, Ryder continued. "Also, there've been reports of a rash of robberies not too far from here. So . . . putting rumors and facts together . . . someone had to investigate all the possibilities."

Reno stiffened and glared at his ex-friend. "And I suppose the Coulter family, close kin to the James's, seemed the logical choice, huh?"

The lawman just shrugged his shoulders.

"And now? Do you still feel the same way?"

"Well . . ."

Mandy walked back and forth in front of the two men, waving one arm in the air. "I can't believe his gall. Staying in our home, eating at our table, and all the while doing his damndest to prove us guilty of some crime, any crime." Actual guilt made her speech all the more passionate and accusing.

"Don't forget the time I put in saving your hides. Surely that should count for something." Ry was relaxed, enjoying Amanda's theatrics. She was upset, and he couldn't blame her, but he'd never seen her more beautiful than now with her eyes spitting green fire, her nostrils flared with indignation and her lips so vibrant and mobile.

"B-but that's beside the point. You owed us for going behind our backs like a sneaky, cheating—" Suddenly it dawned on her how she'd reversed position. The insufferable man just made her so damned furious.

While Mandy attempted to deal with her anger, Ry looked to her brother. "Can you blame me? Your family has been close with Jesse. There's a sudden outbreak of lawlessness. You and your brother disappear all too frequently. Everything seemed to point your direction."

Mandy stomped her foot and turned on him. "You

400

used us, damn you! You used me!"

Reno also turned to Ryder, but the young man read something in the marshal's face that curbed his planned attack. Instead, he took his hat off and dusted it against his pant leg, then settled it firmly on his head. He coughed and started walking toward the front of the cave.

"Well, I've got to get back and check on Jeremy. We can sort through all this later. Ah, when do you think you'll be leaving?"

"He can damned well—"

"I'll be able to ride in a couple of days. And I'll see to it your sister gets home safely."

Reno backed along the wall, worriedly watching his sister's motley face. Man, was she mad. "Thanks, Manning. We'll look for you soon, then." He spun on his heel and made a graceful exit, even though he was in a hurry to check on his horse. He'd left the animal tied for a long time.

Mandy took several steps in her brother's direction but stopped at Ryder's next words. "You've accused me of using you. How so?"

She was boiling on the inside but tried her best not to lose all control. "You know how, you . . . you vile . . . beast."

Ry sank back and faintly put the back of one hand over his eyes. "Sorry, I can't hear you. What'd you say?" Even his voice was weak.

Mandy felt concern gradually replace some of her anger. He'd probably overdone himself, getting up for the first time and now participating in this shouting match. She took several steps toward him and reached down to feel his forehead.

The steely hand that wrapped around her wrist gave no indication whatsoever of weakness when she tried to pull back. Instead she was yanked forward to

401

land amid a whoosh of air upon his hard, unyielding lap. What was he going to do? He wouldn't beat her, would he?

Ry held her in place with one strong arm while the other hand smoothed through her hair and down her cheek until she calmed down. "So I used you brutally, did I? You didn't enjoy the touch of my hands on your skin, or the kisses that we shared, or the lovemaking—which you never willingly participated in. Is that right?"

Mandy's body was trembling from the force of his tender touch. The words, though spoken softly, reminded her of the way she'd unashamedly sought those very acts he was so sensuously describing. "Th-that's not what I meant. You used me to get to my family."

Her skin was on fire under the hot ministrations of his fingers. She helplessly arched toward him as his hand warmed her breast over the soft cotton of her shirt. God, how long could she stand it?

His lips traveled over her cheek and along the firm line of her jaw until her head turned and she tried to catch his lips with hers. The buttons on her shirt appeared to automatically fall open to allow the palm of his hand to cup the supple flesh of her creamy breast. The nipple puckered, then hardened, a yearning bud to be plucked at his will.

Those wondrous lips that she longed to taste were only a breath away when they fanned the moist outline of her own as he spoke. "It may have seemed that way at the beginning, but you've got to believe that I would never do anything to hurt you—or your family. Do you believe me?"

Her lips were searching, pouting, reaching for his mouth when his hands slipped to either side of her neck and pushed her slightly back. "Answer me, sweetheart. Do you believe that?"

Mandy tried to think. Believe what? Oh yes, that he wouldn't harm the Coulters. But did she? Could she? And then, because he had never done anything more than help them, she found that she could, did.

"Y-yes. I believe so."

The breath escaping from his lips caressed and parted hers, and she arched to press against him as the kiss deepened and ignited the smoldering flames of their mutual desire.

When they lay on the pallet, naked, flesh touching flesh, his legs between her parted thighs and the tip of his manhood teasing the pulsing portal of her womanhood, he lowered his arms and rubbed the wiry fur of his chest across the quivering softness of her breasts. "I want you, Amanda."

Her voice was hoarse and throaty as she answered, "I know, and I want you."

"No, I mean, I want you for always. I want to marry you."

Mandy's eyes popped open in startled surprise. Marry? Her? Her heart pumped in triple time as joy flooded her being. He wanted to marry her. Her dreams had been answered. He loved. . . . But he'd never said he loved her, had never even pretended to.

"Why?"

Ryder pursed his lips. Why? He'd never expected her to ask that. All he needed was a simple *yes*. "Well, because you need me. You need to be protected, to have a man around to take care of you."

Mandy's heart ceased its acrobatics and almost quit beating altogether. Needed. Protected. Take care of her. Well, he'd given her an answer all right. "God, what do you take me for? Some kind of mindless infant? I've never *needed* a man in my life. And I can protect myself better than most of you so-called men.

Why you conceited, overbearing jackass—"

Ry cut off her tirade by effectively filling her mouth with his tongue as he kissed mindless. Then his hips thrust forward, and he buried himself within her tight, slippery sheath as she arched in an effort to move away from his overpowering masculinity. In a matter of seconds her protests turned into moans of pleasure, and her fists became grasping claws as she clasped him more tightly to her.

He held himself back until she was thrashing and bucking beneath him, then he plunged one last time to the most intense release he'd ever experienced. As he lay on top of her, their bodies still joined as one, he prayed that maybe this time he'd impregnated her. If he couldn't get her one way, he'd try another.

Then his mind recoiled at the thought. No, it would take too long that way. Something might happen that would cause him to lose her before then, and he wouldn't take the risk. She would marry him, even if he had to use force.

Back at the farm, Reno found Jeremy sitting in the rocking chair with Mandy's Sharps across his lap. His head was rolled to the side, resting on the bony edge of his shoulder and propped by the back of the chair.

When Reno lowered his saddlebags and they dropped onto the floor next to the dozing boy, he had to duck and take cover as Jeremy started and swung the gun in all directions. "Don't shoot. It's me, Jer. I didn't mean to frighten you."

Jeremy's pale cheeks flushed scarlet as he sat back down and picked up the cadence of the chair's rocking. "Sorry, but you never know these days."

Reno glanced around the room, then went to the

kitchen door. "Where's Pa? I thought he was goin' to stay here with you."

"He did but left a couple of hours ago to turn Dusty and the mules out in Mandy's valley. We figured it would be better if there weren't any signs . . . you know."

"Yeah. That's probably a good idea."

Jeremy was looking out the windows and over Reno's shoulder toward the door. "Where's Mandy Jo? She's all right, isn't she? You did find her, didn't you?"

Reno sat down in one of the straight-backed chairs, fingering the faded, calico print ruffle that covered the cushion tied to the hard slats. The stitching was uneven, and gaps showed the pieces of blanket folded inside. He remembered the nights Mandy had spent in front of the fire, sewing curtains, cushions, anything she could make out of scraps to make their empty house a home.

"Mandy's fine, Jer. She's still at the cave. Manning's with her."

"And you left her alone up there? Reno!"

The older brother laughed. "I think she felt the same way. But he'd been shot. She was just taking care of him. What could happen? Besides, I'd better warn you. There's somethin' goin' on between those two. I wouldn't be a bit surprised if Manning weren't a new addition to the family before long."

Both boys grinned at each other. They'd talked about Ryder on the way home, and the idea set good with both of them. Mandy needed a strong man in her life, and Manning sure fit the bill.

"Say, what're you doing up? I gave Pa strict orders to keep you in bed."

"And I was, until a while ago. After he'd taken the horses, I was almost asleep when I heard riders

405

millin' around outside. Barely made it into the tunnel 'fore I heard footsteps movin' through the house. It sounded like Hank and his boys."

Reno grunted and stretched his legs out in front of him as he slouched in the chair. "Uhhnnh. Probably lookin' for you or Mandy, or tryin' to find out if their eyes'd played tricks on 'em when they saw the ghost of Reno Coulter ridin' after 'em."

Jeremy slapped his knee and laughed heartily. "I bet ole Hank about came unglued, don't you? I'd like to've seen his face." Sobering, he reached over and leaned the rifle against the wall by the fireplace. "But if they're snoopin' around this place, it could be dangerous for Mandy Jo."

"Yeah, I know."

As the brothers sat in the growing darkness, both jumped when they heard the reports of gunfire close by.

"What the hell?"

"Where's it coming from?"

Reno ran to an open window and looked out toward the nearest line of trees. "Sounds like it's coming from Pa's still."

As Jeremy leaped to his feet, he grabbed the Sharps from where he'd placed it only moments earlier. "Let's go."

Dust hung heavy in the air over the trees as they ran up the incline, evidence of the hasty departure of several riders. When they broke through the brush into the clearing where their father ran the still, the first thing they noticed was the wanton destruction around them. Shards of crockery littered the ground, and the odor of whiskey was overpowering. Splintered staves from broken barrels caused the men to step carefully.

Then, through the dimming light from behind a

wooden box, Reno saw the soles of a pair of worn-down boots. "Jer, over here."

George Coulter was still alive when they bent over his battered, blood-spattered body. The breaths came in shallow gasps, but the rheumy eyes flickered with recognition when he heard Jeremy call "Pa? Pa, can you hear me?"

The tired, seamed face smiled up, and the eyes cleared somewhat when they encountered Reno. "I've been waitin' fer ya, son." His fingers groped until he found Jeremy's hand, and his eyes swung back and forth between his two boys. "Had ta tell ya how proud—" A fit of coughing interrupted, and bright flecks of blood appeared at the corners of his mouth. "Tell yore ma—"

Reno placed two fingers on his father's eyes and gently closed the lids. George Coulter was gone. Unable to face life and his young family without the woman he loved by his side, he'd retreated from the realities of the world and survived the only way he knew how. At least in the end, he'd died savoring the presence of his sons. And as nothing else could, that knowledge eased his passing in the minds of Reno and Jeremy.

"My God, Jeremy, I can't believe he's gone."

"Me neither. And you know what? We talked this afternoon, just like we would've . . . if nothin' had ever happened. He was a lot smarter than I ever thought." A choked sob erupted from his throat as he asked, "Why'd it happen this way, Reno?"

Reno shakily placed his father's hands over his chest. "What? Why'd he get himself killed? Or why'd he live up here like a hermit all these years?" The questions weren't asked expecting any answers, and he shook his head sadly. "I wish I knew, but I don't. It's such a waste. All I can say is that I'm grateful to've had the chance to see him on friendlier terms than usual before he died."

"Yeah." Jeremy scrubbed at his eyes and looked back in the direction of the farm. "What'll we do with him? Shall we wait 'til Mandy Jo gets back?"

Reno salvaged an old blanket from under the debris. "No, I don't think we oughta wait. It may be two or three days before Ryder's well enough to travel." He looked around the clearing and spotted a likely site under a tall tree. "I think he'd be happiest up here, and in case something happens to the farm . . . well, he won't be disturbed."

It was almost dark, but Jeremy saw a shovel not too far away. When he bent to pick it up, the handle was split in half. "Damn Hank Ford to hell." When he returned to his brother, holding the shortened implement, he questioned, "It was Hank, wasn't it, Reno? Who else could've done such a thing?"

"I don't know, Jer. He's got the nod in my book, too. After all, Pa told us himself that Hank had threatened him, along with you and Mandy. My guess is that Hank confronted Pa and wanted to find out what he knew about you kids. And from the looks of Pa, he didn't tell Hank what he wanted to hear."

A growl came from Jeremy as he bent over and started to dig under the branches of a large cottonwood. The first layer was tough going, but then became easier the deeper he dug. "I'm goin' after him. Just as soon as we bury Pa."

"No, not yet. We both need to rest and gather some provisions. Then we wait for Mandy. We can't just run off and leave her a note. This is something we have to tell her face to face."

Jeremy stubbornly continued to attack the ground, cutting into the earth with savage strokes, even though he could hardly see what he was doing.

"You're right. But the thought of Hank and the scum's maybe getting his hands on Mandy Jo again makes me mad—really mad. He doesn't deserve to live.

"And neither do I." He threw down the shovel and fell to his knees as Reno rushed to his side. "It's my fault. All my fault."

"What do you mean? How could you have caused this to happen?"

"I didn't, exactly, but I told Pa what a bitter taste his last whiskey had, and he said he'd come get a jug from another batch. See? If he hadn't come up here, Hank might not've found him. I killed him."

Reno shook his brother's shoulders until he was ashamed of himself. "Don't say that. Don't you ever repeat it again. If that's the way you feel, then you might as well accuse me of pointing the gun that shot him."

Jeremy looked up at Reno and slowly rubbed the back of his neck. "What're you talkin' about?"

"I put some medicine in your whiskey to make you sleep. That's why it tasted bitter. I had no idea. . . ." He took a deep breath and pinched the bridge of his nose between his fingers.

Then Jeremy stood up, brushed the dirt off his jeans and resumed his vigorous digging. Finally, he stopped and rested the arch of his boot on the top of the spade. His features had lost that boyish quality that always caused Reno to think of him as the "kid" brother.

"The only fault lies with Hank Ford, and he'll pay."

Ryder rested his head on his hand as he propped himself on one elbow and watched Amanda sleep.

He'd been making plans, plans that he intended to carry out the next day. He was feeling pretty good this morning, and with one more day and night of rest, he'd be ready to ride.

And in one more day, Miss Amanda Jo Coulter would become Mrs. Ryder Manning. God, he liked the sound of that. In fact, he could hardly wait to be a domesticated married man. Of course, with a wife like Amanda, life would never be the dull and boring affair he'd always pictured. He only hoped he had the strength for it.

His free hand rested on the curve of Amanda's hip, and he was sorely tempted to run his palm over the smooth, satiny expanse of flesh so deliciously exposed to his view. However, that activity wasn't included in his plans for the day, or in preparation for the coming nuptials. He hoped that abstinence would make their wedding night even more special. Thank heavens it was only *one* day.

So, he pushed himself reluctantly away and rolled to his feet. It felt good to stand on his own again, and he allowed himself to indulge in a spine-loosening stretch until the scabbed wound on his back protested. Then he decided to explore the cave.

It was quite an impressive sight. Obviously an outlaw's pride and joy, it was big enough to hide a large group of men, yet small enough to keep hidden and secret. As he walked toward the back wall of the cavern, he noticed the black space yawning before him. Another cave?

As he stepped through the opening, the aroma of hay, manure and horse gently assaulted his nostrils. The only light filtered from outside through the rear entrance. When a low whicker caught his attention, his mouth creased into a smile. His mustang was stabled next to Amanda's Red Fox, looking fat and

410

sassy and well cared for.

He gave the horse a pat on the forehead and started for the rear of the cavern to see if he recognized any of the country. It was when he got close to the stack of hay that he realized there was another animal in the cave. The dark shadows moved, and a horse snorted, then blew through his nostrils before stamping his front feet.

"Easy there. I'm just passing by." But when he was close enough to see the outline and the exquisite shape of the black horse, he stopped and appraised the stallion with a critical, then approving once over.

The first thing that crossed his mind was that this was Reno's black stud. Evidently the boys had run across the horse on their way home and had brought him there for safe keeping. And what a horse he was.

He had a smaller head than most horses Ry was used to seeing, with a large, muscled jaw. The sleek neck tapered into a huge barrel chest, and the muscles along his ribs and back were hard and lean. His hips were flat and sloped into the tail, and the legs were thick and much shorter than the usual thorough-breds. If Reno was looking for a good stock horse sire, he'd found the best.

Finally able to pull himself away from the animal, Ry continued his trek to the rear opening. Upon seeing the rough terrain and the cliffs to either side, he recognized the hill that he'd chosen as his landmark. What an ingenious setup. It even looked like the trail out had been hand chiseled into the rock and over the steep descent.

A muffled sound from behind gave him a start, and he turned to find Amanda standing close to the stud with her eyes wide and a hand covering her mouth. Surely she couldn't be worried about his being up? He was feeling great, just a little weak.

411

"Mornin', sweetheart." As he sauntered back toward her, he put out his hand for the stallion to get his scent again, then ran his hand down the heavy neck.

"I'm glad Reno got his stud back. This horse would've been a big loss."

When Amanda continued to silently stare at him with those huge, questioning eyes, he sighed and put his arm around her shoulder to gently push her into the main cavern. "I'm fine. Really. And knowing I didn't let your brother down so badly makes me feel a lot better. Now, what's for breakfast? I'm starved."

Chapter Twenty-Two

Mandy had had a trying time figuring Ryder's weird behavior for the past twenty-four hours. He had such a smug look on his face, like he knew a secret that he wouldn't share. Well, that was fine, because *she* knew something *he* didn't. Most disconcerting though, was that he acted like he was afraid to touch her, which was fine, actually, as she was still so angry that she couldn't even speak to him. He'd taken advantage of her, had used his wiles in forcing her to succumb to his erotic touch. Of course, if she didn't love him so much, she could've resisted, wouldn't have turned into a weak-kneed quivering mass of jelly.

It made her angry all over again just to think about it. But he'd made one point. He'd not done anything that she hadn't wanted, encouraged, him to do. She'd been right, too, though. He'd gone about investigating her family in a sneaky, underhanded way, and she still was suspicious about his nonchalance toward Jesse. He was too cool, too casual in the way he mentioned the funeral and in the intensity of his eyes when he looked at her whenever the subject of her cousin came up.

Breakfast was a tense, quiet affair during which Ryder kept looking at her with such a speculative gleam that she could hardly hold her hand steady as she drank her coffee. What was he up to? If he was trying to drive her crazy, he was close to succeeding.

Mandy jumped when Ry asked, "Are you ready?" And she thought to herself, if she wasn't, she'd better be. For anything.

"Ready? For what?"

Ryder threw what was left of his coffee into the fire and watched as it hissed and smoked. "I feel good enough today that I thought we ought to start back. It's getting too close in here. I need to get out in the open, breathe some fresh air, find out what's happening in the world."

She laughed and genuinely smiled at him. "I get that way in here, too. It's a nice place to be, if you're a bear."

"So, any objections to leaving as soon as we straighten up the place?"

"No, but I'll do the cleaning. I don't want you to break open your wound."

Ry flexed his back and shoulders. "It's fine. You did a good job."

"Uh, thanks. It was nothing, really."

"Well, nevertheless, I want to thank you for taking care of me. I appreciate it and hope to return the favor."

Mandy fidgeted under the knowing looks he continually bestowed upon her. She was so nervous that she fumbled the plates and cups she was cleaning and almost dropped them.

Ry left Amanda to the cleaning but was drawn to the horses and proceeded to ready them and their gear. Red Fox seemed leery of the black stallion, so Ryder decided to lead the stud with his mustang.

When he and Amanda were outside the cave and ready to mount, Ry scanned the entire area, then searched the ground. To an untrained eye, everything appeared natural, but he detected the marks left by a branch when scratched over the earth. Who knew about the cave? Or, more to the point, who didn't know? And why was it being kept such a secret now?

His voice was casual as he said, "With all the traffic in and out of here the past few days, there sure aren't many tracks."

Mandy fiddled with her cinch strap and cursorily surveyed the beautiful blue sky. "I came out the other night and wiped them out. Or what I could, anyway."

"Why? Was there something you were trying to hide?"

She turned to face Ryder and burned him with scorching green fire. "Yes, you idiot. Us. Or would you rather Hank Ford had found us while you were unconscious or delirious?"

Ry had the grace to look away first. Damn his suspicious mind. Why had he thought there might've been another reason? "Now don't get riled. I didn't mean anything by it. Okay?"

Somewhat mollified, Mandy swung into the saddle. There was no sense in worrying about covering their tracks as they left. Anyone who wanted to use the cave from now on was welcome to it. But she looked back as they rode away and knew she'd never forget the times spent there, with Jesse, and now Ryder. It had served them well.

"Which way did we come in the other night?"

She pointed and said, "From the east, why?"

When he turned his horses and started traveling that direction, Mandy kicked Red Fox to ride up next

415

to him. "This isn't the way home. Why do you want to go this way?"

He winked and grinned. "Just hold your horses and have a little patience, sweetheart. You'll soon find out."

Mandy seethed as they rode down the hill, but after several miles had been put behind them, curiosity got the better of her. He was so exasperating. If only she could figure him out.

When they reached the outskirts of the little village, she'd finally had all she could stand. She rode up next to Ryder and put her hand on his arm, causing him to pull back on the reins. The stallion minced around and pulled on his lead but eventually settled down again.

"I demand to know what we're doing here. We could've been home by now." As she watched his lips quirk into a grin and saw the dimple in the side of his cheek deepen attractively, she sucked in her breath and forced herself to look directly into his seductive black eyes. "Just what are you planning to do?"

Ry was pleased with himself. They'd made it as far as the town without having a confrontation, and now, victory was his. "Why, my dear, there's a man here I want you to meet."

Mandy couldn't stop him from nudging the horses into a walk, so rode alongside and finally decided to play his little game, for a while. "What man?"

When Ry stopped in front of a large, plain building with a cross nailed to the planking on the door, she looked at him questioning. "Why're we stopping here?"

"Where else would we go to get married, except the church?" Ry was grinning, but he was also wary. His hand was poised, ready to reach out and grab her reins if she should decide to flee.

Married? Church? What sort of diabolical scheme was he hatching now? "And just when did you decide to do this?"

"Night before last."

Mandy couldn't get over the relaxed way he lounged in his saddle, while she felt like an army was marching through her insides. But still, she wanted to find out what had prompted his actions before she raced Red Fox away from him.

"And can you tell me why you decided that we should get . . . married?" He'd told her once, but she was a glutton for punishment. Would his reasoning be the same?

He sighed and wrapped Ebony's lead around the saddle horn. "There's several things I could mention. I think the most important reason, and one that you know full well, is that I want you. And if you think for a minute—" he snaked his hand out and grabbed Red Fox's reins just as she tried to wheel the horse around—"you'll admit that you want me just as badly."

When the horses were calm once more, he continued, "It would be a good idea for us to be man and wife before we run into our friend Hank again. At least maybe it would deter his notion to take you for *his* bride."

As he stared at her stubborn, petulant profile, he added, "And what if our lovemaking has produced another little being? What would you do?"

Mandy choked on an angry retort. This must be her punishment for hinting the same thing to Reno. "I don't care about any of that. I can manage. Would *rather* manage on my own. Do you hear me?" How humiliating. She was about to cry because he still hadn't given her the reason she wanted most to hear.

Now Ryder was getting angry. The brat! What was

it going to take to get the woman to marry him? But Ry had been so well trained at keeping his face closed to his emotions and any expression that he didn't realize just how cold his blank eyes and features made Mandy feel. He gave no evidence of the love consuming his every heartbeat.

With gritted teeth, Ry used his big guns. "Well, sweetheart," he sneered, "maybe you won't mind managing without your older brother."

Mandy's head snapped around so fast that even Ry could hear the bones crack. "What do you mean? What about Reno?"

God, he hated the fear that swallowed her eyes, but he had to make the play. "It seems that while I was conveniently napping, I overheard you and Reno talking. Seems that Reno confessed to riding with the James gang."

Ry looked at the back of his hand and then buffed his nails against the material of his shirt. "I imagine I could find a warrant for him if I looked hard enough." He was only bluffing, playing his last joker, but as he saw her face drain of color and her shoulders sag with defeat, he knew he'd taken the pot.

"So, sweetheart, what's it going to be? Prison for Reno? Or marriage to me?"

To Mandy's mind it was prison either way. Life would be miserable married to a man who didn't love her. She would more than likely end up making a fool of herself, fawning over him, throwing herself at his feet for scraps of affection. And Reno, how could she not protect him?

Then the thought occurred to her that at least she'd have Ry, one way or the other. She could reach out and touch him whenever, maybe even wherever, she wanted. And if she was lucky enough to get pregnant, she'd have a little piece of him to love unconditionally.

"Well? Make up your mind. We don't want to keep the man waiting."

Mandy looked up, confusion written over her face, to see the same little preacher that Hank dragged along a lifetime ago. He was standing nervously, wringing his hands, shifting from one foot to the other. The wary brown eyes kept darting from Mandy to Ryder's gun. He probably feared a repeat of his previous experience.

Her answer was so low that Ryder leaned in the saddle in order to hear her acceptance. "I'll marry you."

But his voice was booming when he hailed the preacher. "Ah, my good man, we'd like you to do the honor of performing a wedding ceremony."

The preacher glanced around as if afraid of seeing the other lunatic at any minute. "You two? Marry you?"

Ryder almost laughed at the timid little fellow but decided it was better to stay on his good side. "Yes, we two, married."

He and Amanda followed the preacher into the church, and he kept his arm tight around his soon-to-be wife's shoulders, just in case she changed her mind.

The preacher wasn't at all happy. "B-but what about witnesses? What about—?"

"Do you have a housekeeper, or something?"

"Why, yes, but—"

"Well, sir, then go get her. This is to be a wonderful occasion. Right, sweetheart? See? The little woman can hardly wait. Run along, please, and hurry."

When the preacher finally left the room, after

turning back several times to make sure they weren't just figments of his wild imagination, Mandy turned on Ry. "Damn you! I can't believe you'd do this to me."

Ry still kept his grip on her but turned his head away. He hoped he wasn't making a mistake, killing the love he knew she felt for him. But he didn't have a choice. She'd refused to accept him willingly, so he'd had to use force. He'd make it up to her somehow.

Seeing that she wasn't getting a response from him, Mandy clamped her jaws together and stubbornly crossed her arms across her chest. She'd make the stranger's life miserable. Stranger? Now that was *strange*. She hadn't thought of him in that sense for a long while.

She knew he was a deputy marshal, knew what his assignment was, knew he liked good horses and homecooked food and knew that he cared enough to give a baby a name even if it wasn't actually created yet. And she knew that she loved him.

Her heart fluttered and then thumped with excitement. Even if this wasn't the way she'd planned her wedding, she would still have the man she loved. And it had been his idea. A smile warmed her from the tips of her toes to the generous curve of her lips.

When the preacher introduced Mrs. Parker, his housekeeper, Mandy greeted her with the most gracious of thanks for consenting to be a member of the wedding party.

Ry watched suspiciously as his bride-to-be shook hands with the preacher and hugged the old woman. What was she up to? It looked like he would have to be on his toes. No way was she going to get out of this.

Standing side by side, listening as the preacher began the ceremony, Mandy and Ryder both snuck covert glances at each other. When asked if she would take Ryder for her husband, her voice was sure and clear while Ryder's answer was guarded and hesitant.

However, there was nothing shy about the way he pulled her into his arms and the thorough way he kissed her grinning lips. He might not understand the change that had suddenly come over her, but he was bound and determined to take full advantage of it.

"Well, Mrs. Manning, what about it? Your place, or mine?"

Mandy was in a jovial mood until she heard Ry's question and became quite serious. "You know, I don't even know where your place is, where you came from, about your family, nothing."

Ry stood beside her and reached out to take both of her shoulders in his large secure hands. "I was born and raised in Indian Territory, but I've been away for a long time. Someday I'll tell you about my family, but let's save it for a cold night in front of a warm fire, okay?"

Amanda smiled and nodded, and Ryder breathed a sigh of relief. They'd have lots of time for discussing family, and he definitely had a lot of questions about hers; but right now he didn't want to get side-tracked from his big surprise.

"I've got a place of my own, Amanda. One that's going to need a woman's touch. It's been deserted for a number of years and won't be much at first, but we can build it together. Will you come with me? Help me?"

His enthusiasm for his home was catching, and Mandy found herself wondering just what kind of a place Ryder would own. And Indian Territory wasn't all that far away. "Sure, it sounds great."

Ryder hugged her to him. "You'll love it, I

know. And we'll have Reno and Jeremy close by for neighbors . . ."

Alarm bells went off in Mandy's brain, and she stiffened until Ryder dropped his arms. "What was that? Just where is this . . . place . . . of yours?"

Suddenly Ry remembered Reno mentioning Amanda's reaction to the idea of moving from Missouri and, most of all, her beloved farm. But she was his wife now. She'd have to go with him. Wouldn't she? So, warily he explained, "My place is a ranch, Amanda. A pretty large ranch south of Santa Fe. From Reno's description of his land, he's not too far from me. A little north and west, closer to town."

Oh no, here it was again. She was going to be pressured to leave her home, her father, everything she knew and cared about. Why? Why couldn't Ryder stay on and work the farm?

"What's wrong with my farm? Why coudn't we stay in Missouri and make it work again? All it would take is a few repairs and maybe some paint and—"

"Whoa, sweetheart. You know better than that. I've seen the farm, remember?"

When Mandy pulled out of his arms and ran to lean against her horse, Ry didn't follow. He hadn't thought about her not wanting to go west with him, had forgotten about how disappointed Reno had been over his sister's refusal to move. Well, he wouldn't mention any more about it for now. Maybe if he gave her room to think about it, she'd change her mind.

They'd been traveling for some time when Ry began to have a nagging doubt tug at his memory. He'd been watching the ground and had picked up a sign that had him racking his brain trying to remember something important about it.

A sign this close to the Coulter farm bugged him for some reason, and a cold chill ran down his spine as he tried to rationalize his worry, and even fear. He knew that in some way, because of whatever it was bothering him, Amanda's life could be in danger.

As they rode into the homestead, the stallion pranced and tugged at the lead shank while letting loose several ear-piercing whinnies. Before they reached the barn, answering whickers could be heard along with the thump of hooves pounding against the board panels of the stalls.

Ry glanced over to Amanda and grinned suggestively. "I know just how he feels. It's going to be nice having a woman around to take care of our needs."

Mandy blushed as her eyes accidently on purpose sought and found the proof of his need. She was embarrassed, yet a sense of pride and well-being pervaded. It was nice to know that the man she loved wanted her so much. The knowledge made her feel attractive and feminine and secure.

Ryder dismounted and tied the grulla to a hitching post before leading the stallion into the barn. There was one good corral that he and Jeremy had repaired, so he turned the big horse into it, watching as the animal bucked and kicked, performing for the six mares kept to be his own personal harem. "Rest while you can, big fella, you're going to need it."

He laughed as he walked back into the barn and saw six heads craned in his direction. Twelve big brown eyes interestedly watched the stud strut his stuff. "Soon, ladies, soon."

As he approached Amanda, now tethering Red Fox next to the mustang, he saw her looking scornfully at the poster nailed to one of the porch posts. If everything worked out as he'd planned, he'd get her away from all of this heartache.

"Hey, sis, when'd you get back?"

Reno and Jeremy rode around the corner of the house, leading the mules, Zeke and Jenny. The boys' faces were drawn and sad looking, and from their rumpled appearance, either they had slept in their clothes, or hadn't slept at all.

Mandy was the first to laughingly express her concern. "You two look like you've just come from an all night drunk, or worse."

Jeremy, dreading the news to come, prolonged her good humor by teasing, "Thanks a lot, Mandy Jo, but you don't look like Sunday-go-to-meetin' your own self."

"Well, I certainly can't argue with you there."

Ry stepped up beside Amanda and pulled her to his side. "Guys, I want you to meet Mrs. Amanda Jo Manning, my new wife."

Both brothers gaped in astonishment. They'd hoped for it but hadn't any idea it would happen so soon, or so unexpectedly. Reno extended his hand to Ryder. "Congratulations, Manning. You couldn't have done any better."

Jeremy hugged his sister, then shyly held out his hand. "Yeah, congratulations. Uh, sorry 'bout the other day."

"It's forgotten. Besides, it's a brother's duty to look out for his sister. And don't think you need to quit now."

Reno cleared his throat and reached for Mandy's hand. "I'm glad you said that, 'cause we've kinda got some bad news."

Mandy's head swiveled and her eyes widened as she looked repeatedly back and forth between her brothers, who suddenly seemed tongue-tied and reluctant to speak. "What is it? Has the farm been sold already? Oh, I knew—"

Reno squeezed her hand and quickly butted in. "No, nothing like that. It's Pa, Mandy. He's . . . dead."

"Nnooo! How? Why?" Again Mandy looked to her brothers, and it was obvious that she was expressing their own questions.

Jeremy's voice was cold and very adult when he told her, "It was Hank Ford. He beat Pa, then shot him. Murdered him."

"But why? For what reason?" At least now she knew how Jesse had gotten the stallion so easily.

"I wish we knew. The only thing we can figure is that he was looking for you or Jeremy."

Ryder had been noticeably silent during the exchange and now snapped his fingers, eliciting the attention of three pairs of eyes, two amazingly green and one startling blue. At the mention of Hank Ford, he'd recalled what was so familiar about the tracks he had seen earlier.

"I saw his tracks, about two miles from here. It didn't click until just now that the broken shoe belonged to a set of tracks I followed that day in the creek bed before I met up with all of you."

Jeremy's eyes lit with an almost maniacal gleam. "Which way were they headed? In, or out?"

Ry looked at Reno and saw the worry in the older brother's features but knew he had to answer truthfully. "They were going east, away from the farm."

Ryder cut across a rolling meadow, heading for some of the roughest country he'd seen so far. There were steep hills intersected by deep canyons, giving

425

rise to bare-faced cliffs and boulder-strewn slopes. He was glad he had a horse as savvy and agile as the mustang under him as he left the last of the even terrain.

He'd split off from Reno and Jeremy a ways back when they'd had a hunch about an old cabin Reno had once frequented. Neither of the boys had blinked an eye when Ryder had slipped on his deputy marshal's badge but had shaken his hand in farewell and wished him luck. Obviously they weren't worried about a stranger beating two home-grown hill boys to the outlaws.

As blind luck would have it, Ryder had only ridden less than a mile into the broken country before he stopped his horse to quietly scan the area. Nothing moved, and there was no sound except his horse champing at the bit. He'd just leaned over to straighten the cinch strap when he spotted a rock that had been recently overturned.

Anything could've stumbled over the rock—a large animal, even a snake if it hit the edge just right—but to be certain, he got off to take a closer look. And there it was: the jagged edge of a horseshoe cut into the freshly turned ground. A broken shoe. Hot damn!

Mandy puttered around the kitchen in between bouts of pacing back and forth in front of the window. How dare the men go off and leave her at home. And Ryder had had the nerve to insinuate that just because she was a married woman, her life was going to change—drastically. Of all the gall, ordering her to stay put and play house for a change.

She threw the rag she'd been using to dust the room into the basin. Well, she wasn't going to do it. Ryder was still weak from his injury, and no matter how hard he denied it, she could see it in the lines around his eyes and the way his shoulders hunched, as if trying to find a comfortable position.

Her face broke into a confident grin. Now that she knew what she was going to do, she felt much better.

Reno and Jeremy reached the cabin about dusk. There was no sign of its being lived in, or even occupied, for years.

"Well, this was certainly a dead end."

"Maybe so, Reno, but it was a good idea to check it out. How far into the breaks do you think Ryder is?"

"Who knows, but don't worry—"

Jeremy took hold of his brother's arm and led him to a bed built against the wall. Reno's face had drained of all color, and he'd swayed and would have fallen if it hadn't been for Jeremy's catching him in time.

"Are you all right, big brother? What happened?"

"I don't know. This has never happened before." Reno shook his head and rubbed his forehead as he sat on the bunk. "Mandy! I've got this feeling. . . . She's in trouble, danger of some kind."

"But we left her at home. What could happen to her?"

"You forget. Pa was killed there, and not two days ago."

"Then we'd better go, huh?"

It was a tough decision to make, whether to go on or wait until morning, but it was so dark that she was afraid she'd miss the trail and have to start all over again the next day anyway. So, she untied her bedroll, then unsaddled Red Fox, tying him loosely

427

enough to enable him to graze on the tall grass sprouting nearby.

Whether or not it was Ryder she was following, she didn't know, but she just *felt* it was. She'd followed the trail of three horses until one broke off in a different direction from the other two. Supposing that her brothers would stick together, the natural conclusion was to take after the single set of tracks.

She wondered if maybe some of Reno's special sense hadn't finally rubbed off on her because she had a terrible premonition that Ryder was riding into danger. And the deeper he got into this rough country, the more worried she became.

The last thing she thought about before she drifted to sleep was that if anything happened to him, he'd die never knowing that she loved him, just like her father.

At first light, Ryder was up and in the saddle. Tracking was slow and time consuming, but he was methodical in his persistance. It sometimes took a quarter of an hour, if not longer, to find the next print, and sometimes he relied solely on his hunches in finding the right trail.

The pace became even slower as he found himself traveling uphill, and the terrain was rockier, if that was possible. Finally he got off and led the mustang, making the going easier on the both of them.

In all of his years of working out of the U. S. Marshal's Office, he'd never felt so driven to run a man to ground. He'd heard some of the old-timers in the field bragging about taking their men dead or alive. Well he didn't much care which way, either, not when it came to Hank Ford, the man who'd dealt his love so much grief.

When he thought of poor George Coulter, he got angry all over again. What had the man ever done to deserve such a violent death? He may not've been the best father, but he'd been a sad, gentle soul who'd kept to himself, never bothering anyone.

It hurt him to think of the way Amanda was suffering. She felt acute guilt over the way she'd ignored her father, and when her brothers had related George's last words, she'd felt even worse. Deep down she'd loved the man very much, and Ry had tried to convince her that George had known. How could he not? Ry was certain that she'd never intentionally hurt anyone during her entire life.

The mustang stopped, drawing back on the reins, alerting Ryder. Damn, he'd been so caught up in his thoughts that he'd failed to pay attention to what was going on around him. Stupidity like that could get him killed.

He stepped back to stand by the horse's head and put his hand on the animal's nose. They stood quietly for a long time, but Ryder neither heard nor saw anything unusual or out of place. However, a faint breeze blew out of the south, carrying a whiff of smoke. Someone had a fire somewhere.

Ryder led his horse behind him until the aroma of a campfire became stronger, then he tied the mustang in a brushy thicket and continued on alone, keeping low and walking as silently as any hunting cat. He only hoped his prey was the men he was so intently searching for.

He climbed all the way to the top of the hill, and there, on a narrow promontory overlooking a winding river and a vast amount of impenetrable country, sat Hank and Ed. Ry's luck was intact. He watched as Hank leaned back against a boulder, tipping his hat over his eyes. Ed held a rifle across his lap, evidently posted as the lookout.

Ry got down on his belly and wriggled along, using his elbows and toes to lift the heaviest part of his body, until he reached a good hiding spot not far from the camp. Both outlaws seemed relaxed, confident of not being taken by surprise in their present location.

Now, while they were unaware of being found, would be his best bet to take them. As soon as a chance presented itself, he'd try to take them alive, but take them he would.

The sun was hot as it beat down among the rocks, and soon Ed let the rifle fall into the crook of his arm while he lifted his hat and rubbed the sweat from his sticky forehead.

This was it: probably the best break he'd get. Ry lunged to his feet, pulling his revolver, and stepped onto the ledge. "Hands up, boys. This is the end of the trail."

Surprise and shock triggered Ed's reaction as he jumped to his feet, letting the rifle fall. Hank sat up, pushing his hat to the back of his head so he could see. Ed, his hands nervously clinching as he held his arms wide, made a foolish mistake when Ryder's eyes shifted to his cousin. In a desperate move, he reached for his pistol.

Seeing the action out of the corner of his eye, Ry swung back and fired, the bullet slamming into Ed with enough force to knock the man to the ground. Before he could turn to Hank, Ryder was rolled to the side as the larger man threw himself against Ry's legs. Hitting the dirt with a sickening impact, the back of Ry's hand slammed against a rock which numbed his fingers so that he lost the grip on his gun. Then Hank was on top of him, grappling, trying to pin him down. This was the way Ry liked to fight, down and dirty, no holds barred.

Mandy heard the shot. She'd lost Ryder's trail when halfway up the side of the hill and had stopped, sitting dejectedly on a fallen log as she wondered where to look next. Her heart stopped, sputtered and began to race. It had to mean that Ry, if it was Ry, was in trouble.

Red Fox's ears pricked toward the top of the hill, and he lunged in that direction the minute Mandy jumped aboard and kicked his sides. When they barreled into the small clearing, she was amazed at what lay before her. Ed was sprawled off to one side, and whether he was dead or alive she couldn't tell. But she forgot about him when her eyes became glued to the spot where two twisting, kicking bodies stirred up clouds of dust.

They were so close to the edge of the bluff that Mandy sucked in her breath and covered her mouth with her hand to watch in wide-eyed horror. She knew better than to wade into the fight, knew that her appearance might distract Ryder's concentration at a critical time.

That was something else her father had taught her. He'd been so wise and practical. Why couldn't he have applied his knowledge and common sense to his own life? Her hand stifled a sob as she continued to take in the swinging, thrashing arms and legs of the two combatants.

Ryder's strength was giving out. His back was hurting, and he could feel little trickles of something besides sweat running down his ribs. Both of his hands were clamped around Hank's wrists, and he barely twisted his lower body in time to avoid a knee to the groin. Suddenly he bent his elbows and pulled Hank's upper body down while raising his knees in the outlaw's abdomen. In one swift jerk, he threw Hank over his head and lunged to his feet, standing spraddle-legged, knees bent, arms outstretched as his lungs sucked in large gulps of air.

Hank was a big man, carried a lot of fat, but Ryder found out that the fat concealed tons of muscle. The man was built like an ox and was just as hardheaded. When he charged again, Ry twisted to the side and brought his right fist under Hank's jaw, then used his left wrist as a club to the back of the outlaw's neck. Instead of falling like any normal human being, Hank curbed his momentum, spun around, roared like a wounded bear and came again.

Ry got in a good solid jab to Hank's gut—he knew that he had because he heard the air whistle from the man's chest—but Hank managed to get his arms around Ry's waist and carried him backward until Ry tripped and fell, hard, with Hank on top of him. The pain that shot through his back and shoulders was almost enough to cause him to loose consciousness, but Ry's adrenaline was pumping full steam, and he fought and twisted until he could get enough leverage to roll Hank beneath him.

As Ry's hands reached for Hank's throat, he saw the outlaw grasp for something on the ground; but fatigue dulled his reaction time, and he was too late to ward off the fistful of dirt and gravel that hit him directly in the eyes. Caught off guard, he was immediately thrown back to the ground, and he just made out the images of Hank's legs as they stepped in close. As hard as he struggled, Ry couldn't get enough momentum to move away. He waited for the finishing blow to the head as he flailed ineffectually and thought of Amanda. How he loved her. He hoped she knew, but she'd even had doubts about her father loving her, let alone the sorry husband who'd forced her to marry him. It was a bad time to die.

When the report of a rifle split the ominous silence, no one was more surprised than Ryder. His fists wiped furiously at his eyes as the blow he'd been expecting never landed. He opened his burning, scratchy lids just in time to see the blurry figure of Hank Ford pitch backward off the steep face of the bluff. Time hung suspended in slow motion until the splash of the body hitting the river drifted slowly to the ledge.

Stunned, Ry twisted his neck. Where had the shot come from? Who'd found them in time to save his life?

Chapter Twenty-Three

Mandy hadn't even been aware that she'd drawn or aimed her Sharps until she pulled the trigger and felt the kick of the stock against her shoulder. She registered thanks to Jeremy, though, for leaving her rifle behind when he'd ridden off yesterday. She and the old gun were a matched pair.

As her eyes frantically searched out Ryder to make sure she'd fired in time, a flash of reflected light hit her square in the face. It happened so quickly that when she turned to look, she wondered if it was her imagination, a delayed reaction to her fright.

No. There, in the trees, swayed a splash of red, the tail end of a sorrel horse just fading into the thick undergrowth. Jesse. It had to be. While she watched, the horse stopped, turned, and an arm raised to her in salute. She waved back, a warm feeling in the pit of her stomach at knowing he'd been there to help. And when the sorrel spun around again, he disappeared, along with the warmth, leaving a sense of loneliness and loss.

All of that had taken no more than a few seconds of time, and she hurriedly replaced her rifle in its scabbard while nudging Red Fox into a lope toward Ryder.

He was sitting up, rubbing his eyes, looking so bedraggled and torn that she swallowed hard to keep from crying. When she stepped out of the stirrup, she grabbed her canteen and ran to his side. After kneeling next to him, she tore her shirt out of her pants and began to rip off a piece of the long hem.

Ry gently took hold of her shaking hand as she poured water onto the cloth. "You're sure hard on shirts, sweetheart. I don't know if I can afford you."

Mandy flashed him a tremulous smile as she ordered, "Tip your head back and let me clean your eyes. Oh, my, they look horrible. They're all red and—"

"I know. It hurts to even open my eyelds. Ouch! Owww. That's better."

She wet the cloth until she could wring the water over his face. As the cool liquid washed the grit away, she leaned closer, just wanting to be as near to him as she could.

When Ryder could at last open his eyes without pain, he was surprised to find Mandy's eyes closed, with tears streaming down her cheeks while she swayed toward him.

"Amanda? Sweetheart, what's wrong? Please, don't cry." He rose to his knees and pulled her to him as she swayed again. Her body trembled, and her mouth pressed tightly closed, trying to keep her teeth from chattering.

"I'm s-sorry. I can't help it. I was so afraid."

"Shh. So was I." He stroked her hair with his hand as he crooned, "I know how terrible it is to kill a man. But, honey, you saved my life. He would've killed me in another second."

435

Mandy pulled back from Ryder but kept her hands on his chest in case he should try to disappear. "N-no, that wasn't why I was afraid. It didn't bother me a bit to put a bullet in that cur. No one's going to lose any sleep over his loss."

"If that's not what's bothering you, what is? Look at you. You're a nervous wreck. Now tell me, damn it. I'm your husband, you know."

A smile cracked the tight set of her lips, and her eyes cleared of the teary sadness. Yes, she was his wife. And she was so proud, she threw her arms around his neck and fell on top of him as he toppled over.

"Ow! Oh, no you don't. You stay right here 'til you tell me what's on your mind."

"But you're hurt. I bet you opened your wound again, didn't you?"

"Could be. But it's a long way from my heart." Finally he resorted to bribery. "If you want to play doctor and make me well faster, you'll hurry and tell me so you can get on with it, won't you?"

Mandy cuffed him on the shoulder. "Oh, all right. I was afraid . . . that you were going to . . . die . . . without knowing . . . h-how much . . . I . . . l-love you." She finally got it out, with a little prodding on Ryder's part, and now she waited for the laughter and ridicule, the hurtful words that would tell her what an idiot she was.

But instead of words, Ryder hugged her to his chest so hard that she was afraid she might suffocate. She could feel the rapid thump of his heart pounding against her breast. It was a wonderful moment, but she couldn't help wondering how long it would last.

Finally, when he felt Amanda gasp for breath, Ry loosened his grip but still held her pressed against his heart. "Want to know something?" When her hair tickled his chin as she nodded, he admitted, "The

436

same thing happened to me just as Hank drew back his foot to— Well, anyway, all I could think of was you and how much I love you and if you knew it or not.''

Mandy pulled back to look into his eyes and saw the truth shining back at her. "Oh Ry, I'd hoped and prayed . . . but we're so different. We've so much against us.''

"Hell, sweetheart, being different is what makes us so exciting. And no one ever said that marriage was supposed to be easy. So? Are we going to give up, or what?''

"No. We're going to give it a try. I do love you.'' She wrapped her arms around his neck as her lips collided with his.

Ry's hands found Amanda's buttocks, and he pressed her tightly against his burgeoning desire. Their mouths opened in an urgent effort to deepen the kiss just as the thunder of approaching horses reverberated the ground.

A gunshot rent the air, and Ryder rolled with Amanda, pinning her underneath him as he shielded her body. Since he'd lost his own gun, he quickly drew her pistol from its holster and pointed the muzzle at the riders.

"Hey, point that thing another direction, will ya? You wanna get us killed?'' Jeremy pulled his horse to a stop next to the two lovebirds while Reno, gun drawn, dismounted and jerked a wobbly Ed to his feet.

"Manning, are you sure you're a deputy marshal? I thought you guys were s'posed to be smart. This fella was just about to make sure you two made it to heaven locked in each other's arms.''

Ryder grimaced, then chuckled at Reno's outraged expression. "I think you've got us confused with the

Texas Rangers." He held out his hands in a placating manner. "Honestly, I thought he was dead, but you're right, I should've made damned sure." Then he grinned at Amanda. "Guess love has made me a mite careless lately, huh, sweetheart?"

Mandy was jounced around on the hard old buckboard seat once too often as she guided Zeke and Jenny over the rough road. At least it was called a road, but was hardly more than two narrow ruts in the ground.

"What's the matter, sweetheart? One of the mules lame?"

"No." She glared up at her husband sitting so easily in the saddle. "Don't you think it's about time we switched places? My bottom is so sore I can hardly sit down."

Ry leered at her as she stood up and rubbed her posterior. "Doesn't look sore to me. It looks—"

"Ryder Manning, don't you ever get tired of . . . of . . ."

Ry dismounted and walked over to lift Amanda from the wagon. He let her lithe young body slide down his chest until her toes barely touched the ground. "I'll never get tired of holding you, touching you, or loving you, Mrs. Manning. It doesn't seem possible to love someone as much as I love you."

Mandy kissed his nose, then leaned back as far as she could to look into his eyes. "It is a bit overwhelming. If anyone had told me six weeks ago that I'd gladly pack my belongings and head for parts unknown, I'd have laughed in his face. In fact, even three weeks ago, 'cause I did, in Reno's."

"Are you sorry?" Ry's voice was hesitant, as if afraid to hear her honest answer.

"Nope, not a bit. You and my brothers were right. There was nothing left for me in Missouri. Everyone important to me is making a new start in a new country somewhere near a place called Santa Fe. Now how could a woman resist the challenge and adventure?"

Ry nuzzled her neck with his lips. *Everyone* important?"

"Yep." Except for the emptiness in her heart as she left behind the memories of a mother and sisters she'd never see again. But she was looking to the future now, not the past.

"Good. Now, let's get in the wagon, shall we?"

"Ryder! No way. We've still got hours of daylight left, and you promised we'd spend the night in a real bed tonight."

"Slave driver. A man can't have any fun. All right, you win. But *you* have to drive the wagon."

Mandy stuck her tongue out at him but kissed him thoroughly one last time as he lifted her back onto the box. In a way, it was scary, how much she loved him. And sometimes he felt as if it were too good to be true. She was distrustful of so much security.

As she clicked the mules into their traces, she wondered how Reno and Jeremy were faring. They'd left for Santa Fe a week ahead of Ryder and herself, too anxious to wait around for Ry's back to heal. The black stallion and six mares had gone with them, and Mandy prayed that they made it to the ranch intact.

Ry sped up to ride alongside Amanda as she slapped the mules with the reins. "Old Zeke's going to be glad to get this over with. From the look in his eyes, he thinks he's cut out for better things than pulling a buckboard."

"He's always had that expression, and only when we hitched him up. Makes you wonder, doesn't it?"

Mandy was thoughtful for a while, then asked Ryder, "What'll they do with Ed?"

"I don't know for sure. He confessed to quite a few crimes, so it could go hard on him. He and Hank cut quite a trail through Kansas and Nebraska, besides Missouri. It was lucky for him that there were witnesses who claimed it was Hank who did the killing, otherwise he might've hanged."

Mandy gulped and rubbed her fingers over her neck, attractively displaying the new carved, gold band on her left hand. And as she glanced admiringly at her handsome husband, she grinned at the new black stetson he was sporting. He'd teasingly wondered how they would manage to squash *it* when she'd surprised him with it for a wedding present.

Ry caught her look and smiled back. "Remember, woman, it was your idea to keep traveling. Keep your eyes to yourself if you don't want to get into trouble."

She saucily shook her auburn curls over her shoulder and presented him with a perfect profile.

"Get uppity with me, Woman-of-Many-Faces, and I'll leave you eatin' my dust."

Mandy held her position as long as she could, then darted a look at Ry's smug features. The beast. He'd known she couldn't resist. "All right, when are you going to tell me?"

"Tell you what?"

"Ooohh! Sometimes I could gladly wring your thick neck."

Ry kneed his horse as close to the wagon as possible before lithely shifting over to ride next to Amanda, leading his horse alongside. "Well, you once told me that I ought to be able to come up with something better than Woman-Who-Grumbles, didn't you?"

"Yes, but why— What did you call me?"

"Woman-of-Many-Faces. It took me a long time to come up with just the right name. There's so many facets to Amanda Jo Manning that you made it tough."

She blushed, and her shoulder tingled where he brushed against her. "I'm nothing special. Just a home-grown country girl."

Ry put his arm around her and squeezed. "You are no ordinary woman, let me tell you. Why, you can ride, shoot and hunt better than most men. And you're a good housewife. You can sew, cook, clean, and you make a helluva nurse. But, then again, there are drawbacks when you turn into a horse thief or a jailbird."

He put his finger under her chin and turned her flushed face to his for a sweet, tender kiss. "You're everything this man could ever want."

Ryder still reclined in the buckboard as Mandy pulled the mules to a stop outside the little burg of Manford in Indian Territory. Like most small towns on a Saturday afternoon, it was bustling with people.

"Well, sweetheart, I may not be able to keep my promise. The hotel might be full tonight."

It was difficult to hide her disappointment, but Mandy managed to shrug her shoulders indifferently and offer a smile. "It's not your fault. We'll make do."

Ry climbed down from the box and tied the mustang next to Red Fox at the back of the wagon. When he again climbed up to rejoin Amanda, he took the reins from her hands and clucked to the mules. It tickled him to watch his wife's neck crane back and forth as they drove down the main street. He guessed correctly that Manford was the largest town she'd ever seen.

Approaching the center of town, they noticed a large crowd gathered in a vacant lot between the only hotel and the blacksmith shop. Rapid gunfire and cheers from the crowd greeted them as Ry halted in front of the appropriately named Manford Hotel.

Mandy stood up in the box and even jumped up and down in an effort to see over all the heads. "What do you think it is, Ry? Can we go see?"

Ry tied the tired mules to the hitch and lifted his arms to his bouncing wife. Her skirts flared and brushed across his face. As much as he liked her bright, feminine attire, he found himself partial to the form-fitting jeans he'd grown to love her in.

"Come on. Hurry. There's a break in the crowd." Mandy grabbed her husband's hand and pulled him along with her as she pushed and elbowed a way to the front row of people. When she could finally see, she stopped so suddenly that Ry rammed her from behind, almost propelling her into the cleared area.

Her face lost the flush of excitement and turned the color of hot ashes. A chill ran the length of her spine, and she clutched her stomach as a wave of nausea gripped her insides. She hadn't known. My God, how *could* she have known? But what else could she do but draw attention from the crowd and suspicion from Ryder if she tried to leave now?

There was a man in the clearing, reloading his guns as an assistant tied strings with buttons on the end of the branches of a dead tree. When the shootist snapped closed the cylinder of one of his S & W Schofield, he nodded to the boy, who then set the buttons in motion, swinging back and forth at different speeds at irregular heights on the tree.

The gunman, dressed in tight-fitting black pants, snow-white shirt and black satin vest, stepped forward, pistols in both hands which hung by his sides, and concentrated on the swinging targets. Then, in a swift blur of movement, his hands raised, and the guns bucked in his fists as first one button after another shattered into flying fragments.

In less than a heartbeat there were no more targets at the ends of the frayed strings. The crowd was speechless, then erupted into shouts and claps of appreciation for spectacular marksmanship.

The shooter turned and, as if drawn by an unknown force, locked his gaze with Mandy's. The pale blue orbs flickered, then lowered to his guns as he ejected the spent bullets and reloaded.

Aided by the young assistant, the man loaded several extra pistols and placed them within reach on a bench. Then the boy ran to the tree and propped up a flat board covered by a sheet of plain paper. The crowd murmured and pressed against the people in the front row, and Mandy felt the assurance of Ry's presence as his fingers squeezed her shoulder and pulled her back to lean against his chest.

Her eyes filled with love as she turned her head to smile at her husband. And when she rolled her neck to look back at her cousin, she caught him tilting his head slightly to wink.

Bets were being placed at the back of the lot, making odds on the chances of the shootist's accuracy, and she watched with interest as Jesse reached into his vest pocket and sent the young boy to join in the wagering. Excitement began to build until all the bets were laid and the man in black took up two of the pistols.

He turned to look at the crowd, bowed his elegant form slightly, then stood poised and confident as the guns barked simultaneously. When they were empty,

443

he laid them on the bench and picked up the next pair while the assistant furiously reloaded.

It all happened so quickly that when the firing stopped, all the people seemed to draw in a collective breath. Mandy gaped in awe at the board, surprise as evident on her features as anyone else's. She'd heard Jesse talk about practicing the trick, but this was the first time she'd actually seen it. For there, in front of all to see, was scored on the paper a perfect silhouette of Uncle Sam. No one said a word until, suddenly, the whole crowd clapped their hands and surged forward to slap the sharpshooter on the back and congratulate him. Smiling faces gladly handed over the money they'd lost on the wager while equally happy men collected, the majority of which went into the sure hands of the assistant.

Ryder's eyes had been glued to the man ever since he and Amanda had walked up. There was something hauntingly familiar about the sandy hair, the thin features, the pale color of his eyes. But the short beard didn't fit the image his mind projected.

As his hands wrapped around Amanda's waist and caressed her invitingly curved body, his eyes strayed to the hotel. His attention span grew shorter and shorter whenever he held his wife in his arms. The stranger could go to hell, for Ryder was going over to get a room if he had to evict present occupants to do it.

Besides, he was a rancher now, had resigned from the U.S. Marshal's Office. It was time he gave up his obsession for the legendary Jesse James, and about twenty other faces he'd memorized over the years, and moved on with his life. Someone else could do the manhunting from now on.

"Stay and watch awhile if you want, sweetheart. I'm going to check on that room," he whispered

444

huskily into her ear.

Mandy had been watching Ryder assess her cousin and was so instantly relieved when his eyes came back to rest on her that her knees almost buckled. It was a good thing he still held her up. "Okay, I'll wait for you by the wagon, darling."

It was the first endearment she'd ever felt comfortable enough to utter, and she was hardly prepared for the urgency he emanated in the locking of his arms and the groan that hissed in her ear. Was it real or just imagined, the soft "I love you" that seemed to drift with the breeze as he released her and almost ran from the crowded lot?

She hugged herself and turned around to collide with the man who'd so engagingly performed his shooting exhibition. "Evenin', ma'am. James Beaugardis, at your service. I trust you enjoyed the show?"

Her eyes and lips smiled in unison as he gallantly kissed her hand. "Oh, yes, sir. It was everything I knew it would be." Her eyes spoke the messages that her lips could not as he continued to hold her fingers.

Finally he gave them an eloquent squeeze, released her to tip his hat and backed toward the sorrel horse tethered in front of the Smith's. "It's been a real pleasure, ma'am. You take care now, hear?"

Choked, and with her eyes moist and starting to well with tears, Mandy watched him place his extra guns carefully in his saddlebags. She should've known he'd fall back on his expertise with a gun to start his new life. After all, it was what he knew best. Her hand was barely perceptible as it lifted in sad farewell when he turned for a final look back before loping out of town.

Later, snuggled in her husband's arms after a

445

frenzied bout of lovemaking, she lazily trailed her finger over his chest, twining it among the curly hairs and then tickling the lean rib cage.

"It was nice, wasn't it, making love in a real bed?"

"Uhhmm. But what do you call what we slept on at my house?"

Ry pressed his lips to her ear, ran his tongue all along its delicate shell shape, then whispered, "That was nothing but a bunch of wild feathers very loosely trapped."

"But it was comfortable, wasn't it?"

"Nope, cause every time I reached for you, I had to fight the damned feathers to find you."

"Oh." As she ran her palm over his hard muscles and around his hip, she encountered a still, pulsating organ and caressed it tenderly, lovingly.

"Damn, Amanda. I do adore you."

"And I love you, darling, more than I ever thought possible. Love me, Ry. Forever."

As they came together in a gentle, mind-shattering union, Mandy couldn't believe her good fortune. She was walking into a new future with the man she loved and life couldn't be better, or more exciting.

Given "lady's choice," her heart had chosen wisely.

<u>FREE</u> Preview Each Month and $ave

Zebra has made arrangements for you to preview 4 brand new HEARTFIRE novels each month...FREE for 10 days. You'll get them as soon as they are published. If you are not delighted with any of them, just return them with no questions asked. But if you decide these are everything we said they are, you'll pay just $3.25 each—a total of $13.00 (a $15.00 value). **That's a $2.00 saving each month off the regular price.** Plus there is NO shipping or handling charge. These are delivered right to your door absolutely free! There is no obligation and there is no minimum number of books to buy.

TO GET YOUR FIRST MONTH'S PREVIEW... Mail the Coupon Below!

Mail to:

HEARTFIRE Home Subscription Service, Inc.
120 Brighton Road
P.O. Box 5214
Clifton, NJ 07015-5214

YES! I want to subscribe to Zebra's **HEARTFIRE** Home Subscription Service. Please send me my first month's books to preview free for ten days. I understand that if I am not pleased I may return them and owe nothing, but if I keep them I will pay just $3.25 each; a total of $13.00. That is a savings of $2.00 each month off the cover price. There are no shipping, handling or other hidden charges and there is no minimum number of books I must buy. I can cancel this subscription at any time with no questions asked.

_____

NAME

_____

ADDRESS   APT. NO.

_____

CITY   STATE   ZIP

_____

SIGNATURE   (if under 18, parent or guardian must sign)
           Terms and prices are subject to change.   2443